A Tainted Proposal

Merged Series

Maxine Henri

www.maxinehenri.com

Cover designed by Sweet 'N Spicy Designs

Edited by Indie Editing Chick

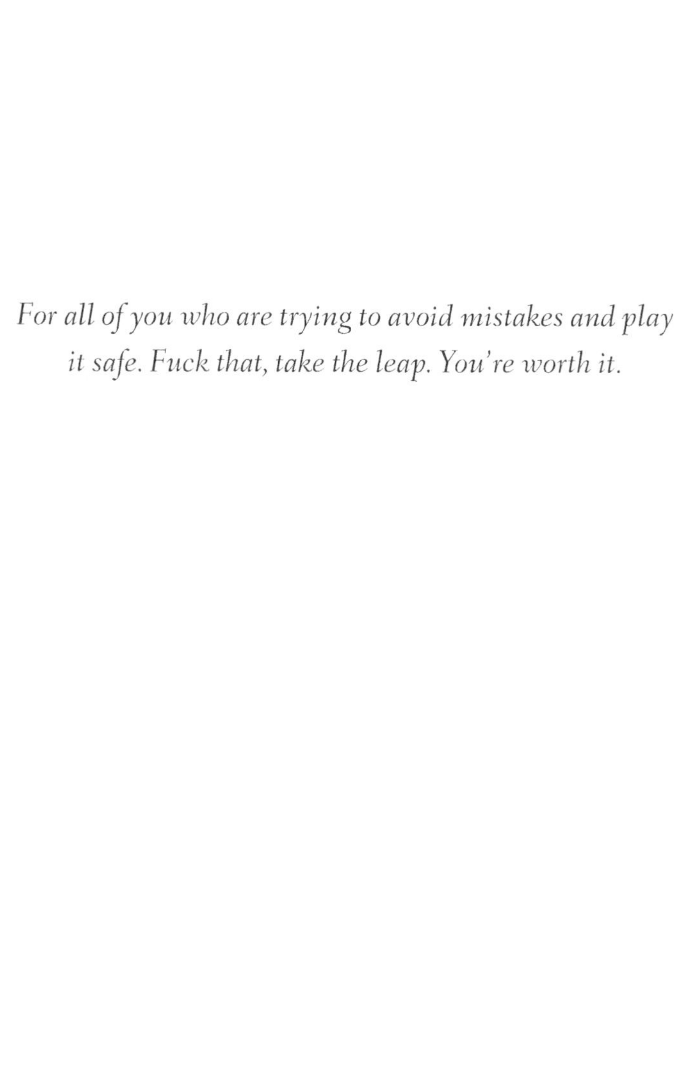

For all of you who are trying to avoid mistakes and play it safe. Fuck that, take the leap. You're worth it.

Chapter 1

Xander

The black dress clings to her like a secret, elegant and dangerous in equal measures. Every curve it reveals is a temptation—and yet, there's nothing overt about the way she carries herself.

Present.

Unbothered.

Unreachable.

"I wondered why you invited her." Cal, my friend and partner at Merged, a company I co-own, elbows me.

It's not a question; it's a statement, like he has some inside knowledge I don't really care about.

"Enlighten me." I glare at him, annoyed by the interruption. Grateful for it at the same time, because what the fuck am I doing?

"She's not interested." He chuckles. "I know that is a tough pill to swallow, but remember, she's my wife's best friend."

"She came with me." I shrug. Though I know she accepted my invitation because her best friends are here, including Cal's wife, Celeste.

She didn't say yes because *I* invited her. It's not exactly a rejection, but it still feels like one, especially since Cal is right, and she is so obviously not interested in me.

She's just happy to be out. Her lack of interest probably got me to invite her to this gala.

She is here with me, but she doesn't see me. Not really. Not the way most women do.

She's completely immune. It makes me feel... something. I love that about her. And I hate that I do.

Because it means I'll have to win her attention. And I always win.

I should be working the room, though.

Shaking hands. Making deals. Nurturing connections to strengthen the empire I'm building. This room is a chessboard of opportunity—and I'm the kind of man who plays to win.

She laughs. Enjoys herself with abandon. Cora Winslow is a woman who doesn't perform for anyone. She simply is. And that presence? It's compelling. It's real.

So fucking real, I almost can't believe it.

No one in my life is this genuine.

I'm not a romantic. I don't seek relationships, but I would wine and dine this woman just to catch some of that uncensored freedom from her by association.

I leave Cal and approach her with her friends.

Her laugh—low, unrestrained, utterly unself-conscious—punches me square in the solar plexus. I've heard women laugh like they're performing joy. Hers? It wraps around me before I can decide if I want to chase it or drown in it.

"May I have this dance?" I wink, and Cora narrows her eyes.

She gives her drink to Celeste and straightens up. "Okay, Stone, you got me to this glamorous event; the least I can do is accept. Let's dance."

"I don't think I've ever seen you dancing." Celeste smirks at me.

We get to the dance floor and... well, dance.

Cora glides across the floor, luminous and completely present, as if the world exists for no other reason than this moment.

There's no calculation in her smile. No desperation in her eyes. No hidden agenda. No points to score.

And fuck, I can't look away.

Though even having her in my arms as I lead her to

the tune, she seems unattainable, and for the first time in my life, I'm lost for words.

Or let's have a dose of honesty here. Everything Cora Winslow is a mystery to me. I first met her at Cal and Celeste's vow renewal. When Cal had introduced me to this woman, she nodded in passing.

Like I was just another person in the line. Mystery number one.

Okay, it might be my over-inflated ego, but that one stung. And increased my interest greatly.

Mystery number two: why did I invite her tonight as my plus one? To marvel at another rejection?

Because, let's face it...

Yeah, I definitely want her attention. Not very convenient. Because mystery number three: why don't I know how to handle her? How to talk to her? She is so different from other women.

And after playing the field for years, I don't know how to behave around a woman when she is not swooning over me because of my sheer presence. Humble pie, anyone?

"How is work?" Yeah, I fucking just asked that.

She groans. "Don't spoil the night, Stone. I haven't been out in ages."

A curl breaks loose from her bun. She doesn't apologize and run to the ladies' room to fix her appearance;

she just goes with the little imperfection, mindlessly swatting it away.

"Why not?" I step back and twirl her around.

"I don't have time. I run a bistro, a family business, and it's been hard lately." She gives out a self-deprecating giggle. "Or always."

She lowers her hand back to my shoulder, and I want her to keep it there longer. Luckily, the music slows down, and I finally get to hold her closer. The moment stills, and she smiles at me.

It's a smile of contentment, and a little mischief. I want to drown in it.

"The harder work gets, the more you need to unwind," I say.

Her lower back is warm under my palm, and I fight the urge to slide it lower.

That is another mystery. I actually fight the urge, because I don't want her to turn around and leave. And I think she would... As I said, Cora Winslow is like a carefully administered portion of humble pie.

I never cared for the taste. And yet, here we are.

"Yeah, that is an excellent theory. My unwind time, however, usually leads me to my bed where I sleep, for way too little time, before I have to return to work."

"Do you plan on expanding your business?"

She frowns. "What kind of a question is that?"

I'm not quite sure what is wrong with the question,

or my conclusion that she works so hard because she's growing her business.

Tonight, my conversation game is off. Derailed by the way she owns the dance floor—not with the practiced elegance of a debutante who spent months perfecting her waltz, nor with effortless, balletic grace.

She moves with something rarer: warmth, quiet confidence, and that grounded, magnetic kind of joy that radiates from people who have nothing to prove.

Simple.

Certain.

Untouched.

By expectations. By judgmental stares. By the salacious gazes of half the men in the room.

Side note: I'm going to murder someone tonight. *She came with me, assholes.*

My partner, Cormac Quinn, the CEO of Merged, which I co-own with him, is glaring at me while he talks to the mayor. His wife and Cora's friend, Saar, smiles and nods beside him, playing the business game she might hate but indulges for him.

I ignore Corm's glare and my obligations and twirl Cora around.

At the bar, Declan, the fourth partner, is whispering something to his nanny—I'm not sure what the story is there.

I guess Corm might be the only one working tonight. Normally, I would be too.

"Don't you usually talk about your business with men?" I tease her, to cover the uncomfortable feeling of being lost. I'm never fucking lost.

"Is that what you talk about with women?" She snorts. At least she is entertained.

She will not unsettle me. Keep lying to yourself, fucker. "Well, I don't really care much about the conversation part," I lower my voice.

"Obviously." She laughs again. "I appreciate you putting in the effort, but you don't have to. This is not a date."

"I'm clearly failing in my efforts."

"I'm guessing that's not something you encounter often."

I'm hyper-aware of the curve of her hip swaying under my touch. "You'd be correct, but I appreciate a worthy opponent."

"I'm not playing your game, Xander. Besides, don't you need to schmooze?" She licks her lips—not seductively; she just wets them, and my entire body—okay, my cock—reacts.

"I'd rather dance with you."

"Doesn't it defy the purpose?"

"Of being here?" I frown.

"Of taking *me* to the gala? Why else would you have invited me?"

Yeah, I'm asking the same question. "Aren't you having fun?"

And can I sound any more desperate? What the fuck is wrong with me?

"I'm having fun, but let's not pretend you're here to be with me. I'm here as a friend of your partners' spouses. To free your time, so you can do whatever networking you men come to these things for. You don't need to entertain me."

She got that right. Partially. I usually work at these events. I bring one of my hookups, and it generally ends up with them complaining they were bored while I worked the room.

But if I had wanted to avoid that, I could have brought our office manager, Roxy.

So yeah, Cora is right. Partially. Because I didn't bring Roxy.

"What if I wanted to spend the evening with you?"

She snorts. "Yeah, right."

What the actual fuck? It's like we are each on a different planet. I'm trying and failing miserably to grab her attention. And she? What? She didn't notice I'm game?

I've never worked hard to get something. Things

come easily to me. Women included. So this is new, but also confusing. I don't get confused.

"I'm having fun, Cora." I go with the truth.

She halts and looks at me with a whisper of suspicion. "Please don't continue in this direction."

"Why not?"

"Because it's ridiculous." She resumes moving her legs, and we stumble back into dancing.

"I disagree. You're hot. I'm hot. You're available. I'm available. There is chemistry. I'm considered a catch."

She laughs—not just laughs—she throws her head back, having a genuinely joyful moment.

I would want to bottle that sound and carry it with me if it weren't at my expense. Fuck, I would probably want to patent it and put it in a vault, so that no one else could enjoy it.

"And he is humble, ladies and gentlemen." She pats my shoulder.

"You're not even a little interested?" Desperate, perhaps, but also realistic.

I can take a rejection.

No, I can't, but let's pretend.

She tilts her head to the side and smiles at me. It's a curious smile, like she is trying to figure me out while feeling sorry for me. That is a first for me.

Fuck, it's like I'm losing my virginity to this woman. And not in a gentle, romantic, movie way.

She doesn't respond the way I'm used to, but fuck, do I enjoy the challenge.

"You're charming, I'll give you that."

"So what's the problem?" The music stops, and I lead her to the bar.

"Just because I can have something doesn't mean I want it."

Just because I can have something doesn't mean I want it.

I've been replaying her words on a loop throughout the night. While we drank at the bar. While we danced more. While we chatted with other guests.

We're being driven home now while she sits beside me, admiring the city lights as we head toward her neighborhood.

She leans back and closes her eyes, and I let myself admire her profile. Her eye makeup is a bit smudged, and I want to reach over to wipe it, but I don't.

"I can feel you staring." A whisper of a smile brightens her face.

I'm not used to a no. I'm especially not used to a no that isn't wrapped in flirtation, in negotiation.

The driver pulls us to the curb, and I jump out before rounding the car to open the door for her. She stumbles slightly.

"I'll walk you up."

She snorts. "I'm not sleeping with you, Xander."

Jesus. "I didn't say you were."

"You didn't *not* say it."

"I'm walking you to your door because it's dark."

The strap of her dress is falling down one shoulder, and it takes everything in me not to reach over and fix it. Or trace the line of her skin. Or say something stupid like, "Please don't go in yet."

She stops at the entrance and turns to me. "Thank you for tonight."

"You're thanking me for not trying to grope you while we danced?" I wink at her.

A laugh escapes her. "Well, that too."

"You really think I'm that predictable?"

"I think you're used to being the one pursued."

"I think you're projecting."

She quirks an eyebrow, but the corners of her mouth lift. "Still charming."

I wait for her to turn and leave, to give me a wave and disappear into the night.

She doesn't.

Instead, she shifts her weight and tilts her head. "Are you hungry?"

I blink. "What?"

"There's a bakery. Open all night. Their pastries will ruin you for all other pastries."

It's past midnight. I have a three-hour meeting block first thing tomorrow. And I've already had enough champagne to justify calling it a night. Also, I don't eat baked goods.

"Yes," I say.

* * *

Ten minutes later, I'm sitting in a cramped vinyl booth across from her, watching her devour a pistachio-filled Danish like it's a religious experience.

Her lipstick is smudged.

There's a crumb in her hair.

She hasn't looked at her phone once.

And I've never been more fucked.

I take a bite. And, okay, it's objectively good. Maybe even phenomenal. Still—

"You're aware that the ceiling in here is crumbling."

She rolls her eyes. "It adds character."

"And the lights are fluorescent."

"So we see the pastries better."

I lean back and watch her lick cream off her fingertip like it's the most natural thing in the world.

"I can't believe you eat here."

"I don't." She shakes her head. "Not often. Only when something's worth celebrating."

"What are we celebrating?"

She looks up and gives me that smile of hers. I can't quite decide whether she's pitying me or just tired.

"I went out. I wore a dress. I danced. That's worth a Danish."

She is a puzzle to me. And that is infuriating and intriguing at the same time. "You're hard to read."

She grins. "You're not." She tears off another piece of pastry and pops it into her mouth.

The bell over the door chimes, and two college kids stumble in, laughing. The bakery hums with low conversation, and the scent of sugar and yeast and something deep-fried. Outside, a bus screeches by.

She stands and dusts off her hands. "Well. That was unexpectedly civil. And kind of... nice?"

I follow her out into the night, still unsure how I ended up in this part of the city, eating pastries with a woman who doesn't see me. Not really. Not the way most women do.

A woman who has no idea she's the most captivating thing I've seen in years.

We walk in silence. The kind of silence that feels peaceful. Maybe we're just both tired. Or perhaps we exhausted all the topics.

I don't need to fill it, though. It's a real moment that doesn't require trying.

No double-takes. No coy smiles. No sideways glances inviting me to make my move.

Just the two of us walking down the street until we reach her building. A bit too soon if you ask me.

Cora turns to me. "Thanks for the sugar."

"Anytime."

I step closer. More on autopilot. There needs to be a kiss after an evening like this. I think.

When was the last time I walked a woman to her door? Never. What are the expectations here?

She clearly doesn't want to sleep with me. I'll lick my wounds later.

I don't want to screw this up. Why do I care? Fuck if I know.

She licks her lips, and her gaze softens as she looks up at me, that almost-smile gone now. Her eyes shine with... Is it an invitation?

Everything goes still as I lean down slightly. But I don't close the distance. Cora Winslow feels like an all-or-nothing girl.

And I'm not ready for all. "Goodnight, Cora."

She tilts her head sideways again, studying me like I'm a half-finished puzzle she doesn't trust enough to solve. Like she is surprised I didn't kiss her. Or I'm projecting.

Just because I can have something doesn't mean I want it.

"Why did you take me out, Xander?"

"I don't know," I admit.

She studies me for a moment longer and then nods once. "Goodnight, Stone."

I watch her go inside and close the door.

She disappears into an elevator, and the lights die, and I still stand there, watching the darkness like a fucking idiot.

Still not having kissed her.

Still wanting to.

Chapter 2

Cora

You all disappeared on me last night.

SAAR

You seemed under the spell of Xander.

Don't be ridiculous.

LILY

Sorry, but I'm sure you had fun.

You left like a ghost too.

SAAR

I'm guessing we have my grumpy brother-in-law to thank for that.

CELESTE

Lils, you didn't have to leave with him, we would have given you a ride.

SAAR

@Celeste, how is your dress?

CELESTE

Ruined by breast milk (sad-face emoji)

How did I miss that?

SAAR

Xander

LILY

Xander's distraction.

CELESTE

Xander's allure.

I'm leaving this chat.

Why didn't he kiss me?

What? Thank God he didn't kiss me.

But it looked like he was going to. And apparently, I wanted him to. In that moment. Because I was under the spell of a great evening, some alcohol, and just the general charisma of Xander Stone.

He plays the game well, I'll give him that. But I'm not a conquest. The man is hot as sin, but he is also spoiled, entitled, and ten years younger.

I enjoyed myself last night because I hadn't been out for so long. And it didn't hurt that my best friends, Saar, Lily, and Celeste, made sure that I was dressed and styled to the nines.

I felt like someone else. And that's a dangerous, potentially addictive premise.

It was wonderful to escape my reality for a society event I would have never been invited to if it weren't for my girlfriends.

And the escape involved a charming playboy who doesn't even seem to speak my language. Because although we may both reside in the same country, we're from such different worlds.

I check the clock beside my bed and immediately forget about the non-kiss, or my companion from yesterday.

The price of my last night's escapism is steep. A light headache. Lack of sleep. And a stressful morning, rushing to the bistro.

Oh, how I hate my alarm. How I hate how exhausted I always feel, constantly playing catch-up. Never on top of work, orders, bills. The business that is in a dire state.

And I don't seem to be able to find a way of pulling it out of that situation. I wish Dad could still work and expand his dream.

I wish I could just sleep for one day.

I wish I could just spend a day without responsibilities. Without the daunting task of managing a business and failing at it miserably.

I wonder if a man like Xander wishes for things like that. For a break. I doubt that. Also, I have no time to think about him.

He's a fantasy. A prince who passed around on his white horse and took this damsel in distress to a ball. For fun. But that's over now.

I push out of my bed, Pitt and Clooney groaning in protest. I allow myself a quick cuddle with my two cats. After all, they own the place, so the least I can do is give them a few moments of attention for letting me stay here. For filling all the voids in my life.

They don't ask for much—just food, a clean litter box, and a place on my lap. And in return, they give me everything.

God, I'm becoming an old cat lady, but fuck it, these two... When the day has been heavy, their purrs smooth the edges, like they're stitching me back together with sound.

They make me laugh, too, with their ridiculous zoomies, and the way they chase shadows like it's the most important mission in the world.

They've taught me that love doesn't always shout. Sometimes, it just sits beside you, warm and patient, until you can breathe again.

Occasionally, I wonder what my life would feel like without them. The apartment would be too quiet, too still.

Soft paws pad after me as I make my way to the bathroom. I take a shower and get dressed.

Finding a headband, I somehow tame my wild curls and make myself an extra-strong coffee. It should last me until I get to work and caffeinate some more.

When I arrive at the bistro—late due to yesterday's indulgence—the place is buzzing with anxiety.

All the tables are full—which should make me happy, but I immediately sense the vibe is off. I practically grew up in this place, so I'm attuned to its energy, and today reeks of trouble, complaints, delays, and mixed-up orders.

I should never have gone to the gala.

My employee, Sanjay, looks at me with desperation as I make my way behind the counter. Steam rushes above the coffee machine. Wet footsteps lead to the kitchen, and something sticky is leaking down the counter.

"Can I get the bill finally?" a customer asks.

This is taking too long. Have they forgotten about my latte? This is not fresh.

The nervous whispers reach me as I try to decide how to help Sanjay without slowing him down.

What a fucking mess.

I should never have gone to the gala.

"Sanjay?" I look at his sweaty face while I get the bill for the impatient customer.

"The cook didn't show up," Sanjay says, dropping drink orders on his tray before he rushes to the floor.

I look around.

That's all I do.

For days... or a few long seconds, I just stand there, paralyzed.

The tables are full, and yet it feels empty—of order, of calm, of anything resembling control. The hum of conversation feels like criticism. Every clink of cutlery is an accusation. A napkin falls to the floor, and no one picks it up.

I don't move.

A woman taps the counter, waiting for a to-go order that clearly hasn't even been started. Someone coughs. Someone complains. The espresso machine lets out a loud hiss.

Behind me, the door to the kitchen swings on its hinge, wide open to reveal... nothing. A few dirty pans. An empty prep station. Abandoned chaos.

No cook.

Sanjay rushes past me again with two drinks balanced on a tray and flour on his apron. "I'm sorry," he says as he breezes past. "I tried calling him, but his voicemail says he's out of town. Like literally says it, like it's normal."

I blink. "He left town?"

Sanjay twists back toward me. "I think he quit."

"Did he say he was quitting?" I sound like an idiot, as if clarity on the whereabouts and plans of my MIA cook is what can save the current situation.

"He posted an Instagram story with a cocktail on a beach and the caption, 'finally free.' I'm reading between the lines here."

Jesus.

Coffee overflows behind me and scalds my hand as I reach for it. Fuck. I grab a rag, clean the cup up, and push it across the counter to the wrong customer, who glares at it like I just served them poison.

I inhale slowly.

Then I walk into the back, find my apron, and start making wraps and sandwiches.

Tomato, lettuce, smear of pesto. Next.

Hummus, cucumber, alfalfa sprouts. Next.

I don't taste; I don't feel; I just move. Because that's what I do. I keep the ship from sinking. Even if I'm bailing water with my bare hands.

"Sanjay," I call out through the open door. "Stop seating new tables for now. We're in triage mode."

"You got it, boss."

The bread is stale.

We're out of turkey.

We're down to two avocados, and one of them is already halfway to brown sludge. But I keep going.

I make four sandwiches in a row before realizing I

haven't buttered a single slice of bread. Doesn't matter. *Just keep going.*

The kitchen smells like wilted greens and burned coffee. My headband is slipping. A drop of sweat slides down the back of my neck. I scrape together something that passes for a caprese wrap.

Sanjay lets out a grateful sigh as he whisks them away.

I grab another tomato and slice it with a little more force than necessary.

I should never have gone to the gala.

Not because I regret the dress. Or the dancing. Or the way Xander looked at me, like I was a puzzle he was desperate to solve.

But because of how easy it had been to forget this.

This chaos. This grind.

This version of myself who lives in reaction mode. Who wakes up already behind, and goes to sleep never quite caught up.

For one night, I pretended I belonged somewhere else.

And this morning, reality welcomed me back with the sharpest claws.

My headache progresses with every slice of the knife. With every completed order. With every chime of the register.

But the work gets done, and the momentary satisfaction seeps through as the day comes to an end.

"Let's close early," I tell Sanjay, an hour before our usual closing time, while I rub a sticky spot on the espresso machine.

I busy myself tidying behind the counter when I finally hear the lock. I almost weep with relief.

Sighing, I lower my head. We did it, just barely surviving, but I kept this place afloat for another day.

"This was delivered as I was locking up. The delivery guy said it's for you." Sanjay approaches me holding a white paper box.

I take it slowly. The logo on the napkin tucked under the string says it all. My favorite 24-hour bakery. My stomach tightens before I even open the lid.

Inside, nestled like a little crown jewel, is a pistachio Danish.

A smile tugs at the corners of my mouth.

I stare at the pastry. It's not just the gesture. He teased me about it. Looked down at the place, the amount of sugar poison.

And yet he got me the exact one I raved about in the early morning hours.

And for a moment—just one—I imagine what it would be like to curl up on the worn sofa, eat it with my fingers, and let the sweetness push the bitterness of the day away.

But the bitterness lingers. I also imagine him spending the day in the boardroom, in his tailored suit, probably making ten times more in an hour than I did today.

What do you want from me, Xander Stone? Why do you bother with someone like me?

I glance around.

The tables are empty now, but there's a stain on the floor no one's mopped. A leaky pipe in the kitchen. A list of unpaid invoices on the counter. A dozen voicemails from suppliers.

This is not a world where pastries solve problems.

This is not a life where I can afford to be charmed by a billionaire who plays games. I don't have time or energy for games.

I close the box gently and hand it back to Sanjay. "Take it home."

He blinks. "Are you sure?"

I nod. "I've had enough sugar for a week."

He smiles. "Thanks, boss."

I manage a smile too. "Go home. I'll finish here."

"For real?" He frowns, but his entire body pivots toward the exit.

"Of course. You were here in the morning. It's my turn. Besides, I still have paperwork to catch up on." Or cry over. Which I definitely don't need him to see.

He leaves.

And I stay.

Sweeping up crumbs that never seem to disappear —so different from last night.

I should never have gone to that gala.

Chapter 3

Xander

Rubber floors. Metal clangs. The steady thud of bass in my ears as I shove the weight overhead.

I love the gym at Merged. My company. A company that I'm building here with my partners.

Something that's mine.

Something I won't fail at.

Something I keep growing and succeeding at. Something I can have.

Just because I can have something doesn't mean I want it.

Why do I keep thinking about that even weeks later? Why can't I imagine that concept in practice?

I want all I can have, don't I?

But it's not just her subtle determination behind

that rejection. It's the smile that came with it. The twinkle in her eyes.

The pistachio cream in the corner of her lips that I didn't lick away. The lips I didn't kiss.

"Why are you smiling like an idiot?" Cal swats me with his towel, sweat trickling from his forehead.

"I figured out how we can save the Chicago deal." I tap my earphones to stop the music.

It's not a lie, because I do have a solution for the trouble we encountered with one of our clients.

The annoying part is that he caught me grinning without me even realizing I was. I'm so fucked.

"If thinking about work puts that smile on your face, you have a problem, dude." He unscrews the cap on the bottle and gulps it down, before basketball dunking it into a bin.

"As if anything else made you smile before you got married and became a father, and utterly boring." I stand up from the bench. "Have you worked out? Or just run on a treadmill like a girl?" I redirect from myself.

"Asshole." He wipes his forehead and tosses the towel over his shoulder. "Take it from the converted, settling down has been surprisingly rewarding. It doesn't compare to the constant, fleeting gratification of partying and hookups."

"I'm too young to settle." I load another disk on my bar, because apparently I want to kill myself today.

"That is a nice story to believe, when the truth is nobody would take the leap." He snorts.

"Are you saying I'm not a good catch?" I pretend-scoff.

"I'm saying you're incapable of dating, let alone of any serious commitment." He lowers himself onto the rowing machine and grabs the handles. "It's okay if that's what you want." He starts rowing.

"I'm capable of commitment." Even to my ears, I sound unconvincing. "I just don't want one. I'm enjoying my bachelor status."

"I'm sure you are," he pants out, increasing his speed. His tone is definitely mocking.

"Let's bet on it." I don't even know what I'm saying. Why do I care about his opinion on the matter?

He stops rowing and frowns at me. "You want to bet on enjoying your bachelor status?"

"No, you douchebag, ten thousand that I can date one woman for at least a month."

He laughs. "That's hardly a commitment, but you're on. In fact, make it twenty thousand."

"You're awfully cocky."

"It's confidence, my friend; it's confidence." He hoists himself up and offers me his hand.

I shake it. "I will date someone for at least a month."

"Officially, and without straying... though I'm not sure how I would check that. And let's put a time frame on it. I don't want to wait for my winnings until I'm retired."

"Six months. If I don't start dating someone in the next six months, I'll pay out."

He smirks. "Easiest money I ever made."

"Don't count on it. I never lose."

He laughs and returns to his rowing. I do one more set of squats, almost breaking under the weight, but enjoying every minute of it.

Perhaps I can call Sissy. Sissy Claremont is an heiress to the largest construction company in the country, and a lovely, if dull, companion.

She is hot, fun, and impeccably groomed to become a wife. For some reason, only her dullness comes to mind as I think of our last encounter.

But she lives far enough from here. A long-distance relationship would be the easiest one to win.

But knowing her, if I showed a bit more interest, she would move to Manhattan and start planning our wedding.

I take a nice long shower before I return to the office.

"You need to leave for the luncheon in an hour." Lindsay, my assistant, looks up and smiles.

Shit. I forgot about the schmoozing event we're all attending. The networking part is easy—I don't need to prepare for that—but the plus-one part is something I should have thought about.

Especially since the other three Merged partners will be there with their better halves.

Grabbing a remote, I plop behind my desk and turn on the news. The large screen on the wall across from me comes to life, with the markets' green and red numbers ticking along.

Mindlessly watching the stocks—and more often than not engaging in the game—has always helped me to problem solve.

Not that there truly is a problem. I can easily call one of my regular hookups. I fish my phone from my pocket and stare.

Perhaps there is a problem.

I haven't hooked up with anyone for a few weeks now—not that I would openly admit that. I have a reputation to uphold.

Unfortunately, I can pinpoint the exact day when all women on my usual roster paled into the background.

The stupid gala. Where Cora Winslow made it

clear she's not interested, and I decided not to fuck up my non-existent chances by not kissing her.

That was a first for me. A normal, grounded man would just give up. Take a clue.

Me? I haven't stopped thinking about her.

The way she descended the stairs in her black dress, all curves and grace, completely unaware of her beauty: her wild ginger hair tamed; her face glowing; her green eyes sparkling; and her body cased in black velvet.

That fucking dress... It wasn't anything special, but its simplicity only added to the allure.

So yeah, it's safe to say I haven't stopped thinking about her. Which is annoying, because the only person I've ever allowed to have a hold over my thoughts has been my father. And that clusterfuck of dysfunctional is frankly enough for several lifetimes.

Cora Winslow, the temptress. An elegant fox.

Goddammit.

I jump up and rush out of my office, and collide with our office manager, Roxy.

"Who are you chasing?" She smirks.

"I don't chase, Ro; I attract." I wink at her.

She hates it when people call her Ro, which we tend to do a lot. Frankly, it may be the only weapon against her because this woman is unflappable, her ability to hold her ground around us admirable.

She glares. "You call me Ro one more time and I swear I'll forward my file on you to HR."

I know she is bluffing. Not about having a file on me—I'm pretty sure she could blackmail any of us in the blink of an eye. But she wouldn't use it uselessly by starting an HR investigation. It wouldn't lead anywhere, and it would have no impact on us.

She is smarter than that. She would use it wisely.

"What do you need, Roxy?" Without waiting, I start toward the elevators.

"When was the last time you were back home?" She trots beside me, and I slow my gait—the woman is a foot shorter than me—even though I don't want to have this conversation.

"Why are you asking?" We pass by my team's cubicles. "Double-check column H," I tell a junior analyst hunched over a spreadsheet.

He looks up, gaping at me. "How did you even...?"

"I'm sure you would have spotted the error in no time." I tap on his partition and continue my escape from Roxy.

We reach the reception, and I hit the elevator's call button.

"I need to go, Roxy, so unless you have something work-related to discuss, I'm stepping out."

As if on cue, the elevator dings and its doors slide

open. I don't wait for her to explain, but I catch her expression before the door closes. Fuck.

She's biting her bottom lip, her nose wrinkled. I'm not the best at reading faces, but she is not her usual smug self, so I hit the button to reopen the door.

"What is it, Roxy?" I sigh.

"Your father called."

Fuck. My. Life.

The Manhattan traffic is at its usual. Loud. Hectic. And slow. So fucking slow, I start to doubt my mission makes any sense.

At the red light, I glance at my phone in the dashboard holder, my dad's phone number mocking me in my mind's eye.

Coward. Just call him back. I push the gas as the light changes. Saved by the bell—or rather light in this case. I'm not calling him now.

Talking on the phone while driving is all sorts of ill-advised. Because suddenly I'm obeying the traffic rules.

As I said, coward.

I avoided my father for almost two years. Why would he call now?

For a moment, I consider that something bad must

have happened. But I dismiss the thought because Lottie would call. I have been in touch with my sister regularly since I left.

She's the only family member who saw through my bullshit, and refused to accept my version of the events that forced me to move as far from them as possible.

While I don't understand her loyalty, I appreciate it. If something bad had happened, Lottie would have made sure I heard about it.

She wouldn't pressure me. She would accept my decision whether or not to visit. She would just fucking be there for me. No matter what story I would feed her.

And as ashamed as I may be, I would feed her some fabrication, because it's been easier than facing the past.

But I haven't heard from my sister, and that begs the question: why is my father making an effort to get in touch with me? And an even bigger one is why I would rather crawl into a box full of vipers than return his call.

I pull my Lambo to the curb in front of the bistro. At least one thing is working in my favor today. I got an extremely convenient parking spot—something unheard of in the middle of Manhattan.

The other Merged partners have drivers and rarely drive in the middle of the day. I guess it allows them to catch up on work while they commute. I like to take my cars for a daily spin. Driving has always calmed me down. It's my thinking time.

Usually, I don't even mind the horrendous traffic jams. My best ideas and most prolific phone calls have happened in the midst of a gridlock.

I step out of the car and stroll into the bistro. I've never been here before, and I don't know what I was expecting, but it wasn't this.

It's small. Quiet. The kind of place that doesn't try to impress. And yet it's welcoming.

A handful of patrons linger at plain, rectangular tables placed haphazardly around the floor. Or perhaps with intention—I'm not sure.

To my right, a raised platform runs along the wall—a built-in booth upholstered in beige. Three round coffee tables break the space. Cozy but communal.

Across the room, a long counter anchors the place. It's not flashy, but the mismatched mugs on a rail and a chalkboard menu give it character.

The whole place is warm, personal but somehow feels unfinished. Like it hasn't reached its potential yet.

A halo of red curls catches my attention. I shift my gaze to the swinging door behind the counter. Fuck. I haven't seen her since the gala, and the sight hits me right in my solar plexus.

A headband holds her hair out of her face, barely

taming the mane. She's wearing a green apron, and if it isn't the sexiest thing ever, I don't know what is.

The only improvement would be if she were naked underneath. But then I would have to claw everyone's eyes out, so I guess the dress is okay.

With minimal makeup, her face is flushed, glistening with a film of sweat. She juts her hip to keep the door open and hands something to the guy behind the counter.

Too distracted by the curve of her breast, and that sexy-as-fuck swing of her hip, I don't realize she's spotted me.

When I snap out of my ogling, my gaze collides with hers. Her mouth forms an O, her eyebrows lift. I walk over, my lips curling up.

Not because I'm used to dazzling women with my dimples. It's not the automated grin I use to manipulate. I'm actually smiling, without forcing it.

"Isn't this a bit far from your beaten path, Stone?" Cora grins and steps to the counter.

"And how would you know my beaten path? Have you been researching me?"

She snorts. "Researching you? Who does that?"

You would be surprised. How would I know where you work, for example?

I ignore her question. "I came to invite you to a

charity luncheon. You proved quite a suitable plus-one last time."

She laughs. "That's one enticing invitation. I'm flattered," she mocks, her hand on her chest for dramatic effect. "When is the event?"

I glance at my watch. "In forty minutes."

She raises her eyebrows, her eyes twinkling with mirth, but then she frowns. "You are serious?"

"Okay, I recognize it's kind of short notice, but in my defense, I forgot about the event." I shrug, taking my smile up a notch.

She folds her arms across her chest. "Are you for real?"

"Always." That's a lie, but well, it's a harmless one.

She studies me, half-smiling, half-frowning, like she is entertained but at the same time not sure what's going on. That makes two of us. Why am I even here?

I guess she would be a safe and refreshing option to win my bet with Cal.

"And there isn't a bored socialite who would be happy to join you?"

Now I'm not sure if she's still mocking me, but based on her glare, I decide to tread carefully. "I'd much rather spend time with someone with more personality."

"I'm going to take that as a compliment. Thank you for your invitation, but I will have to decline."

What? She might not have succumbed to my charms (yet), but she did enjoy herself at the gala. It was a much-needed break for her. "On the grounds…?"

She shakes her head slowly, a wry smile tugging at her lips, eyes narrowing with a blend of interest and disbelief. "I'm working."

I look around. Only two people remain here. "Close the shop."

A snort-like laugh leaves her lips while she shakes her head again, but then her features harden. "You *are* serious?"

"You asked that already." Mild frustration edges into my composure. I guess I should have invited a boring socialite.

"I can't close the shop. I need the revenue."

I look around the empty place again, and then at her, deadpan.

She turns as if she's done with the conversation. "The lunch rush hour is about to start."

"Then you better close now."

"You're out of your mind."

I walk over to the front door and flip the sign to the 'closed' side. "Here, easy." I return to the counter. "Come on, Cora, don't tell me you don't want an afternoon off."

After a few drinks at the gala, she told me how

tired she was, and how hard it's been to run this business. The shadows under her eyes confirm it.

"I can't take a day off. Some of us have bills to pay."

One of the remaining customers comes to the counter and settles the bill. Cora's employee deals with him while I lean closer. Her scent wafts to me, and I almost close my eyes and inhale deeply.

"How much do you make a day here?" I look into her eyes, the emerald green in them gleaming with indignation now.

"That's none of your business." She jerks her head back.

I reach into my pocket and throw a wad of cash on the counter. "I will transfer another four K to your account."

She eyes what must be about ten hundred-dollar bills. "Did you hit your head on the way here?"

"That may be, but you will benefit from it." Why is she so stubborn?

She purses her lips and pushes them to the side, studying me like she's trying to decide if I have an infectious disease.

"Come on, Cora. You get a break, you won't lose money, and we both can have fun."

She shifts her pursed lips to the other side like she is really chewing on the idea. "As ridiculous and as inappropriately appealing as the idea is, I don't have a dress to wear for a fancy event."

She says it as if it's an obstacle. It's not. A challenge, maybe, but I always play to win.

"I'm Xander." I turn to her employee, offering my hand. "What's your name?"

"I'm Sanjay. Nice to meet you." He shakes my hand.

"Sanjay, your boss is leaving. Would you mind closing the shop once the couple over there leaves?"

"I didn't say I'm leaving," Cora huffs.

"You said my offer is appealing. That's as good as accepting it."

"You're obnoxiously bossy."

I smirk. "I have yet to get a complaint about that, sweetheart."

She rolls her eyes.

"Chop-chop, or we're going to be late."

"Stop. Right. Now." She steps back.

"Okay." I raise my thumb. "One. Do you want to make five K without grinding here?"

She glares at me, but doesn't negate the point.

I raise my index finger. "Two. Do you want to have an afternoon off while being catered to?"

It takes a moment before she nods—or rather shrugs—reluctantly.

"Three. Do you want to have fun with one of the

sexiest bachelors in Manhattan, according to several prominent online outlets?"

She perks up. "What? Why didn't you tell me Julian Franco is going to be there?" She fans herself, like the fashion-brand heir incinerated her underwear just by existing.

She thinks she can deter me that easily. Game on. "Okay, Coraline, shed the apron, and let's go."

She flinches. "My name is Cora," she snaps, but pulls the apron over her head. "You forgot about the dress."

"No, I didn't." I lean in her direction, offering her my arm.

She bends down and pulls out a monstrous-sized purse before she rounds the counter to snake her arm through mine, a disbelieving smile playing on her lips.

She eyes me with a dose of skepticism. "I feel like a hidden camera crew will reveal the prank any minute now."

"What prank? This is not high school." I open the door for her. "What do you carry in that bag?"

"None of your business, pretty boy."

"You find me pretty." I unlock the car and she stops, eyeing the ride with an expression that looks anything like the admiration my Lambo usually gets.

"You really are loaded, aren't you?" We walk to the passenger side.

"Don't hold that against me."

She mutters something I don't hear and sinks into her seat. I lower myself into the driver's side and rev the engine, showing off just a little.

Cora snorts, shaking her head, but one glimpse at her lit-up face confirms she is enjoying herself.

I've never tried to impress a girl—a woman—before, but apparently, around this one, I turn into a desperate asshole.

And I don't mind it.

"This one is perfect." I check my watch again.

At this rate, I'd be happy if we make it for the dessert. I might need to increase my fucking donation. Corm will bite my head off; his mother organizes this event.

I tap my foot. We've been at the hotel's boutique for fifteen minutes, and Cora is still in her outfit

Though I don't mind it at all. She is wearing a black wrap dress that has a small hole in the side.

She is underdressed, even compared to the shop assistant who is giving us a fake smile, and yet she is a hundred times more attractive.

I have been trying to dissect my irrational attraction to her, but I'm coming up empty-handed. I usually go for tall, leggy types. She is the exact opposite. And yet…

"Did you see how much it costs?" she whispers, the tag dangling between her fingers.

"No. I don't particularly care. It's a dress. How much could it be?" I shrug.

"It's three thousand," she hisses, and glances at the shop assistant while ducking a bit. Like she can hide from the price.

She acts like it was a hundred thousand. I snatch the dress from the rack. "Do you want it in more colors as well?" I shove the dress into her hands. "Get changed."

Her eyes widen before she looks at the dress again. She wants the dress, the desire all over her face as she chews on her bottom lip.

I groan. We're going to miss the whole thing.

"You really are desperate not to show up solo if you're willing to cash out such an insane amount of money to take me."

"Insane?" I would pay ten times more to spend time with her, but I just hike my shoulder and take out my credit card. "Just hurry up, finally."

She shakes her head as she enters the changing room.

* * *

"Wow, I didn't expect this to be such an eventful occasion." Cora kicks off her heels and leans against the balustrade.

The heat and humidity cling to us on the outdoor patio of the venue. We're standing under a canvas awning, in the shade, but the sun is still beating down on us.

"And you didn't want to come." I lean beside her, shedding my jacket.

"If I had known Declan would punch someone, I would have gotten front row tickets." She giggles and takes a sip of her cocktail.

Yeah, that happened. My partner caused a scene, but I guess the other asshole asked for it.

"You got front-row tickets." I turn and lean on my elbow, studying her profile.

Most of the guests have left, with only a few still loitering around, but Cora doesn't seem ready to dash. And I'm not going to rush her. She seems relaxed and carefree, just like she was at the gala.

The few minutes in her bistro were not enough to judge, but it's like she breathes with more ease after she steps out of there.

"You're staring." She looks at me, rolling the small straw from her drink between her lips.

"You're beautiful."

She cackles. "Yeah, I better be in a three-thousand-dollar dress."

She picked a deep green color. The fitted bodice hugs her torso, and a flared skirt falls just below her knee. The cut is classical, and yet she makes it look sinful.

The neckline is too high for my taste, but fuck if she isn't sexy wearing it. I *should* have bought it in all the colors for her.

"You increased its value tenfold."

"Oh, you're good." She grins at me.

And I grin back. This woman makes me feel lighter. Carefree. Liberated.

All the things I've been faking. With her, they sneak in uninhibited.

"Let's go." I put her drink on a nearby table and take her hand.

"Where?" She snatches her shoes from the ground and lets me lead her back inside, so we can get out of here.

"Since I practically hired you for the rest of the day, I plan to make the best of my time with you."

"Hired me?" She snatches her hand from mine, glaring. "Fuck you, Xander."

Chapter 4

Cora

I'm marginally aware of the staff tidying up the banquet hall where the luncheon was held, but I don't care about the audience.

I knew I shouldn't have accepted his offer. It was ridiculous to begin with, but I'm so bone-deep tired that the illusion of an escape won me over. Who would pay that much money just to take me to an event?

This cocky playboy, who made me feel beautiful and normal for a few moments.

I've been busting my ass in my father's bistro for years, which feels more like an eternity at this point. I have nothing to show for it—just debts, a deep feeling of failure, and exhaustion that painfully claims my joints and muscles.

So, yeah, the carefree, fun, entitled man in front of

me offered me a ticket to forget my reality for a moment, and I jumped at it.

I recognize that the concept of our transaction does little service to feminism, but can't I be selfish for once in my life?

Apparently, I can't.

It's one thing to silently berate myself for accepting his money, but it's entirely different when he throws it back at me. How dare he?

He raises his arms in surrender, his boyish grin lighting up his face. "That came out wrong."

I let out a laugh of disbelief. "Is that your apology?"

He gives me a lazy smile. A smile that has disarming qualities. And he knows it, because he's been using it like a weapon. "Apologies are for the weak. I don't do that."

God, I wish I'd never taken his offer, or that I could pay him back. An entitled rich boy. Fuck him. "I don't want your money. I'm going back to reopen the bistro."

I spin and march through the carpeted room.

"Cora." He catches up with me. "Come on. I promise you will not regret staying closed today."

To my dismay, his boyish grin does exactly what it intended. It makes me want to relent. Not necessarily because I want to spend time with him. But because the idea of spending time away from work is too appealing.

I work six days a week. I'm only closed on Mondays. And even then I'm working, ordering supplies, bookkeeping, paying bills... So much admin work. Being closed today without losing revenue is a gift. A relief. A chance to breathe.

What I want is to go home, cuddle with my cats, and spend the day in bed, just chilling. But there is that nagging sense of duty. Xander is reimbursing me for being here instead of at work.

I glare at him. His pale blue, almost gray eyes, usually lined with small crinkles of mirth, are downcast as he pleads with me through his unfairly long lashes.

The man is handsome, and rich as sin. He's also fun to be around. Partly because of his personality, and partly because he's so disconnected from reality.

Do you want it in the other colors as well?

He wasn't even kidding when he offered to buy me the dress in other colors. I'm pretty sure my entire wardrobe costs less than this one. I wish I didn't love it so much.

"Why?" I ask.

"You need to elaborate. Why does the sun shine today? Why isn't it Friday already? Why—?"

I roll my eyes. "Explain why you want to spend the day with me. It's one thing to have me fill in as your plus-one—though your approach was extravagant—but the event is over."

His pretty face grows serious, and he glances away for a moment, his jaw ticking, his hands in the pockets of his gray suit pants, all the dominance he bleeds effortlessly leaving him for a brief moment.

"I'm in the office twelve-plus hours a day, and when I need to decompress, I party. It might look glamorous from the outside, but it's fucking exhausting, and even more lonely."

I expected him to jest and bullshit his way to answering. Instead, he shocked me with his vulnerability. His honesty.

He rakes his fingers through his thick, light brown hair. It's buzzed on the sides, but longer on top, and his impromptu combing makes it stick up in a mess that makes him seem even younger.

He shifts his weight from one foot to the other, looking at me with an expression of capitulation.

He gave me a peek at the layer underneath his veneer, and I wish he hadn't. Because now my sense of duty kicks up a notch, and there is no way I'm going to deny him my company.

I still don't understand why he isn't with someone from his circle, with one of the long-legged bombshells he probably spends time with normally. Why me?

I shouldn't spend a day with him. It makes no sense. I'm a decade-older woman with a failing business who lives in a small apartment in Brooklyn.

He is rich, powerful, successful, and a ridiculously attractive playboy. There is nothing we have in common besides a group of friends—his partners who seem to have snatched up all my girlfriends.

His chin dips as he stares at me, and there is a veil of honesty in his expression I haven't seen before.

And as much as this friendship, or whatever this is, makes no sense, I realize we have something in common.

We're both tired and lonely.

I clear my throat. "There must be someone—"

"I had more fun with you at that gala than I had in as long as I remember. You're real, genuine... unlike anyone in my circle. Sue me for wanting more of that."

I expect him to joke or bullshit me, selling me a version of himself he so skillfully dazzles the world with. While his words ring true, I don't think he would freely confess his feelings to his peers. He trusted me. Perhaps because we're not close.

It's easier to confide in me. I don't matter in his life. I won't use his words against him. Perhaps that's why he'd want me to fill the gap.

And if I allow myself a moment of selfishness, the idea of one day that is completely different, almost illicit—stolen away from the everyday grind—sounds very appealing.

"Where would we go?"

The smile my question brings to his face is blinding. It's not his usual grin, which I'm starting to think is about as real as a wax figure's smile.

"Let me surprise you." He winks, and the playful playboy is back.

And while I find this side of his personality annoying, and quite frankly ridiculous now that I suspect there are other layers to him, I'm willing to put up with it.

"No shenanigans, Stone," I warn.

He offers me his arm. "It has never crossed my mind."

Of course it hasn't. I'm not his type. But for a moment, as I snake my arm through his, I allow myself to picture how it would feel to be chosen by Xander Stone.

Forget the age gap, the financial gap, and all the other gaps that separate us... I have a feeling we could have a lot of fun together.

I banish the thought as quickly as it blossoms, because it's a ridiculous fantasy.

"Don't make me regret this." I sigh.

"You're going to ask for more. And that's a guarantee." He gives me his cocky grin, and I roll my eyes.

Xander offers me his hand to help me out of the car. We're in the underground garage of a swanky hotel on the Upper East Side.

"A hotel? Really?" I glare.

"You will like it here." He locks the car, and we walk to the elevators.

"We agreed no shenanigans," I scold, but my admittedly rusting lady parts weep.

I have been buried at work, and it's been too long. Unfortunately. Because hooking up would be preferrable to my current celibacy.

But also because with an active sex life I would be immune to my current company's charms. I think.

I wish I could allow myself more freedom. Xander Stone certainly has the body and experience to deliver orgasms. My body would be on board, but my mind and my heart would fuck it up for me.

"Have some faith, woman." He puts his hand in the open door, so I can enter safely. The small gesture should not cause butterflies to fly amok in my belly.

"What are we doing here?" I hike my bag up onto my shoulder.

"What are you carrying in there? It looks like it weighs at least ten pounds." He hits the button for the reception.

"Leave my purse alone. I carry things I might need."

Perhaps three different notebooks are overkill, but I don't know which one I might need, so I carry all of them. Just in case.

"Like what? Bricks?" He smirks.

"Exactly. I use them to hit people with annoying questions." I look away, trying not to grin. This verbal sparring with him is more fun than it should be.

"It's a good thing I'm charming. I wouldn't want to walk around with a gash in my head."

The elevator stops, and he steps forward to keep the door open for me again. His hand lands on the small of my back for a brief moment as he ushers me out gently.

The contact sends electricity through my body, culminating at my core. Oh my, I'm really starved for human touch.

I'm so shocked by my reaction that I recoil, making a weird, inelegant step forward to avoid his touch.

The cool air of the foyer reaches my lungs, but my skin prickles with heat. What's going on? Premature hot flashes?

"Good afternoon, Mr. Stone." A suited man greets Xander with a smile. "They are ready for you."

"Thank you, John. I appreciate your help." Xander shakes hands with the man and pats his shoulder.

"Anytime, Mr. Stone; enjoy your afternoon." John,

who is wearing a name tag and must work here, nods a polite silent greeting to me.

"You come here often?" I ask as we walk down a hallway, my heels sinking into a light beige, spotless carpet.

How do they keep it this clean? My friends are rich, so I'm not completely new to the lavish world, but I can't help but look around in awe.

The dark wood paneling and gold decorations are minimalistic, but still feel opulent. The silence around us is another weird thing. Like we're no longer in Manhattan. This must be the only hotel undiscovered by tourists.

"I live here," Xander says as we reach a double door. A sudden scent of wood and floral surprises me, but not as much as his answer.

I stop, searching his face for signs of teasing. "You live in a hotel?"

He shrugs and taps a card against a small reader beside a double door. It clicks open, and Xander steers me in.

Before I can satiate my weird fascination with his living situation with more questions, I'm rendered speechless.

The air smells like eucalyptus had a love affair with lavender—clean and expensive.

A receptionist smiles at us. She looks like she floats

to work, her smile serene and glowing. I'm sure she's never yelled into a pillow or cried herself to sleep in her life.

Behind her, a waterfall trickles down a slab of stone that probably cost more than my apartment.

Soft music plays from invisible speakers. I feel like I should have moisturized more aggressively this morning, but at the same time, my frayed mind is drawn to this blissful oasis.

This place doesn't just whisper luxury—it recites it, with perfect diction and a posh British accent.

Xander leans in, and his breath fans my skin, snapping me out of my awe. The shiver his closeness sparks is another issue I'm going to ignore.

"Have I achieved the unheard of and rendered you speechless?" Even his whisper sounds obnoxiously loud in this room.

"This is a spa," I say, my eyes wanting to close just from the scent. This place oozes relaxation.

"Beautiful and smart," he teases, but I stare at him, robbed of my ability to quip back. Xander frowns. "Are you okay?"

How many times have I wished for a spa day in the last few years? Too many to count. Actually, I banished any thought of pampering and relaxation as soon as they sneaked in, because I don't have the luxury of time or money for such frivolity.

To my horror, tears prickle behind my eyes. I blink them away quickly. The receptionist says something, but Xander raises his arm to stop her, stepping in front of me, shielding me.

Like he knows I need time to compose myself.

Jesus, this is embarrassing. Maybe I'm so tired that the whiff of some downtime unlocks something I don't want to examine. The other thing I don't want to examine is why this practical stranger intuitively gifted me exactly what I needed.

"Thank you," I whisper, and he smiles and turns to the receptionist.

I got a two-hour-long facial and the best massage ever, and now I'm enjoying myself in the relaxation room stocked with fruit, nuts, and cucumber water in a crystal decanter.

Fuck, I can get used to this. But I guess even if I could afford it, it would become ordinary after a while.

I scribble a verse in my small notebook and put it down, sighing. Closing my eyes, I sag onto the soft mattress.

"This is the softest robe ever," I mew to myself, stretching on a lounger that is frankly more comfortable than my bed at home.

"Talking to yourself?" Xander's voice is all playfulness and gravel. It wraps around me more softly than the robe.

Has he always sounded like this? My mind must be so shocked from the onslaught of peace that it plays tricks on me.

I open my eyes to tease him back, but if I had any quip ready, it dissolves as I take in the sight.

Holy fuck.

Xander Stone stands across the room in nothing but a towel. His skin glistens, droplets of water beading across his broad shoulders.

Even with his clothes on, it has always been clear the man is ripped. But for the love of my trembling ovaries, I wasn't prepared for this level of magnificence.

He picks up a decanter and pours himself a glass of water. The ripple of his muscles as he executes this mundane task is like catnip for a woman who hasn't had sex in... Let's not go there.

He turns to me, raising his glass like he's toasting to something. Oh, he knows what he is doing to me. Asshole.

"I was just complimenting the softness of the robes here." I rub my cheek on the collar to emphasize. "You should definitely try them." I reach for the bowl of nuts to distract myself.

"Nah, I'm good."

I busy myself with the nuts like Cinderella sorting the peas and ashes, but I'm still acutely aware of him sauntering over and plopping onto the lounger beside me.

On the periphery of my vision, I see him putting his hands behind his head. I refuse to look at him, because God knows what happened to his towel as he flopped onto his bed.

"I needed this." He sighs.

A smile curls my lips up, and I put the nuts down and lower myself. I keep my eyes closed for the sake of sanity. I'm not going to let a half-naked man distract me from this visit to paradise.

"Thank you," I murmur, because as ridiculous as his infiltration of my day is, I can't argue with the facts: no one has ever done something like this for me, and I haven't had a day to myself in the longest time.

"You thanked me already." The bed squeaks a bit as he moves. "What happened out there earlier?"

Based on the proximity of his voice, he must have shifted to lie on his side. I swallow, painfully aware he's probably watching me.

If I hoped he'd let that moment pass, I was being naïve. He might have shielded me from the receptionist, but he wouldn't miss the opportunity to tease me.

But then I'm grateful for this experience, and he did offer a sliver of vulnerability today, so I decide to reciprocate. "I don't remember the last time someone did something like this for me."

"Taken you to a spa?"

"Allowed me to be selfish." I want to look at him, but then I remember he's practically naked, so I throw my forearm over my eyes for good measure.

"Self-care isn't selfish. I could see you were tired. You mentioned at the gala how much you work... You deserve a brief break. I'm glad I could organize one for you."

There is that cocky undertone in his voice, but fuck if his words don't stir more emotional turmoil inside me.

I almost wished he had said he wanted to come and just tagged me along, but he brought me here because he thought this was what I needed. A man who had only met me a handful of times before.

My emotions clog my throat, and I think my swallow must be audible. Tears threaten their reappearance, so I change the topic.

"Why do you live in a hotel?" I reach to take a sip of my tea.

"Why not?"

I whip my head toward him. "Are you for real? It must be expensive, and wouldn't you want a home instead of an impersonal space?"

He shrugs. "I never got around to finding something since I moved. At first, I didn't know where I'd want to live, and then I got too busy at work. I enjoy the service that comes with a room here. I'm comfortable, and it's convenient, which I value more than a painting on the wall and a picture on a nightstand."

I blink a few times, trying to understand his view, but I fail. Though I guess it must be nice not to cook, clean, or do laundry, or even grocery shopping. "But it must cost you a fortune."

He picks up an apple and takes a generous bite. The juice rolls from the corner of his lips, and his tongue darts out. A sexy apple bite. God help me!

I lie back down and force my eyes to stare at the ceiling.

"It's a fraction of what I make."

"That must be nice," I snort.

In the few beats of silence, the robe becomes incredibly uncomfortable, the sweat trickling between my breasts and down my spine.

I contemplate how different our worlds are, and with sadness, I realize that his world feels so much easier than mine.

"I don't think a piece of real estate creates a home. It's the people you share it with," he says casually, but the sentiment behind his words is anything but casual.

He moved here from San Francisco to start

Merged, I think. I paid little attention to what my friends said about him.

Thinking about it now, we had one lengthy conversation at the gala, but he somehow made me talk without sharing much. How did I not realize that?

"Do you miss your family?" I turn to him, hoping I've somehow built immunity to his muscles.

Unfortunately I haven't. But it doesn't feel like I should have this part of the conversation while talking to the ceiling.

The room fills with a heavy silence, and I regret taking this direction immediately. My family situation is something I never discuss, so why would I ask him that?

"I miss them, but this is where my life is now."

The statement sounds like a sentence of exile more than a decision, but I don't pry anymore. It's not like we're close enough to share details. Besides, I don't want to talk about my family, so let's leave it.

"And what a life! I can get used to this." I smile.

"You're welcome anytime." He winks.

"Don't tempt me."

My words are innocent... or that's how I meant them, but his pupils darken, and the air between us thickens with suggestion.

He gives me that slow, sinful smile that seems very

familiar, but which didn't seem to affect me before today.

"Maybe we can continue this upstairs in my room?" He reaches to tuck a curl behind my ear. The robe becomes a furnace as I try, and fail, to regulate my breathing.

"We agreed no shenanigans," I rasp, the words barely passing my throat. The devil on my shoulder throws a tantrum, questioning my sanity.

"I wonder, though, why you suggested it? What are you afraid of, Cora?" he drawls.

That is a good question? What am I afraid of? Because if I judge by my body's reaction to his touch—his mere presence—I'm fighting something, and I don't even know why.

I haven't been in a serious relationship for almost ten years, protecting my heart at all costs. I used to choose my casual hookups carefully, with men who felt safe. Men who wouldn't call the next day.

Even if there were a slight indication they would, I would just give them a wrong number. Yes, protect my heart at all costs, while potentially stomping over theirs.

I'm pretty sure Xander won't call the next day, but I'm also quite sure the loss would sting. He's not a safe option.

His hand lingers near my ear. It sends micro-explosions throughout my body. Swatting it away, I sit up.

"Don't be ridiculous, Xander, you're a decade younger. This makes no sense." I laugh, but it's strangled.

This man is good, I'll give him that, but he won't fool me. A playboy like him would have another woman on his arm within hours of sleeping with me.

He sits up as well, and as he pivots, his legs bracket mine. I glance down, but at least the towel is long enough to cover what seems like a growing erection. The awareness of his cock in such proximity makes me press my thighs tighter.

"Age is just a number. I don't care how old you are—"

"You should," I croak.

Nothing that happened today is ordinary for me, and yet all of it has been wonderful. Why can't I just be reckless for a bit longer?

"Now who is being ridiculous?" Xander says.

"I'm being realistic—"

"No, you're being stubborn."

Asshole. "Has it ever occurred to you I might not be attracted to you?"

His dimples make an appearance. "No."

"Well, that's presumptuous." At least his cockiness cools my inconvenient desire.

His hands settle on my thighs. I didn't even realize the robe had parted—not until his touch meets bare skin, and I freeze. My breath hitches. Goddammit.

I should swat him away, but it's like I have a point to prove—though I have no idea what I'm proving or to whom—so I don't move.

He doesn't advance any farther—just traces short lines up and down my inner thigh with his thumb. Even that feather contact makes me want to spread my legs.

I want to look away, but for some reason I'm a prisoner of his hooded gaze.

Okay, he's right, there is chemistry. Or my body is just so sex-deprived that it reacts. Not that I can tell him that.

"Coraline, we're both old enough for lies like that. We share an attraction, and I have a feeling that burying my cock in your pussy would be unforgettable. Because I'm not going to lie, I invited you to that gala because I wanted to get to know you. And since that gala, I have been thinking about all the ways I can make you scream, and believe me, you would enjoy every single one of them and ask for more."

Fuck, if he puts it like that… I pant by the time he finishes his declaration. One that sounded more like a threat.

It's not just the promise he so casually, but so

passionately, threw between us. It's not that he's just admitted he's been thinking about this for weeks.

It's the way he used Coraline for the second time today. My father is the only person who used my given name. Until he stopped.

I lick my lips, and Xander's gaze drops. He reaches to trace his thumb where my tongue was. It's slow and seductive. "Stop overthinking it."

He is right.

The thought feels so liberating, a smile stretches across my face. Before I get to nod and let him deliver on that delicious threat, we both jerk as my phone starts dancing on the table beside us.

Fuck.

I look at the screen, and dread replaces all the lusty fire in my veins. Tessa, my sister, never calls.

Groaning inwardly, I straighten my spine and answer.

"Finally. Where are you? Dad was robbed."

Chapter 5

Cora

Tessa's eyes practically hit her hairline when Xander helps me out of his expensive sports car. If I weren't so frazzled by the circumstances I would have insisted on taking a cab, or having my sister pick me up.

But I couldn't have gotten here fast enough. The ice bucket that Tessa's call dumped over us was a blessing in disguise, because what the hell was I thinking?

Xander Stone is the king of playboys, and I really don't have room for that in my life. It reeks of heartbreak and self-loathing. The latter I secretly practice with the utmost dedication regularly, so I don't need to add extra reasons there.

"Let me know if I can help in any way." Xander awkwardly kisses my cheek, but I'm sure he can't get away from here fast enough. I don't remind him that I don't have his number. He doesn't need my level of family drama.

Though he jumped into action the minute I'd received the call, and I'm grateful for that. The silence in the car on the way here was awkward as fuck. I was calming my hormones and my nerves at the same time.

He probably regretted the offer of a ride.

"Thank you… for everything." I tuck a strand behind my ear and cut the awkward dance between us short, dashing across the street.

The engine revs, but I don't look back. He's gone, and that's good.

"Who was that?" Tessa's tone is laced with accusation, which shouldn't surprise me because it's her signature intonation.

"A friend." I march toward the care facility entrance, but I know there is no way to avoid this conversation.

"Since when do you have friends with Lamborghinis?" she huffs, her heels clicking as she tries to keep up with me.

I stop. Does she really want to talk about this now? "Have you ever met any of my friends?" I deadpan.

This time, she huffs without the commentary. I resume my walking.

Tessa, who is usually a poster child for inflated self-confidence, always gets weirdly self-conscious when we visit Dad. In fact, I don't even think she ever visits by herself.

It might be the reason Dad rejoices every time we come. I'm not proud of that, but it makes me feel like my visits don't matter to him. As I said, not proud of those feelings, but I can't seem to curb them.

And while he is always thrilled to see her, Tessa behaves as if she'd secretly smoked weed on the porch before entering his room, all anxious and uncomfortable.

The tension grows with every step as we approach the building where Dad has lived since his stroke.

While my mind reels with all the possibilities, trying to solve the robbery before I understand what happened, Tessa blabbers inconsequentially about her life, mostly about an event she is putting together.

With her successful, handsome husband, a luxury mansion on Long Island, a villa in the country, and two perfect children—who I adore, so I can't hold them against her—Tessa has never worked in her life.

She keeps herself occupied with a never-ending series of charitable activities. I mean, I guess volunteering counts as work.

I hold a grudge because when Dad couldn't take care of his business, she never volunteered her time or money.

I'm being unfair. The deal was, Tessa picks up the bill for his care, and I take care of the business. I'm bitter because the business is barely surviving, and every time I visit my dad, I'm drowning in guilt.

"It's so unnerving. Can you believe a caterer canceled on me at such short notice? People in the service industry can be so unreliable."

She stops, her hands on her hips, her fingers tapping.

What I *can't* believe is how she can talk about this while we rush to console our father.

The foyer is busy with caregivers and visitors, the phone ringing in the background.

"How dare they?" I say, just to annoy her. I don't think she even realized I *am* a person in the service industry.

Her eyes widen. She opens her mouth, but changes her mind and waves her hand. Good. I continue toward the elevators.

She doesn't seem to follow, so I sigh and turn. My sister stands in the middle of the commotion, seemingly unaffected by it. With her lips pursed, she blinks away fake tears.

This is always the case: she offends me, but acts like it was the other way around. Plus she doesn't ask for help, but guilts me into offering it.

If I compare her life to mine, I guess her approach

has rewarded her, unlike mine. I hate how bitter I am every time we're together.

We need to get to our father, so I sigh and give in. "Send me the details, and I'll prepare the catering for you. But you have to source the staff; I can only get you food."

She raises her chin. "Thank you," she says, in a voice like she did me a favor, not the other way around, and marches away as if she is being chased.

"So sincere," I grumble under my breath, and follow her.

"Where were you anyway? Can you afford to close the shop? Nobody was answering the phone." She pushes the call button in quick succession, because apparently we're in a hurry, finally.

This is what I get for closing the bistro and indulging myself at a rich-people luncheon and a freaking spa. My father couldn't reach me, freaked out, and got my sister involved.

If I had stayed at work, this whole situation would have been manageable. An hour ago, I was blissed out of my mind, and the effect has evaporated so quickly.

And since when has Tessa been interested in the bistro? She insisted on selling the *money pit* when our father couldn't manage it anymore.

I take a deep breath. "I took a day off. And I have a cell phone, as you ended up remembering." Now it's my turn to jab the call button with a sense of desperation.

Every time I'm with Tessa, I feel less, and then I act less. Less kindly. Less mature. Less reasonable.

I hate that version of myself.

"Dad tried to reach you and couldn't, so he called me," she accuses.

The elevator comes, full of people, which saves me from screaming, slapping her, or worst of all, defending myself as if I did something wrong.

Why she is annoyed that he needs help is beyond me.

By the time we reach Dad's floor, my body doesn't feel any effect of the afternoon of pampering I just had.

I have been thinking about all the ways I can make you scream.

Jesus. As irrational as it is, I blame Xander for all of this. The stupid massage made me miss my father's call. Why didn't I check my phone? It was right there.

"Both together? Mr. Winslow will be so happy," a caregiver greets us when we arrive at Dad's ward.

Tessa greets her as if they are the best of friends. At least she doesn't speak to me anymore before we reach Dad's room.

"Tessa, you came!" Dad stretches out his arms, inviting an embrace, looking even smaller in his wheelchair than the last time.

Tessa gives him a quick peck on his cheek, and I approach and hug him, feeling him tense under my touch.

"What happened, Dad?" I sit in the chair beside him.

He looks at me with that absent gaze of his that I wish would clear one day. It breaks my heart every time I visit—he survived the stroke, but his life seeped out of him regardless.

He turns to my sister. "How are the kids? And how is that handsome husband of yours?"

Tessa walks around, tracing her finger along a shelf. "Everybody is all right. You really need to make sure they come to clean your room every day, Dad. We pay them to do that."

"Dad, tell me what happened." I try to get him focused.

I know this emergency is probably as fictional as any other we've had over the years, but still, let's not just chit-chat.

I find my blood boiling as usual when the three of us are in the same room. Tessa ignores Dad, he ignores me, and at the end of the visit I somehow end up feeling like a failure.

"Have you been drinking?" He raises his eyebrows.

"I had a glass of wine at an event earlier." I search my purse and pop a mint. "What happened, Dad?"

"Well, you remember how you put the bank on my phone?"

His slurring is always more pronounced when he's frustrated. I cover his hand with mine, trying to comfort him.

With his other hand, he clutches his smartphone to his chest, protecting it. I bought it for him so he could video call his grandchildren.

He seemed to have enjoyed the technology, so I installed a few other features to make his life easier. Including a banking app. What was I thinking?

I was happy that he took to the phone so well, and now plays solitaire and Candy Crush like a pro.

Not yet sixty-five, my dad doesn't belong in a long-term care home. But as he never fully recovered from my mother's betrayal, and after he suffered his stroke, we had no other options.

"I thought you enjoyed using the app." Okay, this robbery makes less and less sense.

"Yes, but someone stole my money." He holds his phone even closer, as if to protect what's left in his bank account. Which wasn't much to begin with.

"What do you mean, someone stole your money?" Tessa joins the conversation. "This place is a state-of-the-art facility. Who would steal here? We need to report this." She opens Dad's drawers and closes them again, nonsensically.

"Not from here. From my bank." Dad hesitantly hands me his phone. "I should never have trusted the stupid ape."

"App, as in application, Dad." I sigh.

I look at the screen, swipe a few times, and don't see the icon, so I use the search and find it quickly. I hand the phone back to him. "Type in your code."

I'm regretting that I exposed him, not just to convenience and entertainment, but also to the perils of cybercrime.

Dad takes the phone, his lips pressed tightly together. "Where was it?"

I lean over, and Tessa jumps closer, craning her neck. The initial password page is still on the screen.

"Dad, you need to put in the password first," Tessa urges, as if speaking to one of her teenagers.

Dad stares at the screen and grumbles, "It wasn't here."

"Dad, check if the money is there now." I smile at him to reassure him while my mind is racing. What is happening?

"The ape wasn't there," he says as he types in the password, and then turns off the screen and looks at us with a smile. "Well, I'm glad this unfortunate misunderstanding at least brought you two to visit me."

"I don't understand." Tessa stares at me.

I smile at Dad and take the phone to show him how

to find an app if he accidentally removes it from the home screen.

We chat with him for a little longer before Tessa announces she needs to head home. I promise to come again on Monday, as I usually do, and we both leave.

"Is your ride coming back?" My sister asks when we step outside.

"No, I'm taking the subway."

"I'm calling a cab. It's really unfortunate I had to come all the way here because he misplaced an icon on his phone. I have two children and a lot of work, Cora. Next time, answer your phone so we can avoid these kinds of situations."

"He was happy to see you," I whisper, but I don't think she hears me through her aggressive heel-clicking as she trots to the curb.

I pinch the bridge of my nose. The smell of lemongrass and sandalwood somehow still lingers on my skin. The whisper of the scent carries me back to the carefree afternoon.

I should never have accepted his invitation. What is it good for, getting a taste of the life that I can't have?

No more Xander Stone for me.

Chapter 6

Xander

I lean back in my chair and sip a coffee that tastes suspiciously like Roxy's contempt. The woman is the best office manager, but she doesn't hold back on any weapons when it comes to the four of us, the partners.

I catch her smirking as I spit the concoction back into my cup. Corm finishes a phone call as the other two partners walk into his office. Caleb takes a seat beside me on the sofa.

"I didn't know you worked from the office today." Corm pats his brother.

Declan's been working at home ever since the paparazzi started stalking his family.

None of us knew his nanny wasn't who she claimed to be, and none of us expected the media circus after the secret was uncovered.

"Yeah, me being here is the least of my problems. Lily wanting to go out today, on the other hand. Fuck..." he grumbles and sits down, scowling.

"Oh, yeah, Saar told me it's Cora's birthday." Corm sits down.

"It's not a good idea for them to go out. The photographers will be relentless," Declan scowls.

"No worries. I just spoke with Celeste. She suggested they all come to our house because of the baby," Caleb says. "I was going to force one of you to entertain me, but she just texted me that the girls agreed to postpone the celebration and go out when things calm down."

"Thank fuck for that." Declan relaxes visibly.

Will Cora be alone on her birthday? The idea bothers me more than it should. Especially since she never called me after I dropped her at her dad's.

I expected her to reach out once she had sorted out the situation with her father. I thought we would pick up where we left off. And even if she started overthinking it again, at least she could have let me know everything was okay.

Not that she owes me any explanations, but still...

Fuck. I have no business spending as much time as I do thinking about her.

It's been a week since the luncheon and the spa

afternoon, and she hasn't reached out. I almost barged into her bistro once.

Or twice.

Okay, three times.

I distracted myself instead and went out. But the Manhattan nightlife doesn't do it for me lately.

"Okay," Declan says, adjusting his cuff like he's about to issue a death sentence. "San Francisco."

Roxy picks up her tablet and types before she looks up. For some reason, we all wait for her before we start talking. Sometimes, I wonder who is in charge here.

Cal clears his throat. "Atlas wants someone from Merged on the board of that renewable firm they're acquiring. Part of the advisory clause."

"The clean energy company?" I ask, pushing the ginger curls and green eyes into the back of my mind. "The one whose vision is progressive, but the board smells like old money and older secrets?"

"Vireon, yep. They made some changes recently," Corm says, drumming his fingers on the armrests. "They specifically want one of us. Someone who understands scale, and can talk to the West Coast crowd without sounding like a Wall Street bulldozer."

"So not you," Roxy chirps.

He glowers and then focuses on Cal, who looks at me.

"Folks at Atlas like you," Cal says and pauses,

studying my reaction. "And your name still carries weight in that city," he adds.

Caleb and I met at Wharton, and I was the one who recruited him to join Merged. He's also the only person in the room who has an inkling about my relationship with my father.

Other than Roxy, who's been fielding his calls lately and knows for a fact I never call back.

"Only because half the city still hates my name," I mutter.

Roxy snorts from the corner. "I'd say more than half if we count all the ladies who mourn your departure."

Declan makes a dismissive sound. "Your father is on the board of three of their partner firms. He could open doors."

The air shifts. Just slightly. I crack my neck. "He could," I say smoothly.

Cal glances at me, his gaze not sharp, but measured. Like he's weighing something and already doesn't like the answer.

My heart rate speeds up just at the idea of that phone call. *Hey, Dad, yeah, I ignored your calls for months, but now I need your help, so I'm finally calling back.* Fuck.

I can avoid that by explaining to the men in this

room that my relationship with my family is on shaky ground—the understatement of the century.

But the mistake I made back home was the last mistake I'll ever make. My last loss. I promised that to myself, and I delivered on that promise thus far, bringing in win after win for this firm.

And that's what is going to happen. I will figure it out. Roxy isn't as subtle as Cal, studying me with raised eyebrows.

I look away. "We'll need someone out there frequently at first. Enough to attend the quarterly and smooth the transition. It's a good look for Merged if we show up committed."

Corm snorts. "Funny. Xander Stone talking about commitment. I thought you were allergic to the concept."

I shrug. "I've been committed to giving you a stroke for months. Feels like I'm close."

Declan grunts impatiently. "Xander has been committed to this firm." He turns from his brother to me. "You're our best option."

I nod. "Sure. I'll talk to my father."

The lie passes through my throat, followed by a lump clogging it. I avoid Cal and Roxy's eyes at all costs for the rest of the meeting.

To be honest, I kind of miss most of what's

discussed because my mind wanders. My mind never fucking wanders. It's ultra-sharp.

Today, it oscillates between my father, the San Francisco deal I can't fuck up, and back to my father. Round and round we fucking go.

The loud circus in my head is only interrupted by a certain foxy bistro owner.

"Okay, let's break up this party. Since my wife will be at home after all, I'm out of here." Corm snatches his phone and leaves us in his office.

"This is the proof that marriage should be avoided at all costs." Roxy stands up, jabbing her pen into her dreadlock bun.

"Don't dismiss what you haven't tried." Cal also stands up, but he lingers.

"Okay, I'm out of here, too. Roxy, send us the minutes. Thanks." Declan leaves.

"I thought you didn't speak to your father." Cal doesn't wait for Roxy's departure, because, like all of us, he knows nothing escapes her.

"I know he doesn't." She closes the door, leaning against it.

"Are you two ambushing me? What is this, a schoolyard?" I approach the door, glaring at Roxy.

She rolls her eyes, but steps to the side. "Most of the time, all of you behave like schoolchildren, so the answer to your question is yes. What's the answer to

Caleb's, though?"

"He didn't ask anything, Roxy. A question ends with a question mark, sweetheart." I smirk.

"Sweetheart me one more time and I'll staple your tie to HR's desk." She returns my glower with her own.

And while I question whether this encounter is high school behavior, now I'm the one engaging in a glaring contest. For fuck's sake.

"My apologies, Roxy." I open the door.

"Xander—" Cal follows me.

"I've got it covered, van den Linden. Go hover over someone else."

* * *

"Mr. Stone, will you want dinner in your room tonight?" the concierge greets me when I emerge from the underground garage.

"John, I think I'll just have a bite at the bar. No worries. Have a nice evening."

"If I may, Mr. Stone. The team at the spa found a journal. It only occurred to them now that it might belong to your companion from last week." He pulls a small diary from behind his desk.

I open it, and on the inner cover, I find Cora's name. I slam it shut.

"Thank you, John; I will return it to her."

I stroll to the bar in the corner of the lobby. The place is open to the public from the street side, but it has a private area with tables always available to the hotel's guests.

After ordering a steak and a glass of wine, I pull my phone out. My fingers tap reluctantly until I'm just a green icon away from calling my father.

The events that led to my move to the East Coast flash through my mind. A silent whisper reasons with me, suggesting I'm carrying more blame than I should own. I know my family—they would look the other way, protect me.

And that would only lead to more self-loathing.

Not that I don't hate myself for my role in the sale of our developer holdings, but at least I don't need to do it under the watch of my loved ones, constantly wondering how much of their disappointment they hide.

Some wouldn't even try hiding their contempt. Well, fuck them all. I'm richer than I've ever been, and it's all my achievement.

Yes, fuck them all. The sentiment spurs the reckless gene in me, and I'm about to tap the green call button when the phone rings, and I almost spill my wine.

Jesus.

"Xander speaking."

"Xander, it's Sissy." The sweet Southern drawl hits my ears.

"Sissy, how are you?" I deploy the Xander-Casanova persona, but my heart is not in it.

"I'm in the city, and I was hoping we could go out. It's been too long."

"Sissy, I'm too busy tonight. Let me know when you're here next time."

Busy? Eating my dinner alone? I guess I can always do more work when I get upstairs to my room. And that's what I'll do, so I'm not lying.

"Aw, don't be such a bore, X. Work can wait."

"Sissy, I wish it could, but not tonight."

She whines for a few more minutes before she makes me promise to see her in a few weeks, when she is back in Manhattan.

We finally hang up when the server brings my steak. Well, I guess I can't call my father while chewing.

But it's not like the issue is kept at bay. I spend my dinner thinking about the ways I can avoid asking my father for a favor. I research other board members, and make a list of my contacts on the West Coast who can help me.

I contemplate calling Lottie to see if she could call in some favors, but I know my sister would help, and then feel guilty about sneaking behind Dad's back. I don't want to put her in that position.

"Can I get you a dessert?" The server cleans my table. "The chef made his signature chocolate cake tonight."

"No, thank you. I'm good."

I wonder whether Cora likes chocolate cake. What? I don't wonder that. She probably didn't get a cake for her birthday.

Reaching for her journal, I consider the whole privacy situation for a beat, but open it anyway.

She built a sky-blue cottage for the sparrow with a broken wing.

A burrow with a library for the badger who had no friends.

A tall, pointy-roofed tower for the owl who wanted to feel closer to the stars.

What is this? The words are written in a tidy cursive, and I think it's the same as the one I saw on the blackboard menu in the bistro. Is this a story?

I flip to the back of the journal and find another entry.

Someday…

Own a private island — Tiny. Useless. Mine.

Is this some sort of bucket list?

See the Northern Lights wrapped in a ridiculous fur coat.

Eat my weight in pizza in Tuscany. Maybe live there for a while.

I chuckle. I can picture her there.

Have my stories published.

Are the lines in the front the beginning of a story? Does Cora moonlight as a writer? The need to know is so powerful, I've half a mind to find her and demand answers. Yeah, fucker, as if you had any right to her story. To her answers. To her time.

But then, she is alone on her birthday.

Finally give up the bistro.

Be held like someone's first and last choice.

Something squeezes my stomach. It's like heartburn building in my digestive tract. This place always serves top-shelf wine. What the fuck?

Forgive my mother (maybe).

Another need to uncover what's behind this wish hits me. Why do I care about her story? It makes no sense. I find the woman attractive, but when have I ever wanted to go beyond the superficial?

Fly first class without guilt.

Who feels guilty about first-class flying?

Find a way to matter outside of duty.

Fuck, Cora Winslow, you intrigue me more than I care to admit. More than I have time to explore.

The way her pupils dilated when I touched her thighs at the spa... The way my dick hardened just seeing her on the lounger in that fluffy robe... The way her lips parted... It's all etched on my mind, playing on repeat and without a pause button.

She had a lot of excuses though... like our age difference. I never even thought about her as an older woman. In fact, her being more mature just drives her into a league of her own.

None of the women in my recent past hold a candle to her. Her being mature and not taking me seriously is a fucking turn-on.

Unfortunately.

Clearly, she hasn't thought about me since the spa day, so why the fuck can't I stop thinking about her?

Because it's new? I haven't had to work hard to get a woman for… well, ever.

Is that her allure? That she keeps resisting? That's fucked up.

Maybe I should call Sissy back.

I pay the bill and take the elevator to my room. I don't bother with the lights, the silence and darkness coiling around my nerves.

Why do you live in a hotel?

"Well, Cora, it's convenient, but it's fucking awful," I say to the empty room as I get undressed.

Perhaps I'm staying here as a punishment. As my personal prison to pay for the mess I created back home.

The melancholy latches onto me with its relentless gloom.

Fuck that.

I get changed, grab my helmet, and head to the garage. I know exactly what will help me clear my head.

Chapter 7

Cora

LILY

I don't like you being alone tonight.

Don't worry about it. I'm pretending
it's not my birthday anyway.

LILY

But it is your birthday.

Stop it.

I'm fine. Enjoying Pitt and Clooney
and a glass of Zinfandel.

CELESTE

Sounds so peaceful. I love my
daughter, but sometimes I wonder if I
will ever just chill with a glass of wine.

SAAR

But look, you wrote two long
sentences.

That's an improvement.

LILY

I feel like it's my fault we're not celebrating you. Sorry.

Again. Stop it. All of you. My birthday is in a few weeks when we go party.

SAAR

Love you.

Good night.

I put my phone away and bring Pitt's fluffy, lethargic body closer. At this point, it's more the cat hugging me than the other way around.

Did I want to spend my birthday alone? No. Though I can't argue with a quiet evening. It's pleasant. Isn't it?

I bury my fingers in Pitt's fluffy coat, the vibration of his purring therapeutic.

I understand that Lily is in the midst of a public scandal, and going out with her wouldn't be enjoyable for any of us.

And I know Celeste would pump and come, but then feel anxious about leaving baby Amelie for a couple of hours. At this stage of motherhood, it must feel like an abandonment. Or so I hear.

And she offered her place, but that wouldn't be

much of a celebration. She'd be distracted, and we would all just focus on that adorable little girl of hers.

I didn't want to impose on them, so I insisted we postpone.

As a birthday gift to myself, I left work early, leaving Sanjay to mind the shop. I should review the financials, but no amount of staring at the spreadsheet would make my father's business more profitable, so fuck that.

At least for one day.

Well, technically, a second day of freedom in the span of a week. The lemongrass and sandalwood are long washed out, but when I close my eyes, their scent lingers.

I should have reached out to Xander to thank him. Especially after our outing was halted abruptly. But I almost gave in to his charm, so I'm sure he appreciates my sparing him an awkward dance. I'm glad I don't have his number.

In light of my real life and duties, I realized how unrealistic such an affair would be. He might say he doesn't care about my age, but that proves the point. He is careless, and I need to be responsible.

Besides, I don't think Xander Stone is a guy you sleep with and forget. Not a girl like me. Jesus, I'm thirty-seven, not seventeen, so why do I feel like giving in and having fun with him is akin to sneaking out of my parents' house to meet a boy? What is wrong with me?

Standing up to Pitt's loud protests, I refill my wineglass and search for a journal in my purse. The sunflower-covered one has been missing. Have I left it at work? Perhaps it's in my bedroom?

A knock on the door stops my search. Is that little Pavel? My eight-year-old neighbor visits occasionally. When his parents argue. Sometimes I wish I weren't working so much, so I could give him refuge more often.

I open the door, and my heart swells. "What are you doing here?"

Saar pushes her way through. "I ran out of Zinfandel, so I came."

"Did you really think we'd leave you alone on your birthday?" Celeste gives me a quick hug.

"Happy Birthday." Lily enters, wearing a baseball cap, sunglasses, and an oversized male jacket.

I open my mouth, and she raises her hand to silence me. "Don't say anything. Declan wouldn't let me leave the house unless I disguised myself."

A laugh bubbles in my chest. "How are you?"

"I've been better, but we're not talking about me tonight. I need a night that isn't about me." She sheds the jacket and the cap.

"And I need an hour or two when I'm not a milk

factory." Celeste pulls chips, popcorn, and cupcakes from a large bag I didn't even realize she carried.

"So where is that Zinfandel, birthday girl?" Saar walks into my kitchen.

She used to live here, for a brief period before she married Corm, so she knows where I stash my favorite wine.

It doesn't take long before we're eating junk and treats and drinking wine, while the conversation and teasing flow effortlessly.

Best birthday ever.

The fact that these women showed up like this melts my heart.

"Okay, I will have to leave soon... Leaking breasts..." Celeste rolls her eyes, cupping her tits. "But we never got a chance to talk about the luncheon."

Lily groans.

Saar perks up. "Not about your revelations and Declan's brawl." She looks at me with her eyebrows raised in expectation. "I think Celeste is referring to Xander fucking Stone paying Cora to be his plus one."

Fuck.

"You make it sound dirty." I throw a chip at her.

She catches it and pops it into her mouth. "Spill the beans."

"There is nothing to spill. He showed up at the bistro and wouldn't take no for an answer."

"That sounds like him," Celeste says. "It doesn't surprise me that the man would coerce you in any way possible. And I definitely don't blame you for taking his offer."

Her support plays tug of war with my good-girl complex. "I don't know what I was thinking."

"Wait a minute. We all know that Xander man-whore Stone would charm the pants off any woman. The fact that he was so adamant about taking you is what I would like to dissect." Saar leans forward, her long legs crossed, eager to listen.

"What? Like I'm not worthy of his attention?" I fake my indignation. But the thought has been playing in my mind, mocking me. Questioning my worthiness.

"Hey, if anything, *he* doesn't deserve *you*. I'm more intrigued by his dedication," Saar says.

"He said something about enjoying my company at the gala." I shrug.

Lily's eyes widen. Celeste tuts, and Saar's arm shoots up in victory. "I knew it."

"We went to a spa afterward, and he wanted to fuck me." I recoil internally.

Not because the idea is cringe-worthy, but because the way I described the situation degraded it. But perhaps I've been romanticizing the whole thing.

"Never would I have guessed that Xander is a man willing to put in the work. I thought he walked through life while women threw themselves at his feet." Saar tops up her glass.

"How was it?" Lily, the shyest of us, surprises us with her question.

"I didn't sleep with him." I pick up Clooney who curls in my lap.

"Why not?" Saar asks.

"Wrong question," Celeste says. "We should bow to a woman who resisted his charm."

"Well... more like I was saved by the bell." I shrug. "I got a call from my father and had to leave."

"Is your dad alright?" Lily reaches to touch my hand.

"Yes, he is okay. And once I dove into the reality of my life, I realized that a fleeting fantasy with Xander would be stupid. So there is that."

"And he just gave up?" Celeste frowns, and I nod.

I've been thinking about being saved, but now it feels like I was rejected Whichrationally I know is not true, nor do I care. My stomach still churns at the thought.

"It was his idea to take you to the gala and then the luncheon." Saar slides down from the sofa and folds her long legs under her, elegant as always. "It's weird that he would give up like that."

"Perhaps he realized I was more trouble than he

cared for. He drove me to my father's home. The whole thing just dampened the mood."

"Would you like to revisit it?" Celeste asks.

"No," I say too quickly. "I don't know. At the spa, it was a different world. Later, it felt like a mistake. So I'm glad we got interrupted. Besides, he's been out with several long-legged socialites this week."

"So you're looking him up?" Celeste grins. "Also, you can't be sure those pics are recent."

I sigh. "I hate to admit that my pride is hurt. I wanted him to call and try to pick up where we left off. Not because I want to follow through, but because it felt nice to be wanted."

"You have been single for too long. We need to find you someone," Saar suggests.

"Like a fake husband?" I deadpan.

All three of my friends ended up in marriages of convenience with Merged partners. How ridiculously odd is that?

But I guess those workaholics don't have other social lives other than the ones that came with us. And since Saar is Caleb's sister... well, somehow my close friends paired up with the rich businessmen.

"Touché. But seriously, when was the last time you dated? I don't remember you going on a date in... well, ever." Celeste turns to me.

How have we been friends for years, and I never told them why I don't do romance?

I take a sip of my wine. "I don't do relationships."

"Why not?" Saar cocks her head, her eyebrows drawn together.

This time, I take a long gulp before I place the glass on the table. Clooney jumps down, disturbed by my move.

He walks away to find his peace in my bedroom, and I swear he sighs his annoyance. My cats give an Oscar-worthy attitude most of the time.

"I was engaged ten years ago."

The bomb renders the room speechless. The echo of my words booms in my head. I haven't said the words in... well, a decade.

I brace for the agonizing squeeze in my chest, the tightening of my stomach, and the scorching lava in my throat—the usual manifestations of the memory and the grief—but while sadness descends, my reaction is pale.

I haven't thought of Ethan in a long time. The realization surprises me, and a wave of guilt washes over me.

"He died in an accident a few weeks before the wedding," I complete the sordid story, and the silence deepens.

"I'm so sorry." Saar speaks first, and my friends murmur agreement with the sentiment.

"Thank you. Needless to say, I'm healed from the heartbreak, but not willing to chance it again. So I avoid relationships."

Lily comes over, hugs me, and stays seated on my armrest. Her closeness wraps me in comfort I didn't even know I craved.

"I can't imagine what that must have been like," she says. "But love surprises us, even if we don't seek it. Don't let the grief stop you from living."

"You deserve to be happy," Saar adds.

"Well, in any case, I don't think a lifetime of happiness is what Xander Stone offers."

Saar snorts. "Smart words."

"I agree. If you're avoiding heartbreak, stay away from him," Lily says.

"Well..." Celeste prolongs the vowel in a way that suggests she might have a different opinion. "Maybe you hooked up with the wrong men before, so I wouldn't discount the idea of getting back on the horse." She makes quotation marks with her fingers.

"My last hookup..." I cringe. "The morning after was awkward as hell, and negated the mediocre night completely. I just stopped trying, I guess."

"Oh my God, one shitty experience can't guide your orgasm quest." All animated, Saar pushes to all fours like she could make her point only if she leans closer.

"An orgasm quest?" Lily giggles.

"I can take care of my own orgasms, thank you very much," I protest.

The three women look at me with various levels of skepticism.

"It's not the same." Lily voices what they are probably thinking. Lily, the least experienced one.

"Was Ethan your first?" Celeste asks.

"No," I admit so quickly, and they all snicker. "I enjoyed my slutty early twenties."

"So then you have no problems with hookups." Saar props herself on her forearms on the coffee table between us, her interviewer nature shining through.

I shrug. "I was with Ethan for five years, and he was the one. He kind of erased the guys before him."

"So perhaps the hookups after him were tainted by your grief?" Lily squeezes my shoulder. "You didn't allow anyone close enough."

"When did you become so perceptive?" I tease. Lily is twelve years younger than I am.

"Older man." She shrugs, referring to Declan.

Saar groans, and I laugh.

"Wait a minute," Celeste says. "When was that?"

All three women look at me with expectations. "When was what?" I pretend not to understand her question, because, for some outlandish reason, I'm embarrassed.

"When did you last fuck someone?" Celeste clarifies, frowning in concern.

Heat swallows my cheeks. "A year or so ago?"

The silence after my sad engagement story was filled with compassion. This pause is just plain shock.

Lily leans back, as if looking at me from a different angle would help her understand the words.

Saar seems to have a blinking seizure, and Celeste just gapes.

"Jesus, as I said, I can take care of my own orgasms." I cross my arms over my chest.

"Merde," Celeste utters. The French dancer has never stopped swearing in her native language. "We're definitely finding you a man."

"Unless you *want to* be celibate. We won't judge you." Saar gives me a reassuring smile, and the other two women agree vigorously.

I roll my eyes. "I know you won't judge me, but it feels like you're pitying me."

"It's more like I can't imagine..." Saar takes a gulp of her wine.

"I had no sex for five years before Declan." Lily shrugs. "I didn't have time to even think about it. I understand, but I'm glad my dry spell is over."

"Say the word, and I will have all Caleb's friends line up to wine and dine you," Celeste says.

"Corm would help, too." Saar perks up. "If that's what you want."

"I don't think Declan has friends." Lily shrugs, biting her lip, and we all burst out laughing.

"Okay, okay, I think I'm ready to date," I declare, raising my glass, and we all drink to my declaration. "Though I can't imagine when I would have time to do so."

"Maybe you can close for a week, and we will set you up on fourteen dates. Then you have a pool to choose from." Saar stands up, bouncing with excitement.

I snort. "Fourteen dates in one week?"

"Sure." Saar shimmies her hips. "Two per day. It will require careful coordination, but it's doable."

I laugh. "You're serious?"

"I think it's a great idea. A matinee and an encore," Celeste says, and Lily nods.

"I can't afford to close for a week." I shake my head, chuckling.

"We will cover the lost revenue," Saar offers with such determination, and I stop laughing when I realize my other two friends are equally on board.

"You've lost your minds. Or you're all drunk."

"That may be." Saar takes a generous sip. "But I'm

serious. We will cover the cost. It's our birthday gift to you."

They look at me expectantly. The three of them are serious about this. I'm so overwhelmed by the prospect, I don't even know what to say.

It's such a ridiculous idea, I'm tempted to agree just for the fun of it. It's also disturbing how my friends can throw money around like that while I live from one day to another, often worrying if my electricity can stay on.

"You already gave me gifts." I point to the gift bags in the corner.

"Let us treat you to this," Saar pleads. She walks around the coffee table and sits on it, taking my hands into hers.

I look from one woman to the other, finding love and determination in their eyes. Would it be so bad to be reckless for once in my life?

I take a deep breath. "I can't take money from you like that." I guess my reckless streak lasted exactly two seconds.

"You took money from Xander," Celeste points out. Not helping.

"Yeah, and I shouldn't have. That doesn't mean I'm accepting full-time charity-case status." I bounce my leg, the reckless streak fighting its way back while my pride fights it with vigor.

"You're not a charity case, Cora. And sorry if I

offended you with the idea. Okay, no money, but you're closed every Monday, so let us set you up on two dates every Monday. And if you take one more evening off, it could be three dates a week." Saar is all business.

I let out the air through pursed lips. "I could use an evening off occasionally."

"Yes." Celeste claps.

"What the hell—let's do it." I shake my head, grinning. Maybe we'll sober up tomorrow and realize how silly the idea is.

"Do you want Xander on the list?" Saar asks.

Yes. "That's not a good idea." My ovaries scream in protest.

"That's probably for the best." Lily stands up. "I have to go. Declan probably wore a hole in the carpet, pacing and waiting for me."

Celeste gathers her things. "Have I ever told you that the first time I met Xander was when he walked in on me and Caleb fucking on the st—"

"For the love of God," Saar cries. "How many times do I have to tell you, I don't want to hear about you doing any of that with my brother?"

Lily bursts into giggles, and I join her.

"Stop laughing." Saar shakes her head, but her lips curve.

We say goodbye, and I consider tidying up, but the leftover chips win me over. Munching on the salty drug, I grin. It turned out to be a wonderful birthday, after all.

Knock. Knock.

I frown, checking my watch. I open the door. "What did you forget?"

But it's not any of my friends I find on the other side. My eyes collide with the tousled, sandy hair, gray eyes, mischievous grin… and for the love of my ovaries, the man is clad in tight jeans and a leather jacket.

Xander Stone in a suit is a feast for the eyes. This bad-boy casual version of him is devastating.

I swallow.

He is NOT on the fucking list.

Chapter 8

Xander

Cora's gaze scans me from head to toe, and a part of me would even suggest she likes what she sees.

She is wearing jeans and a white T-shirt, the most simple and casual of all outfits, and fuck, I certainly do like what I see.

What did you forget? Who did she think I was?

"Were you expecting someone else?" I lean against the door frame, making sure she can't close the door.

The simple fact that I'm here should concern me, but I keep banishing the thought. I rode my bike mindlessly to clear my head. Somehow, I ended up at her bistro.

She wasn't there, so I decided to send her a cake. It's her birthday, for fuck's sake. To do that, I needed to bribe Roxy to get me her apartment number.

I don't even want to know how she got it. Or what her "I'll cash the favor later" means.

Instead of ordering the birthday cake, I reached out to my lawyer, who didn't appreciate the late call, but I pay him enough to keep his grievances to himself.

Now I'm standing here with an envelope in my pocket, to celebrate a birthday with a woman who never invited me.

I don't know whether I like the image.

But I know I don't want to be anywhere else.

It took me twenty-seven years to understand the thrill of the chase. That's what I think this is, because the other explanation... Fuck, there is no other explanation. I'm not interested in exploring another angle.

"What are you doing here?" She ignores my question.

I go with the least cool answer: the truth. "I didn't want you to be alone on your birthday."

Her face softens, a smile teasing at the corners of her mouth, but then she frowns. "How did you know it's my birthday?" Her frown deepens. "And how do you know where I live?"

I give her a slow smile. "I told you, I have my sources."

"Are you stalking me, Xander Stone?" Her words miss the bite, and she is grinning, so I take that as an invitation.

"You wish," I deadpan, and push my way in.

I'm immediately in a living room. A jacket hangs on a hook on the inside of the front door. I guess that's the extent of her entry hall.

A sofa, two armchairs, a coffee table, and a dresser with bookshelves above it are all that fit into this room.

An open door to my right leads to the kitchen, or I guess it's just a countertop with a stove and a cupboard. Another open door leads to her bedroom.

Being in close proximity to her bed makes my cock twitch. Fuck, where is this desire coming from?

The two dates I forced myself into this week resulted in my making up some excuse so I could dash out before we even ordered the main course. I had put in the effort, but I just didn't want to be there.

And here I am, uninvited into Cora's apartment, and my cock perks up. Fuck. It must be the unresolved tension from the spa.

"Are you okay?" She eyes me suspiciously. "If you're wondering, yes, this is my entire apartment. Your hotel room is probably bigger," she says sarcastically.

I wasn't wondering about that, but I'm not going to correct her. Fuck, she is right. My hotel suite's entry hall is larger than this place.

"I like it." I shrug.

I'm not even lying. It has character. It smells and

feels like Cora. It is also full of mess and clutter. I cringe; maybe I'm lying a bit.

Cora snorts.

Fuck, now she thinks I'm a pompous prick. She's probably been thinking that anyway.

"Did you get me another Danish?" She eyes the white box in my hands. "You need to stop sending—and now bringing—them over."

"You like them." I shrug, handing her the pastry.

I refocus on what looks like party leftovers on the coffee table: three bottles of wine, various wrappers, bowls with crumbs, chip bags.

"That looks like—"

She cuts me off. "Like your sources were wrong, and I wasn't alone on my birthday? The question is, do I need to file a restraining order?"

"Depends." I shrug, shoving my hands into my pockets.

She cocks her head. "On?"

"Do you want to miss out on my company... on the *fun* I offer?" I enunciate fun in a suggestive way that leaves no room for interpretation.

She snorts. "Careful, pretty boy, my apartment isn't big enough for your ego."

"Let the record show she thinks—not for the first time—that I'm pretty." I shrug, rolling on the balls of my feet back and forth, unsure if our current position by the door is a sign she will ask me to leave soon.

She laughs. "Okay, have a seat. Can I offer you anything? I have leftover chips or a half-eaten cupcake, and a glass or two of Zinfandel left."

Her eyes gleam as she grins at me. She's tipsy. Adorably so.

Why did I think she'd be alone? The need to know who was here with her is annoyingly persistent.

I take a seat on the sofa. My feet leave the ground as I sink in much deeper than expected. Fuck, this sofa is worn out. "Do you have Macallan?"

She laughs. "Of course. Do you want a twelve- or fifteen-year-old?"

Is she teasing me? I frown at her, trying to read the situation.

She huffs. "Jesus, you really are from a different planet. Sorry, but it's Zinfandel or Zinfandel."

She doesn't wait, but gets a clean glass from her excuse for a kitchen and pours me what's left in the bottle. One of the bottles anyway.

I take it from her, shaking off the awkwardness. I seem to have a perpetual cultural shock around this woman. It's humbling, but also weirdly refreshing. So different from anything I know.

"Happy Birthday." I raise my glass and take a

generous gulp. When have I ever needed liquid reinforcement?

"Thank you."

She sits across from me and crosses one leg over the other. It's an automatic position, but she looks so effortlessly fluid, otherworldly. A queen.

A black headband holds her curls off her face, and I let my gaze roam over her freckles. How did I not notice she had so many?

It's like here, in her domain, I see new layers of her.

I'm about to produce my gift, when a furry creature comes from somewhere and glares at me. Hair stands up on my neck, and I fight the need to recoil. The cat hisses a few times.

While my mouth goes dry, Cora seems immensely entertained. "That's Clooney; you're sitting in his favorite spot."

The cat glares at me, and I glare back. *Let's see who wins, fucker.* I blink a few times because another cat saunters in, joining Clooney, and fuck, I can see they are cats, but their glower turns them into pumas. No, lions.

I scoot to the other side of the sofa, and the two jump up, giving me a shrug, I swear.

Cora giggles, and the sound breaks my silent war with her felines.

"You have two cats," I say, like a complete idiot.

"Maybe I have ten." She shrugs.

My eyes dart around, and she laughs again. Fuck, but I'm still not sure if she's teasing me.

"Ten?" I croak.

"Oh my God, the unflappable Xander Stone is freaked out by kittens." She seems unreasonably pleased with the situation.

"They don't look like kittens." I eye the two beside me, and to my horror, one of them places its paw on my thigh.

I tense. It's not that I hate cats. Or fear them. Okay, fuck it, I'm terrified of them. It's completely irrational, rooted in an unfortunate incident with a feral, rabid cat that Lottie brought home once when I was seven or eight. I shudder at the memory, sweat erupting on my skin.

The cat stretches, protracts its claws, but then it deflates into a tight ball and starts purring. I try to push the discomfort aside. The purring isn't all that bad. Ever so slowly, I lower my hand to its fur.

I caress its back cautiously, and the purring intensifies. "It's like a helicopter."

When I look up, my gaze collides with Cora's, and my stomach flips. She's never looked at me like that.

Like she likes what she sees, an enigmatic smile lingering on her lips. I'm captivated by it, and for a moment I forget I'm in the vicinity of a potential predator.

"That's Pitt, and it looks like you bonded." She stands up and comes to give both cats a scratch.

Her citrus scent immediately reminds me of her naked body in that robe in the spa. Not that I saw what was covered under the plush material, but my imagination offered enough to replay that moment more often than I care to admit.

She looks up, and life pauses. Bent over like that, I get a glimpse of her white bra. It's just a suggestion of the lace, but I still fidget, adjusting for the pressure behind the zipper of my jeans.

But it's not just the sexual calling of her scent and looks; it's her face tonight that is somehow different.

Like she sees me in a different light. Like she shifted her perspective. Like she is open to possibilities.

Her heat warms my skin, and I itch to move my caress from Pitt to her. Our gazes locked, she licks her lips, and my eyes drop.

She is close enough for me to kiss her. Is that why she came over? Those luscious lips part slightly, the air between us crackling.

I'm about to lean forward and claim her mouth when she straightens. "Sorry, I need to pee."

She scrunches her face in what I interpret as

regret? Apology? Like she wanted to lean into the moment, but nature's call was too strong.

"Be my guest," I say, as if this were my place. *Idiot.*

She narrows her eyebrows, her latent grin still present, and disappears behind me. I glimpse the closing door I haven't noticed before.

"Be good to Pitt and Clooney," she calls from the bathroom.

As if on cue, the other cat gets closer and nudges my hand.

"Okay, beast," I mumble and scratch his head. He doesn't seem content with that, and lazily jumps down and saunters away.

I hear water flush, a faucet run, and then some buzzing noise. Is she shaving? Brushing her teeth? I smirk and stand up, because my body is filled with excess energy I need to shake.

Pitt groans and follows his brother.

Cora's living room is small, but it doesn't feel crammed. A pile of journals on a dresser reminds me of the sunflower one in my inner pocket.

I don't think she would appreciate my reading it, or even knowing I opened it, so I decide to add it to the other ones.

"Don't touch those." Cora's voice startles me.

I drop the notebook and pick a random photo frame beside the journals before I whip around. "Is this your…" I glance at the picture of young Cora with a man. "Your father?"

Thank God it's not a picture of her cats. It would solve the question about their number, but make me scramble for a way to finish my question. And I've felt weirdly inadequate enough times tonight already.

She comes around the sofa and peeks at the picture.

"Yes, that's me and my dad." Her breath is minty… She *did* brush her teeth. It feels like a win.

The chances are it has nothing to do with me, but I'm not going to entertain that. She's planning to keep that mouth of hers close to me. And I don't mind.

"How is he doing?" I put the picture back beside the others. A few more with her dad and some with her friends. There are no cat pictures, so the mystery continues.

"He's fine. It was a misunderstanding. He deleted an app icon from his home screen." She shrugs and points toward the sofa, moving us away from the dresser.

I can't be sure, but there is an urgency in her seemingly subtle attempt to relocate us. Like the dresser contains secrets she needs to protect.

I plop back onto the sofa. "It must have freaked him out. It's easy for our generation, growing up swiping and scrolling, but for him... there must be a learning curve."

Cora's eyes crinkle in another soft smile. She is back in the armchair. Too far from me. "Wow, I didn't expect this."

"What?"

"Understanding instead of mocking the situation."

"I like to keep things light, but that doesn't mean I'm a cynical asshole."

That enigmatic smile lingers. It has a direct line to my insides, warming up my chest and steering things south of there.

"So just an asshole." She tries hard not to smile fully, but she's failing miserably. It's nice to see her like this—like she put aside the weight she usually carries on her shoulders.

"Hey, that was uncalled for."

She giggles. "Okay, Xander, I apologize. And thank you for thinking of me on my birthday, under strange circumstances that make me want to call the police, but... I still appreciate you coming."

"Though it seems you were not alone after all." My eyes beckon to the coffee table.

"Saar, Celeste, and Lily came. We couldn't go out because of the tabloids' hunt for Lily, but a low-key night was perfect."

"Is that how you always celebrate? With close ones only?"

She tips her head to the side. "Who else would I celebrate with?"

"I don't know. My birthday parties at home used to involve hundreds of guests, most of whom I didn't know."

"Hundreds? Whatever for?"

"Mostly networking and business deals."

"Wow, that's... I don't even know what to say. Growing up, I usually spent it with my family. We would go to a restaurant of my choice. Later..." She pauses, and something flickers through her face, wiping away that casual, relaxed smiling expression. "My mother left, and I would go out with my friends, but my father always waited for me with a bottle of Zinfandel. Ever since I was seventeen."

"Illegal." I mock outrage.

She giggles. "He allowed me only a sip or two at first. My first official drink happened when I turned twenty-one. It was more of a ritual than a drinking event. He talked about his dreams for the bistro... After Mother left, he never recovered, and the bistro was his only reprieve."

"He must be so proud you took it over."

She sighs. "Yeah, I hope he is."

She looks away, and I wonder if we went too deep into the personal and spoiled the mood.

"I guess we had very different birthdays growing up," she says, smiling at me again, but the ghost of whatever the conversation triggered prevails in her eyes, now veiled in sadness.

"My version was fucked up, but at least I got a lot of gifts." I shrug.

"I have a feeling you didn't really need anything growing up."

"In a material sense, perhaps not." I'm not ready to dissect that, so I cut the topic short. "Talking about gifts..." I pull out the envelope and hand it to her across the table. "Happy Birthday."

She scoots forward and grabs it eagerly. "What is it?" She opens the flap and pulls out the paper, unfolding it. She frowns for a few moments, which seems to last long enough for me to doubt the gesture. "What is this?" she asks again.

"A deed."

She rolls her eyes. "I can see that. But it's for a piece of land, and there are only numbers and coordinates on it."

"It's an island in the Pacific Ocean."

I have experienced a lot of excitement—fake or genuine—after I gifted a lot of useless expensive shit to women over the years, so I'm pretty sure I fucked up the minute I said the words.

The deed falls from Cora's hands, and she blinks a few times, her jaw slackened. The worst part is she doesn't say anything, so I'm not even sure if my internal freak-out is warranted. Maybe she is just surprised.

"I have a feeling it's not a pleasant surprise," I say.

She opens her mouth and closes it. Then she repeats the motion a few more times before she finally utters words. "I don't want to be ungrateful, but this is the kind of gift you give someone who doesn't need anything. And even then... what am I supposed to do with it?"

"Nothing; it's just for fun, so you can say at parties that you have an island, or have it named after you..." I peter out because the words sound frivolous to me.

Fuck. She may have put it in her journal, but I guess I annihilated my lawyer to deliver on my impossible request for nothing, because when I look around this place, she would have benefited from a thousand other gifts.

The silence between us is next-level uncomfortable. I should probably leave, and avoid her from now on.

"Well, thank you." She lets out a laugh that sounds a bit deranged, her sincerity wiped out by the stupid gift. "You're right, it's a funny gift. Unforgettable, for sure. Maybe next year you can gift me a plane ride to visit my property." She gulps down her wine and refills it quickly.

I don't even know what to say. I have never thought of gifts in terms of their practicality. She was right; I've never needed anything, and neither have people I know. Gifts have always been a question of originality, fun. Now they feel like empty gestures. Fuck.

"Cora—"

"No, Xander, don't say anything. I understand you meant well. I understand we fly in different orbits. But as they say, it's the thought that counts." She drinks some more.

I take another sip. "Okay, lesson learned. But I think our orbits collide more than you're willing to admit."

She looks at me, the smile waning. "You seemed to have a rich social life this week."

We both flinch at her sudden change of topic. Or I flinch at its direction, but it's an opening to dig us out of the awkwardness, so I lean into it.

"Do *I* need to file a restraining order?"

She studies me for a beat, and the spark returns—our previous tension warming back to life. "Depends," she breathes.

"On?"

Cora smiles, uncrosses her legs in a fluid motion,

and stands up. She rounds the cluttered coffee table. Stumbling, she almost lands in the middle of it.

She giggles and sits—or rather falls—beside me. Fuck, gulping down her wine wasn't the best idea.

Not that I ever cared about a woman drinking too much, but somehow I feel responsible for pushing her over her limit. With my stupid gift.

Cora angles her body toward me and puts her hand on my chest.

Her touch burns through my T-shirt, threatening to incinerate my common sense. Our gazes collide. Our breathing stutters.

I shift to face her. "Cora, as much as I—"

She slides her hand lower, not grabbing my dick, but massaging over the bulge in my pants. I groan.

"I can think of a better birthday gift." She bites her lower lip.

I circle my fingers around hers and bring her hand to my mouth, dusting her knuckles with my lips.

"Coraline, believe me, I want to, but you're drunk, and I don't want to be your regret tomorrow."

She pouts adorably. "You're not living up to your reputation."

"And believe me, it pains me." I stand up, and she slides down onto her side, mumbling protests and closing her eyes. Covering her with a blanket, I kiss the crown of her head. "Goodnight, Coraline, and Happy Birthday."

With one last look at her, I step out gingerly like the floor is barbed wire. She doesn't look at me, shaking her head like she is regretting tonight.

I almost change my mind.

Almost.

The door closes behind me, and I stare at its wood with the slightly chipped paint, like staying here will somehow balance out the score... What score? Fuck.

Have I just refused sex?

With a woman I crave?

The worst timing ever to grow a conscience.

Chapter 9

Cora

CELESTE

How is OD?

LILY

OMG, who overdosed?

CELESTE

Operation Dating! (laughing emoji)

SAAR

Having the list compiled, ironing out details.

LILY

This is so exciting.

I can't believe I became your project.

CELESTE

That's not what this is.

SAAR

You will have so much fun.

LILY

You deserve to have fun.

I don't have time for fun.

SAAR

We'll see about that.

* * *

Saar leans against the prep table in the bistro's kitchen and puts her latte down. It's one of those days I can't even sit with her.

"Sometimes I envy the freedom you have," I sigh, immediately regretting my pettiness as I shove dishes into the dishwasher.

Saar stays silent for a moment. "I know you never let us help you, so I'm not going to offer it again. Just know the offer is on the table—"

"Let me stop you right there. As shitty as it sounds, pride is one of the few things I have left."

She lifts her arms in surrender. "Then struggle away. I only brought it up because you mentioned freedom. Only you know which one is more important to you. Freedom or pride?"

I deflate. "The fact that I have to choose sucks."

"You can have both, but it would require some changes. You gave up your life for the family business; maybe instead of struggling to save something, you need to start reclaiming what you really want."

I groan, closing my eyes. What do I want? That train has left the station at the speed of light. "It's not that easy."

"Cora, darling, I know firsthand how hard it is to redefine yourself. But I also know you can't get there when you're overworked, exhausted, and financially ruined."

Saar might have grown up rich, and is now married to a man whose wealth is defined by so many zeros that I don't even care to count them, but she is real.

She experienced a brief period of not having money or work. As a model she was overworked, so I know she speaks from experience.

But she also grew up with a pair of parents who are the worst, most selfish beings in the world. She doesn't understand family legacy. She is close to her brothers, but they don't need her.

My loyalty to my father runs too deep. He needs me, and caring for him—his business—is something I can't change. I don't want to change.

"I know." I sigh. "Hopefully, once you unleash your dating scheme on me, I will get the wind back in my sails."

Fuck, the idea of dating is making me tired, but I can't change the other aspects of my life, so I'm going to let my friends help me in this one.

"I have the first two candidates lined up. Corm is

strangely invested in this." She shrugs, grinning. "But I'm saying this one last time; I can help you with the bistro, as well."

"I'm not tainting this friendship with loans. That's a rule my father learned the hard way when he lent money to his best friend. I love you, Saar, but stop offering."

She nods. "Understood. Let me show you the pics of a potential future Mr. Winslow."

Snorting, I wipe my hands and reach for her phone. "Show me."

Both candidates are handsome and rich. They're both perfect on paper. I should be more excited. Why am I not?

"My sister went to university to find herself a husband," I say. "I always judged her for that. But perhaps a part of me resented her for being able to study while I stayed behind to help Dad."

"Did she find a husband?"

"Yes she did actually."

"Good for her. You will get one soon too, and then your troubles are over. Freedom is waiting." She pokes me with her elbow, teasing.

"I can't believe I'm becoming my sister."

"You're not becoming anyone. You're just overthinking everything. You will date amazing, educated men who can pull you out of your reality once or twice a week. Hopefully it will give you a new perspective. Then you can redefine yourself."

"Redefine myself?"

It's like she's saying something between the lines, but I can't quite grasp it. What new perspective?

"I love you, Cora. Let me treat you to some quality male material." She winks, avoiding a direct answer.

"Thank you." I sigh.

She shrugs. "I'm doing it as a service to your neglected lady parts."

I groan and laugh at the same time, shaking my head. Saar laughs.

I remember something she said earlier. "Why do you think Corm is invested in your matchmaking scheme? It doesn't sound like him."

She purses her lips. "To mess with Xander, I guess."

The mention of the handsome devil makes my insides flip, both in a good and not-so-good way.

Two days ago, the morning after my birthday, I woke up in agony on the sofa, my entire body screaming in protest on the uneven, soft mattress, my head throbbing, my mouth dry, and the memory of the night before churning in my stomach along with the hangover.

While the last moments of the night are kind of

hazy, and seriously dampening my love of Zinfandel, one thing I know for sure.

I came onto him, and Xander Stone left. I thought I would feel bad after hooking up with him. Well, the idea of that aftertaste doesn't compare to the embarrassing sense of rejection etched in my mind after I woke up and replayed the events.

"What does my dating life have to do with Xander Stone?"

Saar raises her eyebrows, unimpressed. "It's crystal clear he wants you."

"Sorry to disappoint Corm and the rest of you, but he most certainly doesn't. There might have been a brief moment of desire the day of the luncheon, but that is gone."

Why did he seek me out on my birthday if that's the case? Was I really so drunk that I repulsed him? Fuck.

In any case, as I sobered up, I knew he had made the right decision.

Xander Stone hasn't kissed me yet, and his taste is intoxicating already.

He hasn't touched me yet, and his touch is burning.

He hasn't claimed me yet, and I feel the aftershocks already.

I would never survive a man like him. I would never walk away with my heart intact. I will never try.

"If you say so." Her smile is coy and telling, but I'm not sure what it is saying.

We walk to the front, and I quickly check the floor, which seems under control, with only a few patrons enjoying their drinks.

"Speak of the devil." Saar snickers.

I follow her gaze and land on the flashy Lamborghini, its owner leaning casually against the hood in his expensive suit. The picture is arresting. He looks untouchable.

Dangerous awareness ripples through me. The sight makes me feel off-balance.

Saar squeezes my hand. "I know we said Xander is off the list, so just say the word and I'll send him away."

I study the suit-clad sin, and I realize one thing. If I want him to stop messing with me, I need to tell him off once and for all.

His constant showing up unannounced is fogging my mind, and giving me false hope about something that makes no sense.

Remembering the deed tucked in my sunflower journal, which I finally found, I consider sending Saar out to tell him to get lost.

But I'm a grown-ass woman, and I need to take care of myself.

"I'll deal with him." And hopefully survive it.

"Still on for the date later this week, though?" Saar asks.

"Absolutely."

She kisses me and leaves, just as Xander enters.

"What are you doing here?" I put my hands on my hips.

"You ask that a lot." He leans against the table closest to the counter.

It's like he knows how devastating he looks. Like the front page of a magazine that causes spontaneous orgasms.

"And you keep showing up uninvited." I don't look away, no matter how much the sight eats at my defenses.

"But not unwelcome," he drawls.

His signature boyish grin stretches across his handsome face, and for a moment I wish I were that girl. A girl who is carefree enough to dive into the unexpected.

Who isn't protecting her heart at all costs. Who can enjoy herself without the crippling sense of guilt.

"What do you want?"

"Is that how you treat your customers?" He takes a seat.

"Xander—"

"I'm driving you home."

"I'm not closing because of you again."

"Fair enough. I'll wait."

I sigh, and am about to send him away when Sanjay appears. "What can I get you?"

Traitor.

Xander smiles and orders coffee. I shake my head and return to the kitchen to prepare what I can for tomorrow's lunch.

"Is he still there?" I ask when Sanjay brings dishes in.

He nods.

I put away the pre-cut veggies for tomorrow's wraps, and sighing, I decide to leave early. I'm not going to have the talk with him here, and clearly he can't be deterred easily.

I grab my things and say goodbye to Sanjay.

"Let's go." I sigh without waiting for Xander. He follows without a word and helps me into the car.

"You seem tense," he comments, gliding in beside me.

"What do you want?"

He winks at me but returns his attention to the road. "Obviously, I want to get into your pants."

I roll my eyes. "You're the ultimate romantic."

He shrugs. "Do you want a romance, Coraline? Just say so."

I can't help but snort. A part of me is kind of

curious how Xander's version of romance might look. I squash that notion quickly.

"Stop calling me Coraline. And you had your chance." I cringe, sounding more needy than I care to admit.

"You were drunk. You know it was the right call, but the case of blue balls worsened, so I would like to continue where we left off."

Direct much? "Keep dreaming, Xander." I sound bitter, and I don't like it. To strengthen my resolve, I add that to his offenses.

He seems completely unperturbed by my irrational venom. "I've done a lot of that lately. I'm after the real deal now. I want to make all our fantasies come true."

"Ours?" I scoff.

He glances at me, his eyebrows lifted. Like he's so sure I feel the same. The infuriating part is, he is right.

There have been fantasies. Don't blame me; he's the only man I've interacted with outside of work besides my father in a while.

As soon as I go on a date or two, I won't be like a starved stray, happy with the first crumb she finds.

"I'm sure there are plenty of candidates to caress your blue balls."

"For sure." He stops at the red light and turns to me. His gaze burns me. Not just my skin—it detonates inside me with such intensity I want to jump out. "But I want your touch, your moans, your cum to coat my face, my hands, my cock. Only yours," he rasps.

Jesus. I should be appalled by his words. I should slap him for the crass declaration. I should... I don't know what I should have, but it certainly isn't hitched breath, racing heart, and clenching pussy. Yet it's the latter that wipes out my ability to speak.

The man is fucking infuriating. A loud honk forces him to refocus on the road, and I'm grateful for the opportunity to breathe.

I need to save myself.

We drive in silence until he pulls to the curb in front of my house.

I sense his gaze on me, but I don't look at him, speaking to the windshield. "Look, Xander, I know women fall at your feet. I know you can buy them, woo them, or coerce them, perhaps. And I'm pretty sure that many of them fall for it, and some of them simply risk it."

"Risk it?" His question is laced with genuine confusion.

"Yes." I turn to look at him finally, his face impassive. "You might not realize it, but your light can illuminate and burn equally, Xander. And I'm not willing to risk it."

He studies me, the imaginary clock ticking loudly

in my temples, almost deafening. I was honest with him, and I don't think he knows how to deal with it.

Will he respect my boundaries, or will he consider my truth a weakness in my defenses that he can exploit?

"Cora, you want me, and I want you. Why are you trying to complicate it?" he asks finally.

For some reason, now I wish he called me Coraline. What's wrong with me?

"Because I'm not interested in what you're offering. I don't want to be a notch on your bedpost—one of many. I don't want to be photographed as your arm candy. I don't want to join the women who hope you give them more than you're willing to."

He frowns. "So you want to be exclusive?"

Out of all the messages in my speech, this is his takeaway? Fuck, I wish I had the ability to see only solutions instead of problems.

"Yes... No. No." God, the man drives me crazy.

"Coraline," he drawls, and fuck no, I don't want him to call me that. "What is it then? It seems like your head is telling you a story you don't really want to follow."

He reaches to trace my cheek. The struggle not to lean into his touch is real. It's a feather-like caress, but it makes me question my determination.

"We can be exclusive," he adds.

"You want to date me?" I sputter.

The conversation is getting away from me and my plans, and I don't know how to stop it. What the hell is happening?

He flinches, like the idea of dating is seriously off-putting, which I'd bet it is for him.

"Friends with benefits?" he smiles.

It's kind of disarming how he's trying to fit me into his way of life. It's also alarming. "One of us—I bet me—is bound to get hurt."

He frowns. "We haven't even slept together, and you're already thinking several steps... or rather disasters ahead? It's a pretty fucked-up way to go through life."

I snort. "It's the only way to survive for some of us. To prepare for the worst, Xander. And this only proves how different we are. I'm sorry, just find yourself a new conquest."

The words feel like a dagger to my own heart. Like I'm betraying myself, my chance at something fun and carefree. My chance at a sliver of freedom amid the cage of my life circumstances.

Xander drops his hand, but keeps me imprisoned in his devastating gaze.

I wish I knew what he sees. With his jaw set rigid, his expression is void of his usual playful grin.

I don't know what he thinks, but I feel the weight

of disappointment. I'm probably projecting, but I can't shake the feeling he isn't disappointed by my rejection but rather in me.

Or perhaps it's me who mourns the opportunity to be someone else with this man. Because that woman feels more like me than the version I settled for.

I can't bear his eyes on me anymore, but I can't look away either. Xander is the first one to break the silent duel.

He opens the door and steps out, and I let out a long sigh, followed by the first full breath since he entered the bistro.

Tapping the hood, he rounds the car and opens my door.

He helps me out of the car. He closes the door behind me. He puts his hands into his pockets.

He's right here, but it feels like he's avoiding me.

I hate every minute of this interaction. I stood up for myself, so why do I feel like a wreck?

He starts turning.

"Why are you pursuing me, Xander?" I'm not sure why I'm asking. I should be content with the completion of this nonsensical chase.

But somehow, around this man, I don't mind touching the flames. It's like I want to get burned.

He pauses to look at me. "I don't know." He shakes his head. "I like a challenge—"

"Wrong answer, young man," I cut him off.

As I thought, I'm just a conquest for him. An exciting chase he would tire of soon enough.

His jaw ticks, and then he shakes his head in what feels like silent exasperation. "Good. I'd better go find myself a new conquest."

The bitterness in his voice matches the aftertaste of our conversation I feel deep in my stomach.

Asshole.

Fucking asshole.

How dare he make me feel bad about my choices? How dare he saunter back into his car and drive away, leaving me there in a pool of regret?

I let myself mope for a moment. Then I stew for another one. Fuck him.

Chapter 10

Xander

"So there is no man I need to threaten?" I ask seriously, and Lottie snorts.

"Stay away from my dates. It's bad enough I have my dating life monitored by the rest of this family." Her eye roll comes through in the tone in her voice. "Besides, you would have to be here to threaten anyone."

She got me there. "Just be careful, and don't trust—"

"Men like you, Lex?" she quips. Only Lottie calls me Lex, a childhood habit.

"I'm a good catch." I walk out of the elevator and nod my greetings to our receptionist.

"If she wants to catch STDs." Lottie snorts.

"I'm perfectly safe, Lottie. And right now, I'm not

thrilled I called you," I grumble, entering my office and turning on the screens.

"Aw, brother, did I hurt your feelings?" she sing-songs, and I snort, shaking my head. "And don't think I didn't notice you skillfully avoiding my suggestions about being here to be able to threaten anyone."

I stop at the window wall behind my desk and let my gaze trace the Manhattan skyline, sighing. "I live and work in New York, Lottie. I'm busy."

"Yeah, yeah, blah, blah, building your own empire, blah, blah... The excuses are old by now; even you couldn't possibly believe them anymore."

"It's not an excuse." I close my eyes, pinching the bridge of my nose.

"I call bullshit. Mom misses you terribly."

The wave of guilt sweeps through me, like always when my sister brings up Mom. "Lottie..." I sigh.

"Look, Lex, I know Dad has been trying to reach you. I think enough time has passed for you to grow some balls and stop hiding."

Fuck.

"When you put it like that..." I grumble.

"So you will take his call?"

"I don't think I will, but I will be in San Francisco soon, and you and me can grab lunch."

"Really?" Her excitement hits me right in my solar plexus. Fuck, I miss her. I miss them.

"Only if you promise not to tell anyone."

She remains silent for a few beats. "I promise, under duress."

I laugh. "Let the record show I did not pressure the witness."

"Agree to disagree. I miss you, bro, so I will play by your rules, but that doesn't mean I agree with them."

"Duly noted. I'll call you later this week."

"Wait, don't go yet. You made me spill the beans about my dating life, and you didn't share shit."

"There is nothing to share. I haven't been out with anyone in weeks." If I don't count the woman who stubbornly pushes me away. The only woman I want to go out with.

What?

I want to go out with her? When did I upgrade my interest from the bedroom? Fuck.

"Don't tell me you are now avoiding human contact like Liam?"

Our brother has been chronically anti-social for the past ten years. Not in a dramatic way—just slowly shutting everyone out like it became his hobby.

"No, I'm just not interested lately."

"Oh my God, you met someone!"

How did she get that from my generic answer? "No. Yes. Kind of."

"And you're stuttering. I hit the nail on the head. Who is she? Is it serious? Do I know her?"

"Stop with the twenty questions. There is nothing to share. She is not interested."

The last time I felt like a failure was before my self-inflicted exile from San Francisco. It's infuriating that the less I score with Cora, the more I want to win. At this point, I don't even know if it's an attraction or just petulance.

Somewhere, deep down, I feel her rejection is half-hearted, based on some bullshit she made herself believe.

She wants me, and I want to show her she doesn't have to deny herself. It feels—let's face it, I don't know enough about her life—like she's been denying herself a lot.

"I want to meet her." Lottie sounds annoyingly excited.

"Did you hear I say she is not interested?"

"That's why I want to be her friend." She practically squeals with delight. "I wish she lived here."

"That's just cruel, Lottie."

She gasps. "You really like her."

I'd like to bury myself in her, breathe Cora's scent until I'm high on it, touch her until she is desperate for more, claim her until she screams my name. That's what I'd like to do.

"I have to go, Lottie; I'll talk to you later." I disconnect the call before she can interrogate me further.

Someone knocks, and I whip around, plastering a smile on my face as if I were in the mood for visitors.

Lindsay sticks her head in the door. "Would you like me to get you lunch before the partner's meeting?"

"No, thank you. I'm going to hit the gym."

I get changed and take the stairs to the gym on the upper level of the building. After a few sets of chest presses, deadlifts, and squats, my foul mood improves slightly.

Wrong answer, young man.

Only because she didn't let me finish. She is more than a challenge. But what was I going to say anyway? That I can't stop thinking about her? That her freckles and curls are on my mind all the time?

That I like even the exhaustion lines on her face, and I wish I could wipe them away. That seeing her relax is like a gift. Like, for the first time in my life, I draw joy from making someone laugh, relax, be carefree.

And all of that is made even more infuriating because it comes in a sexy package that makes my balls swell.

I wouldn't have told her any of this. I know it's just my infatuation throwing tantrums because it can't get a toy.

But I wonder if, at this point, I'm still trying to win with Cal or to win the girl.

Because the yearning remains. The need to conquer her is stronger than ever before.

Who am I kidding? I've never felt a pull this powerful. It must be her resistance. Because at the end of the day, she is right. We're from different worlds, different backgrounds.

Perhaps it is the novelty of her world.

Whatever it is, I don't think I will shake it until I have her. This interest must be quenched somehow, and then I can move on.

Or perhaps I can turn the challenge around. What if I win in resisting her? That must be it.

After I finish my workout, I head to the partners' meeting.

We always meet in Cormac's office, as if we didn't have boardrooms. But then he hoards the best vintage Macallan, so I don't mind invading his space.

His door is open, so I walk right in and find him with a visitor. "Oh, Saar, how are you? Did you come to make sure his muzzle is well fastened?"

Corm's wife laughs. "I wouldn't want him to bite anyone. It's just messy."

"I'm right here," Corm scoffs.

Saar kisses his cheek. "You're right, darling, you

need to put *them* on shorter leashes, so they learn respect."

Corm rolls his eyes, smirking. "Okay, off you go, woman, before you completely destroy my team's morale."

"What morale?" Roxy walks in.

Saar laughs. "Roxy for President."

"I have better things to do." Roxy sits in her usual armchair, swinging her legs over the armrest.

"Okay, I'm out of here." Saar gives Corm another peck. "Make sure Ed Reynolds shows up."

"Jesus, he said he'd be there. I'm not a dating service." He walks Saar to the door, his hand caressing her lower back.

"Are you setting up Ed Reynolds?" Roxy rubs her hands. "With whom? I need details."

"With my friend Cora," Saar says cheerfully, sends everyone an air kiss, and leaves.

"Where is Caleb?" Corm asks as the latter walks in, his hair still damp from the shower.

"I'm here." He sits down.

The entire exchange is happening while I'm standing rooted. Ed fucking Reynolds is a boring tech guy whose firm is two stories down from ours and covers our IT needs. What on earth does he want with Cora Winslow?

And why would she refuse me and then go on a

date with that clown? The fucking Quinns are setting it up? What the hell?

"Are you just going to stand there?" Corm raises his eyebrows, all my colleagues eyeing me with various degrees of puzzlement.

"I have a solution for the Chicago issue," I say, and sit beside Caleb. "Is Declan dialing in?" I dive right into the meeting, hoping it will stop my blood from boiling and help my mind refocus.

"He won't be dialing in today," Roxy informs us. Declan left for London. To win his woman, and help with the Merged branch there.

All my colleagues have settled down. When did that happen? We were all blissfully single when we started this firm not even two years ago. And suddenly, I'm an outsider.

"Do you care to share?" Corm growls when I don't speak. I snap back into work mode, but barely focus on projects while the image of Cora and Ed together flickers through my mind.

I explain my take on the Chicago project and try to answer all concerns, but it's an uphill battle. All the pent-up energy I worked out in the gym is back in a full-blown attack of nerves.

"What about the..." Corm turns to Caleb, and I tune them out.

She thinks she can date?

"Why are you setting up Ed Reynolds?" I spit out, before I can stop myself.

Silence follows as the three people around me stare, Roxy hiding her grin behind her notebook.

"The IT Ed Reynolds?" Caleb asks, puzzled. "What setup?"

Fuck.

Fuck.

Fuck.

What is wrong with me? At this rate, I would have been better off not getting up this morning.

I played racquetball with fucking IT Ed a few times, and now I seriously regret not smashing the ball into his face. Multiple times. That would take him off the market.

"Saar—God bless her—strong-armed Corm into setting up a date between Cora Winslow and Ed," Roxy drawls, glee practically oozing from her voice.

"I wish I had time to play matchmaker." Caleb rolls his eyes.

"I got pulled in." Corm shrugs. "They set up some system to send her on a date at least twice a week, and I had to bring all the single men I know to the table."

What the actual fuck? She is going to date at least twice a week? "Did you put my name in?"

Corm scoffs. "She is one of my wife's best friends, so no."

"What is that supposed to mean?" I glare at him.

"That I'm one step closer to winning twenty K." Caleb chuckles.

"There is a bet I don't know about?" Roxy turns to him.

"Enough," Corm snaps, annoyance rolling off his shoulders as he cracks his neck. "Where do we stand with the Vireon board appointment?"

The topic should snap me back to reality, and it does, but the simmering annoyance refuses to fade.

"I will report something next week," I say, adjusting my tie. Idiot! That's my tell when I'm obscuring. And the people in the room most probably know that.

"What's taking so long?" Corm asks.

"My father has been overseas." The lie slips out effortlessly.

I haven't felt like a failure since I left San Francisco. And here I am failing again in all aspects of my life. Losing a woman I never had, or who doesn't even want me, and derailing our efforts on the West Coast.

This is becoming a pattern. One I don't much care for.

"Okay, get in touch with him ASAP, or find another way in." Corm stands up, adjourning the meeting.

I zip out of there like my ass is on fire. I pass by Lindsay's workstation and enter my office.

Fuck. I need to hit the gym one more time. Or go downstairs and break Ed Reynolds' ugly face.

"You know, I gave you labels over the almost two years we've known each other..." Roxy's voice startles me.

"Ever heard of knocking?" I snap, and grab a fidget cube from my desk.

She leans against my library. She wears a schoolgirl miniskirt and a granny cardigan. Her sense of fashion is plain weird, but she makes it work. The simple outfit today is the only innocent-looking thing about her.

She ignores my comments. "Fitting labels. Playboy. Asshole. Idiot. But never have I thought you'd deserve to be called a liar."

There is something we can agree on, but at the moment, I don't give a flying fuck about the San Francisco deal.

"Find out where he is taking her!"

Talking about labels, I'm pretty sure I just lost the "genius" label I've been coined with... clearly unjustly.

She folds her arms across her chest, raising her chin. "First, admit you've been lying to everyone."

"Isn't that the reason you're here?" I click the toy, flicking it between my fingers, and try not to pace.

She already has the upper hand in this conversation. I don't need to show her my desperation.

Fuck. I *am* a desperate man. I just can't pinpoint the moment that transformation happened.

"You should leave that poor woman alone."

"So I've been told."

By the said woman, multiple times. I put my hands in my pockets, still tapping the metal parts of the toy. "If you're not going to help me, then go do your job, Roxy."

"Why would I want to help you?" She purses her lips like she is really musing about the answer.

"I swear to God, Roxy—" I walk around and sit behind my desk. The toy snaps into pieces.

"Wow, you really care about her."

I glare at her, and she takes pity on me, laughing. "I'll see what I can do."

"Do better than that." What am I even going to do with the information? While my sanity raises the question, it doesn't improve the situation because I ignore it.

"For someone who wants something from me, you're awfully obnoxious."

I inhale. "Roxy, please find out where Ed Reynolds is taking Cora and when."

"I want a raise."

Only returning to San Francisco would be worse than this woman. "Okay."

She opens her mouth in a mock gape, then glares. "You're not authorized to promise me that."

"I will fucking pay you out of my pocket."

I'm officially insane.

And this moment right now marks the first occasion that renders Roxy Moretti speechless. She stares at me for a moment, and then her lips stretch into a gleeful smile. "Well, well, well, Xander Stone."

She closes the door and sits on the armrest of the chair in the corner. I'm not sure what's going on, but I've already established I'm insane, so I don't care much.

Roxy clicks a few times on her phone and then taps the headset she never takes off at work.

"Saar, sorry to bother you. I ran into Ed Reynolds, and he wanted a suggestion for a date-suitable restaurant. Since I happen to know who his date is, I thought I'd better check with you. Where would Cora like to go?"

She doesn't even flinch. Impressive. And mildly disturbing from the woman who called me a liar.

"Oh, he already confirmed with you. I guess he was second-guessing himself." Roxy fake-giggles and listens. "You're right, it's adorable, and that is a great space."

She hangs up and winks at me. "One down."

Scrolling quickly, she taps her headset again.

"Hello, I'm Evelyn, Mr. Reynolds's assistant. I'm calling to confirm his reservation tonight at seven."

She listens, smiling triumphantly. "No, no, my mistake. It *is* for eight. You're right."

Roxy hangs up and types on her phone. My phone pings with a text. I open it to find the name of the restaurant.

"That was—"

"The last time I help you, Xander." She stands up.

I frown.

"At least until you man up and call your father." She reaches for the door.

"You're strangely invested in my relationship with my father."

"Just protecting my bonus." She shrugs and leaves.

I glance at the text on my screen.

"And Xander?" Roxy sticks her head in the door again. "Don't ruin that woman's chances with a decent man."

And for the second time in a few weeks, my conscience comes knocking.

Chapter 11

Cora

"I went to a few fancy events lately." I shift from one foot to the other. "You would have hated it."

The tombstone doesn't answer, so I continue my monolog. "My friend is going through a rough patch, and she moved to London. You would have liked her."

What do I know? I never got a chance to see what kind of person Ethan would become nearing his fortieth birthday.

"I have a date tonight. Geez, let's hope it's like riding a bike. I don't even understand how the years went by, and I never truly moved on. Do you mind that I'm going out? Even if you do, I'm going to go through with it. You left me first, after all."

I try to picture his face, his smile, but it's too hazy.

As much as I try to hold onto the memory of him, it's fading with time.

Right after he passed, I had to save the bistro, helping my dad. It was the best antidote for grief... or an avoidance tactic.

"I'm still mad at you for it. And I fucking miss you."

I squeeze the bouquet in my hand, and a green leaf falls onto my shoe. I better save the flowers. Squatting, I lay them down beside the stone, because the vase that is attached to it is filled with roses.

Ethan's mother must be coming here regularly. A part of me wishes I would run into her. We didn't get along before, but perhaps we would now. Bound by tragedy.

I don't come here as often as I used to. Somehow, these visits became a reminder of what I lost, and stopped bringing any solace. Stopped healing me.

I decided to cut down on my visits after I realized it was holding me back. Not that I moved forward afterward.

But being here today feels therapeutic. Like the moment I decided to do something for myself, I freed up some energy to allow myself closure.

Like that tiny step forward—God, I hope the date will be exciting—gave me hope. Hope that I can forge a sliver of my own amid a life driven by circumstances.

"Well, duty calls. I'll come again. I enjoyed our chat." I snort silently and walk away.

The peace of the cemetery lingers when I walk into the bistro. Sanjay greets me while he steams milk for a cappuccino. I'm relieved to see we have a quiet pre-lunch hour.

It's going to be a good day.

Putting on the apron, I dive into lunch prep, taking stock of morning deliveries. We offer salads, wraps, and sandwiches here, and one meal of the day. Today it's a curry, and I cooked that yesterday, so the prep is on the lighter side.

"Boss, do you have a minute?" Sanjay leans against the door frame, monitoring the floor.

I've heard this line enough times to recognize the pattern—the question, the pause, the inevitable resignation—and dread coils in my stomach. "Sure. Is everything okay?"

"Soooo..."

Oh shit, he is hesitating. That's not good news. *Sanjay, don't leave me.* I don't have the mental or physical capacity to cope with everything by myself.

"Sooo?" I prompt him. "Just say it. Don't keep me in suspense."

"I know that money is tight around here at the moment, but I thought maybe I could take on more responsibilities. I'm not asking for a raise right now, but if I prove myself, and it contributes to your bottom line..." He glances at the restaurant. "Shit, sorry." He dashes to take someone's order.

I follow him and wave to a couple of our regulars. Sanjay comes back and starts preparing the drinks.

"Have you just offered to work more for the same amount of money?" The skeptical me is looking for the catch.

"Look, Cora, I think there are things we can implement that would bring in more customers and revenue. If you allow me to take on a bigger role, I will prove that to you. Then we can talk about my cut." He shrugs, smiling, while he glides behind the counter, preparing coffee, tea, and lemonades.

"I don't have money for investments in improving anything, Sanjay."

"I get that, but some of it is just a question of investing some time. To modernize the process, the menu presentation, and special offers. I would take care of that. Let me test some of my ideas for a month or so, and if you don't see the impact... well, I'll be embarrassed, but you have nothing to lose."

I blink a few times. I should be excited about his willingness to put in more effort, but I'm still half-skeptical. "Okay. But answer one more question. Why?"

He sighs. "My wife wants a baby. And me, too, but I need to make more money. I went through many hospitality jobs, and you're a good boss. I value that more than anything. And one day I would like to open my own place, so you'd really give me free training."

I know there are minor changes that might lead to better financial performance, but there is a part of me that wants to keep this place the same as my dad left it. Like I'm preserving it for him to return to, which is a silly, unrealistic notion, but I can't help it.

The mounting bills and the financial mess he left behind have prevented me from doing it as well. And at the end of the day, I don't have the energy to change anything, so I just plow through, hoping that the same action will produce different results.

"Thank you, Sanjay." For some outlandish reason, tears prickle behind my eyes, so I go hide in the back, blinking them away.

Accepting help is akin to a root canal to me. Why? I wish I knew. After years of doing everything solo, I've developed a co-dependent relationship with my own stubbornness.

I hate that Sanjay noticed the financial struggle and assumed that's why we're stagnating. Yes, that's a big part of it.

But...

Every time I even think about changing something, it feels like I'm betraying my father. Like adjusting the menu or having a happy hour equals admitting he failed. Or worse—I did.

I know that's ridiculous. I know the bistro is outdated, that it's barely surviving on nostalgia and caffeine.

But the truth is... stuck feels safer than risking something new. At least stuck is predictable. Familiar. Exhausting, yes, but I know how to survive in it.

I'm tired—but I don't know what I'd be without the weight. Letting go may feel like a relief. Or it may feel like giving up.

And honestly? I don't have the energy to find out which.

"I hope I didn't offend you." Sanjay pokes his head in, interrupting my mindless rearranging of bowls and utensils.

"I have a hard time changing anything here, but I'm not going to curb your enthusiasm. This place needs a financial boost, so be creative."

There is a big part of me that is completely sincere. But the vise on my stomach reminds me that I'm probably taking a much-needed leap I'm not ready to take.

"I'm freaking out." I pace around my living room.

"Calm down. You look great." Saar's voice comes from the screen I propped on my coffee table.

"Can you stop for a second, so I can see you?" Celeste says.

I halt in front of the tablet's camera. I'm wearing a dark green jumpsuit, and for whatever reason, I feel naked in it.

It's too tight. Too revealing. Too much.

"You're stunning," Lily squeals enthusiastically.

"Seriously," Saar offers. "Your boobs and hips look great. The cleavage is just slutty enough, while the whole look is classy."

"I agree," Celeste says. "The green brings out your eyes, and your hair down like this, with that green matching headband, is perfection."

"You're ready to dazzle him," Lily says.

"What are we going to talk about?" I shake my shoulders to shed the nervous energy.

"Weather," Saar teases.

I snort and sit down, turning the camera toward me. "I'm being ridiculous, am I not?"

"Just a little bit." Celeste smiles.

"As someone who went through a dry spell myself, I can relate, but don't let your nerves stop you from having fun," Lily says, sipping her tea.

Her words should provide comfort, but they do the exact opposite. "Oh my God, hooking up is so much easier. You pick a guy at the bar, and you don't have to go through the awkward dinner and conversation. Do I have to sleep with him tonight? Or is the three-date rule still in effect these days?"

"Jesus, relax finally." Saar laughs. "You do whatever you want."

"This is the worst idea ever. If I don't like him... You guys know him. Corm will hate me."

Saar snorts. "Corm doesn't give a flying fuck about most people. Don't you worry. Just enjoy yourself."

"And if he's not a perfect gentleman, we will have Caleb cancel his contract," Celeste cackles, but something tells me she wouldn't hesitate.

"You have nothing to worry about. If you don't click, text me, and I'll call you with some emergency," Saar says.

"And if you click, that's what you groomed your lady parts for." Lily giggles.

I let out a strained laugh. "Okay, thank you for this emergency call. I don't even know why I'm so anxious."

"For one, it's been a while since you dated, so it's natural to feel nervous. But what isn't helping is your thinking about other people's feelings too much. Like what would Corm say?" Saar folds her arms across her chest. "Fuck that. We set you up to make you happy, not for you to worry about offending us. Be free of that shit for one night, Cora."

Freedom.

It seems to be the theme of the month, and yet so unattainable. "Okay, I better go put on some makeup."

Saar checks her watch. "You better; your car is here in twenty minutes."

"What car? I thought I was meeting him there."

"Yes, yes, but don't you think we would let you traipse around on the subway. The car is my treat, and before you protest, you can pay me in unlimited lattes."

"You already drink lattes for free." But for once, I'm grateful for her insistence on making my life easier.

"See? I owe you. Enjoy yourself."

Okay. Fuck it. It's been a pretty good day so far, so let's ride the wave.

My good day took a downward trajectory about five minutes into the date.

Ed may be a perfectly eligible bachelor on paper—the looks, the status, the career—but there is no chemistry between us.

"Aren't you glad you let me choose the wine?" He takes a sip of the super-expensive Sauvignon.

I wet my lips. The wine is as acidic as my sourness over his earlier comment that Zinfandel is too common a wine for the occasion.

I should have insisted, but I told myself that foregoing my typical choice is part of the novel, new journey in this new phase of my life.

Perhaps he's as nervous as I am. Or he's a selfish asshole who simply doesn't care about my preferences. I don't mind dominant, but both parties need to draw satisfaction from it.

The only thing I'm drawing out right now is time, stretching the silence, hoping he's vain enough to forget his own question.

No such luck. He stares at me with expectation. And the worst part? Based on his smug expression, he expects me to praise his wine selection.

"It's... smooth." I finally find a word that hopefully doesn't offend his choice. "I still prefer Zinfandel," I murmur.

"But I'm changing your mind on that one."

Again, he keeps his gaze on me, expecting me to... what? Agree with him? God help me with this conversation. I should just shut up and praise his choices? Is that what he truly expects?

"Sure," I lie, with the brightest and most pretentious smile known to man.

He nods with a self-confident smirk, satisfied.

Read the room, asshole.

How can he not see or feel I'm faking it? We don't know each other, and yes, I'm being more polite than he deserves, but he can't be *that* self-absorbed.

Ed digs into his steak—and who drinks white with red meat?—chewing with such vigor I avert my gaze to my dish.

My pasta is delicious, but I can't focus on savoring it because I'm resisting pulling out my phone and texting Saar.

If I have her rescue me from this date, it would be a premature capitulation. She went to so much effort organizing this, and seems even more excited than me. I don't want to disappoint her.

I'll sit through this, focusing on the positive. I'm out on a date. It's not perfect, but at least I'm practicing.

The restaurant is amazing. It's expensive, but nothing here makes me feel uncomfortable. I'm sure Saar suggested it.

The food is good, and yes, the company is lacking, but it's not that bad.

Chewing, Ed points his knife at me. "We landed a new client this week. This will..."

I tune his words out. Unfortunately, I can't tune out the open-mouth mastication he practices while talking about his work.

Don't cringe. Don't cringe. Don't cringe.

"Are you okay?" Ed frowns at me.

Fuck, I guess I cringed.

"I love this pasta." Even the couple beside us turns at my exaggerated enthusiasm.

"Great." He grins, as if he were the chef here. "Pasta isn't the best choice for your hips, but let's indulge."

Fucking asshole.

"Let's." This time, I don't even try to hide my sarcasm. I dig into my dish and stuff my face with one forkful after another. My hips love it.

Ed seems a bit taken aback by my lack of manners in eating, like this is the first meal I've seen in ages.

He blinks a few times before he returns to his steak and his rant about his business success.

I wonder if we will ever get to the part of the date when he actually asks me something about me and my life. His ego probably doesn't have that setting.

I imagine stabbing him with my fork. What should I aim for? His hand? His eyes?

"Coraline."

The name and the voice wash over me like molten chocolate.

It's only momentary bliss before my mind engages. What the fuck?

Chapter 12

Cora

My gaze collides with Xander's, and he is grinning. I know the man can wear a suit like a sex god, so why does the sight of him keep dazzling me?

"Xander." Ed stands up, offering his hand. "What a coincidence."

"I wouldn't call it that." Xander ignores the hand or its owner, his gaze firmly latched on me. "Are you ready to leave?"

"I don't think we are," Ed says.

"I wasn't talking to you," Xander snarls, his gaze still holding me in its claws.

Is this a modern version of a knight in shining armor who comes on his white horse to save the princess?

I mean, I'd give anything to end this date, but I'm

not a fucking damsel in distress. And why is he here? This question is getting tiresome when it comes to Xander.

I haven't seen him since I rejected him the last time... One of the times... Wow, we really have a fucked-up dynamic.

The worst part? I'm glad to see him. It's probably because the other man in this equation is as charming as fungus.

"What are you doing here?" I stammer.

Besides providing a sliver of entertainment on this otherwise horrible night. Not that I would ever give him any credit.

He flashes me one of his self-assured and annoyingly charming smiles. "Rescuing you from a boring date."

"Excuse me?" Ed voices his indignation. It's like he was on a different date than me.

Xander finally looks at my companion, though it's like he's looking at an annoying insect. "You're excused. In fact, the sooner you get the fuck out of here, the better." He is about to turn back to me when he changes his mind and adds, "Especially if you want to keep using your hand in racquetball."

I was going to aim for his hand too! My internal cheer might be inappropriate on some level, but I don't care. I do, however, bite the inside of my mouth to stop myself from grinning.

"What the fuck, Xander? You know each other?" Ed's eyes dart between me and Xander.

I should say something. But, as horrible as it is, this is the most enjoyable part of the evening thus far.

Both men stare at me with their eyebrows raised. God, I just want to send them both away and enjoy my pasta.

But the good-girl syndrome kicks in. "Stop threatening my date." I sigh, glaring at Xander.

Xander snorts. "I wouldn't need to if he finally fucked off."

"Cora?" Ed croaks.

Is this man seriously asking me to defend him? Xander's behavior is abhorrent, but grow some balls, Ed, for fuck's sake.

When I say nothing, he repeats. "Cora?"

"Dude, read the room," Xander scoffs. "And if I find you anywhere near her again, you will have bigger problems than lost dignity. Lost clients and broken bones come to mind."

"You're out of your mind." Ed snatches his jacket and, without looking back, storms out of the restaurant.

Xander's warning scores big time with me, and I'm not even questioning my sanity anymore. I really don't want to picture how he would deliver on that threat.

Fuck his tactics, though. He saved me from a dreadful evening.

If I find you anywhere near her again... That was hot. And disturbing.

Xander turns to me, sporting his cocky grin. He takes Ed's seat and gestures for the waiter who almost trips, trying to reach us as quickly as possible.

"Mr. Stone." He bows.

And, of course, he knows him by name. I don't even try not to roll my eyes.

Xander grips the Sauvignon bottle and takes it out of the ice bucket. "Take this back, and bring us your best Zinfandel."

"Of course." The waiter scurries away.

I wish the whole caveman routine, softened by his wine order, wouldn't send a kaleidoscope of butterflies amok in my stomach.

"Where were we?" Xander smiles at me. And this time, it's not the cocky smirk. It's a genuine smile. I think.

"There is no *we* here. *I* was on a date, and *you* ruined it for me." I should thank him, but his ego is big enough already.

"You look beautiful."

He takes my hand and brushes my knuckles with his lips. It happens so fast, I don't get to snatch my hand back.

Also, I don't want to. The feather-like touch reverberates through me with a need I really don't want to feel.

"What are you doing?" I croak, finally yanking my hand from his, clasping it to my chest as if it were injured because he touched it. Or precious. I can't decide.

This man is good at many things, but he excels at stirring conflicting feelings in me.

"Trying to salvage your date night." He pushes Ed's unfinished plate to the side with his index finger.

"Well, your heroic attempt isn't appreciated."

It's exhausting how much I fight this attraction. At this point, it's hard to remember why.

"Really? I've been sitting at the bar for the past twenty minutes, and I would bet my kidney you were looking for a reason to bolt."

"Are you stalking me?"

"Are you telling me you had a good time?"

I open my mouth, but I can't disagree with him. I had an awful time, but that doesn't justify his behavior.

"Were you here just by chance?" I don't know why this is what I need to know, but his showing up randomly in my life is a bit unhinged.

This time, he opens his mouth, but then closes it.

Save yourself, the devil... or is it the angel on my shoulder whispers.

"This is insane." I push the chair back.

Throwing the napkin on the table, I march out of the dining room. Turning right, I decide to head for the bathroom. Hopefully he won't follow me there.

I barely close my stall when I hear a bang—probably the entrance door hitting the wall—and my hope that he wouldn't dare evaporates.

"Cora?"

"Go away, you lunatic." I lock the door.

"Just come out."

The slight hitch of vulnerability in his voice is almost imperceptible, but I hear it. I wish I didn't.

"Just wait outside." I sigh. "I need to pee."

He doesn't say anything, and my bladder refocuses me. When I'm done, I turn the lock slowly. Xander yanks the door open, startling me.

"What the hell?" I glare at him, and he glowers right back.

This is getting out of hand. I close my eyes and shake my head. At the situation. At him. At myself.

Because as much as I fight this, his stalking, his showing up unannounced, and sadly, his company thrill me. They excite me, despite my best efforts.

Rooted in a weird stalemate between us, we stand in a silent duel. Or perhaps it's a dialog. Though there is no way we can find understanding. We never do when we use words. But this pent-up energy must explode somewhere.

Xander looks like he's fighting an inner battle of his own.

"You're driving me crazy," he rasps. "You're... making me forget that I don't even believe in this kind of shit."

We glare at each other, heaving as if we just ran a marathon.

His words jog my memory, and I remember why I'm fighting this. Because he's younger, reckless, and a playboy who doesn't believe in "this kind of shit."

And yet... In his eyes I find raw need, and unadulterated desperation.

It's a heady feeling to have so much power over someone. To have someone show me how much I stir their darkest desires. To force someone—just by existing—to act without restraint.

He practically vibrates, his shoulders trembling. Like his whole body is straining not to take. Not to devour.

His chest rises and falls, every shallow breath dragging out the heat between us. His jaw is tight, but his lips are parted like he's on the verge of saying more—more desperate, more reckless, more final.

But he doesn't move.

Doesn't touch me.

His hands hover at his sides, like he's afraid that if he lays even one finger on me, he won't be able to stop.

And I feel it too—this magnetic pull that's half desire, half destruction.

I swallow, willing my heart rate to settle into a more comfortable beat. I don't know how long we stand there, and by sheer luck, nobody interrupts the moment.

I don't even know what this moment is, but it calls to me on a visceral level. It's like, in slow motion, I feel my defenses dropping, or perhaps dissolving at my feet. I don't care about keeping them to protect me.

"Fuck it," I pant, taking a step.

Fisting his jacket, I pull him to me. Our lips collide.

A moment of hesitation, or perhaps surprise on his part, is immediately erased when Xander snakes one hand around my waist to yank me closer and cups the back of my neck with the other.

His tongue teases the seam of my mouth, and I part for him. I might have started this kiss, but he takes over and dominates my mouth, my body, my reactions effortlessly.

God, I don't think I've ever been kissed like this. It's full of roaring frustration, untamed desire, unleashed emotions.

Xander feels like Zinfandel. Bold, juicy, spicy but smooth. It's addictive. It's spellbinding. It's dizzying.

He groans, stepping forward, forcing me to stumble backward. My back hits the wall while he leaves my waist and cups my cheeks to angle me to his liking.

I feel the kiss in my core, slowly but surely dissolving any objections I had to this union, however short and purely physical it may be.

I melt under his touch, and with it melts any notion of this not being a good idea.

Oh, it's a terrible idea, but fuck, it feels good. Some mistakes are worth the pain.

"Let's get out of here," I murmur into his mouth.

He peels his lips away, resting his forehead on mine, his gaze burning and awakening parts of me that have been in slumber for way too long.

His breath ragged, he stares at me with such intensity, goose bumps sprout on my skin.

He owns me with that look.

It scares and elates me at the same time. We stand there frozen for I don't know how long.

Having given my consent, I thought he would drag me out of here straight to his bed. But he doesn't. He remains motionless, his breath fanning my face, our bodies flushed.

Okay, one part of him is in motion: the growing bulge in his pants.

While he pauses, I would expect a sliver of doubt

creeping into my mind, but the hunger in his eyes doesn't allow for any unease.

"You will be the death of me," he sighs, the words brushing against my lips.

There's no edge in his voice, no tease—just quiet, aching resignation. Like he's already accepted the sentence.

Closing his eyes, he shakes his head slightly. His lashes fanning against his flushed cheeks, he clenches his jaw like he's biting down on a scream. I can feel the tension rippling through him.

He's not trying to seduce me. Not trying to win.

He's unraveling. One shallow breath at a time.

It hits me then.

This isn't a line. This isn't a game.

He means it.

Somehow, I've gotten under his skin and past his armor, and now he's standing here, pressed against me, asking me not to do the very thing he knows he can't stop.

Fall.

But this is Xander Stone, I remind myself. And yet I trust this moment more than any preconceived notions I had about this man.

Maybe this ends up being a good day after all.

"I think you'll survive me with ease, young man," I

tease, but it's bittersweet because I don't say the other part.

I know, irrevocably, that I won't survive him.

"I appreciate your confidence." He gives me a lingering kiss. "And stop calling me young man."

"Or?" I bite my lip.

"I'll take you over my knee." He growls, grabs my hand, and finally drags me out of the bathroom while I giggle like a schoolgirl.

We don't make it far. As soon as we stumble a few steps down the corridor, Xander stops and cups my face again.

His lips fuse with mine. This time, the kiss is less desperate, more playful, but still urgent. Not necessarily foreplay. More like he—we—can't get enough.

It's as if, after weeks of dancing around, we at last fell into step, and we can't help but marvel at the newly forged, tender, and probably dangerous bond.

His hands on my face are just a whisper of touch, yet it screams loud throughout me with longing and with joy.

For one night, I can be reckless. And enjoy the hell out of it.

Someone clears his throat, and Xander groans but disconnects the kiss. He leads me out of the restaurant.

"I'm sorry I interrupted your date," he teases.

"Are you?" I grin.

"Not in the least. I told you, that's a sentiment for the weak. Why the fuck would you go out with Ed Reynolds?"

I snort. "To find out I don't want to date him."

"I could have told you that."

On the street, the evening breeze is warm on my skin. "How did you even end up here?"

He cocks his head, looking at me through his lashes. "By now, you should know I have my ways."

"By now, I should have called the police." I try to sound stern, but my lips quirk with laughter. My sanity is on vacation, apparently.

"And what does it say that you didn't?" He yanks me to him. "You may fight this, Coraline, on many rational grounds, but this pull between us... it defies logic, gravity, and all our beliefs."

I reach to touch his cheek, his words scraping my mind blank. His effortless handsomeness is devastating, but it's his wit and raw honesty that strip me naked in front of him.

He is right. He is also brave. Braver than me. Or maybe he is just less broken. Less tainted by past experiences.

"Well, I guess we better discover what it means."

"You, Coraline, are a discovery by itself." He kisses me and then offers me his arm. "Shall we? Good that you're wearing pants."

"So you can literally get into my pants." I laugh.

He pulls me to him, slapping my hip gently. "That, too, but mostly because of our ride."

I follow his gaze and stop in my tracks. I step to the side to untangle myself from his hold. My heart rate hammers in my temples so loud, the city seems to have drowned under water.

Images I tried to erase flash freely in my mind. My mouth goes dry as I try to refocus, but the sight of his motorcycle renders me motionless. Speechless. Scared witless.

"Cora?"

Xander's voice seeps through the panic roaring in my head.

My vision blurs as I shake my head. I focus on that motion, hoping it grounds me. "Absolutely not."

My legs move toward the road.

"Cora?" Xander's confused voice is more insistent.

But I raise my hand and, miracle of miracles in Manhattan, a cab pulls to the curb.

"Cora—" His hand brushes against my arm, but I jump in, not looking back.

"Go," I urge.

The driver gives me one concerned glance and steps on the gas. I shouldn't be spending money on a fare, but the sight of that bike...

Jesus.

A stray tear rolls down my cheek.

Five minutes into the ride, my cheeks are wet, but my panic subsides. The relief is immediately followed by an irrational bout of anger. At myself.

If Xander Stone wants to kill himself on a motorcycle, it's his choice. It has nothing to do with me. I didn't have to run like an unhinged person.

But the sight triggered a reaction beyond my control.

Too many agonizing memories.

Chapter 13

Xander

What the fuck has just happened?

Chapter 14

Xander

"How long are you planning to stall?" Roxy doesn't knock and saunters into my office like it's her space, not mine.

In the corner, she pulls a bottle of Macallan from behind a book—of course she knows where I keep it—pours herself a glass, takes a sip, and sighs with delight.

"Feel free to answer anytime." She sits across from me in the chair on the other side of my desk.

She is wearing jeans with an intricately made lace top that belongs on an evening gown. Her haphazardly curled bun sports a pen, a pencil, and what looks like a laser pointer.

"Last time I checked, this was still my office," I retort, and swirl in my chair away from the monitor to face her.

"Not for long if you keep avoiding Daddy dearest."

She takes another sip while she checks her manicure, as if she is bored with the conversation she started.

"Don't you have an intern to fire, or a supplier to harass?"

She sighs. "Xander, you're an asshole most of the time, but we both know it's just a pose. Deep down, you're a decent human being. You're also smart—"

"Don't try to sweet-talk me, Roxy. You're better than that."

If there is something I want to do less than discussing my father with Roxy, it's actually talking to my father.

After another sigh of exasperation, she continues. "You're also smart, even though you're set on acting like a dumbass. What did your father do to you?"

"I didn't know you were promoted to office therapist." I pick up my smoothie.

"Xander, was he abusing you?"

I spatter the green liquid. "No! Jesus, why would your mind go there?"

"It's not that outlandish, but I'm relieved to hear it's not the case. Which begs the question, why are you avoiding him? Whatever he did, grow up, forgive, and move on."

I lean back in my chair. "It looks like you might be the one with daddy issues."

She flinches. "We're talking about you."

Whatever is behind her reaction, unlike her, I don't believe I'm a therapist, so I let it go. "I'm just curious why you assume he did something."

Her eyes flicker with something that looks disturbingly excited. "It was you who fucked up? Were you exiled?" The unabashed thrill in her voice draws a laugh from me.

"It's not a soap opera, Ro."

The hated nickname wipes the glee from her face. "Whatever you did, Xander, your father has been trying to reach you, so I'm sure you're forgiven."

By him, maybe. "I'm not ready to talk to him, so drop it."

"Is it so bad that you're going to let down Merged?"

She might have just verbalized the burden that has been weighing on my shoulders. "I'm looking for another solution. He's not the only one with connections in San Francisco."

"Another solution?" She looks at me, unimpressed, swirling her drink.

I nod.

"How is that going for you?" She doesn't hesitate to call me on my bullshit.

I've been going through my contacts, but most of them have a connection to my father. That's what happens when I built my name in his shadow.

Honestly, I haven't had a chance to really try because I've been distracted.

Whatever happened four days ago with Cora... I might not understand it, but that doesn't stop me from thinking about it. Nonstop.

When I try and fail to sleep. When I work out. When I'm in meetings. When I'm attempting to work.

The way she grabbed my lapels and pulled me to her. Fuck, that was the hottest thing ever. I have kissed many women, but never has a kiss evoked as much thrill as hers. Right there and then, I knew a taste wouldn't ever be enough.

"Look, Roxy, I appreciate your concern, but I'm still your boss, not the other way around. I'll get it done. I always get things done."

"Can I have another one?" She raises her empty glass.

"For fuck's sake, it's not even five." I shake my head.

"I had a shitty day, okay? I'm hiding here because Lewis from HR wants to discuss something, and he bores me to death."

I snort. "Go at it. I'll have one too."

She shimmies her hips in a little dance. "Finally, the fun Xander is back."

"I've been here all the time."

She unscrews the bottle. "Yeah, but since you

started chasing Cora Winslow, you're… I don't know… different."

"I'm not chasing her," I reply out of habit, defending my playboy status. I'm totally chasing her, and the worst part—or maybe the best—is I don't mind at all.

Roxy snorts. "Really? Taking her to events, going to her house, crashing her date…" She brings over two glasses. "How did that go, by the way?"

"Ed fucking Reynolds is an idiot."

"Agreed." She clinks her glass with mine. "So why have you been moping?"

"I'm not moping."

"You're awfully defensive today about everything. That's not your jam. Tell me what happened. Was she upset you interrupted her potential lifetime of happiness?"

"Take your drink somewhere else."

She laughs. "So, remember how you owe me?"

I take a gulp. "What do you want?"

"I want to know what happened." She leans forward, as if attentive listening is the only thing on her agenda.

"Out of all the things I can make happen for you, you want me to recount that insane moment?"

"Look at that! You're self-aware enough to recognize you act insane." She cheers with a smile.

"You really need to live a little." I take a sip. Perhaps a female perspective won't hurt. "There is not much to share. She hated the date, she pretended to hate I interrupted it, but after Ed left, we kind of hit it off."

"What did you do?"

"What the fuck, Roxy? Why would you assume I fucked something up?"

"You're a self-absorbed man. It's an easy conclusion to draw."

"Why am I even talking to you?"

"Okay, okay, what happened?"

"I don't know. We left the restaurant, and then she suddenly changed her behavior and bolted for a taxi."

"No explanation?"

I shake my head. "I considered calling her, but I've done enough stalking. She just... I don't know, she saw my bike and—"

"Oh," Roxy utters knowingly.

"What does that mean?"

"This is not my story to tell..." She takes a sip.

"Well, now you have to tell it."

"She needs to explain that herself."

"Is this some sort of female thing I'm not aware of? I really don't fucking understand what happened. If she is scared of riding a bike, she could have just said so."

Roxy hums pensively.

"What?"

She shakes her head, refusing to explain.

Well, if this is the game she wants to play, I pick up my phone. "I'm calling Lewis from HR that you're here."

She jumps to snatch the receiver. "Don't you dare."

I move my arm out of her reach. "Explain."

She slouches into her chair, sighing. "After you asked for her home address, I put together basic facts about her."

"You profiled her?" I might act with shock, but in reality I'm barely stopping myself from asking for that file.

"Like I do for our business partners." She scrunches her nose. "I like that part of my job," she adds a little too quickly.

And she is great at it. "I want to see the file."

"You know that is all sorts of—"

"Don't finish that sentence. Bring the file, Roxy, or I will not only call Lewis, I'll make sure he has a weekly one-on-one with you.

"You can't do that."

"Watch me." Something in my determination—and I've been riding the unhinged train with dedication lately—makes her pull out her phone.

A few swipes, and a lethal glare later, a notification

pops up on my screen. I click on the attachment, and my jaw tenses. "The password," I growl.

Roxy stands up, finishes her drink, and with a smile, walks to the door. Before she opens it, she looks over her shoulder. "First, I'm going to send you your dinner reservations for tonight. If you show up, I will give you the password."

"You want me to take you out?"

She laughs. "I have better things to do. This dinner is a kind request from Mr. Stone Sr." She hitches her shoulders innocently. "And Xander?"

I meet her eyes, trying to hide the turmoil her blackmail caused.

"If you care about Cora... if you're even a tad serious about her, I wouldn't look at that file."

Fuck. My. Life.

Don't be a pussy.

I'm ten minutes late for dinner with my father. Not because I got delayed. Mostly because when it comes to my father, I turn into the little boy whose balls haven't dropped yet.

I've been sitting on the balcony level of the swanky steakhouse for half an hour. Senior came, immediately owned the room, and is now sitting and waiting, motionless, his gaze locked on the entrance.

If he was on the phone, or reading or flirting with the waitress, I might have descended already. As it is, he feels like a statue, not a human.

Fuck it. This is how losing feels, and I'm not good at that. In my current situation, either I show up or not, but it still feels like a defeat.

Grow some balls, asshole.

I stand up, fasten the button on my jacket, and adjust my cuffs. I walk to the curved staircase, wishing it was at my father's back behind his table. It's not.

Two more steps and he will spot me. Two more steps and I will have to face him. Two more steps and I will have to confront my demons.

Fucking Roxy.

But as my foot touches that second step and our eyes meet, I'm kind of glad she coerced me into this meeting. It's not like I can avoid him forever

I might have come here because a part of me I don't recognize, much less know how to tame, wants that file. It wants to uncover Cora's secrets. No, it *needs* access to her world, her needs, her troubles, her joys.

But if I'm honest, I don't know if I want to find out through Roxy's skillful sleuthing. I want Cora to share her world with me. But the stubborn woman is fucking exasperating. Why doesn't she let me in?

If not for Cora's file, I might have come here only for my father's help with the Vireon business, but the reality is different.

I should have come here to reconnect with my father. And now, as I approach him, I'm glad I'm here. Still dreading the conversation, but what is the worst-case scenario? We'll return to the status quo, which would suck, but I have my life here now, anyway.

"I had a call, and it took longer..." Good job, starting with a lie.

He stands up and wraps me in an embrace. I tense. I don't remember the last time we hugged.

"It's good to see you, son," he rasps.

I pat his back before he steps back. "It's good to see you, Dad."

The biggest surprise? It really is good to see him. I was prepared for the wave of guilt, blame, shame. Fuck, I was even ready for a stern dressing-down or an argument.

I wasn't ready to deal with the flood of sap that cruises through my veins at that moment. I didn't realize how much I missed him.

I've been so buried in my shame, in avoiding the issue, and running away from it, that I didn't allow myself to feel the hurt of our estrangement.

"I took the liberty of choosing the wine. This

conversation is perhaps more suitable for a tumbler of whiskey, but we're at a steakhouse."

That's my dad alright, always leaning into expectations and norms, even if it's against his own preferences.

He gestures to the waiter, who approaches with the decanter and pours me a glass. It's an organic Zinfandel from a small vineyard in Napa Valley, and my mind immediately wanders to the ginger nymph who has been escaping me.

Would she like this vintage?

What is she doing?

Why did she run away?

The last question is returning with annoying frequency.

I raise my glass and take a sip, desperately thinking of a way to lead this conversation. My father is the only man I know who makes me search for words. It has been like that forever.

The thing is, when Senior speaks, everyone listens. I grew up in the light of that awe and respect he so effortlessly commands. As a result, I always measure my words with a care that borders on self-censorship.

Like I'm trying to mimic his authority while second-guessing every word that leaves my mouth. Like every syllable is a test I didn't study for, but can't afford to fail.

The lifelong habit is only emphasized given the circumstances of our encounter. I fucked up. I left. I ignored him. How does one start a conversation after that? Fuck.

"I'm sorry I made you feel that leaving was your only option." He dives right into it.

"You didn't—" Or maybe he did. Who knows anymore? But what staggers me is his apology. Whatever happened to the Stones never apologizing?

"Look, Alexander, you have a brilliant combination of intelligence merged with street smarts. You have a drive that pushes you beyond and above. But we didn't realize how smart you were early on, and you went through the school system with such ease, you never learned one important thing."

I frown in question.

"You never learned what it is to fail. We had enough worries with your siblings—"

"It's not your fault..." Are we going to dance around it and blame it on the school system?

"Maybe not, but I think we should have challenged you more. Instead, you learned that everything comes easy to you, and when you faced your first challenge—"

"You lost a company because of me," I snap, finally naming the issue that had spun in my head since I'd caused the situation but had never verbalized.

He raises his eyebrows, and then frowns. I'm not

sure if it's because I've never interrupted him when he speaks, let alone this many times, or because my admission surprised him.

"The company is just an asset. I replaced that several times over since then." He takes a sip of his wine, looking away. "I lost way more."

Not sure if I'm as smart as everyone tends to think, because I never considered his angle. I never considered his loss.

The regret in his tone, in his expression, in those averted eyes, is as potent as the one flooding through me. Even though he's not looking at me, lost in his own emotions, I look away.

I'm so fucking sorry. About my wrong decision. About his company. About running away. About missing the time with my family. About disappointing him.

And most of all, I'm sorry I can't say it. I can't apologize. That word has never been in my vocabulary. The man across from me taught me that apology is a sign of weakness.

"You must be disappointed," I swallow around the lump in my throat.

"You're my son. You can never disappoint me. I'm proud of what you've accomplished here. And perhaps the situation back home triggered you in the right direction. One you would not have entertained otherwise."

"Silver lining," I mutter, his pride wrapping around me like a prickly coat.

One of the reasons I lean into sarcasm, playfulness, and jokes is so that people don't take me too seriously. I grew up being praised by everyone because I just learned things faster and more easily.

Being praised constantly doesn't help you find friends, or even keep the peace with your siblings. So I dumb it down.

Even now, as a grown-ass man, my father's praise gives me shivers.

This meeting is unraveling deeply hidden traumas I really fucking don't want to address. I think childhood shit should stay right there, in my fucking childhood. Meeting my father after almost two years is stirring shit up, whether I like it or not.

I expected to rehash the situation that led to my exile. Instead, all sorts of other rehashing is happening, and the last thing I want is to show that weakness to my father.

He shrugs. "Perhaps a silver lining. Or just the way things were supposed to be. I don't like how you got here, but I think you're where you should be."

I nod. "How is Mom?" I redirect before I suffocate in my own bullshit.

"Busy with her annual gala, driving everyone crazy,

and claiming this is the last year she's organizing it. The usual." He chuckles. "But I'm sure Lottie told you that."

I shouldn't be surprised he knows I've been in touch with my sister, but I am. "She did," I admit.

"Shall we order?"

I nod, and he raises his hand. We order steaks and more wine, and he gives me an update about my siblings and some other relatives.

Finished with his meal, he wipes his mouth. "So tell me about Merged."

"I have a feeling you probably know enough." I lean back.

Despite the heaviness of the circumstances, and my still unresolved guilt over the situation from two years ago, I'm enjoying his company.

"I hear your client is expanding to the West Coast."

"It's not a secret. The merger has been announced." I'm just not sure why he brought it up, but I guess I might as well take advantage. "But since you mention it..."

"How can I help?"

I might still take my revenge on Roxy—her meddling is not appreciated—but I'm glad she pushed me here. It might be the first step in reconciliation with my family, and finally get us closer to that seat we promised Atlas.

"I need a seat on the Vireon board."

He nods. "Those assholes will drive you crazy, but I still have some pull there."

I snort. "They drove you to resignation, I hear."

"I'm at the age when I choose carefully who I spend my time with."

"Will you help us?"

"Of course, but I have a condition."

And the plot thickens.

The last time he made a request—demand—my life imploded. I fucking hate that he still has so much power over my choices.

Chapter 15

Cora

SAAR

Why are you not answering, @Cora? It's been four days. How was the date?

Depends

CELESTE

OMG, you can't answer like that.

I just did (winking emoji).

CELESTE

So there is a story to tell.

SAAR

You liked Ed! Should I cancel tomorrow's date?

I didn't like Ed. Sorry.

SAAR

Don't be sorry. We just started.

CELESTE

I still need details.

Six hours later

LILY

I hate being in a different time zone.

@Cora I'm sure the next one will be better (kiss emoji).

"You used to tell me Ethan wasn't good enough for me. Why, Dad?"

I'm not sure why I'm raising the question.

Dad sometimes doesn't remember me; he for sure wouldn't remember my deceased fiancé. And it's not like it matters anyway.

I'm still unsettled from my reaction to Xander's bike a few days ago. Discussing Ethan with my dad will not help me, but he's been on my mind. What are the odds that Xander would have an orange bike as well?

It's like I asked Ethan if he was okay with me dating, so he sent a sign? Fuck, I should call Xander and explain. But as strange as it is, I still don't have his number.

I can ask Saar, I suppose, but that would unleash

the investigator in her and... well, I don't want to dissect what might be with Xander. Or what some part of me still hopes for.

Besides, what would I tell him? The motorcycle is non-negotiable for me.

I still remember the call on that dreadful night, when all my future plans got canceled in a pool of blood and motor oil.

Ethan had only one flaw: he was speeding... until he died.

"He never deserved you." Dad looks at me with such clarity, I almost gasp. We hold our gazes for a moment, all the pain and unresolved feelings within reach to unravel. "You never deserved any of this."

"What are you talking about?" I whisper.

"It's more comfortable for you than living your own life." A hint of disapproval—no, disappointment—flavors his statement.

What is he talking about? Ethan? What does he mean by *any of this*?

"Is Tessa coming?" he asks, his eyes again unfocused, staring somewhere in front of him.

Whiplash, anyone?

"She's too busy with an event at the moment," I say vaguely.

I might not even be lying, though I want to be petty and say *she's too busy to visit you* instead. That wouldn't serve anyone, so I push my unreasonable sibling rivalry to the side.

"Sanjay, who works at your bistro with me, offered to implement some changes." I hold my breath, hoping to engage him.

Not sure why. To absolve me of the guilt I'm feeling about changing anything my father left behind?

Usually when I broach the topic of the bistro, he either berates me, firing suggestions, or he is completely indifferent.

To my surprise, he levels me with another focused look. "It hasn't been my bistro in years," he says, with such indifference that I blink a few times, as if that could bring some understanding.

My visits here are never easy, but today is dredging up something I can't yet pinpoint. Like Dad is laying out a puzzle for me. Only every piece is black, so I can't build a picture from it.

"What are you talking about? It will always be your bistro."

"Oh, Coraline." He shakes his head. "As I said, that man was never good enough for you. He took away your dreams, and then he fucked off, and you settled for chasing mine. Such a shame." His hands shake.

Stunned doesn't even begin to describe how bewildered this entire exchange makes me. I want to talk to him. I want to open a bottle of Zinfandel and hear his opinion, argue my point, find understanding. Like the old times.

But he can't drink wine with all his medication. He speaks in riddles I no longer understand. And… as much as I don't want to admit it, I'm afraid to push further.

This is the most intimate conversation I've had with him in the longest time. It's been unsettling, as well. For both of us.

We sit in silence for a little while longer before I say my goodbyes.

I leave the home in a daze, almost missing my train stop. Above the station, I buy myself sunflowers from a florist on the corner of my street. It brings some joy, pulls me back to the present moment, but the unnerving energy lingers.

My life is unraveling at roller coaster-like speed, and I feel like an observer. I replay my father's words in a loop, but they don't bring any clarity

The farther I am from his home, the more certain I am it was one of his confused statements. From a place where he gets lost in his own world, outside of this time and dimension.

At least at work I can lean on Sanjay. And maybe I should reclaim my personal life and ask Saar for Xander's number. He deserves my explanation.

When I enter the bistro, the hair on my neck

prickles immediately. Everything seems normal. There are no visible leaks, the power is on, and the display is filled with our usuals. I walk toward the counter as a few patrons smile my way.

I can't pinpoint the source of my premonition until my eyes meet Sanjay's.

"What is wrong?"

He looks away, wiping the polished surface around the sink. "We need to talk."

I frown. "Okay."

He unties his apron, still not looking at me. "I resign. Effective immediately."

Relief floods me as I laugh. "Seriously, Sanjay, you scared me."

He snaps his eyes to me, his expression pained. My smile disappears, and the earlier unknown feeling gripping my stomach returns. "You're not joking?"

He shakes his head and looks down again.

"What happened? Earlier this week you were full of enthusiasm to help out more around here. Is it about money? You know I can't offer you more at the moment, but—"

"I got another job. I'm sorry, Cora. I-I hope you understand."

I sigh. "No, Sanjay, I don't understand at all. I really don't, but I guess you made up your mind. Is there any way I can—"

"Please, Cora, just let me go."

His plea is so desperate, I can practically feel his anguish in my stomach. "You want to leave right away?"

"Yes, I have vacation time I'm owed." He moves toward the back door. "You don't have to pay me. The job is closer to my sister. She got sick, so I really have to go." He slips into the prep room, and before I can gather my wits and follow him, he returns with his backpack.

He nods, giving me a curt, guilty glance, and leaves. Just like that, after being here almost every day in the past few months, he just walks out.

What has just happened? Shit.

I don't know how long I stare at the glass entrance, a part of me waiting for him to return and finally confirm it was just a prank. A cruel one, but still a joke.

"Can we pay?" A customer snaps me back to my new reality.

I look at him, still stunned, trying to remember how to run a register I'm perfectly familiar with under normal circumstances.

I finally manage to settle their bill. "Was everything okay?"

The elderly lady and her husband are regulars here. She smiles at me. "Yes, as always. We've been coming here for years."

Smiling, I walk them to the door, but I can barely see them. It's like I'm suspended in a different dimension, just watching myself going through the motions. The lady says something I miss, but they finally leave.

I should call the temp agency. And prep for lunch.

Instead, I flip the open sign to closed and lock the door. My legs carry me back to the counter. I check the register for the open orders and then glance at the tables.

Only three of them are currently occupied, and none of the patrons is waiting for anything. The ingrained instinct is sending me toward the tables to check if they want something else, to clean the dishes, to schmooze.

Instead, I'm standing rooted in place. If I thought I was tired before, the level of weary fatigue that hugs my nerves is so deep, I don't think I can ever move again.

You never deserved any of this.

I don't know what to do with Dad's statement. Or with my current situation. So I stand there, waiting for everyone to finally fuck off.

When I lock the door after the last customer leaves at eleven in the morning, I get to the back room, grip the handle of my largest chef's knife, and stab the wooden cutting board repeatedly.

And then I scream. At the top of my lungs until my throat hurts.

It helps only marginally. The fog in my mind clears slightly, but I'm still just tired of it all, with no drive to look for solutions. I just don't have the energy to keep this boat afloat.

Don't be fucking dramatic, Cora. And now I speak to myself, sounding like my sister. Great.

Okay, this is not the first time I'm left without help. I get my phone to dial the temp agency when a bang on the front glass draws my attention.

"We're fucking closed," I murmur, but whoever is there doesn't leave and knocks again.

Groaning, I shuffle to the front, and when I see the property manager on the other side, the earlier premonition grows its wings and flaps around me like an angel of doom.

I unlock the door. "Mr. Petruch, how can I help you?"

"You're closed? I guess you heard already?"

"What do you mean?"

"The building has a new owner."

I blow a raspberry. "Okay?"

"Look, Cora, I know things haven't been easy, but the new owner wants to double your rent." He hands me an envelope.

I look down at the legal-sized yellow paper and

watch my hand move toward it while my entire being screams, *Don't touch it.* As if not accepting whatever legal document is in that envelope could change its consequences.

"I can't pay double," I say when the paper connects with my fingers.

"I'm sorry." He shrugs.

"I can't," I repeat, and I'm not sure if I'm still talking about the rent only.

He gives me a compassionate look, or maybe it's just pity, then nods and leaves.

And just like that, I lost my father's life's work.

"What are you doing here?" Tessa says as she opens the doors, her eyes red.

"Are you crying?" I forget how soaked I am, because of course, after weeks of sweltering heat, Mother Nature sent us a reprieve right as I was walking from the station.

"Why are you wet?"

Every conversation with my sister is a tug-of-war. Like we grew up one-upping each other, so now we fight for who leads the conversation just by force of habit.

"It's raining." I resign from the argument, not

because I want to act as a well-adjusted adult. I'm just tired and, well, resigned. Let alone shivering from the cold.

"Ever heard of an umbrella?" She isn't moving to invite me in.

"Ever heard of hospitality?"

She opens her mouth, but bites back her retort and steps back to let me in. "Why are you here?"

She's definitely been crying. "What's wrong, Tessa?" The air is arctic on my wet skin. How low is her AC setting?

"Like you care." Her lip trembles.

For the love of God. "Why would I ask?"

She looks so small and broken, I want to give her a hug. The only thing stopping me is that she is wearing a cashmere sweater and I'm wet.

"Paul left me. And the girls took off with him." She wipes a tear, sniffles, and lifts her chin. "You know, living in Florida with Daddy is so much cooler."

"Fuck, I'm sorry, Tessa."

"I don't want your pity," she snaps.

I guess she just needs a punching bag. To use someone to get her anger out of her system. I wish I weren't freezing in soaked clothes, and too wrapped up in the middle of my own business crisis to offer her what she needs.

My shoulders shake of their own accord, and my

teeth rattle. I shouldn't have come here. Fuck my pride. My friends would help me without a blink, but I just couldn't admit to them this new level of low.

Besides, that bistro is our father's. Tessa should care. She never has, but she was still my first natural choice.

She knows how poorly the business is doing, and I don't care about her opinion of me enough to feel embarrassed. I don't need to apologize to her for trying to save our family's heritage.

I don't expect her to jump at the idea, of course. I know she would make me suffer for it, but I still hope she will bail me out.

What I didn't expect was that my perfect, always well-put-together sister would be in the midst of her own personal crisis.

"It's not pity; it's compassion. I'm sure the girls just imagined Florida means an all-year spring break party. They will miss you soon enough."

My words break the dam, and my sister allows herself a moment of complete vulnerability and cries. "You really think so?"

I have no idea. I don't know what really happened between her perfect husband and her, or why her daughters would side with their father. Or if that's really even the case.

I don't know whether they would return. I

wouldn't live with my sister voluntarily. But perhaps this is a time when a kind lie counts. "Of course. Tell me what happened."

Tessa blows her nose into a linen handkerchief, her shoulders shaking. She sits down on a settee in her entrance hallway, her hiccups bouncing around the walls in the cavernous space.

Between her sobs, she retells me the story of Paul's cheating, and how she finally decided to throw him out.

Despite my being freezing and her circumstances, for a moment I feel like we're girls again, sharing our pains like we used to before our parents separated.

Maybe we still are those girls somewhere deep down; we just buried them to cope with the new reality in our lives. I miss those girls.

"We didn't handle it well with the twins. I always hid his affairs. They idolized their father, and now I'm the villain in the sordid story."

"I remember when Paul came to pick you up the first time. Boys used to just honk in front of the house, and you rushed out. It rained that day, and I sat in the window. He stepped out of his car and walked to the door to hold an umbrella above your head. I found it so romantic, I almost fell in love with him." I sigh.

"Yeah, he was very attentive at first." She hugs herself, rubbing her arms. "Jesus, why don't you go get a towel?" she snaps suddenly. "Let me make you some tea. The last thing I need is you accusing me of getting sick."

And just like that, the bonding session comes to an abrupt halt. Tessa shuffles toward her kitchen.

If I weren't chilled to the bone, I would turn and fucking leave. Instead, I venture into her guest bathroom upstairs and take a long, warm shower.

The water loosens my numb limbs, but it doesn't dislodge the lump in my throat, nor does it unclench my stomach.

I might be able to find a new employee. I might be able to find energy to work more and train them. I might be able to implement a few ideas on the menu that may help the bottom line.

What I'm not capable of doing is generating the income needed to pay the increased rent. Not without a sizable investment. One I don't have.

I towel-dry my hair and put on a plush robe I find on the door. I look at my jeans, T-shirt, and underwear, crumpled in a sad, wet heap. The idea of traipsing downstairs barefoot isn't appealing, but I guess that's my only option.

When I open the door, I almost trip over something soft—a neat pile of leggings, a sweatshirt, and a pair of socks.

In the kitchen, I find Tessa sitting on a high stool by

her enormous square island. I take a seat beside her and wrap my fingers around a warm cup. "Thank you for the clothes."

"Have your tea; I'll go put your things in the dryer." She leaves, and for whatever reason—exhaustion perhaps—her act of help brings tears to my eyes.

Jesus, I really need to take some time off.

"What are you doing here anyway?" Tessa asks when she returns.

Gathering the strength to broach the topic, I study her for a long moment as she moves around the kitchen doing I don't know what.

"The rent at the bistro has just been doubled."

"Good," she mutters.

"What do you mean good? With that kind of increase, I may as well file for bankruptcy."

She sighs. "Perhaps that's what we should have done the minute Dad bailed out."

I slide off the stool. "How can you say that? He got sick."

"Okay, but he got it into the state it was left in. You took the responsibility of saving it for him. Whatever for? It's not like he's coming back."

I blink a few times, her words floating between us viciously. "I knew it was a mistake coming here."

"What did you expect? That I will finance the operation? If I had ever thought it was a good idea, I would have offered help a long time ago. You need to stop idolizing Dad, and finally get rid of that stupid bistro and live your life."

"I guess all daughters idolize their fathers but yours." I throw her earlier words about her twins back at her. The stab doesn't make me feel better, and I regret it immediately.

Tessa's eyes water.

"I'm sorry." Bowing, I shake my head. "I'm stressed and—"

"Cora, even if I wanted to help you, I don't have any money."

"What do you mean?" I look around her kitchen, which is at least three times bigger than the bistro.

"I mean I'm one of those stupid women without a prenup who is now at the mercy of her husband."

Fuck. "I'm sorry."

"I said I don't want your pity. But take my advice and fucking close that bistro. Dad doesn't care. Whatever you're trying to achieve, it's not worth it. Especially since you don't want to do it."

Especially since you don't want to do it.

You never deserved any of this.

The two statements live rent-free in my head with

relentless dedication. They play on a loop when I get rejected for loans at two different banks. When I try to reason with the building manager.

Even when I finally confess to Celeste and Saar about my issues. All the while, I lie to them, feeling like shit, when I tell them my sister is stepping in and helping.

I love those women. Money would fuck up our relationship, and let's be honest, it's the only thing I have left.

Tonight is my next date, but I'm running a fever, so I canceled. Saar will understand. I'm in no shape to go out, even if I didn't have this horrible flu.

Being tired, broken, and sick is the most potent combination for sadness. I've been feeling so sorry for myself, even Pitt and Clooney went to purr somewhere else.

I need to change my shirt and sheets, probably, but I can barely get to the bathroom. Unfortunately, nature calls, so I slide out of my bed to start the almost Olympic-level task that is getting to the toilet. Never has my place felt this big.

I rest on the sofa on my way, my bladder almost bursting, but the last few feet seem insurmountable. I've always enjoyed living alone, but I've only ever been this sick... well, never. What I would give for a roommate now.

I should call someone to help me. Where is my phone? I whimper when I realize it's on my nightstand. In an absolute display of indignity, I collapse to the floor, ready to crawl toward the toilet, when a knock on the door draws another whimper from me.

The front door is closer than the toilet, so I shuffle to it. Still on my knees, I reach for the lock and twist it.

And then everything goes black.

Chapter 16

Xander

Caged lion.

That's how I've been feeling since Cora's door unlocked but never opened. Fuck, I've never been as scared or powerless as I felt when I found her collapsed on the floor.

The ambulance took three lifetimes to arrive. And it took another one to finally hear that she was okay, just severely dehydrated along with her nasty flu.

Her face is transparent as she lies in the huge hospital bed. Her nose looks even redder against the ashen background of her beautiful face.

What would have happened if I wasn't there? If I didn't come to her uninvited yet again? I had some doubts about my visit, which I stubbornly ignored. But those faint voices of reason were erased the moment I saw her.

The doctor reassured me she'll be fine. They broke her fever and pumped all sorts of drugs into her, to keep her sinuses clean and her body hydrated.

And still I'm wearing holes in the sterile floor, waiting for her to wake up and scold me for something, so I know she is okay.

I stop to check my emails. It's almost midnight, but at this point I'd do anything to distract myself from waiting. Leaning against the wall, I tap my foot while I review a few proposals.

"What's the tapping?"

I drop the phone on the windowsill and rush to her bedside, her raspy voice the most beautiful sound I've heard all day.

"You're up," I say like an idiot, leaning over her, gripping the frame of her bed to stop myself from touching her, hugging her, holding her.

She squints. "Xander? Where am I?" Her eyes move from me to her arm, and up the tube to the IV bag, and then back to me. "What happened?"

"You had a fever and fainted, but there is nothing to worry about; you should regain your strength soon."

"I fainted?" She closes her eyes, frowning.

"Are you in pain?"

She shakes her head. "You found me?" She licks her cracked lips.

Unable to stay away, I caress her head, her hair

sticky and warm under my touch. "Luckily, you unlocked the door just before you lost consciousness. Here, have a sip of water." I reach for the cup and bring the straw to her mouth.

She blinks a few times and takes a sip. "It was you knocking?"

"Yes."

She closes her eyes again. I want to pepper her with questions to make sure she is not suffering. I want to call the doctor and demand they run all sorts of tests to make sure she's alright. I want to berate her for not calling someone sooner when she fell sick.

I don't do any of those things. I just watch her, the caged-lion feeling restraining me again.

I don't know how long I stand there as she drifts back to sleep. I just resume my pacing, and when she groans, I'm back at her side so quickly I almost topple over a chair.

"I was on my way to the toilet when you knocked," she whimpers, embarrassment coloring her cheeks. She covers her face with her forearm. "Did I?"

"Don't worry about it." The state she was in will forever be etched on my mind, but that minor detail is inconsequential. I peel her arm from her face. "I was there; that's what matters. And you were perfectly decent, I promise."

Groaning, she looks away. "Thank you for that charitable lie," she murmurs.

Fuck, she is adorable. Always. In her anger. In her defiance. Even in her unwarranted embarrassment. "Look at me."

She does reluctantly.

"I'm just fucking glad you're okay."

"With no shred of dignity left," she whimpers.

"It's going to be a good joke one day," I tease.

She widens her eyes, but the corners of her mouth twitch. "Don't you dare ever mention it."

"I promise." I pat my heart.

"Thank you," she says again. "How long have I been here?" The momentary peace disappears from her face, her forehead marred with lines.

"Too fucking long." I sigh, but she attempts to sit up, so I add, "A few hours."

"I need to leave now." She tries to turn to swing her legs over the edge, but stops. Eyeing the drip, she bites her lip.

"Okay, woman, what's the problem? You were half-dead an hour ago. Let them treat you, so you can regain your strength."

"I can't stay here, Xander." She whispers, despite us being alone in a private room.

"What are you talking about?"

Is she still running a fever? Did she hit her head

when she fell?

"Why would you get me a private room?" She sags into the pillows, covering her eyes with her free arm.

I open my mouth, but I realize I don't have an answer to that. I called Corm on the way here because his mother is on the board, and this is what followed.

I look around. "It's the best they have."

"I can't afford it," she whisper-snaps at me, glancing at the door as if someone were eavesdropping.

Shit. I sit on the edge beside her. "It's a good thing I'm paying for it then."

"I'm not accepting your charity," she says, like she had options here.

"It's my birthday gift redo." I wink.

She glares at me. "This is not much better."

"But at least it's something you need."

Her eyes pierce through me, first with fierce disdain and then with something akin to resignation. "Thank you."

Good girl.

"Stop thanking me."

It may be just the drugs and her fatigue, but I can almost see how the tension from her shoulders leaves. Like she's finally accepted the reality and decided to let go of her independence for a moment.

For some reason, it makes me feel like I won some sort of prize. Like I tamed her stubborn streak or something. It's fucked-up and intoxicating. I've never cared for anyone. I never needed or wanted to.

And it's not even about helping her, which is strangely rewarding, and it slightly lessens the latent panic from earlier when she was lifeless in my arms.

It's about her surrender. About her letting me help her that makes me feel like I conquered Mt. Everest.

Our eyes locked, I wipe sweaty hair from her forehead, letting my fingers linger near her warm face. Even pale and congested, she is breathtaking.

She parts her lips, wetting them with her tongue. I want to lean down and take that taunting mouth.

Fuck the germs.

If I could, I would take the sickness from her. But I don't think she would appreciate my mauling her while she can barely breathe.

Cora puts her hand over mine and inhales to say something.

"I see you're up, Ms. Winslow." A nurse walks in, and I jump away as if she caught me stealing.

She did, kind of. I was trying to steal a moment with this woman who stole my attention, and refuses to let go.

The nurse gives me a stern look and turns to Cora. "I'm Doctor Chen. How are you feeling?"

Oh, so not a nurse.

"I'm good. Can I go home?" Cora's voice is laced with hope.

I groan. Still fucking stubborn.

Dr. Chen glances at the half-empty drip and pinches Cora's wrist between her thumb and index finger while she checks her watch.

"I don't see any reason to keep you here longer. As soon as the drip is done, we'll discharge you."

"I discussed a CT scan with your colleague," I interject.

Dr. Chen smiles at me. "I heard of that, but it's really not necessary."

"What if she hit her head when she fell? We're not leaving here until we've discounted all the options." I barely keep my voice at a decent volume.

"I'm sure Ms. Winslow appreciates your concern," Dr. Chen says, with a sweetness that's anything but sincere. "But you don't have the power of attorney here, so I think we will discuss Ms. Winslow's health without your input, Mr. Stone."

She knows who I am, so clearly she knows I know people on her board, and she still plays this game.

"I'm sure a negligence lawsuit would look great on your resume," I snap.

"Xander, please, tone it down. I'm sure they would run a CT if there were a reason for it. Thank you, Dr. Chen."

"Good. I'm going to prepare the discharge papers. The nurse will come back with medicine and instructions for your home care, but it's pretty straightforward. You have an infection, so I'm prescribing antibiotics. Stay hydrated while your body copes; come back if you feel worse or can't break the fever with over-the-counter meds. But I'm sure the antibiotics will kick in soon, and you'll be as good as new."

"Thank you," Cora says, and Dr. Chen leaves.

"What the hell, Xander? They know what they're doing. Why did you have to bully her?"

"Bully her? I just demanded she do her job."

"And what gave you the right to demand anything here?"

Doesn't she understand?

"Fear," I snap. "When I found you... I've never been so scared in my life."

* * *

"You really don't need to—" Cora whines.

"Can you shut up finally?" We enter her apartment. "Over my dead body I'm leaving you alone here."

"I'm fine," she says, like I hadn't heard her the first ten times since we left the hospital.

"You're still under the influence of drugs. And when your fever spikes again?"

She rolls her eyes. "I will take more drugs."

I drop her keys on the coffee table. "Now you're just being stubborn. I'm not leaving."

"You can't stay here." She leans against the doorway leading to her bedroom. The woman barely has the energy to stand, but she uses it to argue. "I don't have a guest room. Besides, I doubt you can cook chicken soup or even prepare a cup of tea."

I put my hands on my hips. Fuck, I'm tired after the adrenaline roller coaster and lack of sleep. "Tea is my specialty, and I can have the best chicken soup here in under twenty minutes. I bet it takes longer to cook it."

She groans and shuffles into her bedroom. "Can you get a guest room built in twenty minutes?"

"I'll sleep on your sofa."

Now it's my turn to lean against the door frame, because as much as I want to—need to—take care of her and make sure she's better, something stops me from entering her bedroom. Like I'm a fucking vampire who needs an invitation.

"With Pitt and Clooney?" She gives me a teasing smile while she leans against the footboard. Her smile is in such contrast with her grumbling, it's adorable. But she needs to get to bed ASAP, so I snap out of it.

And yeah, the cats.

"At least I can finally count them all," I retort.

"Oh, they hide well. Especially with a stranger around here."

I narrow my eyes. I'm ninety percent sure she's messing with me, but fuck, ten percent can make a significant difference in negotiations, so I'm still wary. "Just get into bed before you faint again."

She rolls her eyes for the hundredth time. "I need to shower and get changed. And these sheets are gross."

Fuck.

"I can help you shower," I suggest, because she's right, I'm not qualified to help her in any reasonable way. And if I'm honest, I'm staying for my own peace of mind as much as for her.

"Why don't I shower while you change the sheets, since you're insisting on helping me?" She opens her tiny closet and takes out some clothes.

My concierge service must be able to get someone here quickly. "Sure, I'll call my—"

"You can't change the sheets?" She snorts and walks past me.

I don't miss the way she is supporting herself with her hand, using the wall and furniture as a cane. And the stubborn woman said she could cope by herself.

"Of course I can," I respond quickly. Just because I've never done something, it doesn't mean I can't do it. How hard can it be? I glance at her queen-size bed. "Where are the clean sheets?"

Fuck, I'll make an idiot of myself just to see the entertainment on her face. She points to the dresser and leaves for the bathroom.

Taking the sheets off is a breeze.

Wrapping the obstinate sheet's corners around the mattress is a fucking nightmare. What sadist invented these things?

They stretch, they snap back, and they absolutely refuse to stay put. This corner holds; that corner pops. It's like playing whack-a-mole with what definitely isn't Egyptian cotton.

I grunt as I try again, wedging the corner down and using half my body weight to hold it in place while I snake around to the other side.

This mattress has no give. Why is her bed so heavy? What's it made of? Concrete?

I finally trap one corner, then sprint around to the next, like a man trying to tame a wild animal. Which, I now realize, is exactly what this is. A white, elastic-mouthed, passive-aggressive beast.

By corner three, I've broken into a sweat. Not in the sexy, glistening-from-a-workout way. In the I'm-a-fucking-loser-with-no-practical-skills way.

"One more corner pops loose, and I'm setting you

on fire. I've survived boardrooms with actual sociopaths. You're just cotton," I mutter.

With a final push, I jam the last corner down and straighten—hands on my hips, glaring at the now-pristine bed like it insulted my ancestors.

And then I hear it.

A strangled chuckle, and a sniffle.

I turn slowly toward the doorway. Cora leans there in a T-shirt and flimsy pajama shorts, damp curls piled on her head. She's not wearing a bra, and her legs are calling to me in a way that is utterly inappropriate given the circumstances.

I peel my eyes off her body and meet her eyes. Amusement practically drips off her flushed, slightly feverish face.

"I've never seen someone threaten inanimate objects with such conviction." She grins. "You okay there, soldier?"

I fix my expression into one of dignified suffering. "That sheet was objectively hostile. I was defending myself."

She laughs, then winces and coughs. "Well, thank you for making my bed."

"Anything to earn your undying gratitude."

We grin at each other for a few beats, before she coughs again and walks in slowly, eyeing the bed. "It's not terrible."

"Please. It's a work of art."

Cora sits on the bed, patting one corner. "You tucked this one in like you were afraid it might explode."

"Because it tried to. Twice." I shrug and get the pillows fluffed for her to lie down.

She smiles, tired but soft. "Thank you."

I shrug, suddenly not sure what to do with my hands. "Figured if I can run a billion-dollar company, I can probably tackle a fitted sheet."

"Barely." She chuckles, lying down.

I smirk. "Still counts." I cover her.

Propped up against a pillow, like the queen of sass and sniffles, she gives me another weak smile.

"I'm going to order the soup. Do you want some tea?" I channel all the caregiving instincts I've never used.

Cora raises an eyebrow. "You know where tea comes from, Stone?"

"Boiling water. Leaves. Magic." I wave my hand. "Don't worry. I've seen people do it."

She lets out a breathy laugh. "Right cabinet. Above the sink. Kettle is electric. Try not to burn down my kitchen."

I scoff and head in, rolling up my sleeves like I'm about to perform surgery.

First problem: there are six different boxes of tea.

Some are labeled things like "Sleepy Soul" and "Goddess Calm," and one just says "Witch's Brew." That one feels like a trap.

I go with mint. Safe. Mint doesn't emotionally challenge you. I fill the kettle, press the button, and wait. The button clicks off five seconds later. Nothing happens.

I stare at it. Tap it again. Nothing.

"Oh, come on," I mutter. "You had one job."

I try a different socket. It hisses. Progress. I drop the bag into a mug and pour like I've just invented the concept. Steam curls up triumphantly.

I open the fridge. Oat milk? Okay, I guess. Does milk go into mint tea? It wouldn't hurt, would it?

I spot a small, bear-shaped bottle. Honey has healing properties. I squeeze. Nothing. I squeeze harder. The bottle farts out a pathetic wheeze and dribbles honey down the side.

By the time I bring the mug out, it looks like I've been in a low-stakes bar fight. I hand it to her.

She blinks down at the sticky mug, then up at me. "Is that honey on your shirt?"

"It resisted."

She takes a careful sip. Pauses. Blinks again. "You made mint. With oat milk."

"I made a choice." I plant myself at the edge of her bed. "And I stand by it."

"You're lucky I don't have the strength to sass you properly."

"You say that, but I can still feel the judgment radiating off your pores."

She hums, eyes closed now, but there's a smile ghosting across her lips. And for some reason, I feel like I just won something important.

* * *

"Jesus, creepy much?" I jerk when I open my eyes and find Cora sitting on the coffee table watching me.

"Why are you here?" she asks.

I sit up and put the back of my hand on her forehead. She doesn't seem to have a fever. I've been watching over her for two days, and she was significantly better yesterday. But her question... is she hallucinating?

She swats my hand away. "I mean, why did you come to see me in the first place?"

"You seem better." She has more color in her cheeks, and her eyes don't have that glassy, sick veil.

"It must be the oat milk mint tea." She deadpans. "You should have that patented."

"I'm glad you feel better." The relief is akin to an adrenaline shot. It's not the boisterous boost I get from a workout. It seeps in quietly, injecting comfort into my veins.

"So why did you come?" It's like her mind dealt with the sickness and rewound, and insists on filling in the blanks.

"I heard about your financial trouble."

Perhaps not the best way to start, but in my defense, I spent two nights fighting for this couch with Pitt or Clooney, or one of the ten cats.

And then I tossed and turned, because this sunken mattress is a death trap.

She grunts and bows her head. "Of course, you did."

Okay, definitely not the best way to start this conversation.

"Let me guess," she drawls, her eyes skating over me like I were something stuck to her shoe. "You'll bail me out if I sleep with you?" Her tone is pure disdain wrapped in silk.

I smirk. "That wasn't my original proposition, but I'm not against it."

"Maybe I can sell the fucking island to save the business." She stands up and sways.

I'm on my feet immediately, supporting her elbow. The scent of her shampoo, and something more primal hits me, and I wrap my hand around her waist. No longer to steady her, which we both know, I'm sure.

Our eyes lock, electricity zapping between us. I can feel her nipples through our shirts. Her curves mold into me in my embrace. I can twist us around, and she'd be under me. I can dip my head and get another hit of her taste. I can bend her over the coffee table and—

"I'm fine; I just stood up too quickly." She puts her hands on my chest like she's going to push me away. She doesn't. She steps back, her hands lingering on my pecs.

"You're not fine." I check my watch. "The breakfast is here in fifteen minutes." I scoop her up.

"What are you doing?" She swats at me half-heartedly.

"You need to rest." I carry her over to her bedroom and lay her gently down before I cover her.

"I'm done resting. And what do you mean breakfast is here in fifteen minutes?"

"What part of that sentence is challenging your comprehension ability?"

"Just go home, Xander," she grumbles, glaring.

Shit, I can verbally spar with her for days and not tire of it. But I had an agenda when I came here, and since she seems better...

"I came to propose marriage."

Chapter 17

Cora

I snap my eyes to him.

I blink.

I squint.

And I wait.

But the punchline doesn't come. Xander is standing there, all six feet, one hundred inches of a god-like male form, with that latent smirk.

He's waiting for my reaction.

But I'm not getting the joke. It is a joke, isn't it? He can't be serious.

A laugh escapes me. Even to my own ears, it sounds a bit deranged.

"What do you mean, *a marriage proposal*?"

"Let's wait for breakfast, and then we'll talk. I need a shower anyway."

"Xander," I warn, but he saunters out of the room. "Xander!"

The bathroom door closes. I plop back onto the pillow.

My first thought? At least there are fresh towels for him on the shelf. What the fuck? He drops a bomb and leaves me hanging, and I care about his comfort?

I didn't even invite him to stay in the first place.

But if I'm honest, I'm grateful he stayed. The atrocious tea aside, as much as I wanted to ascertain my independence, I was in no shape to cope alone.

And if he hadn't shown up—let's not think about the alleged reasons—it could have ended up way worse.

Plus, the sheet-wrestling show was strangely arousing, but perhaps my fevered brain was sending the wrong signals. And him constantly re-tucking me in has been annoying and endearing at the same time.

As uncomfortable as it is for me to rely on someone, having him around hasn't been bad at all.

The man is an ultra-rich business genius with no practical life skills, but he didn't call his helpers to make my bed.

He probably made his first ever tea for me. Not that he got any better with the third or the tenth, but he put the effort in.

And all the food. He's been sourcing nutritious

meals for me while I sweated in my bed and barely took a spoonful.

A thoughtful Xander.

If I stop fighting the help, ignore the guilt from accepting it, and surrender to the situation, I must admit it feels really good to be cared for. I haven't experienced that in the longest time.

The universe probably sent me this moment of receiving, so I can continue giving. Perhaps it's not selfish to indulge in his care. Maybe it's fine.

Besides, the sexual tension between us is a plus. Or a minus—I'm not sure yet.

A marriage proposal, though? What the fuck? Is that some fucked-up way to help me? Why would he want to go to such lengths? It makes no sense.

"Even in the shower, I could practically hear you overthinking," Xander says from the living room. "The breakfast is here."

"I don't have time for breakfast. I have to go to work." I push to a sitting position as I hear him open the door, murmur something, and close it again.

Fuck, I need to go prep and open. The idea brings tears to my eyes.

"You're not going anywhere today," Xander calls from my kitchen, while he opens and closes all the cabinets and drawers by the sound of it.

I wouldn't need to if I were married to you.

My mind trips over the thought and stumbles. What the hell? He mentions a proposal, and I immediately give up my independence?

What's wrong with me?

Still, my tired brain wanders there, and for a moment I let myself linger with the idea. It feels so peaceful not to worry about money. I close my eyes. I could revitalize the bistro and bring it back to life.

I could probably get better care for Dad.

I could take days off.

It's the last thought that spreads hope through my chest, as if taking a break is the only need in my life.

"Cora?" Xander whispers.

I open my eyes, and fuck... Xander holds a tray, filling up the doorway, wearing only a towel. I repeat, the man is wearing only my white towel.

I've seen him like this at the spa, so I shouldn't be this spellbound, but I can't drag my eyes away for the life of me.

All the ridges and planes of muscles still glisten with droplets of water. His torso is a perfect triangle, narrowing into lean hips. His body is firm, perfectly defined, like he spends days training instead of sitting in a boardroom.

"I'm glad you like what you see." He smirks. "You can touch whenever you want," he drawls, and saunters in.

I may imagine it, but he walks slower. Just to torture me with every move. God, I want those arms to toss me around.

I want that body to cover me and consume me whole.

"Your breakfast." He places the tray on my lap.

The smell of quiche finally distracts me from the half-naked man standing beside me. Smoked salmon and avocado sit neatly on the plate, with a bowl of fruit and a small salad off to the side.

"I don't have time for this. I really need to go to work," I protest, but it's more of an autopilot response. Like I know deep down I'm staying, but my sense of duty hasn't gotten the message yet.

Xander doesn't say anything and leaves, but before I have a chance to react, he's back with two cups.

"I think this time I got your tea right." He puts the mug on my nightstand, snatches a slice of salmon from my plate, and sits at the foot of my bed with his cup.

"This is really nice. Thank you." I take a bite of the mini-quiche and moan. "Jesus, this is good."

"Wait until you try their eggs Benny. I didn't order them because they need to be eaten fresh, but I'll take you."

"So now we're making plans?" I cock my head, teasing.

"Of course." He shrugs.

"Because you want to marry me?"

"Look, I..."

He stands up and turns to the window. Like it's difficult to explain to my face. It's so out of character for a man who oozes confidence like it's his birthright.

"I have an important business deal in the works that requires a seat on the board of a firm in San Francisco. My father can open those doors, but he wants to see me settled to help me out."

"That's fucked up."

Xander turns to look at me. The sight pulls at my heart. He looks like a little boy in trouble, and my need to help him is strong. But Jesus. This really is all sorts of fucked up.

"I left the family business after I made a wrong move, a terrible one. The business I was in charge of suffered because of that. My father wanted to save the situation by pawning me off in marriage to a business associate, a potential investor. I couldn't stomach the idea of an arranged marriage with someone I barely knew, so I left. The company I sank filed for bankruptcy afterward."

"I don't even know what to say. That's horrible. You're his son, not a chess piece on his empire's board."

"This is his way of doing things. I grew up being groomed for that world, but when it mattered, I couldn't do it." He turns back to the window.

The shame he feels may not be justified, but it's real; it resonates from him.

Putting the tray to the side, I slide from the bed to stand behind him.

I put my hand on his tense back. "You did what was right for you at the time." The tension melts slightly under my touch. "I think you're judging yourself too harshly for what went down. What changed?"

He turns around, frowning. "What changed?"

His scent of sin, and the warmth of his freshly showered skin distract me, but I try to stay focused. This conversation is important.

"Clearly you're ready for an arranged marriage now. To help your business endeavors. What changed?"

He bows his head and sighs before he looks at me, this time not hiding his vulnerability but facing it.

"I guess I accepted I'm not that different from my father. Also, I'm choosing the bride this time." He winks, snaking his arm around my waist, yanking me to him. And the playful Xander I know so well is back.

I put my hand on his chest, the contact burning. The way he's looking at me is intoxicating. How does a man make me feel like a goddess, when he hasn't really touched me yet? "You have to stop looking at me like that."

A gentle frown touches his face. "Like what?"

I lick my lips. "Like you really want me."

"That's impossible, Coraline. I can't look at you any other way."

My breath hitches, the room's temperature skyrockets, and I kind of want to step back and get closer at the same time.

"So, will you marry me?" His playful grin gives me the opportunity to breathe in.

It's like he sensed I was getting aroused and freaked out at the same time, so he dialed back.

I'm forgetting why *him and me* are not a good idea. The list of warnings about this man seems to have been wiped from my brain. Or it's buried under lust.

"What's in it for me?" I tease.

It's not like I would ever accept it.

Why not?

Fuck. The fever must have burned some of my gray cells.

"Besides mind-blowing orgasms?" He caresses the small of my back, sprouting goose bumps on my skin. His touch is gentle, and I can barely stop myself from leaning into it.

"That theory hasn't been tested yet." The air crackles with yearning, accentuating my taunt.

"And whose fault is that?" He cups the back of my neck and fuses his lips with mine.

I missed his kisses—it's the first thing that invades my mind, but it's the last coherent thought I have.

After that, it's just heat.

The press of his mouth, firm and hungry. The glide of his tongue, coaxing mine into answering. The way his thumb brushes the side of my throat like he's memorizing my pulse.

This isn't sweet or tentative.

This is Xander taking.

His mouth claims mine like it's already his.

Like the question was never *if*, only *when.*

His grip tightens at the back of my neck, anchoring me in place while his other hand curls possessively around my hip, pulling me into him until I can't tell where I end and he begins.

And I should stop this.

I should push him away, say something cutting, remind us both that this is a terrible idea—

But all I can do is gasp against his mouth and open for him. Every kiss from him feels like a decision already made.

Like he's rewriting my body's loyalty with every stroke of his tongue. My bones, my blood, the traitorous thrum low in my belly—

They all lean into him. I melt. I fight it, but I melt.

Because kissing Xander is a full-body experience.

It's chaos with intention. A slow slide into surrender dressed up as play.

And God help me, I want to drown in it.

I moan, and he groans, disconnecting the kiss. "A preview." He winks.

"A kiss?" I retort, but it's only a weak breath.

"Hmm, Coraline," he drawls. "Tell me you're not wet right now. Lie to me if you want, but it changes nothing. We will fuck, you will scream my name, and it's going to happen very soon."

My knees buckle, and I try to push away from him, my chest heaving. "How soon?" I whisper.

"As soon as you answer my question."

I could drown in his gaze—it's dominant and adoring at the same time. "What question?"

He laughs. "Keep up, woman, we're negotiating our nuptials."

The words finally snap me out of my stupor. It's like he sprayed the air with lust that fogs my mind.

I finally step back. And no surprise, I miss the closeness immediately. Grabbing the plate, I march to the living room. I'm not doing this on an empty stomach.

"How would that even work?" I sit cross-legged and dig into the plate with the vigor of a dedicated stress eater.

"We marry, and we fuck." He sits across from me.

Fuck, he's still in that stupid towel. A towel that is tenting visibly.

"Can you be serious for a moment and get dressed for fuck's sake?"

"Yes, ma'am." He stands up and fucking drops the towel on his way to the bathroom. Oh, he plays the game well.

His ass is firm—no surprise there—and just delicious. I look at my plate. This quiche *is* delicious. Jesus. I'm a mess.

"Stop calling me ma'am. Right now. You don't want me to remember I'm older than you."

"Coraline, not this again," he warns. "Stop overthinking."

"It's a business arrangement. I might not be good at running companies, but I need to make sure I'm not signing up for something that I would regret."

"So that's a yes." He returns in his briefs only. Seriously? He could have stayed in the towel.

I groan. "Let's talk rules and conditions, and—" I take a breath, struggling to think about the needed conversation. Am I really considering this?

Xander raises his hand. "Okay, okay... what are your conditions?" He leaves again and returns with our mugs.

I take a sip of now-lukewarm tea. Perfection. "What is this?"

"Shit. Did I fuck it up again?" He sits down across from me, with the coffee table between us.

"You made it? It's delicious." I take another sip of a perfectly steeped black tea with a splash of milk. Even lukewarm, it's divine.

"I'm glad. I watched a few videos."

"You watched tutorials about tea preparation?"

Does he even know what these small deeds do to me? I don't think he does. He is self-assured as fuck, but that comes with his pedigree and his looks.

But caring for me, for anyone, seems a new concept to him. The persistent "why is he doing it" dominates the back of my mind, but the feeling of being cared for? It occupies the rest of my head, heart, and soul.

No one's ever done this for me. Not really. Part of me wants to flinch, to push him away before it becomes something I learn to expect.

But I just sit there, swallowing around the lump in my throat, pretending this doesn't matter more than it should.

Because this feeling is new.

Of being seen.

Of being worth the effort.

It's only stupid tea, and yet, I'm aching in places I didn't know could ache, just because someone thought to care.

"Don't get me started. I clicked on a three-minute

one and ended up down the black hole of tea ceremonies and traditions for like three hours last night." He throws it out there casually, like he didn't just shake me to the core.

I need to regain some control here. "If I agree to your proposal, I want you to help me save the bistro."

"Okay, how much do you need?"

I hate when he reminds me of our money gap, even though I know he doesn't see it as an issue. "It's not just about money. I need help to actually bring the business back to life."

"Okay, I'll hire people who will work to turn it into a profitable venture within six to eight months."

I blink. "It's not that easy. My rent has just been increased."

"Don't worry about that. You will work closely with your team to make sure they follow your vision."

My team? My vision? I wish Dad could see this through.

"What other conditions do you have?" Xander takes a sip from his mug.

"I don't want you to fuck other women."

He looks offended. "I wouldn't cheat on my wife."

My wife. Jesus. Am I really doing this? "Not even in secret?"

He studies me for a moment, his jaw ticking. "Trust me, this arrangement will be exclusive."

"Why?" I blurt out. I still can't believe this man is choosing me.

The circumstances aren't romantic, but his choice is loud.

"Because it's you I want."

He doesn't speak of a challenge like the last time. I shouldn't, but I believe him.

"Aren't there women in your circles who are more acceptable candidates?"

"If I wanted a forever with a socialite and a miserable existence, I would have married the woman my father chose for me."

A small part of me craved he would say in words what he shows me with his devouring gaze, but I guess I can't have it all.

"Cora, stop thinking about other women finally. I'm fucking here. I came to you with my problem. You're my solution."

I might fall before we finish these negotiations. What did he put in my tea? I take another sip. "There is one more thing that would be a deal-breaker."

"Hit me," he says, impatient.

"I don't want you to ride the motorcycle."

Oh, how many times had I said this sentence before? Too many to count, and I never won the argument. Until the bitter ending.

"Okay."

"I'm serious, Xander," I urge.

"Okay. I sold it already," he says, tapping his fingers on the armrest.

"You sold your bike?" I put the plate down, leaning forward as if I can understand better when I'm closer. "You sold your bike," I parrot. "Why?"

"I anticipated this demand." His voice is laced with annoyance, but it pulls at the corner of my mouth.

He sold the bike because the last time I saw one, I ran. I didn't even get a chance to explain. And yet here he is, pre-emptively complying with my demand.

"Xander, I need to explain."

"You don't have to—"

"I should. I mean, you sold the bike. I can at least explain why I'm so averse..."

His jaw ticks like he really doesn't want to talk about this, even though he doesn't know what this is.

He trusted me with his story, and I owe him mine. Especially if we're to co-exist like this.

"Ten years ago I was engaged, and Ethan, my fiancé, killed himself on a bike. It was a senseless accident when he went for a joyride, speeding recklessly. Luckily, he didn't kill anyone else," I explain.

For the first time, I recount the sordid story with an unexpected detachment.

Xander studies me for a moment before he rounds

the table and squats in front of me. "I won't ride a bike, Coraline."

The words hit me in my stomach. The raw commitment behind them, the intensity of his promise, dislodges the shard of Ethan's betrayal from my heart. Like ten years later, a man shows up in my life and softens the feeling that I wasn't enough.

"Thank you."

We stare at each other for a moment, the delicious tension from the kiss earlier seeping through slowly.

And I realize one important thing: I never had a chance.

Escaping Xander Stone was never on the table.

Surviving him… I can only hope that chance is still mine.

Chapter 18

Xander

Her heartfelt, genuine thank you seeps through me, warm and intoxicating, like the best Macallan. Fuck it, not even the best whiskey makes me feel this powerful and powerless at the same time.

Like my next breath already depends on her next thank you, her next smile, next sass.

If I were a better man, I would acknowledge that this cloud will hit the truth head-on.

It will burst into a storm of epic proportions. But I let myself float on it, anyway. Fuck the consequences. I want to collect these moments with her.

I drink in her gratitude and just study her for a moment. She's feeling better, and she said yes to my fucked-up scheme.

This morning couldn't get any better.

The talk about her good-for-nothing fiancé dampened the mood a little. I don't feel in competition with the guy a decade later. I still hate his guts for knowing her before me, as irrational as that is. For winning her before me.

But that's not the real problem here. I should tell Cora what a douche he was, but I would have to explain where my information comes from.

Roxy's file on Cora wasn't the most comprehensive, but it was informative enough. I didn't even think twice before I sold the bike. She doesn't need that kind of trauma in her life.

"Do you have any other conditions?" I rasp, the moment between us tightening my throat.

"I think I covered all my concerns. But I have a question."

The air is thick with our need, and I stifle the groan. "Ask away."

"How long do we stay married?"

Forever.

And fuck, why is she already thinking about the end? We haven't even started. I'm not planning to be done with her anytime soon.

It makes no sense. It's not my usual modus operandi. It's inconvenient. But I still don't want to change it.

Coraline Winslow is mine.

"One year maximum, to make sure I can deliver on my side of the bargain. Or we can divorce as soon as I get the board seat," I lie.

I don't even feel bad about it. It's a placating lie, so she stops overthinking this.

"Okay. And then what? We just stop pretending in front of people? Your father will see through that."

Even in a moment like this, giving up her freedom, she thinks of my relationship with my father. It's satisfying and infuriating. Has she ever put herself first?

"Let's worry about that when the time comes."

If the time comes.

It won't.

"Okay. I'm concerned about meeting your family, though. I don't belong in your world."

"Cora, the last time I checked, you've been a part of my world for a few months now. Stop feeling less, stop projecting this *you're not enough* attitude. It doesn't suit you. You sass me all the time; I'm sure you can stand your ground in any situation."

She lets out the air through pursed lips, her expression skeptical. "I wish I had your confidence about this, but okay. Do you have any questions?"

"How many cats do you really have?" I ask, to lighten the mood that got too serious for my liking, but also because, fuck, I really hope it's just the two of them.

She laughs, and it's like the most moving musical score. I want to make her laugh. All. The. Time.

"You will have to count them yourself." She bites her lip.

"I'm going to fuck the information out of you." I fist her hair and fuse my lips with hers, lowering myself to my knees.

She whimpers into my mouth, and I almost blow into my underwear. I've been half-hard for hours, for fuck's sake.

She leans into the kiss, her nails scraping my skull, and I want her to draw blood and never stop.

Hoisting her legs around my hips, she slides on her seat closer to me.

Only a flimsy fabric is between her clit and my cock as she seeks friction, gyrating her hips. Jesus, this woman will be the death of me.

"I thought it was we'd marry and then we'd fuck," she murmurs into my mouth. Her words are at odds with her actions.

I hook my fingers in her shorts and yank. "Stop stalling, Coraline, or my dick will fall off."

She laughs again and lifts her hips, so I can peel the garment from her hips. But the way she is positioned, wrapped around me, I don't get it low enough.

"Fuck it." I rip it off.

Cora gasps and then chuckles. "It's a good thing you're filthy rich."

"Finally, you understand the advantage. And the filthy I'm about to show you will make you revisit all your beliefs."

I scoop her legs and throw them over my shoulders. She loses balance and collapses into the armchair with giggles, her back hitting the cushion while I lift her pussy to my face and blow gently.

"Fuck, this is the prettiest pussy ever."

"Xander," she breathes.

"Call—and scream—my name freely, Coraline. I will make sure you have enough reasons to do so." I look at her from between her thighs, grinning. I like this vantage point very much.

"You're overly confident."

"I've dreamed about this pussy for long enough to deliver." I look down and spread her with two fingers. "Look at that pretty cunt of yours. So ready for me." I blow on her clit again, and she buckles. "And greedy."

She moans, and the sound is a pure aphrodisiac, dripping need through my veins. I lower my head and inhale her, the primal scent adding to the intoxicating feel.

Cora tenses, her thighs fighting to close. "What are you doing?"

"Getting high on you." I run my nose up her thigh, licking and kissing her silky skin. "Relax, Coraline."

"You don't have to—"

"If you're under any illusion I'm forcing myself to do anything here, you're still delusional from your fever, sweetheart."

She is still strung, her hips locked. "Ethan didn't like—"

"Have you just mentioned another man while I have my head between your legs?"

She stares at me, bewildered. "I don't want you to do this."

I lean back on my haunches, gently putting her ass down on the seat. "You don't like a man going down on you?"

She blows a raspberry and straightens up. "We probably should talk."

"There is too much talking involved in this for my taste, and not the right type of talking." I yank her closer, wrapping my arms around her and tucking a loose strand behind her ear.

She rests her forehead against my shoulder, tapping it a few times like she's trying to knock some sense into herself.

I kiss her hair. "I'm not going to do anything you don't consent to, but I have a feeling you're basing your reaction on some shitty experience with a man who didn't deserve you, and certainly didn't know what he was doing."

She groans.

"Talk to me, Cora."

She leans back and looks at me. "I thought there was too much talking for your liking."

"Don't be a brat."

She lets out a long breath. "Okay, here goes. I haven't had sex in... a while. And I'm not very good at giving head. And if you do that..." She looks away. "I will have to—"

I cup her face and force her to look at me. "I want to eat your pussy. I want to taste it. I want you to come all over my face. I really fucking want that. It's my fucking dream, Cora."

Her brow furrows, but her lips twitch like she's skeptical, but trying hard not to like what I just said. "Really?"

"Yes, but we can do other things if this is not something you want to do. And whoever made you believe oral is a question of reciprocity deserves a death sentence."

She snorts. "Okay, I'm happy to make your dream come true, but I don't think I'll relax enough, definitely not to come all over your face."

"You know what my favorite pastime is? Proving people wrong."

I stand and scoop her up bridal-style while she squeals. "What are you doing?"

"I'm done talking."

I carry her to the bed and throw her down.

"Hey," she pretend-protests while she takes off her T-shirt.

I stop for a beat, feasting my eyes on the beauty in front of me. The sight hits me with a feral need.

But it's the realization that I will get to touch, kiss, and caress every inch of her that spreads a warm feeling through me.

I don't know what this is, because for the first time ever, I want to stop time. Like this is no longer about my need, but about her pleasure. The feeling is… new, potent, and somehow essential.

Cora squeals again when I yank her to the edge and drop to my knees.

"Open wide," I command, and she obeys. Finally. "This pussy is mine," I hum. "Understood."

"I thought you were done talking." She grins at me.

I want to slap that ripe cunt of hers, but she isn't ready for that. So I lower my lips to her clit and alternate between sucking and licking.

She's tense at first, holding the sheets in a white-knuckled grip. I flatten my tongue and lift her hips to lick her from the back hole, over her entrance, to her clit, a few times, lapping her juices like a starved man.

The feel of her body loosening in my hands, under my tongue, is hypnotic. Her submission strums every string in me. Soon enough, she is writhing to escape and bucking to get closer. To get more.

And I'm happy to oblige, because fuck, this woman stripped me of my free will, and the only thing I've been able to do is to gravitate to her orbit.

I lift my gaze.

She's breathtaking, with her hooded eyes and slightly open lips.

She lets go of the sheets, and her hands are squeezing her tits, her fingers playing with her nipples. The sight is arresting.

Cora cranes her neck. "Why did you stop?"

"You're fucking beautiful. Just..." I return to her clit before I make an idiot out of myself and say something we're not ready for.

She moans. "Yes, there, there." She pants. "More."

Her fingers grip my hair as I add a finger to the mix, first teasing her opening and then plunging one and immediately another digit in. She is tight as fuck. God, I can't wait to sink my cock in there.

Her reactions. Her response. Her eagerness. It's everything. And not enough at the same time.

"Come for me, Coraline." I crook my fingers and suck on her clit.

"Xander," she cries, and I almost blow as I feel her

walls tighten around my digits, her muscles rigid before they loosen again.

It's like her body is an instrument I was always meant to master. I haven't even fucked her yet, and I'm satiated just from her reactions.

This shouldn't be this different. This shouldn't be this addictive. It shouldn't feel this novel.

I continue pumping and licking while she comes apart, letting her ride the wave while I desperately need to take care of the painful situation in my briefs.

But there will be time for that. This woman trusted me to finally get closer; she deserves a couple of orgasms before I take one from her.

Her body is still twitching with the last waves of release when I pull myself up, kissing my way along her ribs, the swell of her breasts, her clavicle.

I look up, grinning, but my smirk disappears when I see her. She immediately covers her face with her forearm. Is she crying?

"Are you hurt? What's wrong?" For the second time in a brief span of barely three days, my heart rate spikes from worry. What the fuck happened?

She sniffles. "I'm fine." She rubs her eyes with the heels of her palms. "I'm more than fine."

I sag beside her, flipping my leg over hers. "Look at me, woman."

She sniffles again and turns to me, her eyes glistening. "I'm sorry."

I wipe a tear from her cheek, my hand tracing her cheekbone. I want to pry answers from her, but I don't think she needs to be bullied right now for the sake of my ego. So I kiss her instead.

"Fair warning. I'm officially addicted to your pussy."

She giggles. "Thank God for that."

I take her nipple between my lips, and she arches into me. "So fucking responsive. I love it."

She watches me through heavy lids, flushed and slightly dazed. I kiss her lips again, slow and deep, her taste still on my tongue. Her arms wrap around me, and for a moment we just breathe together.

"As much as I want to slide home, condoms are in my pants."

"Condoms? Plural?" she grins.

"Only two, unfortunately. I will have more delivered."

"Oh my God, don't you dare. I don't want a delivery man bringing us condoms."

"Using condoms is responsible. It's like a PSA for safe sex."

She laughs. "Having someone deliver condoms to us is public service?"

I nod, kissing her forehead. "Stop distracting me." I jump out of bed and rush to find the condoms.

I tear the wrapper with my teeth as I return. Her breath catches as I roll it on to my stiff cock and climb back, hovering above her on my elbows. "You okay? No regrets."

She nods, biting her lip. "Stop talking before they consume me."

I position the tip of my cock, brushing against her entrance. "I'll make you forget your own name before I let you regret a second of this."

I thrust slowly, watching her face as I fill her. Her lips part, brows knitting in a perfect mix of pleasure and surprise.

"Jesus, Xander—"

"I know, sweetheart. You feel like fucking heaven."

I give her a moment to adjust, savoring the way her body stretches around me, gripping me like it already knows what we are.

"Move," she rasps.

I obey. First with long, deep strokes. Her legs wrap around my waist, and her nails drag down my back.

She lifts her hips to meet me, every motion matching mine, her walls clenching around me like she's never going to let me go.

Her moans, my grunts, our bodies sheathed with sweat—they all blend into a haze of sensation rippling through us. We're fused into one as our pleasure builds.

"Harder," she gasps.

Fuck, this woman *will be* the death of me.

I pull out and flip her over, hiking her hips in the air. "You better hold on."

I ram into her, and she cries a prolonged yes. From this angle, I hit the spot that makes her tremble and gasp.

"You're mine, Coraline," I growl, thrusting harder.

"For now," she moans, but her voice cracks.

Fucking woman. The death of me. Nothing comes easy with her. I fist her hair and pull her to me. She angles her face, and I take her lips. I take it the way I take her body—completely.

And then I stop moving.

She groans. "What the fuck, Xander?"

"Say it. Say you're mine."

I don't know where the need is coming from, but it feels like a vital surrender on her part. Like that is the missing piece of the puzzle in this relationship. One that is not conventional, and probably doomed already.

Her concession wouldn't mean anything in this context, and yet I'm obsessed and need to coax it from her.

"You're insane."

I slam into her, making her gasp again as she falls to her hands. "Say it."

She pushes her hips to me. "I'm yours. Fuck. I'm yours." Frustration and truth lace her words. Or at least that's what I want to hear.

I start a piston-like tempo, chasing the release we both need.

She tightens around me when she comes again, her body arching into mine. I groan, my climax slamming into me like a freight train, and I spill into her with a curse, burying my face in her neck.

In the sea of orgasms I have experienced in my life, this one takes me by surprise. What is it about this woman?

We collapse beside each other, tangled in sweat and breathless satisfaction. She brushes my hair back from my forehead, her fingers light, affectionate.

"You still don't know how many cats I have," she murmurs.

I grin against her skin. "Oh, sweetheart. I've got all the time in the world to count them."

And for once, the idea of forever doesn't feel like a trap.

It feels like a plan.

Chapter 19

Cora

SAAR

Are you alive?

CELESTE

I stopped by the bistro but it's closed.

LILY

Jesus, go check on her at home.

Chill. I've been sick and took a few days off.

SAAR

I didn't know it was that serious when you canceled the date. Can I get you anything?

CELESTE

Do you want me to come?

You don't need my germs. I'm fine. I have everything I need. I promise.

* * *

"Xander," I scream for the third time. My legs quiver, my pussy clenches, my mind is wiped blank.

With my legs wrapped around his waist, I tilt my head back and close my eyes. The water streams down my face, its warmth in contrast with the cold tiles of my shower.

The man has stamina. I give him that. And he is strong as fuck. How he manages to hold me and pump into me at the same time is beyond me.

Yet here we are, and the handsome devil chases his release and looks like a god of sex. On his face are only desire and bliss, no exertion.

I guess he's my fiancé now. Jesus. I'm really doing this, am I not? Though at the moment, satiated to the brim, my system flooded with happy hormones, I am probably the happiest bride-to-be in the world.

There is a small part of me that the orgasm-induced bliss hasn't reached yet. That part keeps reminding me that this will lead to heartbreak. Because we might have negotiated the conditions, but this is not a business arrangement.

This is a relationship.

Physical only.

But still a relationship.

And even that part isn't completely true, because if it was only physical, Xander wouldn't show up in all the ways he did.

He took a Cinderella to the ball and never let go. He pampered me with massages and a facial when he saw how tired I was.

He didn't want me to be alone on my birthday.

The way he showed up for me when I got sick.

The man sold his freaking bike.

When I close my eyes and only feel his body flush against mine right now... his muscles straining under my fingertips on the background of his thrusts and my moans, I allow myself to fantasize that this weird union can somehow work.

But I remind myself it's only temporary. He will get his deal, and he will move on. Get a few more years of fun under his belt and then settle down with a woman his own age and start a family.

And me? I will hopefully be able to remember this as an exciting affair. One that helped me get out of the shell I grew around myself post-Ethan.

"Fuuuuuck," Xander roars, his cock twitching inside me.

It's a heady feeling to see him undone like that. And apparently, there is no justice when it comes to him; even his orgasm face is pretty.

He bows his head to my neck, panting before he

lowers me with care. Cupping my face, he seizes my lips, his tongue exploring gently.

It's no surprise he knows what he's doing, his reputation preceding him. And yet his attention is overwhelming and unexpected.

Xander Stone is a generous lover.

He puts me first. And he fucking clearly draws satisfaction from it. It's addictive. And an addiction is the last thing I need with this man.

That first orgasm rammed through me on a wave of emotions that brought tears. I expected him to run away. Who wants a crying woman in his—technically my—bed? Instead, he kissed my feelings away, without ridiculing me.

If he keeps it up... *Just stop thinking, Cora.*

"You're gorgeous when you've just been fucked." He pivots me away from the shower stream.

I laugh. "As romantic as ever."

Xander lathers his hands and starts washing me. "I might not be a poet, but the fact remains..." He soaps up my back, his touch gentle and attentive. "This back is a piece of art. These tits..." He steps closer and washes my chest, his fingers flicking over my nipples. I arch into him.

"They are masterpieces." He moves his hands down to my hips and ass, lathering my skin. "Works of beauty."

It's the reverence in his voice that breaks me. I swallow around the lump in my throat, hoping the tears will stay hidden this time. I really don't want to cry from sheer joy twice in front of him.

"And this pussy..." He sinks to his knees and kisses me between my legs before he looks up at me.

The sight is striking. Xander Stone worships with his entire being, and I'm the lucky object of his affection. Pure bliss.

I swallow again.

"This pussy is the holy fucking grail." He slaps my ass gently, winking as he stands up and starts washing himself.

And just like that, he's played every one of my strings—pulling until I am taut—only to ease the tension with a well-timed tease, lifting the heaviness like he knew exactly when I needed some air.

I squirt some body wash into my hands and lather his chest. "Let me."

My hands roam over his skin, and if I'm honest, it's for my benefit as much as his. The bulges and valleys of his body are a study in contrast—hard muscle beneath smooth, heated skin.

Every inch of him feels sculpted, carved from determination and ego, and just enough recklessness to make it thrilling.

He's solid in a way that makes me feel unsteady.

My fingers trace the deep line between his pecs, slide down over his abs, and I swear his skin pulses beneath my touch.

He's all tension and heat and restrained power. Like something barely leashed. And yet he's letting me touch him like this—slowly, reverently—as if he's mine to explore.

And maybe that's the most dangerous part.

"Careful there, Coraline, that was our last condom," he rasps, raking his fingers through my hair and pulling me in for a kiss.

I hum into his mouth. "I guess we will have to go buy more."

He squeezes my ass. "Go?"

"Yes, I need to get some nasal spray, or we won't be able to use those condoms. I can barely breathe." I turn the water off.

Xander reaches for a towel and hits his elbow. "This shower is the worst offense to humanity. This whole closet of a bathroom is."

He dries my skin, wrapping me in the towel.

"You're so spoiled." I roll my eyes.

He turns, and half of the things on a shelf by the shower tumble to the ground, mocking me. Xander says nothing, just looks at me, deadpan.

"You paid them to do that." I pout.

He leans to pick up the scattered tubes and bottles

and drops them into the sink.

"Let me put them back." I reach, but he grabs my hand and pivots me to him.

"Later." He kisses me, reaching for my robe on the door at the same time.

Okay, this is a tiny bathroom, and it feels even smaller with Xander here.

He drapes the soft fabric over my shoulders.

"I can put on my robe," I croak, the steamy room filled with emotions.

"I know." He kisses my forehead.

I swallow... This man's natural attention, this gentle thoughtfulness, is unraveling me.

"You're still recovering. You need to rest."

His concern is my undoing, but I can't let him affect me like this, taking me apart. "Keep dreaming, young man; you will fuck me until I can't walk."

He laughs. "Your wish is my command. Let's order everything we need."

"What we need is to get out of here for a bit."

I don't tell him I need an opportunity to assess whether his effect on me finds reason during non-bedroom-related activities.

Also, I imagine there will be many occasions in Xander's world in my future, so it wouldn't hurt to take him for a test drive into my mundane world.

"I don't see why," he grumbles.

He towel-dries his hair. It's sticking out in all directions, but with his boyish grin, he still looks like a model.

"To buy you a toothbrush." I ogle him as he leans against the counter, not bothering to cover any part of himself.

"Am I moving in, Coraline?" He smirks.

I laugh, but then I realize that's a valid point. "Shit, where are we going to live?"

Picking up my hairbrush, I try to untangle my hair.

"Let me." He takes the brush and starts gently brushing the ends of my hair.

My poor heart.

"You have to stop taking care of me like this," I protest while I lean into him.

He lifts his gaze, and our eyes meet in the mirror. "You didn't seem to complain when I was taking care of you with my tongue between your legs."

To make his point, he snakes his hand around me and cups me roughly between my thighs. I gasp, despite enjoying the gesture.

It's the ease he brings into this that is... just perfect. There is no awkwardness, no hesitation, no second-guessing on his part, and it overflows into the energy between us.

God, I could get used to this.

God, I can't get used to this.

"Here is the thing, darling fiancée." He massages my clit, and I kind of forget what we're talking about. "You can't pick and choose what attention I'm allowed to give you. It's all or nothing."

"You promised to do only what I consent to," I breathe, referencing our earlier conversation.

That was a revealing moment for me. Ethan had never gone down on me. And he told me I was shit at giving head. That pretty much buried the idea of oral for me. Until this man.

He removes his hand, leaving me breathless and needy while he casually returns to combing my hair.

"I will honor that promise." With his skilled fingers, he returns to my clit and draws another moan out of me. "But I'm sure you'll consent to everything. So yeah..." He flicks my clit, driving me crazy. "All or nothing, Coraline." His breath fans my skin.

Something tells me all or nothing in Xander Stone's world is something I have no reference for. Hurricane. Tsunami. Earthquake.

Life-threatening.

Unavoidable.

Out of my control.

And yet I jump into the experience willingly.

* * *

"When was the last time you were in a drugstore?" I bite my lip.

"High school," Xander answers casually, not looking at me. He picks up a box of cereal, turns it over, and frowns at the label. "Maybe college. We were going through a lot of condoms with Cal."

"You went to school with Celeste's husband?"

"Yep. This thing is poison in a pretty box." He puts the cereal back on the shelf.

"For some, it's a cheap source of energy, often the only source."

He frowns and glances at the box again. "I never thought of it like that." Then he shakes his head. "Scratch that; I never thought about those kinds of struggles."

It's not regret—more an observation. The slight shift in the mood is noticeable enough for me to regret not opting for the delivery.

Maybe this is too much, too quickly for him. We should still be in our own bubble, and here I am confronting him with poverty.

"Let's get you that toothbrush," I say.

He glances at the box again, and then takes my hand and leads me through the aisles. I should revel in the contact, but instead I fight the urge to pull my hand from his grip.

I thought bringing him here would be immersing him in my life. He adjusted just fine. It's me who focuses on the looks of other customers.

Even in his casual attire, he is so obviously rich. And I'm so obviously older, especially with the red nose, no makeup, and bags under my eyes.

At the cash register, he pulls out a black credit card. The cashier flips it in her hands a few times before she decides she trusts it enough to try it.

"Did you bring me here to humble me?" He pulls me to him and kisses my temple when we step outside.

I guess he noticed how he stopped the usual flow of things in there. Even though he didn't show his awareness.

Why the fuck do I care about strangers looking? Where did the need to appease people I don't know—or try to be invisible—come from?

"I don't think that's possible. Your ego swallowed this entire zip code the minute you set foot in it," I tease.

He snorts. "But you were tense there. Why?"

Goddammit, he has keen observational skills. "People were staring."

He looks at me sideways, frowning. "So?"

His confusion is so genuine, it shocks me. He really doesn't care. Or perhaps he is used to it.

"It really doesn't bother you that I'm older? Or that I'm not draped in luxurious clothes? We're so obviously different."

He stops and pivots me to him, his gaze piercing through me. "Would I be here if that were my concerns?"

I shake my head.

"Stop looking at all our differences. They are inconsequential." He's transmitting the message with his entire body. His perspective is so freeing, I have no choice but to accept it.

Not because the man is a force to reckon with, and I lose all my arguments under his passionate gaze. But because he is right. Those differences are inconsequential.

Rooted in societal expectations, I accepted them at large without really thinking about our specific connection. I can be happy without strangers' approval.

"You're right." I smile at him.

He brings my hand to his lips, brushing my knuckles, glancing at me with his pantie-melting bedroom eyes. "Besides, my cock fits your pussy perfectly, so fuck any other differences."

I laugh.

"And it's not ego." His features harden, no longer

jesting as he returns to my previous comment. "It's confidence, sweetheart—something I'm going to instill in you. And from now on, we're getting deliveries. I've never considered myself a snob, but apparently, you proved me wrong."

He turns to walk again.

"So, no humbling on the agenda?" I grin, loving the way he holds me close to him, the plastic bag in the other hand.

"You, darling Coraline, change me enough already." He kisses my crown, walking as if he didn't just blow my mind. Or pierce my heart with a honey-coated arrow.

We remain silent, slowly meandering down the street toward my place. Despite the humidity, the companionship is pleasant, and I almost regret that the walk is so short. But then there is a large box of condoms in the bag, so I guess we can take a long walk another day.

"I think Chelsea or Tribeca would suit us well," Xander says when we enter the elevator.

What? "I think Brooklyn suits us well, too," I respond, just to be silly.

He nods, frowning. "It's a long commute for both of us, but if that's what you want, we will make it work. I'll call my realtor."

Oh, our living situation. Shit. I got completely distracted. "You would move to Brooklyn?

He shrugs. "I would bitch about it, but if that's what you want."

I laugh. Who is this man?

"I like Chelsea." I squeeze his hand, the idea of living somewhere else, even if it's temporary, exciting me. "But you choose, because you will be left with the place after the divorce."

He flinches, but then gives me his signature grin. "Maybe you'll hire a better divorce attorney."

"Oh, the angle of cleaning you out financially hasn't occurred to me. Good thinking." I grin.

He studies me for a moment, a dark shadow over his handsome face, and then he steps closer. His body flush against mine, he captures my lips. The kiss is urgent, feral, almost desperate.

It's arousing, like everything about Xander, but it takes me by surprise. It's like he's saying something with that kiss, but I don't have the dictionary to understand it.

I take it anyway, and I give back, because there might be a gap between us in many ways, but physically, we just blend effortlessly.

The elevator jerks to a halt, and we stumble out, kissing and moaning. My back hits the wall, and Xander groans into my mouth.

"Merde." A familiar voice jerks us apart.

Heat swallows my cheeks. Down the short corridor, Saar and Celeste stand in front of my unit.

"Fuck, and we thought you were unconscious on the floor." Saar folds her arms across her chest, smirking.

"That's yesterday's news, ladies." Xander saunters to the door, pulling my key from his slacks.

"I don't have pockets in my shorts," I say, like explaining Xander doesn't own the keys to my place is the most pressing issue here.

Saar snorts. "We thought you were sick."

"What is he doing here?" Celeste asks, as if *he* wasn't standing beside her.

"Wasn't that obvious?" Saar's lips twitch.

"Still warrants an explanation." Celeste doesn't even try to hide her grin.

I look at Xander for guidance, but he is as cool as a cucumber, leaning against the now unlocked door.

I groan and push past him, letting everyone in. "Saar, Celeste, meet Xander, my fiancé. Xander, these are hopefully still my best friends. But you know each other already anyway."

With my glare, I try to communicate the rest, or rather ask them to leave.

"Merde." Celeste leans against the chest of drawers beside my entrance.

"What do you mean, fiancé?" Saar's eyes dart between me and Xander.

To his credit, he stays close but doesn't crowd me. He gives me his silent support without running his smart mouth.

He's letting me decide how I want to handle this with my friends. Why does he always know...? Fuck... I really need to write a list of his flaws and read it daily as a reminder.

"Xander needs my help, and I need his, so we are fake-engaged at the moment." I know that my succinct non-explanation is not going to get them to leave. But it's not like I can tell them to fuck off because I want to have a lot of really, really, really hot sex right now.

I can't ask them to leave after they showed up because they were worried about me.

"What help do you need?" Saar turns to Xander, more accusing than inquiring.

He gives her that handsome grin and hikes his shoulder. "Hand job, blow job..."

Saar covers her ears, and Celeste snorts.

"Xander!" I pinch the bridge of my nose.

Of course he would joke. That's his personal brand. And while he showed me there is more behind that veneer, I can't expect him to change his personality for the benefit of my friends. I wouldn't want him to.

"Thank you for checking on me. I'm feeling much better. I'll fill you in later." I walk to the door.

"Will there be a big fake wedding?" Celeste asks, but at least she angles herself toward the door, like she got my not-so-subtle attempt at ushering them out.

I look at Xander. Fuck, there is a lot we need to discuss.

"There won't be a wedding. We will donate to a few organizations in lieu of a big party," Xander answers, and fuck, I like that solution.

"Okay, I guess you don't need us at the moment." Celeste gives me a hug. "You good?" she whispers in my ear.

I nod and grin, and she winks at me.

"I get that you're fake getting married, but what are you in real life now?" Saar hugs me.

"Friends with benefits?" I shrug, avoiding Xander's eyes. I don't think there is a definition of this.

After I promise we will get together soon, they finally leave. Closing the door behind them, I lean my forehead against it. Shit, I didn't want them to find out like this.

Strong hands whip me around, and before I manage to gasp, I'm pinned against the wooden surface, my hands above my head in Xander's tight grip.

We stare at each other. His gaze burns, incinerating all nerve endings in my body.

"I'm going to punish you for that, Coraline." His voice is dark, but the threat sounds like a promise.

"For what?" I breathe.

His erection rigid between us, Xander kicks my legs apart with his knee. He thrusts forward, his hips holding me in place. Somehow, he holds both my wrists in one hand while he brings the other to my throat.

My pulse must be hammering against his touch. I can practically feel it bouncing off his fingers. He squeezes a little, and my breath hitches. "For calling me a fucking *friend* with benefits."

My entire body hums with need and want, but I'm completely at his mercy, unable to touch him. Somehow, that heightens my arousal.

"Isn't that what you suggested when I asked you what you wanted from me?" I croak, that conversation in his car feeling years away.

Xander lowers his mouth to my ear. "There is nothing friendly about the things I want to do to you."

"Promises, promises." I pant, and Xander groans, thrusting forward again, practically locking me between him and the door.

"Oh, Coraline, you think you can provoke me? Make me lose control? Let's see who is in charge here?"

His words should appall me. Instead, they ruin my panties.

In one swift move, Xander spins me and pulls my shorts and panties to my knees. With my cheek pressed against the door, he fists my hair.

I cry out as he shoves two or perhaps three fingers into me without warning. Not that the last few seconds suggested any other development. Not that I wanted to *not consent* at any point during this assault.

It's delicious. It's wild. It's ridiculously hot.

He pulls out and pushes back in almost aggressively. And it still isn't enough. The need to be filled by him is visceral.

"I. Am." Thrust. "Your." Thrust. "Future." Thrust. "Husband."

Can I come in under one minute? Probably, yes.

Do I enjoy the savage attack? Definitely, yes.

Xander might be dominant and seemingly out of control, but he's still putting me first.

My former fiancé never did, even though I didn't know it at the time. My current fiancé has yet to do anything selfish during sex.

I can barely breathe with his weight against me, but I meet his thrusts with wanton abandon. The pleasure builds up, flooding my entire body, ready to crescendo.

"Yes, yes, yes," I chant, probably scandalizing all my neighbors.

My knees tremble, my pussy throbs, my breathing is ragged.

And then cold air hits me. I almost collapse to the floor, completely dazed. He's gone.

"What the hell, Xander!" I turn.

He sits in the armchair, tapping his fingers on the armrest. "I don't feel very friendly right now."

The bastard. I'm going to kill him.

"You can't just leave me like this." I step forward but almost tumble, my shorts still around my knees. I shove them down and step out of them, my legs still shaking, my arousal wet between my legs.

"And yet, here we are," he teases.

Asshole. His cock is practically tearing through his pants, so if he wants to play this game...

"If you don't fuck me right now, Xander, the deal is off. What did you want me to tell them? What is this even?"

He rakes his gaze from my hairline to my tiptoes languidly. It's like he is touching me, his stare burning my skin. I wish I didn't enjoy this game.

I'm still going to kill him, but this delay is strangely provoking in a very tantalizing way.

"I'm your husband. And you're *my* wife."

There is something in his tone that speaks directly

to my core. Maybe the emphasis on *my* wife. Or perhaps the desire in his eyes. He sits a few feet from me, but he owns me.

I should laugh. I should protest. I should assert my independence. The entire exchange is ridiculous, and yet the undercurrent of commitment rings in his words. And that's what my hormone-crazed mind latches onto.

It must be the hormones, because I shouldn't get turned on when my fake not-yet-husband claims me like that... like I truly belong to him. Like we just said our vows.

"You're not. Not yet," I breathe.

His hooded gaze speeds up my heartbeat. I feel it in my stomach where a kaleidoscope of butterflies flutters. That heated, worshiping look burns in my core.

"Take off the shirt," he demands.

I blink a few times before my hands flee to the hem of my shirt, and I pull it over my head. It floats to the floor and lands at my feet.

"Your bra, too," he rasps, no longer tapping. He is gripping the armrests now.

I unhook my bra and let it fall.

I shiver, not from cold, but from the weight of his devouring gaze. I never thought that standing in front of a man naked could be this empowering.

While I would only see flaws, it's clear Xander sees

anything but. His grip on the armrests is white-knuckled now.

"Crawl to me, Coraline."

Dear God. The air fills with potent sensuality. With wanton filth. With delightful darkness.

He sits there like a king, waiting, dominating the dynamics of this situation. I can refuse, but why the fuck would I?

I lick my lips.

I take a deep breath, my entire body trembling.

I place my hand on the door, because I don't trust my legs.

My head spins with desire. His eyes burn with equal need.

The moment of silence stretches while he dares me patiently, and I stall because the tension is too tantalizing.

He issued the order, but it's me who holds the cards. And I want the fucking experience.

I lower myself to my knees, my heart throbbing in my temples. His eyes flash with approval, and it's all I need to channel my inner temptress. One I didn't even know existed.

The distance is very short, but I take my time, swaying my hips, my chin high, my eyes glued to his.

His jaw twitches.

His gaze is ablaze.

His fingers tremble slightly.

His chest rises and falls unevenly.

All his reactions thrum through my body as I kneel between his legs.

"No touching." I issue an order of my own. The guttural sound that rumbles through his chest is approving and desperate.

"You're enjoying this, little minx." His voice is hoarse, but there is no doubt he's enjoying it equally.

I unzip his pants and hook my fingers in the waistband of his briefs, peeling them out. His freed cock springs out, glistening with pre-cum.

"You might not be my *friend*, but you're not my husband either. You're my fiancé only." I extend my ring finger. "And even that is questionable."

He fists my hair and captures my lips. It's messy and desperate. Tongues dueling. Teeth clashing. Lust growing.

Xander yanks me onto his lap without disconnecting the kiss. I'm straddling him now, his rigid length rubbing against my pussy. The moan the friction draws from me is animalistic.

He reaches for the condoms, his lips and teeth everywhere at the same time. My skin tingles under his touch.

"I need you. Now!" I snatch the condom from his hands, and he chuckles.

Getting rid of the wrapper, I roll it on slowly as we both watch. Once he is sheathed, I lift my gaze, and fuck—

There is no doubt in my mind that he needs me as much as I need him.

At least in this moment.

Chapter 20

Cora

I'm a married woman, officially.

CELESTE

I'm calling a huge HEA here.

SAAR

I can't believe I'm saying it but I agree.

Get ready to pick me up when I fall and he's not there to catch me.

CELESTE

Something tells me he's already there.

SAAR

The way he's been looking at you.

LILY

What did I miss?

I hate being five hours ahead.

CELESTE

You live in the future, babe.

Can you check if I'm heartbroken in the future?

* * *

"Mrs. Stone." Gina Cassinetti extends her hand. "Nice to meet you."

"It's Winslow-Stone." I shake her hand, trying the name on my tongue for the first time. I ignore the weird indigestion it causes. Not the name, but my fake claim to it. "Call me Cora."

I've been Mrs. Winslow-Stone for two weeks. Two weeks with Xander that feel just like a normal marriage.

That's the most worrying part.

Xander got a marriage certificate to appease his father and follow through on the business with his client. No problem there. The bistro is getting saved in the process.

He added some amazing sex to the equation. No problem at all. I'm benefiting, and enjoying every moment of it.

But he's also throwing in these little acts of what really feels like genuine care. That is the confusing part. Because how am I to protect my heart?

"Then, call me Gina. You have a great place here."

She walks around the bistro, which has been closed since Sanjay left.

"It's my father's pride and joy. Unfortunately he's sick, and I..." For some reason, I feel like I'm on trial here.

"Mr. Stone said you want to preserve the original concept as closely as possible?" She taps her fingers on the counter, her eyes behind her blue-rimmed glasses inspecting the space with professional scrutiny.

I don't know what she sees, but for some reason I want to apologize. "What is it you do, Gina?"

She faces me with a bright smile. "I'm a consultant in the hospitality industry. My expertise lies in restaurant processes, staffing, and marketing. I work either with new places or with already established places like yours. In both cases, it's my job to help a restaurant succeed."

She speaks with conviction and enthusiasm.

"My father left the place in a dire financial situation."

"Mr. Stone said the budget is no issue."

I guess that's part of the deal. Whatever that means.

"But, of course, I will provide suggestions with pricing options, and you're in charge of choosing what's best," Gina continues. "Will your father want to provide input?"

"I'm afraid he isn't in a position to…" I peter out, because what am I going to say? In a position to care?

"Okay, let's start. I have a gazillion questions." She sits down and pulls out her tablet, saving me from the painful search for the right answer.

We spend almost two hours discussing the current operation while Gina makes notes.

The whole time I'm trying to get excited, but as it's been lately, I still only feel exhaustion.

Maybe it's burnout. Or just overall disillusionment with the way my life turned out. When Gina leaves, I look around the space and sit down for a moment, to reflect on my lack of motivation.

The space, closed and empty, sparks nothing besides an intense relief that I don't have to open, prep, and serve at the moment.

I realize my break is sponsored by the man who will probably move on soon, but I need this to be able to breathe. Besides, I'm helping him as well.

Instead of forcing myself to dream about the next chapter of this venture, I take out my notebook. Escaping to fictional worlds has always helped.

I flip through the pages, but I can't find the lines I remember writing a while ago. Regardless, the story awakens in me with its next lines:

The fox liked the building part best — the

hammering, the fixing, the knowing she'd made something that would keep someone else warm.

But when the sun went down, and the lights glowed in all the windows, she curled up outside, under a tree, and told herself she liked the quiet.

"Foxes don't need homes," she said. "We make them for others."

But she always built them with extra room. Just in case.

The story pours out of me. I don't remember the last time I wrote in such a flow. It's just silly verses for kids, but they fill me with a sense of purpose I haven't felt in... quite a while.

It's like the moment I allowed myself a bit of a break, my mind freed up for creativity.

My phone rings, and I answer mindlessly.

"...I'm calling from the Brooklyn Food Bank Network. I couldn't reach your husband, but his assistant gave me your number. I wanted to thank you for your generous donation." The male voice pulls me back to reality.

"Pardon me?"

"Your donation. Let me tell you, not many people decide to feed the people in need instead of their wedding guests. I just wanted to thank you personally."

There won't be a wedding. We will donate to a few organizations in lieu of a big party.

"You're welcome. I'm glad we could help at least a little bit."

He chuckles. "A little bit. We're covered for at least a year, despite the conditions."

"Conditions?"

He chuckles again. "Don't take me wrong, we appreciate that you thought not only of the financial support. It's true we can't afford to be picky with the food we source. Well, now we can, thanks to you, and I promise we will ensure the food we provide is nutritionally balanced."

I try to mumble something coherent, but no words leave my mouth.

"Are you there?"

"Yes." I finally find my voice. "I hope we didn't create more work for you."

"With the best intentions, so we don't mind. Frankly, it's quite refreshing that someone cares beyond the cheque."

"If you need anything else, just let us know," I say, like I have the resources to assist more.

I hang up, smiling. If nothing else, my fake marriage fed many people. I'm about to send a message to Xander, but a knock on the door has me smiling even more.

"You're still closed?" Saar asks as I unlock the entrance.

"What are you doing here?"

"I missed my lattes." Celeste navigates the stroller inside.

"You came all this way. What if I wasn't here?"

"I had to meet a new dance teacher." Celeste's dance school is half a block from the bistro. "Saar was coming to join me for a stroll with Amelie, and we happened to see you sitting here."

"Are you okay?" Saar gives me a hug.

"She should be—honeymooning." Celeste winks.

I groan. "You would have to wait at least half an hour for your lattes. The machine hasn't been used for two weeks."

"Let's go to the small coffee shop up the street," Saar suggests, and we leave.

As we walk up the street, I realize I locked up and left without a second thought. Like it was the most natural thing to do, leaving the burdens behind me.

I've had coffee with my friends many times, but always at my father's place. Never somewhere else. Somewhere where I can be a customer and fully enjoy the company without thinking about the preparations, patrons, bills, and everything else.

We take a table on a patio. The small coffee shop is

lovely, the coffee is delicious, and the company is great —if not a little nosy.

The freedom is intoxicating.

"Are you going to make us pry it out of you?" Saar asks.

"We gave you two weeks, but I'm dying to hear what the hell is happening." Celeste peeks into the stroller. "First, are you happy?"

I blink a few times, because the question takes me by surprise. How fucked-up it is that I have to pause to think about the answer? But my smile stretches because the answer is unanimous.

"I'm very happy."

"Good sex will do that to you." Saar smirks.

"And let's face it, we all started in a marriage of convenience and..." Celeste shimmies her shoulders. "The rest is history."

"Yeah, but it's different with Xander." I take a sip.

"How?" Saar asks.

"Even if we ended up having a genuine relationship, in a few years he will want a family, and I will be forty by then. There is no way this has a chance of surviving beyond a year or two."

The truth silences our little table.

"The way he looked at you when we came to your apartment, I don't know, I think the man is ready to compromise." Saar shrugs.

"Did you talk about children?" Celeste asks.

"No, of course not. It's a fake marriage." I shake my head.

"With real sex," Saar whispers, but the couple near us gives us a look.

We giggle like schoolgirls. "Yes, very, very real," I say dreamily.

"Again, I think the way he looks at you..." Saar shrugs.

"Maybe he's ready to settle," Celeste says.

"If that's the case, I'm hardly the best candidate. I'm ten years older."

"I think you're making too big a deal of your age gap," Saar says. "From what you told us, he's taking you to introduce you to his parents. Not to remind you of all the women he's been with, but any of them would look like a better candidate... on paper... young, and with a single goal of landing an eligible bachelor—"

"Stop. I don't want to compare myself to the long-legged blondes." I fold my arms across my chest.

"But that's the point. You don't need to compare yourself. He chose you." Saar shrugs.

"For a fake marriage," I mumble.

"Still, Cora, he had options," Celeste says. "I don't think the age gap is an issue for him."

"I know it isn't. That doesn't change the fact that

he will need more than I can offer down the road," I argue.

"Let's not talk about down the road, because right now, you're honeymooning." Saar bites her lip with mischief. "How is the interruption of your celibacy?"

The smile might split my face. "No complaints at all."

"Then stop worrying about tomorrow and enjoy today." Celeste raises her cappuccino to toast to that. "Besides, when a man is with a younger woman, it's not an issue. So let's just fuck the double standard, and enjoy fully."

And she's right.

Also, today is what matters. Even if this relationship is doomed to end, I will always cherish the few moments in life I had with him.

Fuck the age gap. I'm not going to spoil what we have right now.

We chat and laugh, until Amelie announces she's done with this outing with a loud wail. My friends leave, and I stand on the street, strangely lost.

I'm so used to working all the time, I don't quite know what to do with myself.

I decide to visit Ethan. As strange as it is, after spending time with Xander, I need a proper closure with my former fiancé. My fake husband showed me in a couple of weeks how "not enough" my former real relationship was.

The buzzing of the city hums in the background of the peaceful place with its large trees, offering much-needed shade.

I walk down the familiar path, already saying goodbye to the place. I will always remember Ethan, but I think it's time to say a proper farewell. It's strangely liberating, knowing this may be the last time I'm here.

His grave doesn't have fresh flowers, and it feels strangely barren without them.

"I didn't plan on coming today," I say, as if Ethan would expect that I wouldn't show up empty-handed. "I met someone. He sold his motorcycle for me."

Okay, I guess I held too much resentment to release it easily. But I don't have to be spiteful.

"I came to say goodbye. One I should have said years ago, but couldn't. Perhaps it was the anger I felt about your unnecessary death. Or maybe it was just me holding onto the future I lost. In any case, I met someone, and I'm happy. I hope you found your peace wherever you are."

"Hello." A boy comes from behind me and squats by the stone, stuffing a fresh bunch of flowers in the vase.

"Hi." Who is this? I look around for a parent or a grandparent. A woman stands in the shadow.

He turns to me. I blink a few times, because I know those eyes. Before my brain can conjure any explanation, he smiles. "Did you know my father?"

I swallow, my knees giving in. He steps closer, gripping my elbow. "Are you okay?"

"I'm fine, I think. I didn't know Ethan had a son."

"I was born five months after he died. Mom and Dad didn't have a chance to tell anyone about me. How did you know him?"

He looks at me with his huge eyes, full of expectations. A boy who never knew his father, probably hungry for any information about him.

I can barely speak with the lump in my throat. "I didn't really know him that well."

The irony? It's not a lie, despite having spent five years with the man. Jesus.

Making an excuse, I nod to whom I assume is the boy's mother. I'm not interested in unraveling this more. Or meeting the other woman.

I stumble out of there. As soon as I'm back on the busy street, I burst out laughing—it's manic, unhinged, and strangely cathartic.

Ethan, you fucking bastard. Can we truly know someone? Only the parts they show us.

I would have expected to be devastated.

Instead, I'm relieved. Like knowing he was a cheating bastard gives me permission to finally let go. I held on to the memory of him for way too long.

I stop at a bakery and get myself a whole box of cakes when my phone rings.

"Why is the bistro closed?" Tessa accuses instead of greeting me.

"Why do you care?" I say, grinning. I don't even know why, but I feel lighter. Like I shed skin I hadn't needed for a long time, and now I can breathe freely.

"I'm standing in front of it," she huffs.

"Why?"

"I don't want to have this conversation over the phone," she complains.

"Tough shit, sis, you'll have to, because I'm not there."

"Where are you?"

"Buying cakes."

"Jesus Christ, Cora, you're making no sense. I came all the way to the city—"

"You should have called," I interrupt, before she can make me feel guilty for not being where she wants me.

She groans. "Do you have time now?" Her tone changes—more a plea than a demand.

"I can be there in half an hour." I sigh.

Twenty minutes later, I find my sister tapping her foot in front of a place she hasn't visited in years.

"Finally." She straightens and turns to the entrance, waiting for me to open.

I roll my eyes. "Nice to see you too. Maybe next time don't come unannounced."

Fishing out the keys, I angle them to the lock and pause. My hands tremble, the air only reaches the top of my lungs, and my heart beats just a bit faster. Am I having a panic attack? It's like my entire body rebels against me entering the place.

What's wrong with me? This is where I belong.

I balance the box in one hand, but my quivering hand misses the hole.

"For the love of God," Tessa mutters and pushes me to the side, snatching the keys. She waltzes inside like she owns the place.

"Why are you here, Tessa?"

She walks to the counter and drops her purse there. I put down the box and my bag on a table near the entrance.

Ignoring my questions, she walks around, running her finger on the surfaces, exploring. Or inspecting.

"Tessa?"

She finally looks at me. "I'm going to invest in the bistro."

For the second time today, my reaction is utterly shocking, and I laugh.

She puts her hands on her hips. "I'm serious. My family is gone. I feel lonely. I need a purpose, so I decided we will run this place together."

And I laugh harder. When I finally catch my breath, I open the box and walk to the counter. "Have a cake."

"You're acting strange." She approaches me with suspicion and looks in the box.

"I had a strange day." I grab a plate and serve us a large slice. I take a bite.

Tessa plays with her fork, and then gives in and has a taste. "It's delicious. We used to share a cheesecake every Sunday."

"We did." I smile. "So you want to work here?"

She blinks a few times. "Why not?"

"I thought you didn't have money."

"Paul turns out to be a generous bastard, after all."

"Well, you're the mother of his children. That should count for something." I take another bite, the sweetness caressing my taste buds and my soul. "I already have an investor."

"You do? Who?"

My husband. A petty part of me wants to drop that particular bomb, but given the state of her marriage, I don't want to hurt her.

"It doesn't matter. I don't even know what I want to do with this place."

As the words roll out of my mouth, unbidden, we both pause. Tessa looks at me wide-eyed. I probably mirror her expression, because where did that come from?

"You want to close it?"

When she says it out loud, I feel a five-second sigh of relief, immediately followed by guilt.

"I don't know, Tessa. I've been closed for two weeks, and now I have a consultant who is preparing options."

"Is he qualified to advise us on this?"

So it's us already? "She is qualified."

"Okay, I'd like to be involved."

"Is this your new charitable endeavor?"

"It might be my future job. I've never had one and..." She looks away. "It's time."

This might be her antidote to loneliness. I'm mad it took her this long to care, but at the same time, I don't seem to care enough to fight her on it.

If this is what she needs right now, I'm not taking it away from her.

"Okay." I raise my forkful to toast this new collaboration.

She smiles and nods, taking her own generous forkful.

We eat in silence for a beat. I'm grateful for it, because it gives me a moment to soak in the new reality.

I have Gina and Tessa now to share the burden of this place, and maybe, finally, I can make it into something Dad would be proud of.

I enter the hotel to wait for Xander. We moved here last week while waiting for the closing on a beautiful townhouse in Chelsea.

Pavel, the boy from my building, is taking care of the cats, because I don't want to move them around.

I smile at the concierge, exhausted.

I didn't do much today, and yet it was the most eventful day in a while.

Tessa is joining the family business. Something I wished for but couldn't have imagined. Let's hope we don't kill each other.

Ethan had a child while he was engaged to me.

His death might have erased my doubts, but when I think about it, they had always lingered. Ethan never showed up for me. I just created a narrative in my head, a story I wanted to believe.

And perhaps the narrative I have around Xander—an entitled playboy, or a man who will want to settle soon with a woman his own age—is just that. A narrative I believe while ignoring my true feelings.

But there is a lot that no longer fits that narrative.

Xander showed me different sides of himself. He never hid his playboy ways. He never hid his carefree force of nature. He is confident in who he is. No masks.

And right now, he wants me.

It might be just for a moment in time, but it's genuine. He makes me happy. Trying to taint it with my worries about things I can't control makes no sense. The man has shown up for me in many ways already.

I deserve to give him a real chance.

In the elevator, I pull out my phone and text him.

We donated to the food bank?

XANDER

We agreed to do that instead of a wedding reception.

We agreed? His off-handed comment in front of Saar and Celeste didn't sound like a conversation leading to an agreement, but many are benefiting from that non-conversation, so I'm not going to argue.

Thank you.

XANDER

Thank me later with your legs spread.

Jesus.

How do you know I'm not playing with myself already?

XANDER

Don't you dare!

Hm...

XANDER

I swear to God, Coraline, don't you dare touch yourself without me there. I'm in a fucking meeting.

Giggling, I enter our room and toe off my shoes.

Don't worry, just one orgasm before you come. Enjoy your meeting.

I get changed into a T-shirt and leggings. I'm going to write a bit before I shower. As I pull the notebook out of my bag, someone knocks.

I smirk. No way he got here this fast. Has he bailed on his meeting?

But Xander has a key card. The thought comes too late, because I'm already pulling the door open.

And the surprise on the other side makes me wish I'd locked it instead.

Chapter 21

Xander

"Why is this meeting in my office?" I push off my desk, my chair rolling backward.

"Because you got married and never even as much as had a toast with us, asshole," Caleb says, sauntering into my office with Cormac and Roxy.

Fuck. The last thing I want is to discuss my complicated arrangement with Cora. Especially the part on how it came about. They might have opinions, and at least one of them does, based on Roxy's glare.

I'm half-hard from Cora's sexy texts, and in no mood for this.

"I don't remember drinking when you got married." I narrow my eyes at Corm.

"You drink my best Macallan enough times." He

unbuttons his jacket and sits on a chair in front of my desk.

"What's your problem, Xander?" Roxy leans against my bookshelf. Today she's clad in a pantsuit, and a corset underneath. "Since when do you forgo a party invitation?"

"Since he's been pussy-whipped." Caleb chuckles and sits beside Corm.

Fair enough, I've been teasing my colleagues about them falling for their women, so I guess I need to absorb some razzing myself now.

"A party? I thought we were having a weekly update meeting." I lean back in my chair, the situation in my pants finally under control. My fingers itch to check if Cora texted again, but I remain professional.

Well, if thinking about my wife naked, while trying to focus on work, is professional.

My wife.

Why does it feel so essential? Like something I need to survive? I went through my life not caring about anyone much. Enter Cora Winslow, and I'm a fucking goner.

The best plot twist ever, if you ask me.

"Okay, let's toast to Mrs. Winslow-Stone. It pertains to this meeting agenda anyway." Shit, why am I telling them this?

"How?" Corm asks.

I walk to my shelf and pour an inch of whiskey for everyone. When we each hold a glass, I raise mine.

"I'm pleased to announce that my father delivered, and I'm flying to San Francisco next week to get voted in as the new member of the Vireon board."

"Good job." Corm raises his glass.

"How does it relate to your new wife?" Roxy asks, before putting the glass to her lips.

She studies me with her penetrating scrutiny, and I fidget. I fucking fidget like she can see through me and discover the whole truth.

"My father had some conditions," I say vaguely, an aftertaste of manipulation spreading on my tongue.

"He wanted you to marry? Wow." Caleb shakes his head, having experienced parental manipulation firsthand most of his life. I make a noncommittal grunt. "To Mrs. Winslow-Stone." He raises his glass.

"That's quite a sacrifice." Roxy still eyes me with a hint of suspicion. What's her fucking problem?

"I get things done." I shrug, taking a generous gulp.

I really don't want to discuss this any further. Not with them. Corm and Cal started with a marriage of convenience and ended up falling for their women.

If I'm honest, I don't mind that scenario in my case. Not at all. The past two weeks have proved that my bachelor days don't compare to what I have now.

I know Cora looks at this as a temporary arrangement, but by the time we get to that point, she will have changed her mind.

I'll make sure of that.

I want her in my life.

I want her to challenge me.

I want her. Period.

"Which reminds me, you owe me twenty grand." Cal snickers.

"What are you talking about?" Fucking bet.

"Obviously, you're not going to date seriously anymore." My friend shrugs.

"Isn't marriage the most serious commitment?" I argue.

"Not if it's fake." He shakes his head.

Not if I get my way.

Roxy's tablet rings with an incoming video call, and she patches Declan through. Setting the screen on my desk, she angles it so Declan can see us all.

"I hear congratulations are in order," Declan says dryly.

"You heard about Vireon already?" I try to move on from the Cora topic.

"What's with Vireon? I'm talking about your marriage. Just don't fuck it up; my wife is fond of Cora." Declan signs some papers before he looks at the camera.

"All our wives are fond of Cora," Corm points out, giving me that we-will-keep-an-eye-on-you look.

"Thank you for the vote of confidence. I'm not going to fuck it up." I shake my head, annoyance rumbling through me.

As soon as I say the words, my own mind challenges the conviction. I'm going to fuck it up, am I not?

I don't have a frame of reference for a successful relationship. All my relationships with women were chronically short-term by choice.

My professional relationships are based on negotiations, transactions, a dose of manipulation, and endless networking. I'm pretty sure that is not a solid foundation for a romantic relationship.

The situation with my family is still at sub-zero level. Come to think of it, the people in this room are my only friends, but even with them I'm bound by business.

My honeymoon bliss evaporates at the realization.

"What's on the agenda, Roxy?" Corm asks.

We spend an hour discussing business, and for the first time in... forever... I can't wait for it to be over. My usual enthusiasm took a day off.

Between Declan's foreboding warning—not so welcome—and Cora's sexting—very welcome—I'm on the edge.

Corm finally adjourns the meeting, and my

colleagues leave. I glance at the fifty emails I received in the last hour, quickly assessing if any of them are urgent enough.

Before Cora, I would have tackled them all before leaving.

Today, I couldn't care less.

"Did you blackmail her?" Roxy startles me.

"Fuck. I didn't know you were still here." I stand up, snatching my jacket from the backrest, the chair swirling.

I put it on, adjusting my cuffs. "What are you talking about, Ro?"

"Answer the question." Her not scolding me for calling her Ro means she won't let go of this conversation.

"Of course, I didn't." I grab my phone and walk to the door, opening it.

The office hum fills the air immediately, stopping her from further investigation.

"If you used that file to manipulate the woman in any way, I will feed your balls to a stray dog on the street," she warns.

"In that case, I suggest you find a better strategy to deal with hungry dogs. If you don't have any other *work-related*, questions, I have to go now."

"I'm just wondering why a woman who didn't want to have anything to do with you would marry you suddenly." Roxy somehow keeps up, despite my long strides.

I hit the elevator button. "I wore her down the old-fashioned way." I flip my palms upward, shrugging. "What's not to love here?"

I'm so full of shit. I'm also full of urgency. To fucking leave.

To make sure I don't screw it up with my wife. As if getting to her faster would change anything. Jesus, I'm pussy-whipped.

I jump into the elevator and wink at scowling Roxy before the door closes. I whip out my phone and text my wife.

Get naked now. I'm leaving work.

I stare at the screen, waiting for the three dancing dots, but there is no reply.

You better not have started without me, or there will be consequences, Mrs. Stone.

Still nothing. An unfamiliar sense of insecurity—one I really don't like—washes over me. I call her. No answer. What the fuck?

I jump into my Lambo and rev the engine,

speeding from the garage and breaking all sorts of rules.

Until I merge into the traffic. Fucking gridlock.

What's the point of having a fast car when you have to crawl down the street with other cars and buses?

I try to call Cora twice more, not even caring to hide my desperation. Fucking Declan, planting the consuming thought.

Calm down, you idiot.

It's not like I could have fucked it up between our texting and now. She must be taking a shower or something.

For the first time I use the valet parking at my hotel, throwing the keys at the attendant and marching through the lobby like my ass is on fire.

I take the stairs to the tenth floor to work off the pent-up energy. Swiping my card, I open the door and stop in my tracks.

"What are you doing here?"

And where is Cora?

Sissy unfolds herself from the sofa and saunters to me. "Surprise!" She opens her arms, expecting a hug.

I dodge her, my eyes darting around.

"Don't be a grouch, darling. Your maid let me in. She's been taking her sweet time tidying up your bedroom. I asked her to change the sheets." Sissy wraps her arms around me.

"Fuck." I peel her off me. "Go home, Sissy."

I slide the double door to the bedroom open and blink a few times, adjusting to the darkness. The blinds are drawn, but even in the shadows of the room, I spot her immediately.

Cora sits on a bench by the window, her arms wrapped around her shins, her chin propped on her knees.

She turns to me. I can't see her expression, which only deepens the sense of desperation. I want to eat the distance, take her in my arms, and explain this shit show, but something stops me. I observe her from my spot, unsure what to do.

The light floods the room. "Oh my God," Sissy squeals. "No wonder she took so long. I'm calling the manager. You can't take a nap on a job."

"Sissy," I growl.

Even with the lights on, Cora's face is half-hidden behind her forearms, and I can't figure out if she is pissed, sad, disappointed, or all of the above.

She swings her legs over and stands up, her expression unreadable. "I'm not on a job, and I take my naps whenever I want. But I guess you kids need to catch up, so I'll leave you to it."

She eyes me with... is that a smirk? She certainly

doesn't look pissed. That's good. Isn't it? Or is her indifference a sign of not caring at all? I swallow around the lump in my throat.

"Cora..." I extend my arm like I can stop her from leaving.

"You know her?" Sissy gasps. "Seriously, Xander, an affair with staff?"

"As I said, I don't work here." Cora rolls her eyes and moves to the adjacent room. She starts putting on her shoes.

"Sissy, stop insulting my wife."

Cora pauses with one shoe on and looks at me, and then at Sissy, who is white as a sheet, and for the first time ever speechless. For a brief moment. Too brief.

She glances at Cora's hand, searching for a ring, and frowns. "Your wife? You married a maid?"

Cora snorts, and I'm not sure if that's good or bad for me. She walks over to Sissy. "I'm Cora Winslow..." She pauses, glancing at me. "Winslow-Stone, and I'm a small business owner. I live here, and I think it's time for you to leave."

Sissy blinks so hard, I worry her fake lashes may fly off. She looks at me, gaping, and then she huffs. "Why wasn't I invited to the wedding?"

Cora snorts again, and I question my sanity, because I used to spend time with this woman.

"I'm sorry, Sissy, your invitation must have gotten

lost. The postal service these days," Cora says, and fuck, I want to kiss her.

"What a shame." Sissy jumps at the opportunity to save face. "Well, my apologies, Cora," she says with zero sincerity. "Have a nice life." She marches out of the room, the door slamming behind her.

Cora's shoulders shake, her head bowed.

"Cora," I rasp, itching to take her into my arms, but not sure it wouldn't cost me my balls.

She looks at me, her lips twitching, and I realize she is trying to stifle a laugh.

"You're not mad?"

"Oh, I was really mad, but while I waited, I realized that I can't be mad you had a life before this arrangement. I knew how colorful that life was, so I can't blame you for that."

The fact that she calls our marriage an arrangement makes me want to bend her over and teach her a lesson, but this is not the best time. I'm relieved she's laughing off the whole situation.

"Thank you. I don't understand why she would just show up like this." I shrug.

Cora sighs. "After I stopped being mad, I killed time thinking about all the women you used to date."

I wince.

"I don't look like them. I will never be as young or as put-together as they are. I sat in that room filled with insecurities. And then, I remembered what Saar and Celeste told me." She pauses, and I try to regulate my heartbeat. "You chose me."

How does she always surprise me? When I expected a scene, I got a heartfelt confession, her vulnerability forcing me to vow I'd never put her in this position.

"You were jealous." I grin, lightening the load.

She rolls her eyes. "Until I talked to her. I don't understand how you could have dated her."

"We didn't date."

Cora snorts. "Okay. How could you have spent time with her?"

"Fair point." I finally crowd her and snake my arms around her waist, inhaling her scent. "I missed you."

She wraps her hands around my neck. "That's good."

"My cock would disagree." I wink, and she narrows her eyes. "Too soon?" I kiss her forehead. "Thank you for being so understanding."

"I might not be mad, but in light of this unfortunate encounter, I have a condition to add to our arrangement." She plays with the hair on my neck, a mindless gesture I've grown to love.

"Name it."

"We'll live in my apartment while we wait for the closing on the townhouse."

I step back. "Are you..." *Out of your mind* probably wouldn't be the right reaction given the circumstances. "Sure?"

"Yes. The cats are there anyway, and it's only for a few weeks."

"Your shower is tiny." I name one of the zillions of objections that spring to my mind.

She chuckles. "It has hot, running water."

"The commute..."

She folds her arms, scowling.

I sigh. "Okay, we'll live there." God help me. "Can I take you shopping now?" I suggest, because first, Sissy killed the mood, and second, I want to treat this amazing, understanding woman.

"I don't need more islands," she deadpans.

"I was thinking another hospital stay," I tease.

"If I break your nose, perhaps. Not funny. What do you have in mind?"

Laughing, I take her hand. "Let's start with a ring."

"So your girlfriends don't mistake me for a maid?"

I guess she saw Sissy's pointed look.

* * *

Shopping with a woman is generally painful. Shopping with my wife is torture. Mostly because she doesn't want to buy anything.

But the ring on her finger—my ring—improved my mood, so I suffer. At least the world knows now that she is mine.

And hopefully, one day soon enough, she will accept it.

“Let’s just ease you into it. Why don’t we set a budget, and you just forget about what you need and lean into what you want?” I walk through the door of a boutique.

“Okay, so what’s the budget?” Cora asks, her tone light, humoring me.

“Let’s start you slowly. Fifty thousand.” I shrug.

She laughs, but stops wide-eyed. “You’re serious?”

“Not enough?” Fuck, I should have said one hundred.

She shakes her head and walks around. She runs her fingers over the silky blouses on a rack, her eyes scanning the minimalist decor.

Finally, after what feels like half a lifetime, she picks some garments that the shop assistant takes to the changing room for her immediately.

Cora stops by the accessories and browses through the headbands. “You’re awfully invested in buying me new clothes. What’s wrong with my old clothes?”

“I saw how the dress for the luncheon transformed you. You may discount it as something silly or frivolous, but dressing for success is a real thing, sweetheart.”

She eyes me for a moment. "Or you just don't want to be ashamed of me."

I lower my mouth to her ear. "Keep talking yourself down, and I will bend you over my knee right here."

My cock twitches as the shudder reverberates through her body.

"You wouldn't dare," she breathes.

"Try me."

Her eyes flash with heat, and we stare at each other between the luxury clothes while I fist my hands so I don't undress her right here.

I don't know how long we eye-fuck each other before the shop assistant clears her throat, and we jerk away from each other.

"Do you want to join me in the changing room, or do you need a time-out?" Cora grins, eyeing the tent in my pants.

"Depends."

"On?"

"Can you be quiet?"

The earlier sensual energy sparks. Cora looks around and toward the changing rooms. "Depends."

"On?"

"Can you be fast?" She lifts her chin.

"I take as much time as I want with you, Coraline." I lean in, yanking her to me, my mouth over her ear.

"Do you want me to fuck you with my tongue, my fingers, or my cock?"

She grips my shoulders. "Your choice, young man."

Fuck, I hate it when she calls me that. Turning, she crooks her finger, beckoning me to follow with a smile.

A smile that makes me forget she keeps pointing out the age difference.

A smile that has me walking through the store with a fucking boner.

A smile of sin and promise.

It hits me along with a realization: I may think I'm in charge here, but this woman stripped me of my free will.

Unintentionally.

Unequivocally.

Undeniably.

"Which one should I try first?" she asks, standing in the entrance to the changing room.

I step into her space, pushing her inside, and close the door. "I don't fucking care what you wear... What you don't wear, on the other hand..." I take another step.

Her breath hitches. "I need to take off my shirt and my jeans to try these."

I grip her shirt and yank. Cora gasps as the fabric falls apart, and her body collides with mine. "I can take them off for you."

Our gazes hold as the world goes still. Absolutely still, for a hungry moment. I lock the door, and when I look back at Cora, she is unzipping her jeans.

"Did you choose, Coraline?" My voice is low and gravely. I'm barely hanging onto my control.

"I haven't tried anything yet." Her chest heaves.

"We're buying all the clothes. I'm talking about fucking, sweetheart." I whip her around. "Hands on wall." She obeys, and I lean over her, kissing her shoulder. "Cock, tongue, or fingers?"

She moans.

"You promised to be quiet," I whisper into her ear.

"You promised to be fast." She turns her head to kiss me. It's sloppy and fast.

I spank her ass. "Then stop stalling and choose."

"What if I want all three?"

Of course she would challenge me. "Okay."

"What? We can't—"

But her protest turns into another stifled moan as I pull down her underwear and shove two fingers into her tight heat.

"Look at you, ready for me, dripping already. Such a greedy girl. Such a dutiful wife." I pump my fingers in and out, my cock getting harder with every reaction—her stifled moans, her contracting cunt, her shivers.

Cora bites her forearm, leaning into my hand.

When she starts clamping on my digits like a vise, I withdraw from her and lick my fingers.

She swears, and I laugh. Unlocking, I step outside. I need to make sure I can take care of my wife the way she deserves.

"Wait here," I order.

"What the fuck, Xander?" She grabs one of the hangers with an untried dress to cover herself.

"Try a few dresses before I come back."

Chapter 22

Cora

I stand there, my arousal dripping down my thighs. What the hell has just happened? Where the fuck did he go?

I lean against the mirror, the coolness sobering my lust-drunk brain. The bastard. Fuck him. I lock the door.

But now I'm trapped in here, stewing. I should try the dress, but fuck it, I'm so wound up. Minutes tick as I stand there, undecided and pissed.

When I finally pick up my jeans to get dressed and storm out of there, the door handle clicks.

"Coraline." Xander's voice carries a hint of warning.

"Go away," I hiss.

"Let me in."

"Go away."

He raps on the door. "Don't you want me to finish what we started?" he drawls.

Jesus, other customers must hear him. "I finished myself," I lie. I should have.

Xander raises his voice, the undercurrent of warning even darker. "Coraline, open the fucking door, or I will break it."

Jesus, is he for real? I unlock the door. "Are you insane?" I whisper-yell. "You told me to be quiet, and then you yell for everyone to hear."

Instead of answering, he pushes inside, unbuckling his belt.

"What are you doing?" I step back.

He looks around the room. "Do they fit well?" He nods his head toward the clothes I brought in here and unzips his pants, stepping out of them as they fall to the ground.

"I haven't tried them." I put my hands on my hips. "What are you doing?"

He casually takes off his jacket and hangs it on the door with care. The man is impossible.

"You don't need to try them. We're getting all of them anyway." He pulls me to him, completely ignoring my mood.

"We're not." I fail to sound stern because he takes my nipple into his mouth, biting gently through the lace of my bra. "I don't need all the clothes. And where the fuck did you go?"

Goddammit, it's frustrating to argue with someone when I have to control the volume. And when, with his first touch, my body completely forgets I'm mad at him. Treacherous body.

"Hush, I'm back now," he says nonchalantly. "Where were we?" He probes my entrance again, and my knees buckle.

If I wasn't so turned on from before, I would send him away.

Who am I kidding? It took two short weeks, and I'm completely addicted to his touch, his expertise, and his uncanny knowledge of my body.

"You just left me here," I quip, though it comes out whiny thanks to his ministration. God, he is fucking infuriating.

"Let me lick you better," he mumbles and drops to his knees, hoisting my leg over his shoulder.

"Asshole."

"At your service." He winks, that boyish grin of his calling to the deepest parts of my body. And perhaps my heart, which I'm not willing to contemplate.

Xander nips at my clit, and then shoves his tongue inside me. I have to cover my mouth to keep quiet. Or as quiet as possible, because there is no way I can stay mute when his—

"Oh my God," I whimper. "Yes, yes, yes," I whisper-chant.

My orgasm hits me so quickly, it's embarrassing. I put my hands on the mirror, trying to stay upright.

"Tongue done." Xander grins from between my legs, his face glistening with my juices.

I slide my leg off his shoulder and stumble like a newborn lamb. "I don't think I can do more."

He takes me in his arms and kisses my forehead. "That's where you're wrong, wife."

Whipping me around, he sits on a bench across from the mirror and lowers me into his lap, my legs astride. With my back to his chest, the picture in front of me is... fucking hot.

Xander kisses my neck, kneading my breasts, and I watch in fascination at the mess between my legs.

"My wife is the hottest woman in the world. Look at yourself, Coraline."

I'm speechless—and completely spellbound—but I believe his words. For a moment I see myself through his eyes, and I love what I see.

He produces a condom from somewhere, sheathes himself, and lifts me. He maneuvers me with ease and eases me down his length.

I can't take my eyes away from where we are connected. His cock disappears inside me and hits a spot that blurs my vision.

"Jesus," I gasp.

"Just me." Xander grips my hips, lifts me, and impales me again. The sensation is overwhelming. I close my eyes and tilt my head back onto his shoulder.

My entire body trembles with pleasure I don't think I've ever experienced. It's like I floated to a different dimension where the physical body is just a vessel for immense decadence.

I'm completely pliable in his hands, and for once I let everything else fade and let the ecstasy carry me high. Higher. The highest.

"Eyes on me," Xander commands, his voice strained.

I open my eyes, and our gazes lock in the reflection. It's unnerving and elating at the same time.

The man is bouncing me on his lap. His cock is bringing me to the edge. His muscles are bulging. A sheen of sweat covers our skin.

The picture is carnal. Primal. Salacious.

But it's his eyes that hold me prisoner with the reverence of his gaze. We may be fucking, but what I see in his eyes is beyond that. The intimacy in the way he looks at me pulls at the strings of my heart.

I desperately want to look away, because I will not be able to forget this moment. But perhaps I don't have to, because the mirror doesn't lie. And I'm looking at him—at us—the same way.

"Xander," I cry.

The release hits us both at the same time, and I bend forward, almost falling to the ground if it weren't for the firm arms holding me tight around my waist.

His eyes seemed to promise me he would be there when I fell.

Xander peppers my skin with kisses as we both try to come down from that devastating orgasm.

But as if the newly found and entirely unexpected closeness wasn't scary enough, Xander pulls me to him, wraps his arms around me, and shifts me around.

I sit on his lap sideways while he holds me in his arms like I'm precious. Like I'm worthy. Like I'm truly his.

"What have you done to me, Coraline?" he whispers into the crook of my neck.

It's such a soft sigh, I'm not even sure if he really uttered the words. But he looks up, and I see the same question in his expression.

His beautiful face carries tortured stillness, and the depth in his gaze makes my chest tighten.

It's like he's memorizing me. Like he's seeing a miracle, or possibly his demise.

The moment grows thick with things we don't say, because they are too raw and too fragile for what this is.

And perhaps we are not ready to contemplate what this could be.

"I had them ring all the things you selected and a few more, and I'm pretty sure you're still under budget." Xander tuts, shaking his head.

His words break the moment, and I'm grateful for that. Yet again, he reached for playfulness at the right time. Is it to protect me? To protect himself? Or to save us both?

His comment penetrates my daze and snaps me back to reality.

"Oh my God, I screamed your name." I cover my mouth with my hand.

"Who else's name would you bring into this?" Xander slaps me gently.

I stand up, grabbing my clothes like I can salvage anything. "Everyone heard us."

"The walk of shame is going to be epic." He smirks.

"I hate you," I grumble, getting dressed hastily.

"Now you're just lying, Coraline." Xander doesn't show any urgency or care.

Jesus. I completely lost myself in him. He's right; this is going to be some walk of shame. At least I never have to come here again.

"And I'm not getting all those clothes; it's ridiculous."

"Cora," he warns.

When I don't respond, he snatches my T-shirt from me and cups my chin. "You're getting all those clothes.

You're taking everything I ever give you, and I will keep giving until you learn to reward yourself. To put yourself first. Understood?"

I glare, but I have nothing to say to that. This infuriating man not only takes care of me, he's determined to teach me to do the same. For me.

"Understood?" He glares at me.

I nod.

"Good girl." He kisses me. "Why don't you wear one of these dresses, since your shirt is ruined?"

The dress is simple, but the fabric is so soft I almost mew when I put it on. This is the most luxurious thing I have ever worn.

I love it. It fits me perfectly. Not only does it fit, it makes me look so much better than in any of my clothes. Goddammit.

"Beautiful." Xander, dressed, with his jacket hooked on his finger, casually over his shoulder, leans against the wall.

"Thank you. Sometimes it scares me how carefree I am when I'm with you."

He doesn't move, just watches me for a beat. "Coraline, you deserve more than you've ever reached for. There is a difference between existing and living. Life is to be enjoyed. Lean into it."

Enjoyed? I guess I can let him put me first while I learn to do it myself.

"Ready?" He reaches for the handle.

I groan, but I guess I can't hide here forever.

He opens the door and picks up my bag from the floor. "Jesus, I forgot how heavy this thing is. What do you carry in here?"

"Notebooks," I reply before I can stop myself. Shit, am I ready to share that with him?

"Are you a professional note taker?" He swings my large bag over his shoulder.

I snort. "No, I'm not. I scribble stories." I look away, suddenly self-conscious about my hobby.

Besides my father, nobody knows I enjoy writing for children. I guess mostly for me, since I've never shown or read my stories to anyone.

"Stories? What kind of stories?" He doesn't mock me, just asks with a genuine interest.

"Children's stories. I started when I was a teenager, and it's been an outlet for me." I shrug.

"That's amazing." He smiles at me, pulling me closer.

We turn the corner, and I stop in my tracks. The store is deserted.

"Where is everyone?" I look around, bewildered.

"You really think I would let anyone hear you come undone? That privilege is mine, and mine only." He leans in and kisses me.

"But how?"

"I paid them to close the shop." He shrugs, takes my hand, and leads me to the exit.

"Are you... What... Xander!" I'm completely incoherent. "How much did that cost you?"

"You're still under budget, Coraline; we need to work on that." He winks.

Outside, a security guard nods and enters the store. "Have a good evening, Mr. Stone."

"I'm going to die," I murmur.

Xander laughs. "Let's have a bite, because I'm having things moved to your place. Can they have your neighbor open the door for them?"

He holds my hand and leads us down the street.

"Sure." We'd just agreed to live there. "You're fast."

"I always get rid of unwanted tasks quickly." He shrugs and pulls out his keys as we approach his car.

"You don't want to live with me?" I tease.

"I don't want to leave my comfortable hotel suite." He opens the door for me and puts his hand above my head, making sure I don't hit it as I get in.

I'm sure he'd hold an umbrella for me in the rain. The girl in me shimmies inwardly. Maybe this playboy is more than that. Maybe I can trust him with my heart.

"You'll live, young man."

I didn't think he would agree to move out of his hotel suite. When Sissy showed up, I was pissed.

Hurt. But as I cooled down, I couldn't blame

Xander. It didn't take the hurt away. This was a woman who clearly meant nothing to him, but who believed she could have more of him than he was willing to give.

She was wrong. What if I'm wrong about everything too? What if he is the same charming self with her? What if this version of him isn't just for me, but his usual modus operandi? And I'm falling for it hook, line, and sinker?

This insecurity, right after the day I had, is exhausting.

"Why did Sissy show up like that?" I decide not to hide my feelings. What's the point? If I'm to scare him away, I should do it sooner rather than later.

"I thought we were past that." He glances at me, but then focuses on driving.

I roll my eyes. "Xander, I'm just wondering... You make me feel..." Fuck, why is this so hard to say? "I know it's only been two weeks, but I'm falling for you, and it scares me."

My body veers to the side as he swerves the car. Loud honking follows his reckless move before we come to a stop in front of a fire hydrant.

It all happens so fast, I don't even get a chance to yelp. Xander whips around to face me as soon as the car stops. I should turn to him, but a stubborn part of me believes we can pretend I didn't say anything.

But I can't pretend I don't feel anything. That I don't fantasize about us being real.

"Cora," he growls, and I finally shift in my seat.

"Forget—"

"My turn," he interrupts.

"Okay." I nod. The storm of emotions on his face is confusing. The adoring stillness from before is gone. But I don't find indifference or annoyance either.

There is something dark and unreadable in his eyes—a determination, maybe, but I'm not sure of what his intent is. Is it to explain what this really is, so I get my feelings under control?

The imaginary clock ticks in my temple as he just stares at me.

"I'm glad you're scared." He says the last thing I expected.

He shakes his head and cups the back of my neck, pulling me to him. His lips fuse with mine in a punishing kiss.

I'm so taken aback that I freeze, my lips unyielding. But he doesn't give up, and takes until I have no choice but to surrender.

Then he cuts the kiss way too soon.

"Not because I want you scared," he continues, holding my face in his hands. "Far from it. If I could, I would take away all your hurts and fears. That's how I feel about you. Like I'm no longer myself. Like your smile is my only objective. Like your wrath is better than not having you around. Sissy is self-absorbed, and I never gave her a reason to think I have more to offer. And yes, there were others like her, but you, Cora Winslow-Stone, you made me a one-woman man. And I'm grateful for it."

"But—"

"No buts. I'm yours, if you'll have me. And you better conquer your fear, because you're fucking mine."

He must hear my heart as we stare at each other with so much desperation that the air heats up.

"I'm yours," I croak.

He kisses me again. "I need to tell you something."

"Can I tell you something first?" I toy with the hair on his nape, and he nods. "I've just found out my late fiancé had a child with another woman while we'd been planning our wedding. I think I'm going to doubt everything for a moment before I trust again."

"You found out today? Jesus." He pulls me closer, stroking my hair.

"Yeah, it's been the longest day ever. And I was mistaken for a maid." I bring some levity into the loaded conversation.

"You also got a lot of new clothes and two wonderful orgasms."

"Yeah, my husband saved the day." I grin.

"Your husband is a keeper." He winks.

* * *

"What did you want to tell me earlier?" I ask when we drive home after we grabbed a meal in SoHo.

His jaw works for a moment. "I don't remember. Probably that I really like your tits."

I snort. It feels more like he changed his mind, but perhaps the day was eventful enough. I'm sure he will tell me when he's ready. As far as confessions go, we didn't hold back today. That's a good start.

You made me a one-woman man.

The smile tugging at my lips must be permanent.

"Well, I really like your ass," I muse. "And some other parts of you too."

"Some parts?" He kills the engine in a paid lot near my building. "I will have to fuck you until you like the entire package."

"That's a reasonable ambition." I shrug, and he laughs, drawing a laugh from me. We walk hand-in-hand down the street.

My rich husband, blending slowly into my life. We kiss in the elevator, and while I'm exhausted, I don't want to go to sleep. I want this day to keep going.

At the door, I twist the knob and push—only to slam into something solid.

"What is this?" I squeeze through the opening and blink several times, taking in the picture in front of me.

Clooney and Pitt mew and rub themselves against my ankles, but I can't even lean to pet them or pick them up.

My entire living room is full of boxes, suitcases, and two racks of suits.

Xander shrugs, a picture of innocence. "You wanted me to move in." He leans against stacked boxes.

"You own all of this? What do you even have in those boxes?"

"Condoms mostly. Some sex toys, too."

I shake my head. "Jesus. How are we going to live here? Where do we even put all of this?"

"I don't know. And the boutique hasn't even delivered all your shopping." He is not even trying to hide the smirk.

"Mine? You forced me to buy it all."

He yanks me to him and kisses me.

Deeply. Fully. Reverently.

I might have no room left in my home. The room in my heart, on the other hand, swells with joy and affection.

Life is to be enjoyed after all.

And perhaps this thing between us isn't temporary. I lean into his kiss, blissfully unaware that the end is around the corner.

Chapter 23

Cora

SAAR

Proof of life, Cora!

CELESTE

Let her honeymoon (wink emoji).

Sorry, I've been busy.

SAAR

Doing what?

LILY

Mr. Stone.

CELESTE

Xander

How did you know? (evil emoji)

SAAR

TMI. We haven't seen you in a week.
Can't he spare you for a moment?

CELESTE

Let her make up for her celibacy years.

SAAR

Okay, but let's have coffee soon.

The bistro is still closed, but let's try somewhere else next week.

"Are you going to the bistro today?" Xander kisses me, droplets from his shower cooling my skin.

I stretch in my bed, the morning sun streaming through the window. "Yes, I'll go soon. I just need a bit of alone time first."

I don't tell him I've been writing every morning, my creativity bursting at the seams. I'm not sure why I bother with the stories, but my creative escape brings me joy.

He frowns. "Do you want me to stay elsewhere for a night or two?"

I sit up. "Don't you dare. I missed you when you were in San Francisco earlier."

"So the alone time is...?"

He retrieves his clothes from the living room, where we still have an obstacle course built from his possessions. Laying his suit on the bed, he starts dressing.

"I've been scribing a bit." I shrug, swinging my legs over the edge. "Just some silly stories."

Why am I downplaying it in front of him? It's a hobby only, but I don't need to hide it. When I told him about it the first time, he didn't mock me.

"Will you ever let me read them?"

I stop on my way to get my coffee. "You want to read a children's story?"

He shrugs, putting on his shirt. "Or all of them."

I lean in the doorway and watch him getting dressed. It's become a little ritual for me every morning.

One would think that undressing him is more interesting, but somehow, seeing his purposeful preparation for a day ahead is inspiring.

Of course, it doesn't hurt that he looks like a sex god, dressed or not, but I love his morning energy when he's getting ready to take on the world.

"Maybe one day."

He smiles at me. "Whenever you're ready."

Xander starts tying his tie, and I can't help it and step into his space, brushing my hands over his as I take the fabric between my fingers. The corner of his lips quirks up, and he drops his hands.

I realize this is just me helping him with his tie. But

he doesn't need my help. My helping him slows down his morning preparation. But somehow, this feels like he's letting me in, trusting me, surrendering to this thing between us that is blooming beyond our intentions.

I take my time—sliding the fabric through, looping it slow, forming the knot. There's something sacred about the quiet hush between us, the closeness. The way he lets me do this.

I reach to adjust his collar, my fingers grazing the warm skin just above the fabric. His gaze on me is steady, waiting, a little dark with something unspoken.

"I like our mornings," I say, pushing to my tiptoes and pressing my lips against his.

Xander wraps his arms around me and takes over the kiss as he usually does. It's slow and sensual, like he has nowhere else to be but here.

"I like our mornings too. And all other hours of the day." He keeps his forehead on mine, and we just stand there for a moment.

Time is on our side in instances like this. No long hours at his office. No burden of the bistro. No financial gap. No age gap, ailing father, cheating exes, or estranged families with blackmailing dads.

And most of all, no contracts and arranged marriages.

It's us. Plain. Simple. Happy.

"You're going to be late." I step back reluctantly.

"I can still have coffee with you." He slaps my ass gently, beckoning me toward the kitchen.

He prepares two coffees for us in a super-complicated, ridiculously expensive coffee machine he had delivered the day after he moved in.

"How is the bistro coming along?" He passes me my cup.

I let out a long breath. "Are you asking as the investor or as my husband?"

"I'm well-informed as an investor. I'm asking my wife." He takes a sip.

"The transformation is substantial, and I'm not sure..." I trail off, not clear what it is I'm feeling.

"If it's too much... You're in charge, Cora."

I chuckle. "You haven't met Tessa yet. The changes are the right ones. I'm just... I guess I'm not an easily adaptable person."

He kisses my hair. "You adapted well enough to my cock."

I roll my eyes, but I'm grateful he turned this conversation into a jest. It's like he always senses when I need more time, and just gives it to me.

"I'm pretty sure your cock's adaptability is honed by experience."

He squeezes my chin, forcing me to look at him, his eyes darkening. "Not anymore, Coraline. My cock fits your pussy only."

My heart somersaults. The words may be crass, but the deep sentiment of commitment behind them… He can't fake the adoring, worshiping gaze.

"I accept the burden, and the responsibility," I tease.

"I'll show you burden tonight." He kisses me.

I watch the empty space long after he leaves, grinning while I sip my coffee.

Then I sit down and pen a story about a leopard, who was always so playful that no one saw him for the bright, capable, and caring friend he truly was.

A story about not judging, and giving a chance beyond first impressions.

* * *

The drill shrills in the back room as I enter the bistro. I stop at the threshold. Gina and Tessa are huddled over the counter, studying large blueprints.

Their chatter is animated, filling the air with excitement.

I feel like an intruder.

I feel like I'm watching a part of my life redesigned, and I don't know how to fit into it anymore.

A new beginning permeates all the corners of my father's business, and somehow it doesn't reach me.

Before, I tried to preserve everything the way Dad had started it. Now I see the changes for what they are: improvements, the next stage, the road to success.

While I accept them now, they don't excite me. That's the problem.

With Tessa and Gina involved, the burden has been lifted from my shoulders. I'm grateful. Relieved. Unchained. But also somehow misplaced.

When I watch Xander getting ready for work, the purpose, the underlying drive, the mission of it is evident.

Coming here certainly doesn't feel the same. It hasn't felt that way for a long time. I wonder if it ever has.

You never deserved any of this.

Have I spent years here just out of a sense of duty? That is a hard thing to admit to myself, but deep down, I worry it may be true.

I always thought my life was influenced by my circumstances. But perhaps it was my choice.

And perhaps I'm on the verge of making new choices. For me.

What does that even mean? What else would I do if not this?

"Look who showed up," Tessa teases, with her typical accusatory undertone.

"It doesn't look like you missed me," I quip.

Gina looks between the two of us and scurries toward the back room. "I'm going to check on the progress."

We stay in a silent duel, and I'm not even sure what we are fighting about.

"I feel like you don't want me here." Tessa puts her hands on her hips.

"That's not true."

She cocks her head, challenging my statement.

I sigh. "I asked you to be a part of this business time and time again after Dad got sick. You refused, so sorry if I'm wary of your sudden enthusiasm."

While I appreciate—need—her here, I don't trust that she'll stay. Knowing my sister's tendency to switch to a new *cause* every few weeks, I feel she may bail soon.

If I'm honest, it terrifies me. That I'll be left here alone again, carrying the burden. No purpose, no mission, no drive... just burden.

"Fair enough, but I'm not going anywhere, and we need to learn to work together."

"Working together doesn't mean you lead and I follow."

"No, but when you don't show up, I need to take over. I want this project to succeed."

"That's the point, Tessa, you think of this as a project. It's not. It's hard work, long hours, never-ending responsibility, bone-deep exhaustion. Rinse and repeat."

She blinks, taken aback by my words. "Why have you been doing it for so long then?"

"Because someone had to!"

I think I shocked us both with the statement. The unbidden, surprising confession is so loud in my mind that the deafening drill in the back sounds like a whispered lullaby.

"Let's go get tea down the road." Tessa snatches her bag and pivots me toward the door.

We walk in silence and take a seat on a patio, ordering iced teas. Everything around me seems to buzz with intent. I buzz with the realization.

Tessa swirls the straw in her drink. "I understand you think me getting involved is just some kind of a rebound activity post-separation. But I'm here because I want to be, not because I have to be. My promise might not weigh much in your eyes, but I'm not going to bail. For the first time in my life, I wake up with something to do. Something that makes me... feel alive."

I believe her, and I also appreciate that instead of dissecting my earlier admission, she's trying to reassure me about her motivation. It helps. Her words seem to free me a bit from the self-inflicted shackles.

"If you can trust me with the bistro, maybe you can

allow yourself some time off," she continues. "To think about what it is you really want."

The way out she's offering feels good, for exactly five seconds. Immediately after, my inner cynic offers many objections. "But Dad—"

"Dad gave up on this business a long time ago. He gave up on his marriage, and then couldn't live with himself. You can't fix that for him. You shouldn't want to, Cora. He's an adult who made his choices. You can't change the outcome of his choices. But you certainly can make your own.

"After Ethan died, you left your corporate job and started helping Dad. I thought it was a phase of grief. And then Dad had his stroke, and you just gave up on your own life."

When she sums it up like that... The younger sister persona awakens in me, and I sulk for a moment, slurping my drink like a petulant child.

"Since when have you been so perceptive?" I murmur around my straw.

"Since I realized I had done a similar thing and given up on my life. For a rich husband."

Did we? Did we both give up after our parents' separation? Finding something that felt safe?

"Do you think that's what we learned from Mom and Dad? To give up?"

"God, I hope we got more than that from them. You got talent from Mama."

I almost spit out my tea. "What are you talking about?"

She rolls her eyes. "The stories you used to write."

Our mother is a freelance journalist, but I guess I pushed that out of my mind around the time she abandoned us. I never wanted to have that connection.

"You remember my stories?" I wrap my hands around the chilled glass, grounding myself.

"I remember you used to dream, and then you stopped. I remember I used to love the bistro, and I always thought I would take it over, and then the family split... and I guess our ambitions split, as well."

As much as I don't want to admit that, her words ring true. "I thought I was protecting Dad." It sounds so silly when I say it out loud.

"You romanticize all men, especially Dad."

"I don't romanticize Dad; I have compassion for his suffering."

"Suffering he caused himself."

"Don't—"

"You need to start seeing things from other angles than the one that suits your narrative, Cora. Dad cheated on Mom for years. Other women and the bistro were everything to him. He pushed Mom away, time after time. You were younger than me, but you couldn't have been that blind. And when Mom finally found a slice of happiness for herself and left, he realized what he had lost. And selfishly put that burden on you."

You never deserved any of this.

My father's words hit me like a freight train of revelation.

"What are you talking about?" My mind refuses her recount of the events.

"Apparently, something you don't want to hear."

I put the glass down and stare, a thousand thoughts fighting for attention. I want to yell at Tessa and tell her to stop vilifying our father. I want to stand up and run away from this conversation.

But haven't I questioned the narrative she just mentioned? Like the stories I write, where I try to show the good in us... am I only seeing the same in real life?

"I went to Ethan's grave..." I tell her about my discovery. One I haven't shared with anyone besides Xander, because... I'm ashamed.

Tessa sighs. "It doesn't surprise me, but poor kid."

"I guess I loved Ethan too much to see... I romanticized what we had." I chuckle humorlessly at her earlier comment.

"Like all men. Case in point—your romantic notion of Paul with the fucking umbrella... that is not romantic, it's a common decency. You tend to idealize men. And most of all, Dad."

"Why have you never told me?"

"I guess I wanted to protect you. And then we just stopped talking at one point... when I became concerned with protecting only my own image."

I look at her, deadpan. "What image? The cold bitch?"

She smirks. "When you marry a rich, influential man, it's in your job description." She takes a sip.

We both chuckle. "I'd better remember that and sharpen my teeth."

Her eyes widen. "I knew the Lamborghini guy wasn't just a friend. Is he the same guy who is investing?"

Shit. How did she figure it out so quickly? I guess I couldn't hide it from her for much longer.

Especially since we're flying to meet Xander's family, and there are public events to attend while we're there. The last thing I need is for Tessa to read about my marriage.

"The Lamborghini guy is Xander Stone, my husband."

Tessa's jaw falls. She pushes her sunglasses into her hair, and then she laughs, the staccato of it turning heads. "You should be an actress. I believed you for a moment."

"Or maybe I'm convincing because it's true."

She leans back. Her eyebrows narrowed, she opens her mouth, but no words come out for a few attempts.

She stares at me for a moment. "Why didn't you tell me you were getting married?"

"We didn't tell anyone. And you were going through your separation; there wasn't a right time."

"Of course, Miss I-Sacrifice-Myself-for-Everyone didn't invite me to her wedding because she needs to spare my feelings. God, I hate how you always pretend to put others first."

And here we go. But this time, I decide not to revert to our usual dynamic. "Tessa, I'm sorry about your marriage. I'm sorry you're angry, lost, and forced to reinvent yourself. I'm sorry I'm finally happy at the same time you lost your happiness. I should have told you."

She blinks a few times, tears brimming around her eyes. "I guess the cold-bitch behavior runs deep. I hate how empty and silent the house is."

"Let yourself grieve. I'm sure you will bounce back. Every ending is a new beginning."

She reaches over and gives me an awkward hug. "I'm sorry I sprang the Dad thing on you like that."

"Yeah, well, I don't think my brain is willing to accept your words. It will take some processing."

We sit in silence for a moment before she checks

her watch. "We should head back. Gina had a few things to discuss with us."

"If you don't mind, I'll stay here for a moment."

She frowns. "Are you sure?"

I nod, and she leaves before I pull a notebook from my bag.

And a story about a bear who kept forgetting to put himself first is born.

* * *

I push the door to my apartment, forgetting it doesn't fully open because of the boxes. The air smells of Thai food and Xander's aftershave.

In a short time, his scent, his things, his presence have blended into my space, making it more home than it's been for years.

Xander texted he was heading home about an hour ago, but I'm not met with his off-key humming or the financial podcast he listens to.

But the smell of takeout? He must be here.

I slip out of my shoes and peek from behind the boxes. And I see them.

Xander is sprawled on the sofa, one arm resting along the back, the other holding a book open across his lap.

My neighbor and proud cat sitter, Pavel, is tucked

into his side, eyes wide and fixed on the page. Both cats are draped across the armrest and Xander's legs like royalty.

No one sees me, and I pause, taking in the picture. Who even is this man? The question keeps popping into my head.

I grin, but a lump clogs my throat.

The domesticity of the scene does things to my heart. The way Xander reads? Like every word matters. Like he's savoring it. His voice is soft, deep, and rich with intention.

And when Pavel laughs—one of those unchecked, childlike giggles—I watch a smile bloom on Xander's face, unfiltered.

This man—this reckless, annoying, entirely-too-charming man—has been letting me see him in pieces. And here's another one. Gentle. Grounded. Devoted.

I step forward, and the floor creaks beneath me. Four heads swivel toward me. Two humans, two felines.

"Hi." I smile at them.

Pavel's eyes light up. "Cora! Xander fixed my bike!" He leaps off the couch and races toward me. "And then he got me a new one! Wanna see?"

I glance at Xander, who sits there, a king of nonchalance. "A new bike?"

"Yeah!" Pavel beams. "Mine was super broken, and

my dad said he'd fix it, but he never did, and Xander did. And then he said I should have one that doesn't try to murder me on every turn, so he got this one. Look." He points to a bike in the corner.

Jesus, I hope he got him a security system with that. This is a decent neighborhood, but that bike would get stolen tonight.

Pavel squirms, casting his gaze down. "Can I leave it here? My dad might try to sell it." That is as likely as a theft.

"Of course," I say to Pavel, brushing his hair back. "You can keep it here."

He beams. "Dope. I've gotta go feed Miso before he pees on my bed again." He bolts out the door before I can even ask what or who Miso is.

I turn to Xander, who hasn't moved from the couch. One cat is now on his lap. The other is licking its paw with the kind of judgmental disinterest only cats can pull off.

"You fixed his bike?" I sit beside him.

"But then I bought him a new one." He pulls me closer, kissing my crown. "The old one was a death trap."

"When did all of that happen?"

"He brooded like a kicked puppy; what was I supposed to do?"

I glance over at the scattered mess that is our

current living situation. Xander's shoes under the coffee table. A suit jacket on the back of a chair. The new bike wheel poking out from behind a tower of boxes.

It should annoy me.

It doesn't.

"And you read to him?"

He flips the book over in his hands. "Yeah. Kid said he can't read so well. He picked *Where the Wild Things Are*. Not bad taste, really."

My heart folds in on itself. "You didn't know how to make a bed a few weeks ago. Now you're fixing bikes and mentoring eight-year-olds."

He grins. "Give it another week, and I'll be cooking and vacuuming without cursing." He kisses me and then lifts my legs and starts massaging the soles of my feet. "How was work?"

"The reopening is not yet scheduled, but it will be fabulous." I close my eyes for a moment, enjoying his fingers kneading. "Oh, and I found out my father cheated on my mother several times. It was he who broke our family."

"Fuck, Cora, that's... What can I do?" He drops his hands and pulls me closer, holding me in his safe embrace.

He never falls for pity, but always jumps into problem-solving mode.

"Tessa said I romanticize men," I murmur into his neck. "That I make them into better people in my head than they ever really were."

He says nothing for a moment. "Is that why you married me?"

I chuckle. "I married you because you're a sex god."

He laughs. "Good. I married you because you're good for my ego."

"Stroking your ego is the last thing we need." I poke his ribs, and then I lock my gaze with his. "I married you because I was desperate. But I think I'm staying married to you because... you're not just what you project."

"Took you long enough." He winks.

"Why don't you show those parts to the rest of the world?"

He tucks my head into the crook of his neck again. If he needs to talk without eye contact, I don't mind. The fact that he's willing to uncover another part of himself is worth it.

"It's easier to be the party guy. The one no one expects much from. That way I can't disappoint."

I look up at him. "The formidable Xander Stone believes he can disappoint someone?"

His jaw works for a moment. "My siblings are brilliant. But I solved a Rubik's cube at five and negotiated an investment deal with our dad by fourteen. My brother always felt he had to compete with me. So I cracked jokes, bought expensive shit, and crashed motorbikes to endear myself to him."

"And it got you girls."

He chuckles. "Exactly. I had always wanted to win. I still do."

"And here I am just trying not to lose. I guess that's the difference between us."

"Is it, though? Perhaps we're more similar than you care to admit. Only I call it winning, and you call it not losing."

"I just don't feel there is anything I want to win lately."

"You won me over." With two fingers he lifts my chin, mirth flickering in his eyes. "There isn't much left to strive for."

I laugh. "I guess I did win."

He looks at me, really looks at me, and his entire face softens. "And you turn this sprinter into a marathon runner."

Is he really in this for the long run? Maybe I have a tendency to romanticize men, but I know with this one, he is really who he showed me he is. Not the business leader. Not the carefree playboy. Not the reckless billionaire.

Just a caring, funny, smart man who puts me first, while I struggle to do so myself.

"A marathon... Hmmm... I'm not worried about you. I've seen you go three rounds without breaking a sweat." I pivot to straddle him, cupping his neck.

His grin widens. "Is that an invitation?"

"Nope." I lick my lips. "It's a challenge."

"Careful what you wish for, Mrs. Winslow-Stone." He yanks me to him, his hand immediately under my skirt.

I yelp and laugh and surrender to his playfulness, because it makes me forget about the rest of the world, and that's what I need.

"I need you," I whisper.

"I know." He kisses me. "I need you too."

And just like that, the energy between us shifts yet again, pulling us deeper. Better. More.

But as the next few days confirm, not forever.

Chapter 24

Xander

"Are you nervous?" I buckle up while Cora fidgets in her seat.

The flight attendant brings us our drinks.

"If you're asking about flying, I'm super excited. I had one unexpected experience on a private jet, but I've never flown first class." She grins like a kid at Christmas, but then bites her lip. "If you're asking about meeting your family, I'm terrified."

I smile and give her a peck on the lips. "They will love you."

"Let's hope." She turns to the window, her leg bouncing.

She's been distracted since she found out about her father last week. She hasn't visited him. How must she feel about meeting my family while hers is falling apart?

How would she feel about my betrayal if she found out?

I was going to tell her.

I really was. In the car, before she confessed about her douchebag ex-fiancé.

I think I'm going to doubt everything for a moment before I trust again.

And then the night I got Pavel a bike. But she dropped the bomb about her father, and I wanted her to feel better, not worse.

She was so vulnerable, I could hardly have challenged the fragile trust she's awarded me with.

But that still leaves me as the villain in our story. I wish I had never gotten that file from Roxy. I wish I knew whether she would have chosen me even if I hadn't created the ideal circumstances.

I was driven by my obsession with her... one that intensified since we got together, but that has grown into something more.

I'm in love with this woman. And I think she's in love with me. We're both scared of the feelings, but fuck, I'm not going to let her go.

Perhaps it's better I keep my confession for later. After our San Francisco visit. Or never. That seems like the best timeline.

Don't be a pussy, Stone.

I will tell her everything once we return to New York. I will.

Cora's leg keeps bouncing. I put my hand on her thigh, and she turns to me, still biting her lip.

"You know I'll be there with you the whole time. You have nothing to worry about."

She chuckles. "That's not what I'm nervous about. I mean, I obviously am anxious about meeting the Stone clan, but I... I thought that—"

She's uncharacteristically shy about something. "Spill it, woman."

She leans down to retrieve her ginormous bag and pulls out one of the notebooks.

She places it on her lap, stroking it like the edges of the hard cover need straightening. "You said you wanted to read my stories." She hands me the notebook.

I look at the small book in her hand, a beat passing before I reach for it. It's not that I'm worried about reading the story. I saw a snippet in the sunflower notepad.

It's the trust she's handing over that makes the 5x8 book feel like it weighs a hundred pounds. "Are you sure?" I try to sound casual. I fail.

She smiles. "Start reading before I chicken out."

"Thank you."

She grimaces. "Don't thank me yet. From what I know, it might be quite terrible."

"What did I tell you about this constant self-doubt?" I narrow my eyes.

"I don't recall you saying much about self-doubt. You promised to fuck some confidence into me." She licks her lips.

"Wanna join the mile-high club?"

Her eyes flash with something dark and exciting, and she shrugs seductively.

I lean in, her scent as intoxicating as ever, and whisper in her ear, "Let me read first, and then I'll fuck you thoroughly here, Mrs. Stone."

"Winslow-Stone," she breathes, the shudder the words elicit hardening my cock.

"Still mine." I shrug and turn away from her, stretching my legs and crossing them at my ankles before I open her notebook.

My eyes land on the neatly scribbled words, but in my periphery I feel more than see her crossing her legs, pouting.

But she finally decided to trust me with her work—a trust I certainly don't deserve, but I will take it seriously. It's more important than getting her off.

And just like that, I forgo sex, because something else feels more important. What has she done to me?

I read, flipping the pages and grinning while Cora adds tapping fingers to her bouncing leg.

When I finally close the notebook, our gazes lock. Hers is full of expectations while she worries her bottom lip.

Mine are full of admiration, I hope. For her beauty. For her talent. For her.

"You wrote about a wolf whose parents never invited his friends to his birthday?" I recall our conversation at her birthday, marveling at how she turned my fucked-up family dynamic into a teaching moment through her storytelling.

She scrunches her face, pinching the bridge of her nose. "I'm sorry." She looks at me through her eyelashes. Like I would mind that my childhood inspired her.

"So I'm a wolf, and you're a fox," I tease, shoving the book into the pocket of the seat in front of me. I angle my body toward her.

"That wolf should have been a peacock. And I'm not the fox," she huffs.

"The one who builds houses for others? That's definitely you."

She reaches into the pocket. "Give it back."

I snatch her wrist and pull her to me, seizing her lips. She fights the kiss for a breath or two before she relaxes and opens for me. My tongue slides in, and I kiss her with all I have—passion, obsession, adoration.

Telling her without words that we might have started in a fucked-up way, but this thing between us is more than real.

And she takes my kisses as if she believes that, too. Like she is ready to surrender to this growing thing between us. Even if she is not, I'm a patient man.

We might have started all wrong, but I don't regret a minute.

"I think it's really good. I mean, I'm not an expert on children's literature, but you should send it to a few acquisition editors or agents."

"You think?"

"Of course. You have nothing to lose." I shrug.

"I don't know. I'll think about it."

"What is there to think about? You spent time every day writing these, and it brings you so much joy. Why wouldn't you want to share that with the rest of the world?"

"Everything seems easy to you."

"Everything is only as complicated as you make it. My sister has friends in the literary world, so I'm sure she could open some doors."

She smiles at me. "Thank you."

I kiss her knuckles and adjust my crotch before I

ring for the flight attendant. "Can you get us a blanket? My wife is cold."

She nods and goes to retrieve a blanket.

"I'm not cold." Cora scoffs.

Taking the blanket from the flight attendant, I cover my wife and inch my hand up her thigh, dusting the soft skin under her skirt. "Let's get you nice and ready before you go to the bathroom."

I nip at her neck, the essence of her and the promise of what's next making me painfully hard.

I reach her panties and massage her sensitive spot through the fabric.

She stifles a moan. "I don't need to use the bathroom."

"You want the wolf to fuck you here? In front of all these people?"

"Lex!" Lottie skips down the staircase in the middle of the vast foyer and runs into my arms. "I'm so glad you're here."

I twirl her around, laughing. Fuck, it's good to see her. She giggles, and when I put her down, she turns to Cora and hugs her. "So nice to meet you. I still can't believe my idiot brother tied the knot, but I'm so happy you look normal."

Cora's eyes widen, her posture rigid.

I snort. "Lottie, let Cora breathe."

"Nice to meet you, Charlotte." Cora smiles.

"Call me Lottie. It's so good to have you both here."

"Mr. Stone." Our butler appears. "We will bring your luggage to your old room. Will your company be staying with you?"

"This is my wife, Cora, and yes, we'll be staying together."

"Are you hungry, thirsty?" Lottie pulls at my hand. "Let's get you some snacks."

"Give us a minute." I shake off my enthusiastic sister and turn to Cora.

Her eyes dart around the cavernous space, and then she watches our suitcases being carried up the stairs by our staff.

I wish I could hear her thoughts. I grew up in this house; it's familiar and, well, my childhood home. But just this entry hall is three times the size of Cora's entire apartment.

I've been complaining daily about the tiny shower, tiny kitchen, and the general modesty of her space. But two minutes back home and I realize how her place is intimate, warm, and has grown to be my home without me realizing.

Or perhaps it's because she's there. Her scent in

the air. Her signature on all things. Her personality in every corner. She feels like home.

"Are you hungry?" I wrap my arm around her waist.

She doesn't respond—just stares at our disappearing luggage.

"Cora?"

"You have servants?" she whispers.

"I don't think that's what they are called. They're our household staff."

"I need a minute." She looks at me, blinking.

"Where are you, guys?" Lottie calls from somewhere in the direction of the dining room.

"Let's go to my room first." I practically shield Cora with my body, like I can protect her from this house, its people, its burden.

"I knew you're rich, but this is... I'm sorry...I'm shocked. Let's join Lottie. I don't want her to think I'm not grateful for her hospitality. Because I am grateful. She seems really nice and normal. She hugged—"

I fuse my lips with hers. "I've never heard you babble."

"I've never been hit on the head with so much decadence. And... Jesus, I made you stay at my place." She jerks her head back and stares at me, but her initial panic is gone, a latent smile quirking up her lips. "And you stayed."

"And I stayed."

I stayed in her shoebox of an apartment because she is there. I would live under a bridge if she were by my side.

We grin at each other for a moment, and the L word is on my tongue.

"Lex, Cora, come on." Lottie's voice snaps us from the moment of unspoken words, but something tells me we don't need to say them.

We feel them.

Deep. Painful. Exhilarating.

Lottie laughs as she sets down her teacup, her eyes dancing with mischief. "So there we are, this seven-foot-tall Swedish financier next to me, politely nibbling on a macaroon like it's radioactive, and I ask him, 'How do you feel about hedgehogs?'"

Cora laughs, a little hesitantly at first, then more fully. She's seated on the velvet settee beside Lottie, a teacup balanced in her hands. Her legs are crossed, her expression relaxed for the first time since we arrived.

Her laugh is everything. It rings delicate, but grounded. Like her.

I watch her over the rim of my cup. Still in awe. She was wide-eyed when we arrived, the size and opulence of the house hitting her like a freight train of antique mirrors and marble floors.

But now? Now she's settled into the afternoon tea like she was born to it.

After my mother and grandmother welcomed her warmly, she started relaxing, and—no surprise there—blending right in with the women in my life.

Lottie and Mom flank her like long-lost sisters. Nana Sybil reigns over the corner armchair, watching my wife with her sharp gaze.

Cora fits. More than fits.

Despite everything that should make her feel like an outsider, she doesn't play the part. She listens, she teases, she holds her own.

If my heart weren't already bruised with all the lies I'm sitting on, it might burst with how proud I am of her.

"When are Dad and Liam getting here?" I ask, partly to break my stare before someone comments, partly because I want the storm to pass already.

"Dinner." Mom smiles at me. "Sterling's wrapping up meetings at the firm. William's flying in from DC this afternoon." She checks her watch. "He should land soon."

"I want to thank you again, Cora," Mom adds, reaching for a cucumber sandwich. "For interrupting your honeymoon so you could make it to the gala. It's a cause very dear to my heart."

"It's nothing," Cora says quickly, her eyes darting to me. "I mean, not nothing—of course it's important. I just meant I'm happy to be here."

She glares at me.

"Such a considerate girl," Nana Sybil muses, swirling her tea. "And such nice hips. Clearly child-bearing ones."

Cora chokes on her tea.

Lottie clasps a hand over her mouth.

I set down my cup. "Nana."

"What?" My grandmother shrugs, entirely unbothered. "It's true. And it was only a question of time before you got one of your conquests knocked up. At least you chose well."

"Sybil," Mom warns, though her voice carries a barely concealed laughter. "We're just... thrilled for you. We hope you'll consider having a wedding reception here. Even if you want to wait until later. After the baby."

She pats Cora's hand. My wife goes white, blinking, probably hoping to be teleported to another dimension.

"Nope," I cut in. "Not pregnant. We just couldn't wait to be together, that's all."

Cora coughs, and I rush to take her cup from her.

She looks at me with what feels like a death threat in her eyes. I put her cup on the serving table.

Lottie raises her eyebrows, clearly enjoying this.

"Well." Nana sighs. "Plenty of time. Though I'll need at least one great-grandchild before I die. It's getting harder to threaten my body into staying alive."

"I think we need to get ready before dinner," I say, tugging Cora's hand. "It's been a long flight. Time zones, you know."

Mom waves us off. "Go. There's a fresh set of towels in your bathroom."

Cora lets me tow her up the stairs. We reach the landing, and I guide her to the left, down the hall toward my room.

"You okay?" I ask, only once the door clicks shut behind us.

She leans back against it. "We interrupted our honeymoon?"

Fuck. "Technically, we did."

Cora shakes her head with a weak laugh. "So... Nana Sybil... Hips? Seriously?"

"She has a way with words."

Cora laughs. "Jesus, why do they think I'm pregnant? I thought your father would clue your mother in. I feel horrible for lying to them."

I walk to her and place my hands on either side of her face. This is the perfect time to come clean.

"Cora—" I whisper.

"Oh my God." She pushes past me and runs toward the wall of windows, flinging the door to the terrace open. "Is this your backyard?"

She leans against the marble banister, her feet swinging in the air as she takes in the manicured lawn, groomed hedges, and flower beds.

"There is a lake, and a fountain? This place is just... I think I want to live here." She looks at me, her eyes dancing with excitement.

Okay, confession interrupted by the view.

"Slow down. I'm almost thirty; I'm not moving back with my parents."

She laughs. "I never had a garden. I always wanted one."

That wasn't on her list in the sunflower book. "We'll have the largest garden ever."

Her eyes search mine. Shit. My promises and commitments are coming left, right, and center, and we both know we need to talk about this marriage that started on false pretenses.

She rises to her tiptoes and kisses me. And I kiss her back. Deeply. Slowly. Willing every unspoken thing to pass through our lips like this instead.

I kiss her because it's easier than talking.

She leans into me. The tension leaks from her body

like air from a balloon. When I pull away, she rests her forehead against my chest.

"I love your family."

"Wait till you meet my brother and Dad." I sigh, kissing her crown.

"Don't do that. I was nervous about Lottie and your mother, and it went almost without a hiccup. And I love Nana Sybil."

"Only because she likes your hips."

She laughs.

I smooth her hair back, my hand lingering. Her scent settles into my skin, into my bones. This moment should feel safe.

But it doesn't.

Because the weight of the lie I haven't told her about yet sinks deeper into my chest.

She deserves the truth. About why I really asked her to marry me. About my father's true ultimatum.

I stroke her cheek and kiss her hair.

I'll tell her.

After dinner.

Or after one more day where everything feels like it could be real.

Even if I already know...

That the truth will ruin it all.

Chapter 25

Cora

CELESTE

How is San Fran?

I don't know. We're in Hillsborough.

This estate is vast. Like bodyguards and servants.

SAAR

Send pics.

I'm not going to walk around taking pictures. I already feel like an impostor.

CELESTE

Shut up and enjoy it.

SAAR

You belong there, just surrender to it.

I love it and feel guilty about it.

CELESTE

Again, shut up.

Okay, okay, surrendering. By the way, his family thought I was pregnant.

CELESTE

That's rude.

SAAR

Are you?

Apparently, nobody knows his father forced him to marry, so they are shocked he tied the knot so quickly.

SAAR

Are they nice to you, though?

Yes, everyone is lovely.

CELESTE

Then enjoy yourself. And don't get pregnant.

Unless you want to.

SAAR

I got you the dress for the gala.

Xander's father got called away, and Liam never showed up. Perhaps they don't want to meet me. Like I'm not enough for them. It's this house that makes me extra self-conscious, full of doubts.

The Stone estate in Hillsborough spans more acres

than most city blocks. Nestled between towering cypress and redwood trees, Xander's childhood home is beautiful and overwhelming at the same time. And, of course, they have their own dome-covered pool.

The water is warm, almost velvety, swirling around my ankles with the gentle hush of movement, like even the water here has learned to whisper.

The dome is massive—an architectural marvel of curved glass and sleek steel beams that rise like the ribs of a cathedral. The light here is different.

Sitting at the edge of the pool, with my dress hiked up, I kick my feet through the water. The tiles beneath me are of a soft gray marble, veined with silver.

The scent of eucalyptus hangs in the air, subtle but intentional, like everything else in this house.

This isn't just a pool. It's a sanctuary.

And that's why I came here. There is so much I would like to believe. So much I would like him to say. So much I should probably say.

I wish we had started like a normal couple. But would we have started? Would I ever have let go of all my objections to this relationship?

I don't know. I wish I knew.

At the end of the day, it doesn't matter. We're together. I'm happy with him. I just wish there wasn't this nagging need to define who we are to each other.

Because I'm sure as hell that we are not in a fake

marriage. Okay, the marriage is fake, but the rest is real. And yet we have a contract, and our divorce is inked into it.

I trail my toes along the surface, watching the ripples chase each other.

It's ridiculous. All of it. This dome could house my entire apartment complex. Twice. There's a rainfall shower near the sauna that looks like it belongs in a Bond villain's lair. A stocked juice bar that probably has a sommelier. And yet...

Despite the extravagance, there's a strange stillness here. Like I'm not in someone else's life anymore, but paused at the edge of two versions of mine.

A part of me feels like an impostor. The charity-case wife. The fake.

But Xander's mother asked me about the bistro like it mattered. Lottie made jokes like we've known each other for years. Even Nana Sybil, in her terrifying bluntness, treated me like I belonged.

And Xander? God, Xander. With his snark and charm, and that soft look he keeps giving me... I can't hold his money or his upbringing against him. That's not fair. He didn't choose this world any more than I chose mine.

And beneath the layers of privilege and polish, his family is... just that. A family. Messy and loud and awkward, and loving in their own strange way.

We're not so different. Not really.

Most of my objections to this union are proving to be wrong.

The water laps against my shins, a slow rhythmic pulse that almost matches my breath. I lean back on my palms and close my eyes for a moment. Let myself feel it.

Not the wealth.

The peace.

But everyone's suggestion about my pregnancy keeps derailing the calm. Their innocent inquiry and, I guess, not so outlandish expectation, is more like the calm before the storm.

Of course, the reason his father wanted him to marry was an heir. That's what they expect.

I laughed it off, because what else was I supposed to do? It's not like we had a conversation about children like a normal couple would. It's not like Xander would want to have kids with an older woman.

What if he wants a big family?

Maybe he doesn't want any children.

And I kind of gave up on the idea of becoming a mother.

Fuck. I wish we were a normal couple.

"Here you are." Xander appears behind me. "You can skinny dip here if you want. Lottie went out, and nobody else uses the pool at this hour."

I snort. "As if I would."

"I'd join you." He sits down beside me, the splashing water getting his jeans wet.

"Like you needed a pool to get me naked." I look at him.

"Are you crying?" He frowns.

"What?" I swipe my hand over my cheek. I didn't even realize there were tears. Jesus. "I-I, no, I wasn't."

"Cora," Xander warns, cupping my cheek.

I bite my lip, turning away from his touch. "Nana Sybil is something else." I chuckle, but it sounds a bit mad.

"Is it about what she said earlier? Don't worry about it. She is past the age of caring about being diplomatic." He takes my hand and brings it to his lips.

But I can't drop it, so I plunge into it.

"You have this huge family... When I saw you with Pavel... and they are right about expecting heirs. And I know this is not what this is—"

"Hey, hey, hey." He scoops me up and lifts me to sit on his lap. The man is strong as a bull. He moves a strand of hair behind my ears. "What are you talking about? You're making no sense. Pavel? They?"

"The expectation is for you to start a family."

He flinches. "Whose expectations?"

"Xander, don't make this difficult." I turn my face to the shimmering water, away from his piercing gaze.

"Then make it clear for me. Are you asking me if I want to have children?" The usual lightness in his tone is gone.

I whip my head to look at him.

He runs his hand up and down my back. The touch is distracting and comforting at the same time. I want to tumble into the pool to cool down. To drown. To avoid this fucked-up conversation.

I can't ask him if I don't even know what I want.

"The answer depends." He gives me a smile, not waiting for the question. It's not his usual cocky one; it's... I don't know, reassuring? Sad? Contemplative?

I swallow. "On?"

"You."

I groan. "Don't be ridiculous. You should have children with a woman of your own age. One that can give you three or five."

"Says who?"

That is actually a valid point. Says my mind that has been in a gutter for a hot minute now. "Logic?" I look away. Fuck, I loathe my insecurities.

"Look at me, Cora," he growls, but doesn't wait for my compliance. He pinches my chin and forces me to meet his eyes. "I'm with you. You." His gaze burns.

We stare at each other for a beat or a lifetime before he continues, "This conversation should only be about whether or not you want to have children. *If* you actually want to have any. And if you do, you're fucking having them with me." The last sentence sounds like a threat.

"I'm thirty-seven."

Even to my ears, the argument is meager in light of who we have become to each other. I open my mouth to elaborate, to express my fears freely, but I don't get a chance because the water swallows me.

He fucking pushed me into the pool.

I come out, spluttering and cursing. And laughing. "What the fuck, Xander?"

I reach the edge, blinking, looking for him.

He snakes his hands around me from behind. He's right there with me. Both of us dressed and soaked. His body envelopes me, the solid muscles so decadent against me.

"I'm twenty-seven," he says, nibbling on my ear.

"Stop it," I say, while tilting my head to give him access, his lips trailing my wet skin. "Stop pretending you don't know what I'm saying."

"Stop telling yourself lies then. If you want children, we're fucking having children. You and me."

Goose bumps sprout on my skin at his words, or maybe it's his lips. Or his hand reaching into my waistband. Or the water. All at once.

"What are you talking about? This marriage is fake."

Xander moves his hand to my chin and forces me to look at him. "Is it, though?"

* * *

"Why are you not sleeping?" I turn, snuggling closer to Xander's warm, naked body.

He kisses my crown. "Sleep, Coraline."

His voice is veiled with something... Worry?

I lift my chin, adjusting to the dimness. Moonlight illuminates his shadowy figure. "What's wrong?"

"I need to tell you something," he whispers.

I lift to my elbows, willing my brain to wake up. "Okay."

He rakes his fingers through my hair and pulls me in for a kiss.

It's like he needs the intimacy to get through the conversation. Or he wants to solidify how not fake we are.

But something is weighing him down, and I can feel the burden of it in my tightened stomach and constricted chest.

"We don't have to have children," I blurt out, picking up the unfinished conversation from the pool.

He chuckles, pulling me closer to him. "Yeah, we kind of derailed that conversation."

Another lingering kiss.

I feel this one deep in the darkest crevices of my soul. It triggers my cynical mind. He's stalling. Whatever he wants to tell me, he believes I won't like it.

But I feared the children conversation, and it ended up in... well, two orgasms and probably a health-code violation that would require a change of water in the pool.

Without speaking about it, we didn't use a condom. As if that preceding conversation clarified everything.

It didn't.

But hasn't it been like that with us? We feel more than talk. We fight those feelings—well, I do—and end up surrendering anyway.

"You're right." He pushes to sit, leaning against the pillows. "We should finish one conversation before we dive into the next one."

I pivot to sit beside him, cross-legged, covering myself with the silky sheet. "I've been single for too long, and I kind of put the idea of children to the side. I never planned on a serious relationship, and my financial situation didn't leave any room for being a single parent."

He reaches for my hand, but then changes his mind. "But you would no longer be a single parent. Or in financial need."

He's looking at me with intent. Like he dares me to

tell him what he wants to hear, even though I'm not sure what that is.

If you want children, we're fucking having children.

His words earlier—so raw, so demanding, but also so fucking irresponsible. If *I* want children?

"I don't know, Xander. I hadn't thought about it when you asked me to marry you, obviously." I twist the sheet in my lap. "And we *obviously* didn't talk about it."

"We're having the conversation now, Cora."

"Are we though? It feels like you're just trying to coerce me into saying what I want. I'm not sure what I want." I twist the sheets more, and then I look at him. "I don't want you to have children with another woman. There, I said it. I'm jealous of your next wife."

Annoyed with the whole situation, I throw the sheets away and start climbing out of the bed. I don't even make it to the edge before Xander applies his superhuman, sex-god powers and has me on my back.

Covered with his sinewy body, I glare at him. He holds my hands above my head, staring at me, that playful, self-assured smirk making his face even more beautiful.

"There will *not* be a next wife. You're my wife. And for the record, I always wanted one or two children, and that's a perfect number for an older woman like you." He winks.

"Asshole." I kick his shin and struggle to free myself.

But my effort is pointless against his strength, so I default to glaring only.

My glower is my last defense, even though at this point my heart has melted at his declaration.

"You're perfect for me, Coraline Winslow-Stone. A month ago, I thought children and starting my own family were a distant destination I would have to accept at one point. You changed that. Not because the clock is ticking, or because Nana wants great-grandchildren. Because you and I, we're good together. Even if you were eighteen—which I'm very grateful you are not—I would want to have babies with you now."

"We've been together for a few weeks."

"You always find an objection, don't you?" He kisses me gently.

"It's only been a few weeks, though," I say weakly, not really listening to that argument myself.

"Life-changing weeks."

Oh, my poor heart. Yes.

Life-changing.

Destiny-altering.

Permanent-joy-inducing.

We grin at each other before our lips clash. Xander lets go of my wrists, and I wrap my arms and legs around him.

His hands are everywhere at once. It's too much and not enough. It's just the perfect amount of affection.

Lust.

Connection.

Just the perfect amount. Because I'm with the perfect man.

"Shall we make a baby, Coraline?"

"You want to start right now?" I giggle. Not because the idea is absurd, but because it's thrilling.

"We kind of started in the pool." His lips leave a wet trail down my torso. He dips his fingers into my pussy, and I gasp. "Besides, you feel pretty ready for me."

My pussy might be ready, but me? Am I ready?

And for the first time in my life, my mind doesn't offer an objection.

"Fuck, Cora," Xander utters.

"What's wrong?" I whip around, the skirt of my gown rippling around my legs.

Fuck, Cora? Fuck, Xander.

My gorgeous husband is leaning in the doorway of his walk-in closet in a tuxedo. I've seen him in a tux before, and yet the sight remains mesmerizing. The man wears a tux like a second skin. A quiet kind of smoldering power. Like this is yet another skill he's mastered.

Though tonight, I also feel unapologetically radiant.

When Saar offered to get me a rental gown in this neck of the woods, I jumped at the opportunity. Her years gracing the catwalk honed her into a true connoisseur of fashion, so I let her pick for me.

And pick she did.

The gown is a deep, burnished chocolate, with a subtle sheen that catches the light with every movement. It fits beautifully against my skin—soft, sculpting, confident. The bodice hugs me in all the right places, the sweetheart neckline framing my collarbones and the soft slope of my shoulders.

"You look... I don't think we can go." Xander pushes off the wooden frame and strides toward me, gripping the back of my neck and devouring my mouth.

"What are you doing?" I admonish, breathless. "I just applied my lipstick. Why can't we go?"

He twirls me around, his chest to my back as we both look in the mirror.

"Look at yourself." The hunger in his eyes pulls at the corners of my lips, making me stand taller.

He lowers his lips to my neck, the off-shoulder strap slipping lower. I mean, those straps are barely clinging, more suggestion than restraint. Like it was made to slip.

Xander groans, his lips hot on my skin.

I didn't accept Lottie's offer to use her stylist and decided on a natural look. And I'm glad I did, based on Xander's reaction.

"I think I will steal the show," I say confidently. Hmm, I guess he did instill some of his self-assurance in me. Xander and this dress.

"You definitely will steal the show, and I see a long jail time in my near future after I kill all the men who see you like this." He wraps his arms around my waist, his gaze running up and down my body in the mirror's reflection.

"Behave yourself, Mr. Stone." I turn around and kiss him. "Everyone can admire all they want. You, dear husband, are the one bringing me home."

"You're beautiful," he rasps.

When he says it, I not only feel it, I believe it. "Damn right I am. But let me get ready."

"Okay, I'll jerk off watching you, so I don't have to walk with a tent in my pants all night."

I roll my eyes, but the evidence of him liking me in this dress is clear.

I pick the earrings Saar sent me to wear with the gown. "What did you want to tell me last night?" I guide the delicate hook through my ear. "I kind of stole the conversation. I'm sorry."

Still standing behind me, Xander's expression darkens. He looks away briefly and fists his hands.

I frown, picking up my necklace. "Xander?"

He takes the jewelry from my hands, his breath close as he leans in, his eyes firmly on me, no longer devouring, but... I don't know, certainly worrying me.

The cool metal skims my collarbone before it settles into place. His fingertips graze my skin as he fastens the clasp, slow and unhurried, like he's savoring the privilege. Or stalling.

My heart hammers in my rib cage as the minutes tick loudly in my temple.

"I know we have a fake marriage certificate..." His voice is hoarse.

I freeze. "The certificate is genuine, though."

Thump.

Thump.

Thump.

The beat of my heart must be heard back in New York.

"The feelings are genuine, too. I love you, Cora."

I turn and kiss him.

He holds me in his arms, just looking at me like he wants to freeze the moment to never forget it. I know I want to emboss it in my memory.

"I love you, too."

"I love you, Coraline Winslow-Stone," he repeats.

"You do, don't you?" I tease, because I want his self-assured smirk back. It hasn't returned with his declaration, which kind of taints the moment.

I fell in love with the carefree, playful Xander. This serious one is new, and I don't know if it's a good thing or not.

He kisses me again.

"I kind of want to take off the dress and stay here."

Something passes across his face. "Cora—"

"Lex," Lottie calls from behind the door, knocking urgently.

"Not now," he growls.

The door swings open. "Are you two decent?" She doesn't step in.

We pull apart, but Xander holds my hand in his.

"What the fuck do you want?" he snaps.

I jerk my head to him, because his reaction is exaggerated, but also so unlike him. What did Lottie interrupt?

"Sorry, guys, but Nana Sybil wants to talk to you right now, and you know how she is." Lottie steps in, shrugging.

Xander looks at me, his face full of anguish, then at Lottie. He lets go of my hand, sighing.

"Fuck." He bows his head for a moment, before he looks at me with urgency. "We'll talk later."

He storms out.

"What's up his ass?" Lottie makes a face.

"I wish I knew."

"I'll see you downstairs. The cars are ready." She rushes out again.

Xander loves me. He loves me. He wants to have children with me, and he loves me.

I just wish the joy wasn't tainted by his weird behavior just now. Is it just a case of not being used to such declarations?

Why did he say it if it doesn't come easily to him?

We'll talk later. About what?

Shaking my head, I give myself one last check in the mirror and remember how confident I felt just a few moments ago. And with a smile, I leave our room to go downstairs.

Re-enacting *Titanic*, I walk down the imperial staircase as Xander looks on, the latent smirk back on his face.

"Wow. A true showstopper." His voice is cold and detached.

The way he's looking at me is weird as well. It's like the tender moment earlier hasn't happened. Like he's back to his predator ways.

Only it's not even back to that familiar distant

memory of Xander when I first met him. It's colder, more aloof. Less him, for sure.

What happened?

What changed?

Did his declaration scare him? I wasn't demanding his love. Hoping for it, perhaps, but he said the words first.

By the time I reach the last step, I'm positively annoyed.

He prowls toward me, fisting his hands and I fight the urge to step back. He is so close now, but it's like my body doesn't recognize him.

It's Xander, but it's not.

"Stay away from her, asshole." The voice that *is* Xander's booms.

Chapter 26

Xander

Cora whips her head to me, and Liam exhales a small, humorless sound.

"Step away, I said," I growl at my brother.

He finally does, and I rush to wrap my arm around her waist, pulling her to me. To save her from my brother, but also to reassure myself she is still mine.

I came to the dome yesterday to tell her the truth. I was going to tell her again last night. And then before Lottie barged in.

Every time, the conversation gets derailed. Or I let it derail.

Maybe it's a sign I shouldn't tell her.

Instead of the truth, I told her I love her.

That is the truth. The only truth that matters.

The businessman in me already knows the probability that the truth will matter to Cora is greater than I care to accept. I would even go so far as to admit the odds are not in my favor.

I'm an investor; I take risks all the time. Yet here I am, avoiding one simple conversation with my wife. Because it's not simple.

In my defense... Fuck it, there is nothing I can say in my defense. I fucked up, and I need to get my head out of the gutter and deal with the situation.

"Wow, this one is a keeper," Liam drawls. "I see why you would break our pact." He turns to Cora. "My apologies, it's the habit of deception my brother and I enjoy playing. I guess no longer." He shrugs. "Liam Stone. You must be Cora." He kisses her knuckles.

"You never told me you had a twin." Cora looks at me wide-eyed.

"You didn't tell her you have a brother?" Liam asks.

"He told me about you, but he never mentioned you were twins."

"Identical." Liam sighs, like it's a burden. "Maybe we know each other better than you think," he deadpans in his dry way, and Cora looks at me, shocked.

"Fuck off." I lead her away from him.

I love Liam, but he's a cold-hearted asshole who loves to play with his victims. No way am I submitting Cora to his kind of cynicism.

"We're taking the same car," he mumbles, trailing behind us.

"What pact was he talking about?" Cora asks.

"Never mind." I put my hand on the small of her back, and nod to the footman who is holding the door for us.

"We vowed never to get married," Liam says.

Cora picks up her skirt before she enters the car. "I thought if you were born to all of this"—she beckons her head toward the house—"you're obliged to provide an heir."

"She caught up fairly quickly. Beautiful and smart," Liam says dryly, like the praise annoys him. It probably does.

"You're awfully chatty today," I quip. "What have you been drinking?"

"Enough to tolerate humanity, given the current social obligation." He drops into the seat without ceremony.

"It's our mom's most important occasion of the year." I take Cora's hand in mine.

"Relax. You set the precedent." He pulls out his phone and leaves the conversation.

Cora eyes me curiously.

"My brother hates events like this," I explain.

"Oh, darling sis-in-law, the occasion might be

perfectly palatable. It's the people I hate. No offense." Liam doesn't even look up from the screen.

"None taken." Cora smirks.

We spend the forty-minute ride in thick silence. Liam avoids small talk at all costs. Cora appears to be mesmerized by the scenery outside, though I guess it's just to avoid eye contact. Not that my brother looks up.

I... I fucking regret letting Liam into this car. I need to talk to my wife. At this point, it might be the worst timing ever, but I can't wait any longer.

"What did Nana Sybil want?" Cora turns to me.

"She wanted my advice on a gift for you."

"Seriously? I don't need any gifts."

"Modesty. That's new in this family," Liam grumbles.

I ignore him. "She wants to welcome you to the family."

"She doesn't need to—"

"Do you want to tell her yourself?" I smirk.

Cora huffs. "Fair point. What was your advice?"

Just to deal with the internal turmoil, I lean in, my lips brushing her ear. "That I keep you naked most of the time, but jewelry suits you well even when spread-eagled for me."

Cora gasps, a shudder reverberating through her body. "Xander," she warns.

"Get a room," Liam grumbles. "Tell me, Cora, how do you feel about meeting Tawny tonight?"

I groan.

"Who is Tawny?" Cora looks at Liam.

"Xander's ex-almost-fiancée." The fucker finally puts his phone away.

Cora's eyes flicker to me, and then she leans forward, her attention fully on my brother. "Tell me, Liam," she mimics him. "How do you feel about being the asshole in the room?" She gives him her brightest fake smile.

"Actually, I don't mind it at all." He shrugs, but I don't miss a glint of approval in his eyes.

Cora swings her hand around my shoulder and plays with the hair on the back of my neck. I love when her fingers mindlessly swirl there. "Well, at least I can be sure I married the right brother."

The ballroom gleams with candlelight and polished glass. Crystal chandeliers hover above, their sharp glitter catching on every sequin, every diamond, every artfully highlighted cheekbone.

Classical music hums in the background, smooth and stately, but it's all white noise to me.

I glance at Cora, radiant in a chocolate gown that

hugs her as if it were stitched by lust itself. Her hair is pinned up, with a few defiant curls loose by her neck.

When I saw her earlier in the room, my heart stopped and restarted in some disjointed rhythm that doesn't seem normal, but it feels right.

I wanted this woman the minute I laid my eyes on her. Then later, the thrill of the chase played a role—I enjoyed her sass, and loved that she was resisting.

Somehow, she grew on me. I wasn't exaggerating when I told her she made me a one-woman man. I wasn't lying when I told her I loved her.

I only wish we had started differently. Without the false arrangement hanging over our future.

The crowd parts as we make our way into the heart of the room. Lottie and Mom flit between guests like they own the place.

With many eyes on us, I introduce my wife to several people, and greet even more. It's a whirlwind of small talk and pleasantries, and Cora handles every introduction with quiet poise and quick wit.

An art I mastered a long time ago, but it feels different with her by my side. Less pretentious?

She leans in, her voice barely audible above the music, when we finally have a moment alone. "The golden boy returns. How does it feel?"

"I'm no longer the golden boy."

"Based on the reception line we just got, I beg to differ."

I smirk. "I burned that title to the ground years ago. They're all tripping over to meet you, dear wife."

She beams. "I always wanted to be the talk of the town," she says with sarcasm.

I laugh. "Careful what you wish for. Do you want to take a break and find a corner to make out? I know a few nooks around here."

She runs her fingers down my arm, sliding into my hand like she was always meant to be held by me. "I don't even want to know why and with whom you discovered those nooks." She pretend-glares.

"I still can't wait to take that dress off," I whisper in her ear, her laughter spreading inside my chest.

When I lift my gaze, my spine straightens.

Sterling Stone.

Silver-haired, impeccably dressed, hands clasped behind his back like he's already halfway through a keynote speech, he gives me a curt nod.

The last two years apart haven't dulled the steel in his posture, or the cool precision in his eyes.

I consider pretending I didn't see him, but he starts toward us.

"Son." He nods curtly and turns to Cora, smiling. "I'm sorry I missed you last night; you must be Cora.

So very nice to meet you." He clasps her hand in both of his.

"Cora, this is my father, Sterling Stone. Dad, this is my wife."

"It's so great to have you here with us." Father smiles at her. "Marianne worked so hard on this event, and having the whole family here means a lot. I hope we will see more of you."

He finally lets go of her hands and looks at me. I know that look well. Not triumph. Not manipulation. Just a silent satisfaction. He got what he wanted. His family reunited.

"It's good to be back, Dad," I choke out, and it's the fucking truth.

Dad pats my shoulder. "I have some more mingling to suffer through, but I'll see you kids at the dinner table."

"He's nice." Cora cocks her head, searching my face, evidently surprised by the civility of the encounter.

That's because I'm the villain in this story. "I need to—"

"Ladies and gentlemen, please take your seats," the announcement interrupts me.

Yet again. For fuck's sake. It's like the universe doesn't want me to be honest with her.

Perhaps I'm making too big a deal out of nothing. Just like I did two years ago when I fled from here.

We pass under arches of white roses and soft, gold lighting toward our table and settle into our seats.

Nana Sybil is already seated, wearing a pale lavender turban and at least three heirlooms from the Stone vaults.

"I told the designer I wanted a train," she complains to Lottie who is seated beside her, "and the old bastard gave me a bustle. I look like a peacock in mourning."

"Hello, Nana." I kiss her cheek.

"You look great, Sybil." Cora smiles, and my grandmother pats her hand.

Dad and Mom join us.

"I love your dress, darling." Mom kisses Cora as she takes her seat on the other side of Dad. "Where is Liam?"

"I'm here," my brother grumbles, and falls into the last empty chair.

Nana Sybil holds her champagne flute aloft like a weapon. "I told the waiter if he bends over one more time, I'm going to tuck a twenty in his waistband."

Lottie snorts. Cora stifles a laugh, squeezing my thigh.

"Welcome to the Stone family." I shrug.

"I guess I know where you got your playful gene." She snorts.

"Mother," my father says mildly, "please don't harass the staff."

"Oh, please do, Nana." Liam raises his flute. "This evening needs a bit of spice."

"William," Mother says sternly.

"Oh, please..." Nana waves her hand. "He winked at me first. If I were thirty years younger and slightly less unhinged, I'd take him home like a party favor."

This time Cora spits into her napkin, while I snort.

Soon enough, we settle into small talk, and I watch my family warm to my wife like embers catching.

She fits here. She really fits.

For a moment, I forget what's coming.

Until Dad raises a glass. "To Marianne—for hosting the gala of the season. And to Xander—for finally joining the family again."

My mother beams.

Cora stiffens beside me. "Not without *encouragement*," she says, sarcasm coating her words.

I squeeze her thigh. Please, for fuck's sake, let's not unravel this here and now.

All she is doing is defending me against my father's blackmail, as she calls it.

Dad frowns at her frosty tone. "All I asked was that

he attend tonight—for his mother, and the legacy she's built with this event."

Cora blinks. Her eyes narrow faintly. "That's all you asked?" She snorts.

Mom's head jerks, and Dad looks puzzled, while Lottie, Liam, and Nana lean back, wine in hands, like this is the most riveting performance they've ever seen. At my fucking expense.

Dad clears his throat. "Of course. Marianne deserves to have her family under one roof again."

Cora turns to my mom. "I'm sorry, Marianne, but you should know your husband forced Xander to marry. He made it a condition for helping him with a business deal."

The entire table stills.

"And the plot thickens," Liam gloats.

"What?" Mom's voice is a whisper, her eyes darting between me and Dad.

"Son?" My father studies me, his expression a mixture of concern and surprise.

Cora's gaze swings toward me, her eyebrows drawn. "Xander?"

"What's going on?" Lottie asks.

"Hush," Nana admonishes. "We reached the main program."

Liam snorts.

"What is Cora talking about?" Dad's voice can cut steel.

I open my mouth. The words don't come. Because the lie—my lie—is sitting at the center of the table now, fully dressed in candlelight and linen.

"I'm sure this is some misunderstanding," Mom chirps. "This chestnut bisque is fantastic."

All heads swivel to her at her effort to salvage the situation.

"Excuse me." Cora pushes the chair, throwing the linen napkin onto her plate.

I move to pursue her, but my father grips my arm. "No scandals," he warns, whispering.

Jerking away, I slouch in the chair. Cora's soup soaks through the napkin, drowning it like I'm drowning under the weight of my lie.

Chapter 27

Cora

I rush out of the ballroom, my heels digging into the carpeted floor of the long hallway. Oxygen is not reaching my lungs, the shock of the revelation spreading through me painfully.

Images flicker through my mind. Ethan proposing. Dad coming home late. Ethan laughing when I begged him not to drive recklessly. The little boy who looks like him. Dad falling to the sofa when Mom closed the door behind her, leaving us.

The feelings are genuine. I love you, Cora.

You turned this sprinter into a marathon runner.

I became a one-woman man.

He lied.

He lied.

He lied.

Just like Ethan. Like my father.

He tricked me.

I get to the end of the hallway, a gray double door mocking me. A fire exit. Fuck, I ran the wrong way. A part of me wants to push the crash bar. The shriek of an alarm would be better than the screams in my head.

But I spoiled Marianne's evening enough. Well, her son did.

I let out a stifled scream, but the chaos in my mind is still louder.

Calm the fuck down, Cora.

I lean against the wall, grateful that the vast space is abandoned. I stand there for what feels like several lifetimes.

The jumble of images of all the betrayals quiets down slowly at one point as I slide down to the ground.

Numb.

Disappointed.

Disillusioned.

How do we bounce back from this? What else did he lie about?

There is a minuscule part of me—an emotionally exhausted part—that believes that we had started with a lie, but the rest was real.

I always knew he was an entitled rich boy, and I fell anyway. Fuck.

He said he loved me. Just a few hours ago, he

declared his love. It should count for something, but it almost makes the whole situation worse.

He made this relationship real while he's been lying to me.

I groan. My mind is spinning fruitlessly. I should leave. I should take a cab straight to the airport and get the fuck out of here.

It's not like I want to face the Stones, and especially not their golden-boy son right now. Goddammit.

The exit door opens, and two members of staff enter. One of them jerks their head, staring at me in shock.

Yeah, I'm sitting on the ground here in a several-thousand-dollar gown. A fucking Cinderella. They must think I'm drunk.

"Are you lost?" one of them asks.

I sniffle and stand up. "I am very much lost. Would you mind if I sneak out here?" I beckon my head toward the exit the other guy is still holding open.

"We shouldn't—" he starts.

"Let her." The other one shrugs, and her colleague opens the door wider.

I step into a narrow alley and pause. The passage is shadowed and reeks of old rain and cigarette smoke. The sky still holds the final flush of evening, but down here, it feels later—darker.

I hug my arms around myself. The wind sneaks

into my dress, curling around my legs. The light on each side of the passageway feels quite far. How big is this venue?

Lifting my skirt, I start walking. So much for a beautiful dress and stealing the show.

Asshole. He spoiled the night for everybody. And it doesn't even seem he cared to run after me.

He probably did... in the right direction, unlike me.

Instead of spending a lovely evening in a beautiful venue, I'm in a smelly corner in the middle of junkie alley. Just great.

In the span of the past half an hour, I went from betrayal to anger, to annoyance to sadness... rinse and repeat.

The wall juts out in places, flaking brick and graffiti. A fire escape on the wall beside me blocks almost the entire width of the pathway. I turn sideways, slipping past it, wrinkling my nose at the odor coming from a pile of garbage under the metal structure.

A shape moves. A rustle. A low grunt.

A figure stirs in the shadows, and I freeze. My heart stutters. My breath catches. My pulse spikes into my throat, pounding in terror.

Another shift. Jesus, it's a person. They cough and mutter something unintelligible.

I scream. Loud, raw, involuntary.

I try to run, but the heel of my shoe catches. The

hem of my dress snags on a jagged bolt sticking out of the fire staircase. I twist, tugging it violently, panic rising in a wave.

Swearing, I yank again, the fabric giving with a rip that echoes too loud.

I whip around and scream again, my body colliding against a solid wall of muscles.

Strong arms wrap around me.

I twist, panic still gripping my chest, but I know that scent. That warmth. That hold.

"Cora," Xander breathes against my hair. "It's me. It's just me."

His voice is a balm. A grounding rope thrown into my swirling storm.

I collapse against him, exhausted. Not physically, not from fear or from anger. From everything else that refuses to stay locked inside.

His heartbeat hammers against my cheek. He holds me tighter like he needs the reassurance, too.

"Don't," I whisper. "Don't act like you care." Despite my protest, I don't push away.

Perhaps I'm a liar too. And right now, I want to soak in this illusion. For a moment, I want to be a damsel in distress, finding refuge in the arms of my knight.

Because the other reality is just too sad. In our real life, I need to be a strong, independent woman who fights for her values. Who doesn't let him walk all over me. Who does what she thinks is right in this situation.

But fuck, if I don't want to just forget and move on.

"I do," he murmurs into my hair.

"You lied."

"I know."

We stand there in our own agonizing impasse, holding on to each other for dear life, knowing it's a fleeting opportunity before we must address the things that will probably break us.

And if I shut down my rational, offended, disappointed mind, all other pieces of me want to lean into him more.

My body. My heart. My soul.

"Did he hurt you?" He rubs his hand down my back, and I want him to keep it there forever.

I hate this roller coaster of emotions, which makes no sense while it makes all the sense in the world.

"No, just scared me."

"Let's get out of here. The stench is nauseating."

I nod and let him hold my hand, leading us out of there. As I try to hold my skirt up with my other hand, I see the tear is huge.

"God, this dress is a rental. It's going to cost a fortune."

We reach the street, and I snatch my hand from

his. As comforting as it felt, I don't want him to think the issue is resolved.

Xander reaches into his pocket and pulls out his wallet. He hands me a small golden card. A credit card.

When I don't reach for it, because what the fuck, he sighs. "It's yours." He shoves it into my hand.

I blink at my name embossed on the golden card, and my anger returns full speed. "I've just found out about your betrayal, and now you hand me a credit card? Is that your solution to everything? Just throwing money at your problems."

"Yeah, pretty much," he snaps. Then he sighs again, shaking his head. "Fuck. That's not what I... I had this issued for you before we left New York. I just didn't get a chance to give it to you."

"And you pick this moment. You're impossible."

"I didn't want you to worry about the dress, besides everything else..." He looks away.

Jesus. This man, with his well-intended, fucked-up gestures.

"I shouldn't be surprised. This started with you throwing a wad of cash at me."

He flinches, but doesn't respond.

Vibrating, he paces a few feet forward before he turns back, the nervous energy radiating from him.

"Fuck, when I heard your scream, I... I..." He takes

hold of my shoulders and just stares at me, scanning me for injuries, or perhaps memorizing me.

His frown and wild gaze, full of anguish, have a direct line to my heart. But it's his fault we both feel like shit right now.

"Thank God you're okay," he breathes out, and steps closer, but then stops himself and lets out another loaded breath.

Despite my shock and bitterness, I want to reach out for him. But I hold back, because trust is earned, and he has stomped all over mine.

He pulls out his phone and starts texting. "I'm having the car come around for us."

"I'm not getting into a car with you." I lift the ruined dress and start marching, as if I know where I'm going.

"Cora," he growls. "If you don't get in the car with me, then what? We will do it here and now?"

I whip around, glaring. "Do what?"

"Talk."

I put my hands on my hips. Is he for real? "A bit too late for that."

"Cora." He sighs again.

He dares to sigh again.

"Don't fucking Cora me. Has all of it been a lie?" I guess we're having the conversation here after all.

He bows his head, exhaling, and when he looks at

me I step back, because the agony in his expression hurts me. And that pisses me off, because he has no right to make me feel sorry for him.

"Cora, I love you. I care about you. You must know that's true."

"I also thought just a few minutes ago that your father is a manipulative man who refused to help you unless you marry."

"You never believed I wanted you for you. You didn't allow yourself to even try to be fully in... because I have more money, because I'm younger, because I fucked other women before you. So many fucking objections. There was always something you would hold against me. Never have you tried to see me for me. And now you finally have a real excuse to bolt."

He lets out a snort, thick with bitterness—but beneath it, there is something fractured. Hurt. Desperation. Misery.

His words slice through me like the sharpest knife. Like a double-edged sword. Because he is right. I tried so desperately to talk myself out of this relationship. I didn't allow myself to get to know the real him.

But that doesn't give him the right to accuse me of forcing him to lie.

"You're too entitled to take *no* as an answer. How dare you blame me?"

He shakes his head. "The lie is on me, but I didn't

see any other option at the time. That night you attended the gala with me... you bewitched me. And I couldn't let go. I tried; believe me, I fucking tried."

"So you tricked me," I sneer.

In my periphery, I notice heads turning.

"I fucked up," he grits out. "People fuck up, but people in relationships talk about shit, make amends, and forgive."

"Since when are you an expert on relationships? Making amends? I haven't heard you saying sorry."

He stares at me for a moment, the anger evaporating. I can almost see the fight leaving him, flying out on its dark cloud as some strange sadness sets in his features. I can almost imagine his internal struggle to reconcile deeply ingrained beliefs with the current need.

It's like he is tasting the words in his mind, but they are so foreign, his brain is rejecting them. "You know I don't believe in that."

My heart breaks. Not only for me. Only for us.

But for the little boy who grew up in a world where apologizing is not acceptable. "Saying sorry doesn't make you weak, Xander. It makes you stronger."

He hangs his head and then looks back at me, pleading. It's the strangest thing, seeing a man larger than life so broken. So vulnerable.

"I love you, Cora. The man I used to be when we

met was a short pit stop in my life while I waited for you. Can we please move past this?"

"I don't know." Another piece of my heart shatters.

"What can I do?"

And this is the reason I'm not yet at the airport. *What can I do?* That question is his apology.

He can't say the words, but he showed me time and again with his actions. Sometimes his actions are completely outlandish, but he always tries to do things for me. To care for me.

And unlike at the beginning, when he would give me a random island, he tunes in now, he tries, he asks for guidance.

That breaks my heart further, because I don't want to be in this situation, but I don't know how to get out of it.

"I don't know." I let out a loaded breath.

"I wanted you so badly that I lied. But the underlying sentiment behind my abhorrent action should count for something."

On the opposite side of the value scale, across from his genuine loving care, sits his entitlement. And that, too, is something that is a part of his personality.

Something I admire at times because I lack in that area. But right now, it fucking pisses me off.

"So I should just be happy and move on?" I throw my hands up in exasperation. "When you were standing in my bedroom, telling me about your father the day you proposed, I thought you were vulnerable, opening up to me. I thought we were bonding. And you were just spitting lies."

"The reason for my proposal was fabricated, but the story wasn't. My feelings that day were real. As real as they are today."

"You know what I learned over the past few weeks? The revelation about Ethan and my dad? That nothing is what it seems."

"Don't you fucking compare me to them."

I let out a bitter laugh. "I almost started believing you were more than an entitled rich boy... but I guess, sometimes, things *are* what they look like."

He steps closer, his chest heaving. "I made a mistake. I wanted to tell you many times."

I snort. "And I should believe that?" I turn to leave finally. This is such an unproductive conversation.

He grips my arm, forcing me to look at him. "Remember in the car after we went shopping? And when you came home and found me reading with Pavel. Or when I sought you out in the pool yesterday, then last night, and today... Today, we got interrupted by Lottie."

I jerk my arm away. "So you tried a few times... that makes me feel so much better. You failed to try for the gazillion other minutes we were together."

Xander's nostrils flare. We're riding on a wave of emotions that forces snarls from us we may regret. I guess that's better than keeping it bottled up.

On the edge of my mind, something screams at me to stop. I'm arguing with him, while I desperately want us to put the argument behind us.

I can't live without him.

The thought invades me with staggering clarity, at the same time as I'm blinded with a flash.

"Fuck," Xander utters under his nose, grabbing my hand.

I'm stomping behind him, my heels tearing the dress even more as the paps follow. Xander ignores them, barreling through, rushing us to the car.

"I'm not leaving with you," I say through my teeth, not wanting anyone to record the words.

I also don't attempt to wiggle out of his vise-like grasp. Cameras click, and words are shouted. I don't hear any of it, my focus on the touch of his hand around mine. On the fact that he's dragging me to safety.

I stumble again, the hem of my skirt now stamped with the sharp spike of my heel. Someone pushes us. I keep my head down, more feeling than seeing the phones of onlookers angled at us.

Xander in New York is fairly anonymous, but clearly on his home turf it's a different story.

One of the suited guards from the estate appears from somewhere, and with his help we reach the waiting car, engine running.

Before the car barely moves, Xander pulls out his phone and yells at his lawyer. My pulse is slowly finding a regular rhythm. The adrenaline spikes in the past hour can't be good for my health.

"No, let's not wait and see..." Xander growls into the phone. "If there are any fucking pictures of my distraught wife anywhere, you're fired."

He ends the call and turns to me. "Are you okay?"

I sigh, closing my eyes. "That is kind of a loaded question at the moment."

"At the moment." He tastes the words and squeezes my hand. "That gives me hope."

I want to pull away. He doesn't get off this easily.

But however many objections I have, I know I will forgive him. This man who never says sorry, but threatens to fire his lawyer because my pictures may appear in the media.

This man who made up a lie, but married me because he really wanted to. As fucked up as it is. Maybe not out of love, but because he wanted to help me. Or be with me?

"Don't get ahead of yourself." I turn to the window, but I keep my hand in his.

Not holding—just letting the touch slowly rebuild the shaken walls of our union.

"Fair enough." He brings my knuckles to his mouth.

"I only wanted to protect myself." The adrenaline crush seeps into my bones, the exhaustion growing.

I turn to him, his beautiful face frowning.

"You were right," I continue. "I did see you as a young, rich playboy. But I also saw this playful, carefree, confident, and generous man, who made me laugh and who challenged me. I wasn't sure which version would hurt me more. But I saw you for you, Xander. Always. The problem was, I never saw myself as someone who belonged at your side."

We stare at each other, the space between us filled with tension, sadness, and frustration. But also with an ever-present pull. A pull I had tried to ignore when we met. A pull that has been prevalent between us beyond logic, expectations, pre-conceived notions.

I move my fingers slowly to wrap them around his, holding his hand back.

Xander squeezes with a sad but hopeful smile.

And then something snaps in me, and I push off my seat, swing my leg over, and straddle him.

Xander's eyes widen with surprise before I fuse my mouth with his. The kiss is desperate and frustrating, because it doesn't fully satiate the burning need inside me.

This might be adrenaline. This might be a mistake after all that transpired today, but for once, I need to take what I want. Not what I should. Or what others might expect.

My hands yank at the clasp of his pants. I pull his zipper down. Xander grips my wrist before I can reach into his waistband, and I groan. I fucking groan.

"Are you sure this is what you want right now?" His voice is strained. He's about to lose it, but he's making sure I consent to what I started… He's giving me pause, so I don't regret my impulsiveness.

"I'm not sure about want, but I need it. I need you to make the hurt go away. Make me feel better."

It's like I released a trigger. Xander grips the neckline of my dress and rips it apart.

"It was ruined anyway." He shrugs and latches onto my nipple.

He bites and soothes with his tongue.

He squeezes with his hands.

My back arches as a primal moan leaves my lips.

"Take. Out. My. Cock. Coraline."

My skin throbs with need. My mind is dazed. My heart is pounding. My body needing. Needing more. So much yearning.

His cock is hard like a rod, pre-cum glistening on

his tip. I squeeze his base tight, and Xander growls. He pulls me in for another kiss, fisting my hair.

And then he moves my underwear to the side. "Look at you, beautiful pussy, needing me so much."

I practically drip into his hand. Good, because I don't want to waste time; I want him to fill me.

I push his hand away and position his head at my entrance. We watch as I lower myself. However we got here, this is where I want to be right now.

The anger still sizzles, the hurt still lingers, the damage exists. But no road is without obstacles, and deep down, I know he didn't want to hurt me. Deep down, I know his lie wasn't a betrayal.

It was manipulation, for sure, but we can get over this. I can get over this, because we love each other.

"Fuck me, husband," I drawl as a form of absolution.

He didn't apologize.

I forgave.

I shouldn't have.

Chapter 28

Cora

SAAR

When is the housewarming?

I'm still unpacking.

CELESTE

Is the bistro open yet?

No (eye-roll emoji). It's a never-ending project.

SAAR

It's going to be great.

That's what Tessa thinks.

CELESTE

We need to find a new spot to hang out. I miss you.

I miss you too. I'm sorry, it's been a crazy month.

SAAR

Let's have lunch together soon.

* * *

"Thank you for meeting with me," I say, my hands clammy as I shake Andrew's hand.

Andrew Sinclair is a literary agent who called out of the blue and wanted to meet me, raving about my stories.

Out of the blue is incorrect, because I know Xander is behind it. A part of me wanted to fight him on it, but I'm learning to accept help from others.

We order lunch at a swanky restaurant on Madison Avenue and East 61st Street, while he tells me what he loved about my stories and goes through a detailed list of notes about suggested revisions.

My initial unease and nervousness evaporate within the first five minutes. Andrew is very easy to talk to, knowledgeable, and his suggestions are great. Most of them, anyway, but he lets me express my opinions without pushing me in his direction.

Our creative brainstorming flows so naturally, I don't even realize what I ate until the plate is empty.

"I have a confession, Cora. When Xander called, demanding I read your stories, I did so out of obligation. But I'm glad I read them, and I agree with him; they shouldn't stay in your drawer."

"Thank you."

"I invited you here because I wanted to see how difficult you are to potentially work with." He takes off his glasses. "And I'm pleased to see that you're smart and creative, but also flexible with your artistic vision, which is a brilliant combination."

"You have a great sense for storytelling, and certainly more experience than me. I enjoyed this creative session. It wasn't as slaughtering as I feared." I smile at him.

He laughs. "I'm glad to hear that. I would like to represent you. I also think Xander's idea for the book launch is fantastic, but would better suit a smaller publisher. Are you okay with that?"

"Xander's idea for the launch?" I'm barely accepting that I may share my stories with the world, and he's already planning the launch?

"To launch it at the schools that partake in the healthy lunch program you run."

I giggle nervously, trying to hide my confusion. "What are you talking about?"

"I thought you ran it, since it's called C.O.R.A."

I blink a few times. "I don't run it." I remain vague, because Andrew may reconsider his collaboration with a woman who either has memory loss or is completely oblivious.

"Shit, I hope I didn't spoil any surprises."

I laugh, sounding only slightly deranged. "It's too soon to talk about the release event anyway."

* * *

"I need you to approve these changes to the layout." Tessa pushes blueprints and spreadsheets in front of me as soon as I enter.

"Hello to you, too."

I plop down on one of the two chairs left in the place. The space has been stripped to its bare bones.

I spent all my childhood birthdays here. I drank my first Zinfandel here. I have slaved here for the past few years.

But it's like my memories belong to a different space. It's unrecognizable. Yes, it's still under construction, but it's been reshaped, changed, and... improved. It will take a moment before I find my place here again.

"Hello." Tessa sighs. "I'm sorry, I've been here since six o'clock, and I need to move on with these. What do you think?"

I'm kind of grateful she wants my opinion, but also annoyed. Her enthusiasm doesn't reach me. It kills the creative flow that carried me from my lunch with Andrew.

I entered the bistro eager to share my news with my sister, and instead I'm being pulled into this. I mean, it's my business and my job, so why does it feel like a distraction? Like a nuisance?

The idea squeezes at my stomach, but it's more because the whole concept of this business lingers in the past.

"What am I looking at?" I squint at the drawings in front of me.

"Jesus, don't sound so enthusiastic," Tessa huffs, but immediately launches into a detailed explanation of the proposed changes.

"I didn't know we would remodel the whole place. We hired Gina to help us with publicity, profitability, and reopening. This is way above and beyond—"

"Cora, Cora, Cora." She sighs. "We've been closed for weeks now, so why not spruce up this place to its maximum potential?"

"What would Dad say?"

As the question falls between us, I realize I asked on autopilot, not because it matters or because he cares, but because somewhere deep down, I still live the reality of preserving his place, his legacy. Of him caring about it.

"It doesn't matter. He's not coming back. Besides, you haven't visited him since you learned about the real reason behind our parents' break-up, so I'm not sure why you ask."

Yeah, I haven't found it in me to face him yet. It's

not even about forgiveness. He broke our family and has lived with the consequences ever since. I don't need to add my disappointment to it.

I forgave him, I think, but I still can't go there and just pretend things are what they used to be. Nothing is what it used to be.

"You're right. I think these are great. Let's move forward with them."

"I'm going to visit him later today. Do you want to come?"

I should. I really should. But today has been wonderful so far, and I'm not ready yet.

"I still have a lot of unpacking to tackle." It's not a lie. Nor is it a good excuse, but here we are.

"Okay, but go see him sooner rather than later." Tessa, who's spent about a tenth of the time with him I have, sounds all sensible and concerned.

Maybe this project did change her in a good way. And maybe that is the best legacy from what Dad started.

"You know what. I'll go with you."

The visit is like any other, and completely different. Dad is quiet, deep in his own world, and I, for once, don't feel the heavy duty of pulling him out.

He made his choices. Those choices affected my life. But I can't change the past. I can only embrace the present, and make better choices about my future.

Holding Dad's hand, with my head on his shoulder, I let Tess chirp about the bistro. It's a surreal moment with our little family.

My sister is different. My bond with Dad has shifted. Despite everything, we're still us.

A small, dysfunctional family.

So different from Xander's.

I think about the distinction as I make my way to the townhouse. Our upbringing and family dynamics are another gap between us I would have held against him—us—a few weeks ago, but getting to know my husband, I realized we all have many facets, and I can't judge and assume.

Even Dad, with his own drama and betrayal, still showed up for me in many ways. The Zinfandel birthdays were real. He was there for me after Ethan.

These are the memories I'm going to cling to.

And similar loving, joyful memories are what close the gaps between me and Xander.

Kindness means we give the other person a chance. Perhaps they prove us right. Hopefully, they will surprise us pleasantly.

Not giving a chance means potentially robbing myself of a beautiful experience.

On the way home, I buy a bouquet of sunflowers. Getting the vase, I find a small box with my favorite pistachio Danish and a note on the kitchen counter.

I love you, Coraline. X.

Every day I find something from him that makes me feel seen. Happy. Content.

It's the little gestures like the notes, a rare vintage of Zinfandel, a book, or an ice cream. So much more meaningful than the island.

I smile, inhaling the scent of my home—sunflowers, moving boxes, Xander's cologne. Perfection.

Xander has been extra attentive in the past two weeks since we returned from California. He couldn't say he was sorry, but he's making sure he shows it to me.

I walk into the living room looking for the cats. The bay window alcove has quickly become my favorite place in our new home. The house is still a war zone with boxes and haphazardly strewn furniture, but here I find peace. Here I write my stories. Here I wait for Xander to come home.

And here I find Pitt and Clooney, who quickly claimed the upholstered bench as their own. I scratch their heads, sit, and finally search up C.O.R.A. online.

Community Outreach for Responsible Appetite is a project run by a woman I don't know—not me or Xander—and the spokesperson is Pavel. My neighbor

Pavel. His school is where the healthy lunch initiative started.

Xander Stone, when on earth did you manage this?

He comes home later, looking his usual gorgeous self, and finds me still at the bench.

"I'm finally sure we have only two cats." He leans against the wall, smiling at me.

We have two cats.

"Maybe the other eight are hiding."

"They are not. My wife isn't an old cat lady."

I laugh. "Isn't she?"

"How was your meeting with Andrew?"

Still wearing his suit, with one leg crossed at the ankle and his tie loosened, he looks both a powerful business executive and a playful man who brings lightness to my life.

My smile widens. "Great. Thank you for taking the first step for me."

"Any time, love, any time."

Pushing off the wall, he leans in to kiss me. Pitt protests loudly and jumps down. Clooney stretches his paws and follows.

"Finally, they know who the boss is," Xander murmurs and sits beside me, his lips on mine.

I giggle into the kiss. "Keep thinking that."

He hoists me over, positioning me on his lap, straddling him. "I will need to stuff that pretty little mouth of yours with my cock."

His words zip through me like an electric current. I'm instantly aroused. And interested, even though we've never done that after I shared my feelings about blowjobs.

He snakes his arms around me. "Just talk." He peppers my collarbone with kisses, staying true to his promise we'd only do what I'm comfortable with.

"I'd like to taste you."

He lifts his gaze. "Are you sure?"

"It might be a very mediocre blowjob given my lack of experience, but it will be an eager one." I bite my bottom lip.

"I want to be chivalrous and tell you it's not necessary, but I'm a simple man, and your offer redirected my blood from my brain to..." He looks down, to where his erection strains against his pants.

I lift my hips and unzip him. "We need to help you with that. But before that, let me think about any benefits I could gain from that lack of blood in your brain."

He laughs. "As if there was anything I would ever deny you." He kisses me while he fists his cock. "I don't even need to be dazzled by your pussy."

I slide down to kneel in front of him. "I might need some instructions."

"Wrap your mouth around my cock and enjoy. Just like a lollipop or an ice cream."

I roll my eyes. "I want to do it right." I wrap my hand around his girth, and he hisses.

That simple sound gives me confidence.

"Coraline, take my cock into your pretty mouth. Just discover. We have a lifetime to perfect your skills."

We have a lifetime.

I lick my lips and then flick my tongue over his tip, tasting the clean saltiness of him. He hisses again, and I look up, our gazes clashing.

"Warning, I don't think I can last," he grits out.

His struggle, along with his heated gaze, spurs me into action, and I wrap my lips around him, slowly taking as much of him in as possible. It's not much, but I try to compensate with my hands.

"Fuck, Cora, such a good girl. You... are... doing..." he pants, "so good."

I find a rhythm, feeling my own arousal pooling in my panties. I didn't expect this heady feeling. This satisfaction. I didn't appreciate how intoxicating it could be.

Xander's hands curl into fists at his side. He's trying to hold onto some control, letting me lead. Even in this, he puts me first.

The intimacy of the moment spreads in my chest, burning, consuming me.

"I'm coming," he groans, pushing me away.

But I don't let go.

"Cora," he cries, and spills himself inside my mouth before he collapses against the window.

"You taste good." I wipe the corner of my mouth when he looks at me, his eyes burning with desire and adoration.

"That was the best head ever." He pulls me up, settling me back astride his legs, my skirt hiked up.

"You don't have to lie to me, but I enjoyed it."

"I can see that." He smirks, eyeing the wet patch on my panties. "And I'm not lying. Everything is better, bolder, and new when love is a part of the equation."

I kiss him, playing with the hair on his neck.

"Thank you for the Danish."

"Had I known you'd suck my cock for that, I would have gotten one sooner." He winks.

I laugh. "You did get me a few before."

We stare at each other, grinning, like this is the only place to be. Like the life outside of this bubble doesn't exist.

I give him a peck. "Before we continue with the evening program, would you care to tell me about C.O.R.A.?"

He raises his eyebrows. "What is the evening program?"

"It will be unpacking if you don't start talking."

"It seems like you already know." He shrugs.

"Why didn't you tell me about it?"

He trails my chin with his finger, the touch light and reverent. "I don't know; it felt like bragging."

I snort. "It's called sharing, you idiot."

He grabs the back of my neck and pulls me in for a kiss. It's deep and passionate. "I'll get better at sharing, I promise."

And I know he will.

"I love you, Xander Stone. Unconditionally."

He cups my face in both his hands, not kissing me, just holding me. "No one has ever chosen me without conditions."

"No one has ever believed in me the way you do."

"I guess we're meant to be together."

"I guess it's always been inevitable." I kiss him gently. "Besides, you named a charity after me," I tease.

"What can I say, Coraline—I used to think profit was the only metric worth chasing. Then you handed me a cereal box and rewired my brain."

We grin at each other, before he scoops me up and carries me to the bedroom where we enjoy each other, foolishly believing we've found our forever.

Chapter 29

Cora

"Do you think we can expand that fast?" I look at the projections.

"I think we need to up our fundraising efforts to make sure we're not dependent on your family's donations only, but I think we can," Britney, C.O.R.A.'s managing director, explains.

"Okay, let's do it. Let's schedule a brainstorming session about potential ways to find additional funding sources. Let's invite some close-to-us teachers and parents, and I'll talk to Xander to get a few business people in. Different minds, different ideas."

After I found out about C.O.R.A., I got involved immediately. That was a month ago, and things are getting busier every day because we're adding new schools to the program. I love it.

"Good." Britney smiles. "I will send you potential

dates, and we'll see who is available to help us prepare the plan."

I used to judge my sister for her involvement with different causes. All of them were in need, but her involvement didn't feel genuine. Like she did it just to fill her time. Like many other wives of rich men, in my previous limited viewpoint.

And now I'm one of them, but I see a different angle: I enjoy the freedom of spending my time where it matters, because I don't have to worry about making ends meet. Spreading kindness because I can and want to, not because duty calls.

"Let's also plan a few activities for the holidays. We still have a few weeks to put something together," I suggest.

"On it." She salutes me. "Before you go, could I get your input on the menu for next month?"

We spend another hour talking about menus. For years at the bistro, designing the menu has been a chore—always looking for ideas that are economical and appealing at the same time.

Here, we're looking for economical and nutritious ,while appealing to picky children, and none of it feels like a chore.

After I finish, I call Tessa. "Will you need me today?"

"Playing hooky again?"

"I want to review the manuscript revisions, but I'll come if you need me."

"I'm good. Go do your thing. I hope you show up for our opening."

"When is that again?" I tease.

"Too soon if you ask me. So much work. You wouldn't believe—" She launches into retelling me all her grievances with a carpenter, a furniture supplier, and the city approval process. Today, she also adds a few anecdotes from the interviews with potential employees.

I listen, grateful she tackles so much with pretended reluctance. Grateful she found something that makes her happy. And grateful I don't have to deal with all of that.

Finding a small coffee shop, I order a latte and open my laptop. Time flies as I dive into revisions.

When I finally stretch, I find a message from Xander.

XANDER

Do you want to grab lunch together? I'm free at noon. Just come by my office. Xoxo

I'll be there. I hope you feed me well.

XANDER

My cock is waiting.

I laugh and start packing up my things. The café is warm with the scent of cinnamon and ground espresso, bustling but calm.

When I lift my gaze, I see a familiar face. "Sanjay!"

I'm on my feet before I can think, a smile stretching across my face. God, it's good to see him.

Of all the people who kept me sane during the last year at the bistro, Sanjay was my lighthouse. He believed in me when I didn't believe in myself. He was the first person who motivated me to even contemplate changing things up.

He startles at the sound of his name. "Cora?"

But his voice isn't nearly as joyous as I feel. He steps back slightly, clutching a green apron as if it's a shield, his knuckles white against the fabric.

I falter, mid-stride. "Do you work here now?"

He glances around, like he's afraid someone's watching. "I only came back because my sister is sick."

Came back?

My brow furrows. "I'm sorry to hear that. But... I thought you *left* because she was sick. I thought she lived in Chicago."

He goes still. His mouth opens and shuts like he's trying to breathe underwater.

"I don't want to get into trouble," he says quickly, almost in a whisper. "Let's just pretend you didn't see me."

"Sanjay..." I lower my voice, stepping closer. "What are you talking about? I'm happy to see you."

His eyes flit toward the exit. Fight or flight? Something is very off.

"Look, Cora, I regretted it the second I took the money." The words tumble out too fast. "I mean, my family needed it. But I never—I never wanted to betray you. I relented only because I knew he'd fix everything."

My stomach drops, and I don't even know why. He makes no sense.

"What money?" My voice is careful now, trembling at the edges.

Sanjay swallows. "Please know I would've never left you. Not unless—" He breaks off, guilt etched across his face. "But I knew he would take care of things for you. I knew you'd be okay."

A beat of silence stretches, taut and unbearable.

"Who?" I ask, even though I already know. I feel it in the clench of my jaw, in the sudden throb behind my eyes. But I fight that thought because... no, no, no.

He looks at me like a kid caught in a lie. "Mr. Stone."

Xander.

The air around me thins, warping like heat off the sidewalk. "Xander paid you to leave?"

He nods, just once. "I'm sorry. I—I didn't know

what else to do. He said you needed a fresh start, and he could fix it faster without me in the way. And he was offering enough to—" His voice cracks. "I was trying to do what was best for my family. But it was wrong."

My hands tremble as I clench my notebook to my chest.

The betrayal stings sharper than I thought it would. Not because Sanjay took the money—I can understand desperation.

But Xander.

Another lie.

Another betrayal.

Why?

Why would he destroy my business?

To manipulate me.

In light of Sanjay's admission, the lie about Xander's father forcing him to marry pales.

I manage a nod, though I'm not sure what it's meant to signal. That I understand? That I don't?

"Thank you for telling me." I don't recognize my own voice—flat, as though all the air's been punched out of me.

"I'm really sorry, Cora."

"Yeah." I offer a tight smile and leave before he can say more.

I don't want to fall apart in a coffee shop. Not here.

Not now.

Outside, the city moves around me, uncaring. But inside, something is cracking.

And this time, it might not glue back together quite so easily.

* * *

I don't know how long I wander around aimlessly. The worst part? I can't reach deep enough to find anger or sadness. I'm just numb, completely empty.

Someone bumps into me and I stumble, but it's New York, and crowds flow around me, unaffected by my personal turmoil.

He paid off Sanjay.

I wish I could just laugh it off. I wish I could go back to this morning, when we both climaxed in the shower before I left the house with a spring in my step.

My phone vibrates in my purse, but I don't want to look at it. I don't want to merge back into daily existence as if nothing has happened.

The vibration doesn't stop.

I relent.

I dash into another cafe and shiver as the AC air accosts me.

"Are you in the line?" someone urges behind me.

I shake my head and slouch into an empty chair. I

finally fish out my phone. On the locked screen, I see several missed calls and messages.

XANDER

Lunch is waiting.

Are you running late?

Where the fuck are you?

Cora, I'm going crazy here. Answer the phone.

God, I hope you're okay.

The phone rings, and I drop it to the table, startled. The picture of Xander's grinning face mocks me.

There is no point in dragging the agony out. I answer.

"Cora, for fuck's sake. I got Lindsay calling around the emergency rooms. Where are you? Are you okay, love?"

Love?

I want to find words, but they are not coming.

"Cora?"

I look around, searching for an anchor. Anything to ground me and help me breathe.

I'm sitting across from the Merged offices. I didn't know I'd walked this way. I didn't even know I was here. But the realization gives me a purpose.

"I ran into Sanjay."

"Who the fuck is Sanjay?"

Jesus. It goes from bad to worse. "My former employee."

The silence on the other end of the line is deafening. It whooshes through me with vicious pain.

"Where are you, Cora?" His demand is laced with panic.

"On my way to your office. See you soon." I hang up.

Soon feels like three lifetimes as my numb legs trudge across the street, against the background of honking, braking, stomping, humming, and all the other sounds of the city. It all blends into the monotony of my hurt.

When the elevator door finally opens on the Merged executive floor, I expect to see his face. Instead, Roxy, who looks uncharacteristically panicked, waits for me, biting her nails.

"Cora." She grabs my hand and rushes me across the swanky reception area into a boardroom.

"Where is Xander?"

"He'll be right here. He had a major fight with Corm just minutes ago, but Corm insisted he stay for a call they had scheduled. Do you want something to drink?" The edge of panic in her voice intensifies with every word.

It's weird. I met her only a handful of times, but

the woman oozes confidence. She is the general around here.

I guess, in my current state, everything is weird.

"He took a meeting instead of talking to me?" Bitterness fills the room.

"No, no, he really had no choice. Can I get you anything?"

"Why are you being weird, Roxy?"

She sighs, looking upward as if she needs strength for what's coming. "He didn't get a chance to say anything. He probably wouldn't anyway. But he was so distraught, he almost punched Corm, and... he said I need to make sure you wait here..." She closes the door and leans against it like she wants to make sure I don't bolt. "He said you know."

And the plot thickens. Her words—while I'm not sure how everything relates to her—are like a cold shower, sealing my shattered heart into a box of ice. "And you know as well?"

"Fuck, Cora, I'm so sorry." She sags against the door. "I should never have given him that file."

A file?

I sit, because standing currently requires too much brainpower, and I need all I can muster to unravel this clusterfuck of lies and manipulation.

"A file..." I hope to prompt her to reveal more.

"Shit, you didn't know about the file." She straightens up.

"Talk, Roxy. I'm angry enough to force you, so you better explain." I don't recognize my voice. My tone. My threat.

"Fuck. Look, Cora, you need to know that man was into you since—"

"That's not what I want to hear from you."

She stares at me, her expression twisted with regret. "He wanted your address and... that's my job—to find out about potential clients, partners, employees—and finding your address was super easy, but I got carried away and dug out more. All I could."

"You dug through my life because he needed my address? Who does that?"

"I'm not proud of that. I enjoy a little sleuthing, and I never planned to give the file to him—"

"And that makes it better? Besides, you apparently gave it to him. What was in that file?"

She lowers her head. "Nothing you wouldn't have told him eventually. But he was so confused after you ran away after the Ed date fiasco, and I wanted to help him, I guess. And maybe I had my selfish reasons, but at the end of the day, he probably used the information to... propose."

She knows about my date with Ed? Has everything in my life been orchestrated by others?

"To manipulate me, you mean?"

She sighs. "Cora, he loves you. That man was smitten with you from the day he laid eyes on you. Is his conduct deplorable? Yes. Were his intentions sincere? Also yes. Just give him a chance to explain."

"Do you know he told me his father was forcing him to marry to help him with some client business? I found out about that omission almost two months ago. That was probably the time he should have elaborated."

"He fucked up." She nods a few times, more like shaking the idea out of her head. "Please give him a chance. I will forever regret my hand in it all."

"So I should give him a chance to absolve *you* of your fucked-up ways? Fuck you, Roxy, and fuck Xander. I don't want to be near your kind... entitled manipulators."

I push away from the table, my chair tumbling to the ground.

"Cora, I'm so sorry." Roxy doesn't move.

I snort. "I'm sure you are, Roxy. And I even believe that you snooped through my life only to satisfy your twisted curiosity. That changes nothing about my husband's betrayal."

Roxy propels forward, almost face-diving into the table as the door springs open and Xander's stormy eyes collide with mine.

Earlier today, I thought my life had crumbled into pieces too scattered to ever be replaced. That my heart shattered into a million irreplaceable shards. That my ability to trust vanished into thin air.

None of that compares to the domino effect of my insides folding, and my world collapsing at the sight of the gorgeous man.

I always knew he would hurt me. I always knew he would destroy me. I always knew I would never recover from Xander Stone.

But I never realized how painful it would be to see him suffer in equal measure.

Chapter 30

Xander

The minute my gaze lands on Cora, I know.

I know with unequivocal certainty that we will not recover from this.

I was prepared to meet an angry Cora. A sad Cora. A frustrated Cora.

I wasn't prepared for this.

Her eyes are devoid of emotion. Her face is unreadable. It's like she's gone already. She retreated into a place where I can't reach her. I can't pull at her heart. A place where she can be safe from a bastard like me.

I completely lost it with Corm when he insisted I take a client call with him. At one point, his asking me to step in was a badge of approval, something I was thriving on. At one point, the Merged business took precedence over anything and everything.

And before that, it was my family business.

Always focus on the outcome. On the next goal. On the score.

So inconsequential in the light of the loss I already feel in my veins. My entire life has been built on a false purpose.

In a twist of fate, the only thing that matters is something I finally had to work hard for. But instead, I found a shortcut, and now I will pay the price.

The price too steep to survive.

"I'll leave you to it." Roxy scurries away, closing the door behind her.

Cora doesn't move. She doesn't seem to breathe. I want to say something, but she looks so fragile that a word might break her.

I don't know what to say to make it better.

To explain.

To apologize. To fucking apologize. I grasp that idea with all the vigor and fleeting hope.

"I'm sorry, Coraline. I'm so fucking sorry."

The words feel foreign but right on my tongue. "I didn't think you'd marry me. I didn't think you would want to be with me. Fuck, I wasn't thinking at all. I was just acting. I was being a spoiled brat who wanted you, so I got you. At any cost."

For all I know she's petrified, her entire posture and expression turned to stone.

"I'm sorry, Coraline. Tell me what to do?" I need to

hold her, but I know I have no right to. I fucking gave that up when I made my stupid choices.

"I'm sorry," I say again, and I feel the sentiment deep inside me, twisting with guilt and fear.

"Tell me everything. And don't you dare leave anything out." The ice in her tone pierces through me like a dagger.

I nod. I don't see a point in recounting my actions, but she is in charge here. A humbling experience. "Okay. Do you want to sit?"

"Talk," she snaps.

I take a deep breath. "I wanted you since I first met you at Cal's Christmas party. You didn't take me seriously. You sassed me, and frankly didn't even look at me the way I saw you. I thought that would be it, but I couldn't stop thinking about you. At first, it wasn't that crazy, intense thinking about you every waking minute. The memory of you just quietly crept in. I would remember you here and there. I never thought of anyone but myself before. And the obsession with you grew with every run-in."

She is mere feet away, but the gap between us stretches endlessly.

Sweat trickles down my spine. I've given presentations that have yielded small fortunes. I've negotiated hundreds of millions of dollars. I've dealt with important information, pitched risky ideas.

None of it ever felt as critical. As urgent. As vital.

"I invited you to the gala. I thought I would fuck you and move on. But you... I don't know... You slipped under my skin. And when I took you to Corm's mom's luncheon, and we spent the afternoon together... I saw a possibility, but you were still fighting it. I was desperate."

"And then Roxy gave you a file about me." She folds her arms across her chest, impatience radiating from her.

I nod.

"And you bribed Sanjay to leave me. Why?"

"I wanted you to depend on my help. I didn't think that the story about me needing a wife would sway you."

"Is that all you did? And think carefully about how much you're going to omit. I have no room left for more shocking discoveries." Her chin quivers. She lowers her arms, hugging her midriff now.

The hurt is prominent in her posture, in her expression, in the words she says, and in those she doesn't. If it's only an ounce as agonizing as what I feel... Fuck, I hate this. I will never forgive myself for hurting her this much. For betraying her trust.

"I found your ex-fiancé's son and his mother, and I paid her to run into you."

Her eyes widen. "But what were the chances of such an encounter?"

"It didn't matter when it happened. In my mind, I took the steps to eliminate the competition."

"Like I was a business transaction?" She snorts and leans against the windowsill, spent.

"I paid your employee, and I bought the building to hike up your rent." I recount all my unhinged actions.

She gasps, stumbling to the chair, sagging into it, broken. My insides burn with the poison of my actions. With my inability to take the pain away from her.

The fucked-up part? I don't regret doing it. At the end of the day, it brought us happiness. I only regret that she feels the agony of the discovery.

Desperately, I want to say, 'Look at the bright side,' but I lost any privileges when I made the choices that led us here.

"Is that all?" A tear rolls down her cheek.

"Yes."

She snorts. Like my word means shit. It probably does, considering everything I fucked up.

"I'm sorry," I plead again.

She shakes her head, her eyes downcast. I can't stand it and drop to my knees beside her.

"You didn't believe we could be good together…" I trail off. I don't want to say desperate things that I would regret.

There is enough regret swirling around for the rest of our lives.

"How am I to trust you ever again? You fucking destroyed my business to trick me into this sham of a marriage." She stands, stepping around me.

Fuck.

Fuck.

Fuck.

I spring to my feet, crowding her. She steps back, her back hitting the window.

"Your business? Have you realized this is the first time you're calling it *your* business? It's always been your father's bistro."

"Don't turn it around. I'm not the one who is lying here."

I snicker in exasperation. "No, you only lie to yourself."

"Fuck you." She pushes at my chest, but I don't fucking budge.

"And let's be honest here, your business didn't suffer from my meddling; it bloomed."

"Fuck you," she yells again, trembling.

"And while we're at it..." I control my voice, leaning closer, my mouth just a breath away from her face. "Don't. Fucking. Call. This. A sham. Maybe I tricked you into this... but this between us is real."

She lifts her chin, her eyes glistening. "And so is my hurt."

A punch to my gut.

I can't help it, and I touch her cheek, wiping a tear from her soft skin. "I'm so fucking sorry, Coraline."

She closes her eyes and tilts her head slightly, like she needs my touch as much as I need it.

The feather-like connection should ground me a bit. It doesn't.

We stand there in stillness. Like the hush before the shattering.

That deceptive quiet when everything feels suspended—too calm, too careful. As if the air itself is holding its breath, waiting.

The touch is light. The breath is soft. But beneath it all, the pressure builds.

Unseen. Unspoken.

A silence so complete, it rings in my ears.

Break ups don't always come screaming. Sometimes they tiptoe in, before it all comes crashing down.

She opens her eyes, looking at me with sadness but also aloofness. "You know what's heartbreaking? The first time you say you're sorry, and it's too late."

"Don't say that. Please, Cora."

She pushes past me. "You had a chance to tell me the whole truth when some of it came up in San Francisco."

"I was scared." I admit the fucked-up truth. I wasn't man enough to confess. I was hoping it wouldn't get out. "I was so close to losing you, and I was fucking terrified. I couldn't let that happen. You were so hurt already, I—" I throw my arms up, exasperated. With myself. With the situation.

She looks at me. Like, really looks at me, with a sadness that rips my chest in half.

"And you lost me anyway."

Chapter 31

Xander

It's been two months since we signed the divorce papers.

Two months since my life shattered.

Two months of plowing through the days without purpose.

Lottie said it would get better over time. So far, it's only getting worse.

Cora moved out. I'm staying at the townhouse that, for a brief period, was the happiest home.

I'm staying here, hoping.

Hoping she will come back. Hoping I will figure out how to win her over. Hoping this is just a nightmare I will wake up from.

Instead, the nightmare deepens every time I tumble out of my bed after a sleepless night, feeling shittier than ever.

This morning seems particularly shitty. I'm not even sure why.

The heart is a fucked-up organ. I was smart not to have involved it before. Too late for that now. I hate how hopeless I feel.

I hate how much I miss her.

I hate that I let things go this far.

I hate myself.

They reopened the bistro. Tessa invited me as the investor. And then she eloquently suggested to her former brother-in-law that I shouldn't spoil the party by showing up.

I put on an old T-shirt—by the smell of it, I must have worn it a few times already—and a pair of sweats.

Downstairs, I do my usual routine, which includes glaring at the dried, withered sunflowers that are probably a health hazard by now, but which I can't throw out. Like anything she left behind.

It reminds me of what I lost, and I'm the fucker who enjoys the torture.

I walk to work, dressed like a delivery boy instead of a partner, not interested in any of my cars.

The walk is probably the only healthy thing I've done in the last eight weeks. I'm only wearing a light jacket, and yes, the remains of my logical brain recognize I will soon get pneumonia because the winter is viciously camping around Manhattan.

I just couldn't care less.

I'm not even walking to clear my head—such a state has left with my wife. I'm walking because I fucking hope I'll run into her.

Yep, pathetic much? Absolutely.

Hopeless much? Definitely.

Still obsessed with my wife? Obviously.

And in love. So in love with her.

I get out of the elevator at Merged. For some reason I've been showing up, even though I haven't been working. Not really.

The work has no appeal. It doesn't spark something. It's not even about losing Cora. It's that she showed me there is more to life than work, and now I'm revisiting my future.

It's bleak without her.

But it's certainly not what my past used to be.

"Here you are." Corm turns from the reception where he's signing something. "My office."

No fucking way am I having a conversation with him. With anyone.

"I'm leaving." I call the elevator.

Corm turns to me with that look that makes his worst adversaries keel over. "Now."

Fuck. My. Life. I trudge behind him.

"Look, man, it's none of my business—" he starts when we enter his office.

"Exactly." I pivot to leave.

"I'm going to buy your shares."

That stops me. "Merged shares?"

"Yes, Cal, Declan, and I—we have been covering your shit, but it's been too long. This can't continue. We agreed to buy you out."

For a split second, I imagine the scenario where I leave Merged. Where the one thing that I built without my father's cloud, the one thing that rebuilt me after I left the family business, would be gone.

The post-Cora void in my chest is crater-sized. There is no room for any more void, so I nod. "Okay, draft the paperwork."

Corm's eyes widen. I guess he was bluffing.

He studies me silently, a predator assessing his prey. "Okay. Will do," he says finally, and I turn to leave. Again.

"And Xander, you should try to fix things. I don't mind having a house guest, but it's been weeks, and your ex-wife doesn't brighten up the place."

"Don't fucking call her my ex-wife." He's seen Cora? He knows how she is? Where she is?

"Just facts." The fucker shrugs and saunters around his desk to sit down. "Interesting how losing the company didn't affect you, but mention of a woman you already lost riles you up." He tuts.

I bite at the snarl, because I want him to tell me more. "She's staying with you?"

He nods. "And as a result, my wife is too distracted, which I really don't appreciate. Fucking fix it."

"How?"

"I don't know, but it's been two months, and both of you are miserable. I'm not an expert here, but I don't think this is a time-heals-all situation."

Sighing, I exit his office, only to run into Roxy. The last sixty-one days have been just a blur of agony, but today takes the cherry.

"You look..." Roxy muses, "as bad as usual."

I open my mouth to retort, but why bother? Not that it saves me, but she trails behind me like an infectious disease.

I nod to Lindsay, who looks at me with eyebrows drawn in concern. I swear, every fucking day she just deepens my overall shitty existence with that pity.

"Go away, Roxy," I snarl, and try to close my door. I want to be wallowing alone. "I have a call," I lie, hoping to get rid of her.

"No you don't." She pushes past me.

I sigh and plop onto my sofa, because lying around is the most I can muster lately. Closing my eyes, I put my hands behind my head.

A shadow prompts me to open them again. Roxy

stands above me with her hands on her hips, tapping her foot.

She's wearing combat boots with a little black dress and a biker jacket. I can't hold her fashion against her currently, given I'm dressed like a homeless person.

"If you hadn't blackmailed her, we wouldn't be in this mess," she spits.

"I didn't blackmail her." I close my eyes again. "And there is no *we* in this."

"Yeah, right, you did much worse than blackmail, you lying piece of shit. And there is a *we* in this equation, because I feel responsible."

"Watch your words, Roxy; I'm still your boss."

"A shitty one."

I open one eye. "Leave, or I will fire you."

She snorts, but then her face twists. "As I said, I feel responsible—"

"It was I who used the file to exploit her former fiancé's secrets and her financial situation. You're absolved. Now fucking leave me alone."

"I shouldn't have researched her."

Out of nowhere, shocking both of us, I jump up, almost spitting into Roxy's face. "It doesn't fucking change anything, does it? She is still gone!"

Roxy's eyes flare. "And what are you doing about it?"

"Respecting her fucking wishes to leave her alone."

Roxy cackles. "How is that working for you?"

The spurt of energy vanishes, and I collapse back onto the sofa, hiding my face in my hands.

"You look like shit," she mutters.

"I feel worse," I mumble into my hands.

There's a silence. Not of the gentle kind. The heavy, judgmental kind that Roxy wields like a weapon.

"You think being noble makes you a martyr? Please. You're not some tragic hero. You're just a coward." Her words cut.

I drop my hands and glare up at her. "I lied to her, Roxy. Multiple times. I manipulated her entire life. And when she finally trusted me, I smashed it with both hands."

"Yeah. You did." She doesn't flinch. "And yet somehow, I'm still here. Go figure."

I scoff. "What, you want a medal? Go ahead and abandon me too. You'd do me a favor."

"No. For some outlandish reason... and perhaps to absolve myself for my part in this, I want you to man up and fix this."

I shake my head. "She doesn't want to be fixed."

"She doesn't want to be lied to. There's a difference." Roxy crosses her arms and gives me that look—that older-sister-with-a-baseball-bat look—she perfected in her first week at Merged. "You know what your problem is?"

"Which one?"

"You're afraid she'll forgive you. Because then you'll have to believe you're worth it."

The words hit hard. Like a sucker punch straight to the ribs.

"She deserves better," I say hoarsely. "Someone who doesn't sabotage her life. Someone who didn't start this whole thing with a lie."

The idea of Cora being with someone else twists painfully in my stomach, acid flaring up my esophagus, squeezing poison into my heart.

"She deserves honesty, you moron. She deserves a choice. You took that from her. And now you're still taking it—by deciding you're unworthy on her behalf."

I drag a hand down my face. "What do you want me to do? Show up at her door with flowers and say sorry I emotionally waterboarded you, but I'm madly in love?"

Roxy rolls her eyes so hard, I swear they echo. "Jesus Christ, yes. Start there. At least you'd be trying."

I stare at the ceiling. "She has the right to hate me."

"Maybe," she says. "But she also had a right to know the truth before she fell for you. And now she has a right to know you didn't stop falling just because she walked away."

My chest tightens, and I swallow, hard. "What if I go, and she doesn't even open the door?"

Roxy shrugs. "Then you wait. Or you write her a damn letter. Or you camp outside with a sign like a rom-com idiot. But you don't give up. One of the things I always admired about you is that unapologetic drive to win."

She sits beside me, her voice softening. "You love her, Xander. For once in your perfect fucking life—don't strategize or buy or talk your way around it. Just love her. Be messy, honest, and vulnerable."

She leans her head on my shoulder, but then slides away. "And take a shower. You smell of despair and whiskey."

"She doesn't believe in my love any more, Roxy."

"Then make her believe. Look, you've been hoping for closure for two months now. I think you should try again."

For the first time in days, I straighten up. Really sit up.

Because maybe Roxy is right.

Maybe I stopped fighting too soon.

Maybe the next move isn't about control or pride or punishment.

Maybe it's just about Cora.

I'm not sure what I'm going to do, but a glimmer of purpose pushes me up. I walk to the door.

"Where are you going?" Roxy follows me.

"To feed my cats."

"Jesus, you kept her cats."

"Fuck you," I snarl.

Because, yeah, as unhinged as that is, I refused to give Pitt and Clooney up. They are not even my cats, but I kept them... hoping she would keep coming for them.

I guess the fact that she gave up after a few frustrating tries is testament to how much she doesn't want to have anything to do with me. She gave up her cats.

And me? I fucking used her cats like a bargaining chip.

What the fuck is wrong with me?

* * *

Pitt protests loudly as I snap the carrier's door shut. Clooney gives me an evil eye, but then collapses into a ball, yawning.

I load them both into my Lambo, hoping the engine doesn't give up based on my neglect. Pitt continues to mew and get on my nerves the whole ride to Cormac's residence.

"I know, dude, but you're going back to your mommy, so stop bitching."

I pull into the driveway, kill the engine, and turn to

look at the two heads glaring at me from behind the barred doors.

"I thought she'd fight for you. But I guess that is yet another thing I lost. The fight over you. And now you. I can't believe I'm going to miss you."

And I can't believe I'm fucking talking to cats.

I get out and look at the mansion, wondering which room is hers. Is she hiding behind one of the windows? Does she sense I'm here?

My heart beats like a wild animal, hammering against my rib cage as I lift both carriers from the passenger seat and make my way to the door.

It bursts open before I even reach the landing. I look up, full of hope and trepidation, but my gaze collides with Saar's. A very pissed, glaring Saar.

"Took you long enough." She crosses her arms over her chest.

"Can I talk to Cora?" I put down the cats.

"She doesn't want to talk to you."

"Saar, for fuck's sake, tell her I'm here."

"She knows. And she would be at the door if she wanted to see you."

An engine approaches, and we both turn. Corm gets out of his car. "Hey, baby. Everything okay?"

He takes two steps at a time and kisses his wife on the temple.

"You're home early." She smiles at him, and then

turns to glare at me. "I was just telling Xander that Cora doesn't want to talk to him."

"Fuck, Saar—" I growl.

"Measure your words, fuckwit. This is my wife you're talking to." Corm narrows his eyes.

Saar takes the two carriers and leaves, closing the door behind her.

"How the fuck should I fix it if she doesn't want to see me?"

Corm shrugs. "I'm sorry, man. I'll talk to Saar and..." He trails off, because Corm Quinn doesn't make empty promises.

I get back to my car and drive off, knowing that I have just left behind my only negotiating chip. Or two of them.

But then, this is not a negotiation. This is not a sprint to complete. This is a marathon, and I may have hit burnout, but fuck, I'm going to complete this race, even if it takes me years.

I miss her.

I miss the fucking cats.

I preserved the dead flowers.

Yeah, I bought a spray to preserve dry flowers, cursing myself for not taking care of them sooner.

I have written her ten letters so far. And I'm checking the mailbox for her replies, even though I have sent none of them.

Life moves with fragile tranquility, the world around me flowing unchanged. I haven't been to work for the past three days.

Instead, I took a shower. I wrote letter after letter. They feel more like journaling... getting my feelings out. And figuring out how to make her life better.

Because after I dropped Pitt and Clooney, I had a breakthrough. I outlined the worst-case scenario. One where Cora moves on. Without me.

And without a shadow of a doubt, I know I would never fully move on. So my contingency for that bleak scenario is to make her life better. Even if I have to do so from afar.

It's nowhere near being with her.

But it's slightly less hopeless than living without her. Than dropping the connection completely.

And so I don't go to work, but I write her letters. And I send a generous donation to C.O.R.A. I also talk to Tessa to ensure the bistro is thriving.

I upgrade her dad's care, so he gets the best his facility can offer. In the absence of Cora, improving her life makes me feel marginally better.

I don't expect her to thank me. I don't need that. In

fact, I'm half expecting her to give me shit for meddling in her life.

At night, I wonder if I can survive like this for the rest of my life. Or if I should move to the West Coast and try to forget.

Either option feels like a slow death, but at least here, I'm closer to her, and I don't have an overbearing family interrupting my self-loathing.

I sit on the sofa that still smells like her—or that's what I believe—and consider ordering a takeout when my phone rings.

I look at the caller ID, and my heart almost jumps through my throat.

"Saar?"

"Just so we're clear, I still think you're a despicable piece of shit."

"Agreed." I sigh.

"Don't be cute with me. I also think she really needs you right now."

"What's wrong?" I sit up straight, already searching for my keys.

"It's her dad."

Chapter 32

Cora

The sun shines for the first time in weeks. It seems so unfair. Shouldn't it rain at a funeral? Shouldn't the sky mourn with us?

Tessa sniffles loudly beside me. Dad smiles from his framed photograph next to his coffin. He doesn't even look like himself. Why did we choose a picture where he is still smiling? Vital. Himself.

Alive.

Ethan's was the last funeral I had attended. I was heavily sedated just to get through it. I wonder if his other woman was there. He was smiling brightly in his photo as well, the cheating bastard.

It's been almost ten years, and I forgot grief hurts physically. I fidget in my seat, the minister's droning an annoying buzz in my head.

How old was Dad in that picture?

The grief, the pain, the void are too overwhelming, so I focus on my irrational anger at the photograph.

Tessa stands up to speak. I gave her the privilege. She asked for it. She said she needs to speak, because she wasn't there for him as much as she should have been.

I was going to fight her on that, but this loss came on the heels of my other loss... I just don't have it in me to... exist?

A violent sob leaves my lungs.

And now I'm mad at Xander. For betraying me and for stubbornly clinging to my heart, even if he is no longer in my life.

I can't deal with all the loss. Another sob breaks free, and Paul squeezes my hand. I jerk away. I don't want Tessa's ex-husband to console me.

My niece smiles at me sadly, and I turn back to Dad's photograph. I can't cope with everyone else's sadness. I can't cope with my own.

People chuckle around me. Tessa must have said something funny. I hug my midriff, the chill raking through my body.

A warm hand squeezes my shoulder. It must be Saar, Celeste, or Lily who flew from London for this. They sit in the row behind me, their support the only lifeline I've had in the last few months.

I divorced Xander. I couldn't forgive him for all the

manipulation and exploitation. When I cry myself to sleep, which has been my usual way these days, I regret it.

Forgiving him seemed like capitulation.

Like giving up on myself.

Like letting him win at his shady game.

Forgiving him felt like betraying myself.

Like cementing our relationship on an unequal foundation.

And letting him rule me.

When I signed those divorce papers, something died inside me. Something vital—a piece of me I didn't even know I had. And I had buried a man before.

Stubbornly, I believed time would heal the wound. Tough shit. Don't they say that broken people survive better because they've done it before?

Well, not in my case. With Xander, without realizing it fully, I lost more than I could ever replace.

It pisses me off. This stupid dependency. But when I close my eyes, I know it's love. I love the man, and based on his recent actions, he still loves me back.

He might have acted on the feeling in his deplorable, manipulating way—no one ever showed him differently—but I know he loves me.

And that's the core of the problem. Just because someone betrays you, you don't stop loving them.

Tessa stumbles from the podium and collapses beside me.

I look at Dad's photo and the bottle of Zinfandel I left there instead of flowers, and suddenly, I realize I can't watch his coffin disappear.

I want to remember the smiling, happy dad from the photograph.

I can't breathe.

I need to get out of here.

"I have to go. Sorry," I tell Tessa and stand up.

Dad's brother looks at me, surprised—I didn't even realize he was giving his eulogy. I glance at the photograph one last time, hoping to forever remember that smile, and I rush outside.

My heels echo obscenely as people murmur.

I push the heavy door open and step outside, and almost slip. "Oh, for fuck's sake."

Mother Nature got the message. While we were inside, the sky darkened, and it started raining.

I rub my arms, huddled under the awning. I should call a cab. I'm not even sure where I'd go, but I can't bury another significant man in my life.

Tessa will understand. She will take care of everything. She will be upset, and remind me of my inappropriate actions for the rest of our lives, but I'm putting myself first.

I'm not doing what everyone expects of me anymore. Fuck that.

The hinges creak, and the door closes with a thud again. A large black umbrella snaps open above me.

My knees buckle. I don't have to look to know who is shielding me from the rain. I recognize the subtle masculine scent, the softness of his coat, the warmth of his body.

And I'm too tired to fight it at the moment.

I look to the side, and the well breaks. Holding the umbrella above us, Xander wraps one arm around me, stroking my hair gently, letting me soak his shirt.

He doesn't say anything. He just stands there, a sentry to my grief. A solid pillar to rely on in my darkest moment.

I don't know how long we stand there while I grieve my father and this relationship, but eventually the door is open, and people file out.

Xander moves to step back. "I'll—"

"Stay," I blurt, gripping the lapels of his coat. "I can't do this—"

"Okay. I'm here." He nods and steps behind me, holding the umbrella as I accept the condolences from people who knew my father.

"I'm sorry I told him to come." Saar hugs me.

"It's okay." I hold her for a bit longer, and then do

the same with Celeste and Lily. In the sea of Dad's acquaintances, these are the people I want around.

And the man standing behind me, a silent guard to my pain.

It's ironic that my ex-husband holds an umbrella above me while Tessa's ex lingers in the doorway, keeping his distance.

"I guess you found your gentleman with an umbrella," Tessa says.

Gentleman perhaps.

But no longer mine.

Once everyone is gone, Xander puts his hand on the small of my back and leads me away.

"I got something for you," he says, walking toward his car.

I don't even question the fact that he is not my ride. "I hope it's not another island."

He chuckles, pulls me to him, and kisses my crown. The whole thing is so instinctive, so us, so normal... it spreads pain through my chest all over again.

He opens the door of his Lambo, and I slide in.

He rounds the car and gets behind the wheel. From behind the seats, he pulls something out and then sets it in my lap.

A box of Zinfandel. Not a premium vintage. Not an organic version. Six bottles of a cheap brand he drank with me that night we talked about our birthdays.

"Thank you." I sniffle.

"I know I'm the last person you wanted to see today, but I needed to make sure you're alright."

"I'm not."

He reaches over and takes the box from my lap, shoving it behind the seats. Then he reaches again and buckles me up. His scent invades my senses. It would be so easy to get lost in him. To escape the pain in his arms.

He doesn't retreat to his side, but lingers, his gaze on me, full of compassion and sadness.

He tucks a strand behind my ear. "I wish I could do something, but I learned recently that grief is a beast I can't conquer."

He's been grieving. Us?

"Imagine when you get a double-whammy. Lucky me." In my head, the self-deprecating nonsense made more sense.

Out loud, floating between us, it only deepens the wounds, reminding us of our own loss.

Xander tenses and withdraws to his side. The loss of his warmth is staggering. I hate that he doesn't joke, doesn't lighten up the mood.

The absence of our usual banter is so loud. I hate

that with our relationship, he lost that part of himself. Or perhaps he wants to respect my grief.

I hate how familiar and strange this encounter is.

I'm tired of hating and grieving.

Xander starts the engine. "Where should I take you?"

The raindrops slide down the windshield glass, the life outside the car loud and hurried. I should go to the bistro where we're holding the wake, but I need the silence and safety of this car.

Not because I grew to like the car.

Because, despite all the pain, the driver gives me more comfort than anyone else ever could.

"Could you just drive for a while?"

"Of course."

And he does. I slouch in the seat, letting my thoughts wander. We drive in silence. I sob for a moment, then I close my eyes, then I watch the traffic.

All the while, Xander drives me around without a word. And I feel safe, sad, and spent. Until the silence feels suffocating.

"Say something," I snap, shocking myself.

Xander whips his head to me, bewildered.

"Distract me," I add.

He swirls the car into a parking garage and finds a spot on an abandoned level. I don't even know where we are, or how long we have driven.

Xander taps his fingers on the wheel. "Lottie moved to Paris to learn to paint. Dad is pissed."

I chuckle, sad I won't know these little tidbits anymore. "I'm sure the experience will change her."

"I'm not sure if she'll learn how to paint, but she's definitely having fun with her art teacher." He shrugs, and I chuckle.

"Well, that's an invaluable experience."

"I don't know, she is my little sister; I would prefer her to join a convent."

"That's discriminatory."

"Not really. For all I care, all women can join a convent."

He groans, looking away, the tension sneaking back between us. On some pitiful, pathetic level, I'm glad he doesn't want another woman.

Jesus. How are we ever going to find closure?

"Thank you for returning Pitt and Clooney." I play with the hem of my skirt, the weight between us growing.

"Fuck, Cora, I'm sorry I kept them."

"Thank God they were not in our prenup." I smile.

"Yeah." He chuckles and looks at me.

Really looks at me—the way he used to. With that same raw hunger, the fierce admiration that always made my knees weak. Like I matter. Like he wants me.

Something sparks between us—electric and familiar. It jolts through me—unwanted, but unstoppable. That reckless, consuming pull that never asked permission. The kind we never could resist. Not even when I tried.

Tired of the numbness that's hollowed me out, of the silence where joy used to live, I just want to feel something again. Anything. Something that isn't rage, sadness, grief, or fucking regret.

I don't have the strength to fight against what I think is wrong, but what feels so fucking right. I'm tired of dragging myself through days that don't feel like mine.

Of pretending I'm fine when I'm not.

I need to escape. To feel like myself again.

I meet his gaze, unflinching now. Reckless. Desperate. "Make me feel better."

He looks at me, stunned. I don't know if he remembers I said those words in the car after his mom's event, when I was hurt and needed to use him.

I hike up my skirt and climb over to his side.

"Cora..." he rasps.

"No talking, no analyzing... just make me feel better."

"I don't—"

"Fuck, Xander, you betrayed me, you lied to me, you manipulated me; don't you grow a conscience now when I need you to be reckless with me."

The war behind his eyes should frustrate me—especially now, when need pulses through me like a second heartbeat. But it doesn't.

It calms me.

It's like with our break up, he lost a piece of his recklessness.

And somehow, I gained that part of him that never hesitated.

Somehow, that shift evens the scales.

He doesn't move, but he is barely hanging onto his control. I can see it in the way his jaw tightens, in the way his breath comes rough and uneven. He's trying to hold back.

I rake my fingers through his hair, slow, deliberate. He shudders under the touch, eyes flickering closed for a beat too long.

His hands are fists at his sides, like touching me might undo him completely. And God, part of me wants that—wants to see him fall apart.

But more than that, I want to feel anything but the way I've been feeling since our marriage collapsed.

His breath hitches as I lean in, my lips a breath from his.

The kiss comes slowly. Like a memory. Like a warning. His mouth brushes mine—tentative, hesitant. Not like him. Not like us.

It should feel foreign.

It doesn't.

I breathe him in, and the taste of him cracks something open in me. My fingers fist the hair above his collar. I need to anchor myself in this moment, or I'll drown.

Because I am unraveling. Fast.

Every heartbeat feels like a breaking point.

But he's still holding back. His hands hover at my waist, the restraint coiled in his body like a drawn bow.

He's trying to stay in control—trying to be careful. Or to do the right thing. Finally.

I don't want careful.

I definitely don't want right.

I kiss him harder, pulling him closer. A sound escapes his throat—half growl, half surrender—and then he breaks.

His hands are on me.

Not hesitant anymore. Not controlled.

Desperate.

He deepens the kiss. The kiss that has teeth and history. The kind that says, "I tried to let you go, but I never did."

And when he finally drags his mouth from mine, breath ragged, eyes wild, I know we've crossed a line neither of us can uncross.

This is a mistake that will cause more hurt right after.

But fuck if I care.

Not today.

Xander reaches down, and the seat jerks backward, the backrest reclining. I yank at his tie, unbuttoning his shirt.

He hikes up my skirt, his hands squeezing my thighs in a hungry grip, marking me with his anguish.

"What do you need, Coraline?" He grits out.

"Your cock. Now." I don't even recognize my own voice.

I finally part his shirt and rake my nails down his chest and abs. Fuck, I missed his body. I missed his touch. I missed his warmth.

Miss. Miss. Miss. The longing barrels through me, unexpected, and I claw at him, drawing blood. But he doesn't seem to care.

He unzips his pants, pushes my panties to the side, and impales me in one swift move.

I cry out, the invasion unexpected. Brutal, yet welcome. He stills, his gaze glued to mine. We stare at each other in a limbo of indecision.

In the small space of his car, we're both fighting the common sense that screams for us to stop.

Not only because we're in a public fucking parking lot. But because we're chasing a resolution that will only bring us pain.

Because we're replacing words with actions that don't match the state of our relationship.

"It's a mistake." I circle my hips, and Xander hisses.

"Certainly."

I make another circle. "We will regret it." I don't even know why I voice all these objections.

"Perhaps." He groans when I lift my hips and sink down again, squeezing.

"I don't want to stop."

"Unfortunately."

The regret in his voice registers, but it's immediately replaced with pleasure when he grips my hips and starts bouncing me in a punishing tempo.

One that wipes my thoughts clear, replaces the agony, and finally opens the emergency exit. Exactly what I wanted. Exactly what I needed.

This is not lovemaking.

This is not making up.

This is not even fucking, I think.

It's more like an exorcism. Banishing our pain. Discarding grief. Expelling the regret.

When we both cry out, falling over the precipice together in a raw, unscripted mess of sweat, bodies, and pent-up need, I know that the effect will be tragically short-lived.

Xander gathers me closer, holding me in his arms,

his cock still pulsing inside me. And then the high comes crushing down, and I start crying.

Because I will never get to open another Zinfandel with my dad.

Because there won't be birthdays we celebrate together.

Because he will never see what became of his bistro.

Because I will never go to visit him again.

Because my dad is gone, and even though I'm not a child anymore, I feel like an orphan.

So lonely.

So fucking lonely.

Xander strokes my hair gently for I don't know how long, but when my weary mind registers the feather-like, comforting touch, I realize I've just used this man.

I push to sit up, raising my hips, disconnecting our bodies, hoping we can dislodge our hearts as easily.

"Coraline," he rasps, but I don't look at him.

I climb over to my side, and he lets me. The loss of him is visceral, but I can't let my grief and hormones dictate the situation.

I shimmy my skirt down. "I'm sorry."

"Don't—" His broken voice is a direct hit to my chest.

"This was a mistake... We shouldn't have done

this." I chance a look at him, and the agony spreads from my chest to my entire body.

What have I done?

Xander's jaw is tight. He doesn't move to tuck himself in. He is still leaning back on his tilted seat, watching me. His eyes hooded, his expression wounded, there is softness to him.

Adoration.

Devotion.

Love.

Jesus, I made things worse. I gave him hope.

I wish things were different. I wish I could trust that he would not manipulate me. I wish I could trust him.

"Xander, I don't know what I feel right now. I'm grieving. I'm so sorry."

He reaches to stroke my cheek. "It's okay, Coraline."

"I shouldn't have used you."

"You can use me anytime, love. I'm here for you for the rest of our lives. Anytime you need this or anything else, I'm here for you. And maybe one day, you will allow me to be more. I'm not going anywhere."

Chapter 33

Cora

SAAR

I don't understand why you don't want to come.

CELESTE

The house is beautiful. We would have so much fun.

I have revisions to work on.

SAAR

House in Tuscany is the perfect place for that.

Tessa might need me at the bistro

CELESTE

I call bullshit.

LILY

I could join you.

SAAR

If Lily can work remotely, so can you.

I'll think about it.

CELESTE

That's what you've been saying for two weeks now.

Pitt dances around my legs as I make my way to the kitchen, his tail brushing against my calves.

The cat hasn't left my side since I moved back home. It's like he senses something irreplaceable is missing from my life, and he's determined to fill the void with fur and neediness.

"If you don't stop this, I will end up stepping on you, silly cat," I mutter, scooping him up before the guilt of accidentally injuring him is added to my emotional load.

He purrs, loud and steady—an instant balm for the storm inside me. Placing him gently on the counter, I reach for a mug and turn on the coffee machine.

They say we should collect memories, not things.

But things hold memories. They haunt you with them.

Like this espresso machine with all its fancy, over-engineered functions. The one that Xander bought when he lived here. He didn't keep it. He sent it back to me with the rest of my stuff.

As if brewing coffee could cure heartbreak.

I left it in its box for a while, but two days ago I unpacked it—because apparently I'm a masochist, with a taste for caffe crema and regret.

The hiss and hum fill the silence of the apartment. The rich aroma curls through the air like a ghost. I close my eyes and breathe in deeply, willing it to settle the ache inside me.

Too many memories in such a short time.

Even the empty corners feel full—like the imprint of his presence lingers in the air.

The way he used to toss his jacket over the back of the chair. The way he grumbled about the size of my shower. The way he read for Pavel, right there on that goddamn couch, like he belonged here.

Like we belonged.

The machine beeps. I reach for my cup, cradling it in both hands like the warmth could make me whole again.

My phone buzzes on the counter.

Tessa. I hesitate, then swipe to answer.

"Morning," she says, cheerful in a way only someone who's not walking around in emotional quicksand can be.

"Hey."

"Just wanted to update you—we met with Gina this morning and finalized the new menu layout. She's sending the print proofs later this week."

I blink. "Menu layout?"

"You know... the new menu we discussed? Oh, and the new supplier started delivering yesterday."

I nod, even though she can't see me. "That's great. I'm glad." It's more like I'm completely indifferent, but I shouldn't be, so I fake it.

There's a pause. A knowing silence. "You okay?"

"Sure." More faking. "I'll be there later this afternoon. I have a meeting with my agent."

"Don't worry about it. You don't have to come every day. I have things under control."

When I hang up, the silence returns with a vengeance.

The bistro is moving on. Just fine. Without me.

It's a relief.

But also unwelcome. It's like after Xander, the other constant in my life—the bistro—is gone as well. I'm not there anymore.

Not at the bistro.

Not in Xander's life.

I stare down at Pitt, now curled on the counter, his eyes blinking up at me like he knows what I'm thinking.

"I made a home for everyone but myself," I whisper, remembering the Fox story. "Even you, you little brat."

* * *

"These are..." I stare at the illustrations, spread out on the boardroom table in Andrew's office. "They are exactly what I had in mind. Perfect."

Working on my book has been the only joy in my life in these painful months. On the surface, life is happening as before, unaffected by the aching crater in my chest.

Tessa is still Tessa. My friends support me more than ever. Pitt and Clooney provide cuddles and give attitude.

I still visit the cemetery, not Ethan's but Dad's grave. I still scribble stories. Bills come, bills are paid. Pavel visits me or the cats regularly.

Life seems to flow, but I'm only drifting.

How long can I live like this?

C.O.R.A. grows and spreads goodness in more schools. The work there brings me joy as well, and it has become my refuge, but it reminds me of Xander too much.

My book is the only thing that is just mine. The breeze of a new beginning I'm so desperately hoping for. Even though it was Xander who truly believed in my stories more than I ever had, this baby is mine, and I cling to it with all my might.

The hollow remains. The light is dimmed. The static is loud.

But at least I have this.

The ginger fox stares at me from the illustration, almost daring me. But how am I to build a home for myself if the most important part of me is missing?

The loving and the loved one. The one that belongs with Xander.

I guess, sometimes, we meet our soul mates, but it doesn't mean they are to stay with us. They come into our lives to shake it up, to uproot what we know and challenge what we believe. They touch us to change us.

Love can't replace trust, and sometimes the habits are too ingrained. Xander negotiates huge deals, and is extremely good at that.

Unfortunately, that admirable drive to close a deal, to win, is something that comes as second nature to him.

I will always be at the end of his schemes. Or I wonder if I am.

"I'm glad you like them, Cora. I'll set up a meeting with the artist, so you can discuss your creative vision. I want to make sure I pitch this to the publishers as a deal, so you can retain creative control."

"Wouldn't they want to make those choices?"

"Let's try to do it my way first."

"Okay. Thank you, Andrew."

"May I ask you something, Cora?"

"Of course."

"Are you not happy with my work?" He polishes his glasses with the tip of his tie.

"On the contrary." I smile. Fuck, have I been such a downer that he doesn't feel appreciated? "Why do you ask?"

"Your husband keeps checking up if everything is progressing as it should." He looks at me, studying my reaction, probably assessing if I'm behind Xander's interference.

"I didn't know." I fiddle with my purse.

I'm here for you for the rest of our lives.

Part of me is upset with his meddling. The other part is... I don't know, relieved, grateful, confused. Is he really planning to wait for me? Forever?

I was sure he'd forget soon enough. *Yeah, how is that going for you?*

"Maybe you can tell him to back off?" Andrew shrugs.

"I'm sorry, Andrew. We're actually... We split up." The words scratch my throat, a lump growing. Instead of time healing things, the wound festers.

"Oh, I'm sorry to hear that. He must really care about you."

He does. And that's the worst part. We both care about each other.

I rush out of Andrew's office, my head spinning. I need space. I need air. I need to get away.

Maybe Tuscany.

Maybe laughter and wine and the girls.

Maybe it's time to rebuild myself. Maybe the distance would help us both.

* * *

"I miss Declan and the kids, but I don't want to leave tomorrow." Lily sighs, taking a bite of bruschetta, the toppings falling to her plate.

The country restaurant we've been frequenting this week is small and honest. I love it here. Winter is not really the time to visit Tuscany, but in many ways, it's better.

No crowds. It's like the estate and its surroundings belong to us only. I've found some peace here.

"I think I'm going to stay here longer."

Am I? I didn't plan on it, but as soon as the words are out, they feel right. More right than anything else in my life lately.

Perhaps the lingering hurt, the humming void, the

silent regret will fade faster if I stay here. Maybe I can find a way to stay here for part of the year. The idea, while unbidden, grows so quickly that a flicker of excitement ignites for the first time in months.

Saar, Celeste, and Lily all stop eating and stare at me.

"I'll check with my producer. I'm sure I don't have to return for a few more days." Saar speaks first.

"No. You all have been wonderful staying here with me. It's been the best distraction. But I think I can stay alone. I should stay alone. Would you mind putting me in touch with the estate owner, so I can extend my stay?"

"You're serious?" Celeste asks, stroking Amelie's back as the baby sleeps in her arms.

"Yes, I'll look for something more affordable, of course. The place is enormous, but I need to extend for at least a few nights."

The girls exchange a look.

"Come on, I'm an adult," I argue. "I can stay by myself in a foreign country. I promise I'll be fine. You don't have to worry about me."

Lily looks away. Saar grimaces, and Celeste kisses her baby's head, avoiding eye contact.

"What is going on?" I frown.

"The estate... it's Xander's." Saar scrunches her face like the words hurt her.

I blink. "What?"

"Don't get upset, but coming here was his idea."

"His idea?" I throw the napkin on the table. "Of course he knows better what I need." The shitty part is, he was right. "I can't believe you. Whose side are you on?"

"Always on yours, Cora," Celeste says.

"He hurt you; the least he could do is to pay for your rebound getaway." Saar reaches over the table, squeezing my hand.

"Rebound?"

"Okay, wrong choice of words."

"We've been avoiding the elephant in the room, but you're hurt; he's hurt. Are you sure there is no way the two of you can get past the betrayal?" Lily asks.

The answer should be unequivocal and automatic, but the denial gets stuck in my throat and doesn't come out.

"None of our relationships started with love," Celeste says.

"He betrayed you," Saar adds. "He tricked you, but can you honestly say that what followed was a lie?"

"So you're on his side!"

"He made a mistake, and he's paying for it. You forgave your father. Ethan and your father are prime examples of multiple shades to every story. You're focusing only on the dark side of yours and Xander's." Saar gives me a sad smile.

"You think I should give him a chance?"

"I think you should stay, and if you feel like a piece of you is still missing after all that time, you need to try to forgive," Lily says.

I look through the window. Her words should feel like a plan, but they only spread an ache through my chest. I came here to forget. "I want to stay, but I can't stay in his house."

"Of course, you can." Saar waves my objection away.

"You have to stop rejecting everything based on the right and wrong you accepted at one point in your life," Celeste says. "Do you love the house?"

"Yes," I grumble.

"You can stay there for free for as long as you want. What objections can you possibly have?" Saar asks.

"I'd still feel I owe him something."

Celeste covers Amelie's ears. "Fuck that. He owes you more."

* * *

The vineyards stretch in front of me, their bare vines rising in neat rows from the frost-kissed earth. Winter has stripped the valley to its essence—no flowers, no fruit, only the quiet dignity of rest. The rest I needed more than I realized.

I tug the wool blanket tighter around my shoulders. My stomach growls, but I'm too cozy to go down to the village yet.

I haven't prepared a proper meal in weeks. The idea of doing anything in the kitchen, other than making a cup of coffee, has been anxiety-inducing.

I have some sort of kitchen-related PTSD. I would rather attend a silent retreat with Xander's grandmother than cut another tomato in my life.

Xander.

Staying at Xander's house alone this past week has been amazing. The stillness. The peace. The creative flow.

It's been agonizing. Because if I thought staying in Tuscany would help me forget, staying in his house makes that impossible.

But I stopped fighting it, because I don't think it matters where I live—Xander Stone etched himself on my mind, and forgetting him is not an option. I'm not even sure if learning to live without him is possible.

But I try. I try hard. When I go for a walk. When I write. When I mindlessly scroll on my phone. When I wake up. When I go to bed.

At all other times, I hope he'll just show up. In that

scenario, I try to move past my hurt. The picture usually breaks apart.

To make things worse, ever since the girls left, I've been receiving a bouquet of sunflowers and a fresh pistachio Danish from my favorite New York bakery every day.

I hate him for that.

But I also love him for it.

Fuck.

I take a sip of my tea, and then reach for my notebook and pen.

The air smells of damp stone, cypress, and distant woodsmoke. The comfortable wooden chair creaks, the only sound on the veranda. It's just me here, the hush of the hills, and the whisper of ink on paper.

My pen hovers for a beat before I let it drop onto the page. The first lines spill out like breath:

The eagle didn't remember when it had forgotten how to fly.

Only that one day, the wind no longer came when it opened its wings.

I pause and reread the lines. I have written four more stories since the girls left. Maybe I'll finish another book before the first one is out.

I smile and put the pen to paper again, when I hear

my phone from inside. Sighing, I enter the house and find the offending device on the dining table.

It's Tessa. My finger hovers over the green button, but I hesitate. My sense of duty pushes me to answer, even though I'm ninety-nine percent sure the sole purpose of the call is to complain about the bistro.

About the vendors, the customers, the workload. All the while she's enjoying the drama. I think my sister thrives on playing the victim.

I also think she is the best that could ever have happened to the bistro. I just don't feel like today should be tainted by her attitude.

But I shouldn't avoid her. We've just started communicating better. The phone stops ringing before I cave in.

I grapple with my guilt for a moment, almost calling her back. Instead, I return outside, send her a quick message that I'll call her later, and pen a story about a kitten that learned to set boundaries.

The story pours out of me, and I don't even realize the dusk falls over the hills.

Needing more light and warmth, I bring everything inside. In the kitchen, I re-read the story.

Xander would like this one.

The thought jerks me out of my creative stupor. Goddammit. As much as I try to forget him...

It's this house. Or maybe it's the guilt I feel about using him after the funeral.

Maybe I'll never move on.

With a trembling hand, before my mind gives me a gazillion reasons not to, I pick up my phone and type.

Thank you for letting me stay at your place. I just wanted to let you know I will be moving out on Monday.

I hit send and immediately regret it. I'm not ready to return to the States. I don't have another rental lined up.

But if I don't take the step toward a thorough exit from this Xander-infused world, I will never move on.

The three dots dance in front of my eyes, and my heart is ready to evacuate my chest.

XANDER

Are you returning to New York?

Goddammit. I don't want to lie to him, but I don't want to tell him that... that what? I have no plans?

I don't want to take advantage of your hospitality.

Okay, that's an honest answer, at least.

XANDER

You're always welcome to stay for as long as you want.

That is a nice concept, but it doesn't help heal my heart. Said heart is pounding like a spooked horse right now. From anxiety. And if I'm completely honest, from a bit of excitement.

Talking to Xander after all this time is still thrilling. Even though the conversation itself is just a very awkward dance.

I love it here. Thank you.

My leg is bouncing of its own accord.

It's a beautiful estate.

XANDER

Have you tried the restaurant in the village?

I smile.

Several times.

XANDER

Whatever they're adding to the food, it's addictive.

Do you come here often?

The dots appear and disappear for what feels like hours, while my heart echoes in my temples.

XANDER

The food is worth it.

That took him so long to write? My fingers hover above the keyboard, and then I take the leap.

Maybe one day we can have dinner there together.

I hit send. There. It's done.

What the hell is wrong with me? I started this conversation to cut the ties completely. And here I am suggesting dinner together.

Jesus. A few lines between us in some impersonal texts and I... Well, I didn't pretend.

For a few brief beats, while typing and reading his messages, I forgot about the betrayal and went with the flow.

He doesn't respond, and my tentative excitement, which is overshadowed by my current freak-out, deflates, because he's not even writing and deleting like before.

And what was I excited about? It's not like I could ever trust him again.

You forgave your father. You're focusing only on the dark side of yours and Xander's story.

My eyes land on this morning's sunflowers, and I close them. Like I could ever unsee what they represent. They never come with a note. No words of coaxing, of manipulation, of influencing.

He just sends them.

Because they are my favorite flowers.

The roar of an engine and the shriek of tires yank me from my emotional spiral. This estate has a secured gate—so who the hell just barreled through it?

I don't even make it to the window when a persistent knock on the door stops me. I approach it with careful steps, as if I could stop an intruder.

Craning my neck, I glimpse a large truck in front of the house, the driver's door open, but I don't see who is at the door from this vantage point.

They left the car door open.

Maybe they need help.

I swing the door open, and my knees buckle.

Chapter 34

Xander

Fuck, she is gorgeous.

Her hair is in a wild mess, her face pale, dark shadows rimming her eyes. And still, seeing her expands my chest, while taking my breath away.

Any version of her is simply something I want to keep seeing for the rest of my life.

Even after not seeing her for months, it's comforting to see all her lines and freckles, the curls, the green of her eyes.

If this is all I get—because let's face it, she didn't exactly invite me over—it will probably sustain me for weeks. It would kill me, as well, but let's hope.

Hope is the only thing I have left anyway.

We stare at each other, not moving, as if we're

afraid that the next breath, next step, next word will fuck everything up again.

For all I know, we're still in the agonizing limbo we've been navigating since everything imploded. But, fuck, if her dinner invitation didn't give me hope.

Yeah, hope is all I have left.

It wasn't much of an invitation, but it was a tiny opening, and I'm going to stick my foot in that door even if it potentially crushes me again.

But I just stand here like an idiot, clutching a cat carrier in each hand, and offering all the eloquence of a lamppost.

Pitt mews—loud and offended—snapping me out of whatever haze her face, her presence, her fucking existence has thrown me into.

Her eyes flick to the carrier. "Are they—?"

I nod and gently set them down beside her. "They wouldn't shut up the entire flight. I figured… you might miss them."

I hope you missed me too, is what I want to say.

Dropping to her knees, she moves the carriers farther inside and unzips the front flaps with trembling fingers.

Pitt shoots out first, elegant as ever, tail flicking like he owns the place. Clooney follows, slower and suspicious, before trotting toward a patch of sunlight by the window like a man on a mission.

They roam the room as if they remember it. Like they've always belonged here.

Unlike me.

I'm still standing in the doorway, all six-foot-four of me taking up space I feel I no longer have a right to.

This used to be my house.

But it only took a few moments to see it came alive with her in it. Better. Brighter. Breathing.

Like me in her presence. Finally breathing. Finally feeling slightly brighter. Hoping to be better. For her. For me. For us.

Watching her kneel there, murmuring soft nonsense to those damn cats, glowing with something like relief... I feel it down to my bones.

The reality—one I orchestrated—is still tragic, though.

They're home.

And I'm not.

I'm about to turn around, leaving her to enjoy the reunion, when Cora looks at me.

"You're here," she breathes.

I find purchase with my hand against the door frame, because I want to sweep her into my arms and never let go.

"I didn't want to send them with a stranger." I smile at her.

She blinks a few times. "But you're here."

"Obviously." I shrug, and my foot moves forward, but I think better of it.

"But it's been minutes since my text."

"I—we..." I glance toward the cats that are both fighting for a spot on her lap, lucky fuckers. "Have been staying at the guest house on the other side of the pond." I beckon with my head in the general direction of the backyard.

"Since when?"

Okay, I didn't expect our conversation would take this direction, but whatever. She's in front of me and we're talking. "Since you arrived."

Her eyes widen. She stands up, both cats grunting in protest. "This whole time?"

I nod.

"Why?" Her eyes dart between the door and me. Perhaps she's deciding whether to let me in?

"I didn't want you to be alone."

"I wasn't alone."

The least productive conversation in history, but here I am, grateful for her attention. "Maybe *I* didn't want to be alone."

"But I didn't even know you were here."

I shrug. "You didn't want to know."

She sags against the other side of the doorway. "Now I know." A whisper of a smile touches her face.

I swallow, and consider falling to my knees and

begging for forgiveness. But she doesn't need my platitudes. Those are just part of the game... I don't want to play games anymore. With anyone, but especially not with her.

I clear my throat. "I have cat food, litter, and their boxes in the car. Let me carry them inside."

She nods, and I unload the truck, carrying everything to the kitchen. It's like walking through a minefield. One wrong move and everything explodes.

"Thank you." She fills the bowls with food and water and sets them all down on the floor.

Both cats dance between her legs and ignore the food, just seeking their owner's warmth and snuggles.

Yeah, I'm an intruder here. A jealous one at that.

I'm jealous of her cats.

"You don't need to thank me." My voice cracks. "I'll leave you to it. If you need anything..."

Fuck, what am I doing? What am I saying? She doesn't want me around. I hurt her enough.

"I'm so fucking sorry about everything, Coraline." I look at the door, but my legs don't move.

"You didn't tire of apologizing." She picks up Clooney and scratches his neck, a hint of her usual sass coloring the statement.

"Someone important once told me it's not a sign of weakness." I step closer. "Besides, I owe you a lifetime of apologies."

We stare at each other, and the air fills with something new. Or rather familiar.

She swallows. She licks her lips.

The tension between us shifts slightly.

It's not angry desperation anymore. It's not just unsaid words, late apologies, and pain.

It's something tentative, physical. It's like our bodies act on recognition, while our hearts hesitate.

"I was planning to go to that restaurant tonight." The words come out uncertain, like she wants to stop them but can't.

"You've been going every day."

"Have you been following me?" She frowns, but she smiles. It's the smile I fell for at the gala. The slight curve of her lips with a glimmer of mischief in her eyes, like she is entertained and curious.

"Yes."

"But I never saw you."

"You didn't want to see me. Besides, I have to confess that I'm still not good at accepting rejection."

She opens her mouth, but I add, "Your rejection in particular."

"What are you doing, Xander?"

It sounds like she is shutting down the opening, but it also sounds like a genuine question.

I'm trying to win you back.

"We're going to eat our weight in pizza together," I say instead.

She laughs, not yet with her usual abandon, but it's a genuine laugh. It hits me in the chest with painful joy.

Fuck, I missed her laugh.

"Well, since I was going to go anyway..." There is some reluctance in her voice, but beggars can't be choosers.

I bow. "My car awaits."

She disappears and comes back with her huge bag. Fuck, I missed that clunky sack as much as her laugh.

"It's not a date," she warns.

It totally is a date. "Of course not."

Shit, I'm lying the first ten minutes into my not-yet-confirmed second chance.

I always believed in the ends justifying the means and all of that... but with Cora, I learned it's not always as effective as being honest.

But if it's not a date for her, it is for me. Not the soundest logic, but I'm desperate.

We make our way to the restaurant in silence, filled with reminiscence and trepidation. Like it's us, but it's not. Like the betrayal caused damage that the distance deepened.

But I'm stubborn, and I refuse to accept that the time apart erased the good we used to share.

A short ride later, we arrive and find a table in the corner after the owner greets us.

"You know each other?" Cora asks.

"I'm a silent partner here."

She snorts. "Of course you are."

"He was going to close two years ago. It's an honest, family restaurant, I couldn't have the best pizza disappear."

She smiles at me. "So you helped him."

"So I helped him."

She studies me, another louder whisper of a smile tugging at her lips. We order wine and starters.

"Tell me about your book," I say, and my heart stutters when her eyes flash with excitement at the topic.

She talks about the stories, the illustrations, the process, and more. She hasn't been this animated about the bistro. Ever.

Seeing her sitting taller, shining brighter, vibrating with joy, hits me like a freight train.

I can't fuck it up.

I can't fuck it up again.

I knew I missed her terribly, but only now do I realize how much. I'm getting another dose of her, and this time, the withdrawal will be fatal.

I can't let that happen. But it's not up to me. The lack of control is humbling. But I surrender to it, because she's worth it.

"So… your text… Are you returning to New York?" I ask.

She sighs. "I love it here. I think I want to stay longer. But it doesn't matter where I live. The void you left…" She shakes her head, like she regrets the sentence I want her to finish so desperately. "Not much good has happened in my life lately, but every time it does, I want to share it with you."

I swallow. Fuck. The words rattle through me, leaving me stripped naked in front of her.

She can break me apart with her honesty, and I would let her any time. All the time. Forever.

"Why are you looking at me like that?" She takes a sip.

"Like what?"

"I don't know. Like you—"

"Like I love you?"

She flinches, the joy leaving her eyes as she swallows visibly. "Xander," she breathes.

"Coraline, I love you. I can't help it."

"What are we doing?" she asks again.

"Eating our weight in pizza."

"You know what I mean." She groans.

"Still the same answer. There is no ulterior motive. You said you wanted to eat here with me, and so, I'm here."

"You need to stop this, Xander. This is what broke

us. You forcing your way into my life and *fixing* things. Making things happen, whether I wanted them or not. Taking my choices away." She slouches back, looking away, tears brimming in her eyes.

Fuck.

"I wouldn't force myself if you let me in." I lean back. Fuck the food. I'm not hungry. Other than for her.

She rolls the rim of the tablecloth and unrolls it. She takes another sip of her wine. She wipes the corners of her mouth with the linen napkin. She puts it back down.

"I sense there are myriad objections brewing in your head. Voice them." I put my hand on the table, wanting to take hers and feel her warmth, but I just fist it.

"There is only one." She lifts her chin.

"Which one?"

"I'm scared you're going to hurt me again."

Me too. A platitude, a commitment, a vow is on my lips, but I lied to her enough already. "I'm scared I will fuck up, but not trying to do better by you scares me more."

She breathes in deeply, as if my words deprived her of oxygen. "I don't want to feel the void you left."

The weariness in her tone cuts through me like a sharp knife. Will this hurt forever define who we are?

"Then let me in, Coraline."

She leans back, hugging her midriff, shrinking away. And my completely mangled heart gets squeezed even more.

She's not going to forgive me.

She's already retreating.

"Let's see how tonight goes."

Oxygen leaves my lungs at her words, a sliver of hope blooming. "You mean this date?" I smile.

She sighs, covering her face and shaking her head. "You see... again, you're changing the narrative to suit you."

"But it suits you, as well." I shrug.

Cora snorts. It's not yet a laugh, but fuck if it isn't a symphony this world needed. Well, *I* needed it.

"I want us to try, Cora. To try for real this time—vulnerable, messy, one day at a time—but I don't think I can change completely. I can promise I will be honest with you, but I can't promise to stop fixing things for you."

Perhaps this honesty will cost me dearly, but I can't pretend to become someone else for her completely. I will try to do better by her, but it's me she fell in love with once. It's the same me. With better morals. With less entitlement, humbled. But still me.

"Are we negotiating?" She gives me a lopsided smile.

"No, my love, in negotiations I would make sure the other party knows what they have to lose. Right now, I'm painfully aware of what I have to lose. This is not a negotiation, because all the bargaining chips are in your hands. I'm just begging you to give the entitled rich boy a chance. And I promise, I will never lie to you or manipulate you."

A heartbeat.

She fists her hands.

Another heartbeat.

She looks away.

Thump. Thump. Thump.

She looks at me, her gaze filled with pain but also with remnants of something else... like she used to look at me when she was tying my tie in the morning.

"There is so much hurt and lies... The way we started..." She looks away.

I'm not sure if it's hesitation, or if she is just avoiding the confrontation.

She swallows, playing with a napkin and blinking as she looks through the window into the darkness outside.

God, she's breathtaking.

She was that night at the gala too—but that was a superficial infatuation. A rush of lust and intrigue over a woman who didn't care I existed. Who laughed without self-consciousness. Who danced like nothing else mattered.

Now I know better.

Now I see the layers.

The cracks. The light leaking through them. The way she carries the weight of responsibility—both needed and self-imposed—with a quiet grace that humbles me.

She's still radiant—but it's not the kind of glow that draws a crowd on a dance floor. It's the low, steady kind that makes a house feel like home.

Like she's been through shit, grown through it, and come out softer and stronger.

She sits in front of me now, but the absence of her, the one carved into every corner of my life, is still loud.

I broke the one thing I was desperate to keep.

This is what I did to us. She deserves so much more than all this pain.

I don't deserve to sit here. I'm the villain in this part of her story.

I take her hand. It quivers in my trembling one. The connection is so tender, only reinforcing what I lost.

She definitely deserves so much better. She deserves the space I've never given her.

I graze my lips over her knuckles, get up, and walk away.

Chapter 35

Cora

His lips connect with my hand, and a shiver runs through me. I so desperately want to mend what we broke.

He might have started it with all the lies and deception, but I was the one not giving us a chance from the beginning. And this man fought for us. The us that was so wonderful. The us where I felt safe and cherished. The us where I grew out of my old habits that were killing me slowly.

He fought for us with dirty tactics, but he also didn't know any other way.

Can I trust that he learned the lesson? Can I risk more heartache?

His lips hover just above my skin, his breath warm. My hand shakes in his, quivering with longing, trembling with fear, stirring with possibilities I'm too scared to explore.

Will he fight for us again? Do I want him to?

Before I have a chance to decide, to entertain the tender possibility, Xander gives me a sad smile and stands up.

His kiss lingers, a flame pressed to my skin, small and searing. A farewell? An apology? A sad thank you?

I bring my hand to my chest, fingers still curled, as if I could trap the heat he left behind and keep it from fading. All the efforts to forget him were in vain. The pain he caused is real, but so is the void he left.

It's a void I won't be able to fill properly. Ever. And I'm not sure if deciding I should try was the right one. That's what one meeting with him did.

My resolution is gone.

My determination is nonexistent.

My reason for our breakup is forgotten. But is it also forgiven?

He walked away.

It was the smart thing to do.

The right thing.

So why do I reel from it? Why do I want to call after him? Run after him?

Because for a moment—for the length of a shared bottle of wine—he made me feel whole again.

Lighter.

Like all the pain, the betrayal, the messy past could exist beside us instead of between us.

God, I missed him. Not just his touch, or his naughty smirk, or the way he took up all the space in a room. I missed the way he made me feel.

Seen. Heard.

Understood.

Even when he didn't agree with me, he made space for me. He ruined my business, but only to save it tenfold.

My opinions. He didn't mind the age gap, the financial gap, or any of the gaps I believed were between us.

My grief. Oh, how he let me hurt him, so I could feel better for a moment.

My dreams. I found myself because he was there all the way, just giving me nudges.

How did we get here? Why did we get here? Even under the weight of his betrayal, his love tips the scale.

I should be proud of him for walking away.

For respecting my boundaries. For not trying to fix it all with a charming smirk and a hungry kiss.

It was noble. And selfless. It was all I ever wanted from him.

And it felt like being gutted with a velvet knife.

Because if he'd reached for me... if he'd said come back, or even just I'm not done—

I don't know that I would've had the strength to resist.

And maybe he knows that.

Maybe he is protecting me from the same storm he brought to my doorstep once already.

Or maybe he's changed. Grown. Loved me enough not to risk breaking me again.

I should be grateful.

But all I feel is the ache of absence—sharper now, because for a second, it felt like he'd never really left.

I'm rooted to my seat. A part of me wants to stop him. To force him to try harder. To allow myself to trust again.

But it's not that easy. This man felt like home at one point, but you can't build one without a solid foundation.

The server comes over with a bottle of wine and a clean glass. He pours some for me to taste and presents the label. It's my favorite Zinfandel from Napa Valley. Not the Italian Primitivo, but—

I frown. "I didn't order anything." I shake my head, hoping that will translate my words into Italian.

He smiles and steps to the side. "From the gentleman at the bar."

Oh, for fuck's sake? Can't a girl grieve in peace?

My gaze meets the pale blue eyes I know so well.

Xander gives me that boyish smile that got me into this mess.

Slowly, he saunters over to me. There it is—that familiar swagger, half confidence, half defiance, like the world can throw its worst at him and he'll still come out grinning.

His jacket is slung over one shoulder, shirtsleeves rolled up just enough to show the veins in his forearms. I swallow, my heart fluttering like it never got the memo that it's supposed to be over this.

The tilt of his head is pure Xander: amused, reckless, unreadable.

He looks at me like I'm the only thing anchoring him to this moment. Each step brings him closer to breaking every bit of resolve I've managed to piece together.

"Hey, I'm Xander." He offers me his hand.

I stifle a giggle and shake his hand. "I'm Coraline," I say, for the first time using the name he monopolized when my father couldn't anymore.

He gives me that winning smile of his. "Nice to meet you, Coraline. Do you mind if I join you?"

"I guess you bought me a drink, so it's only fair." I extend my hand toward the chair.

He takes the same seat he vacated moments ago.

For a moment our gazes hold, suspended in this air of

opportunity, second chances, and tender trust. Maybe hope. Not a desperate one. Hope that speeds up my heart rate. I'm not sure what we are doing, but it feels a thousand times better than anything I've felt in the past few months.

"I hope I'm not intruding," Xander says after we order pizza.

"Do you really?"

"I guess I'm intruding, but just say the word and I will leave. I heard that just because I can have something, it doesn't mean I want it. I recently learned, in a very hard, life-changing way, that it works the other way as well. Just because I want to have something, it doesn't mean I can... take it."

His words take my breath away. I'm not sure if it's in a good way or a bad way, but it's dizzying to have him in front of me, trying and hoping, giving me space instead of just taking.

"Do you want me to leave, Coraline?"

I should want him to leave, but I don't. "I would have to finish this bottle alone. That's not a good idea."

He smiles and refills my glass.

"Besides, I have been eating alone for many long weeks. I might enjoy the company."

He puts the bottle down and looks at me with that penetrating gaze that holds me prisoner. "So what is it you do, Coraline?"

I raise my eyebrows, a smile tugging at the corners

of my mouth. Are we going to try to rebuild the missing foundation? "I own a bistro in Manhattan."

"Interesting. I live there. What are you doing in this neck of the woods?"

The smile is automatic now. I can't stop grinning at him. Whatever game we're playing, it's simple and honest. Something our relationship so fiercely needed. "Actually, I'm writing a book."

He leans closer. "Wow, that's amazing. What are you writing about?"

I take a sip. "I write children's stories, animal parables."

"Will you write a story about a tiger who was an entitled dumbass?"

A laugh escapes me, unbidden. "What will be the moral of that story?"

"That sometimes you need to be brave and risk rejection. That losing the girl is the worst fucking feeling in the world, but the fear of it doesn't justify manipulation as a love language."

I sigh, this reminder of the past tainting the moment, but also opening a possibility for me. Perhaps I can start trusting again. Just as he started understanding where things went wrong.

I take another sip. "Tiger, hmm...?"

He grins. "I'm glad you picked up on that."

Our pizzas arrive, and we fall into an easy conversation about anything, retelling things we know about each other, and accepting them through new lenses.

After we pay the bill, Xander leads me outside, and while his hand is absent from the small of my back, his heat is radiating and warming me up, on the outside and on the inside.

"Can I give you a ride?" He clicks his keys, and the truck flashes open.

If we're pretending that this is the possible beginning, I'm going to lean into it. "Aren't I too old for you?"

"Not at all. Besides, a few years mean nothing in the span of a lifetime." He opens the door for me.

"A lifetime?" I get in.

"That's how long I'm planning to fight for you." He closes the door.

My poor heart.

Earlier tonight, we drove in silence. This time Xander talks about the neighborhood, and drives a longer but more scenic way. Even though it's dark, I get a glimpse of sites and places I haven't discovered yet.

Somehow, we do a loop and enter the village again from the other end. Xander brings the car to a stop.

"This is not where I live," I protest when he gets out of the car and gets around to open my door.

"We didn't get dessert."

He leads me through a narrow passage, and we end up in a small courtyard with blue doors.

We enter a small bakery with a few patrons drinking their espresso shots at a tiny counter. It's really just a square room with stone walls, its glass front fogged from the heat of whatever miracle just came out of the oven.

"I didn't know about this place."

"I didn't know about pistachio Danishes, and now I have several pounds to show for it. Consider it my revenge."

"You seemed so scandalized by my bakery back home. And look at you now."

"That wasn't a bakery; it was a crime scene."

I snort. "Was? I ate a Danish from there this morning."

"It's a respectable place since I bought it."

I stare at him. "You bought the bakery?"

"It was the easiest way to make sure you can have your Danishes forever, especially since international shipping is required at the moment. But I might sell it after you try the local goods."

I keep staring, because I'm not sure if I'm impressed or annoyed.

He tugs a strand behind my ear. "Come on, Coraline, I put your sister in charge. The busier she is, the less she bothers you."

Now I don't only stare, I gape. And I realize I'm not impressed, nor am I annoyed. I'm grateful. He might have his fucked-up way of caring for me, my needs, and my issues, but he does care. He does notice. He does see my issues before I even notice them.

To distract myself from the onslaught of emotions, I turn to the counter. A tray of sugar-dusted bomboloni sits in the middle, their golden shells puffed, oozing cream from delicate seams.

The smell alone could knock me over—vanilla, yeast, something citrusy—pure comfort wrapped in nostalgia.

It's the kind of place you'd miss if you blinked. No chrome. No fancy lighting. Just the clink of espresso cups, handwritten prices on curling paper signs, and an older woman behind the counter who greets Xander like he's one of her own.

I glance at him, watching as he leans in to order in perfect Italian, all suave charm and reverent tones like he's requesting access to a private vault.

We take our pastries to the car, and he drives me back to the estate. Killing the engine, he turns to me. "I wanted to kiss you after the gala."

I don't know why we're revisiting that night, but somehow it feels important. "Why didn't you?" I swallow around the lump in my throat.

"I didn't understand it at the time, but you felt

different, and I guess I didn't want to follow my usual pattern."

A wave of melancholy sweeps through me, and I say, "We would have had a one-night stand, probably."

"You would have kissed me back?" He looks genuinely surprised. "I thought you would have just kicked me in the balls."

I burst out laughing. Not because it's funny, but because I need a break from this torture. It feels so good to laugh that the sentiment takes over, and before I know it, I can't stop. Tears rim my eyes, and everything in me releases the tension through a cathartic laugh.

It dies too quickly, and when I look at Xander, I find what I used to expect but forgot how much it meant—admiration, pride, love.

It kills the laughter, because his feelings, written all over his face, are too real. And I don't want to be the person who steps all over it. But we have so much to rebuild, and I'm not yet certain we even can. "I guess tonight is not the night for a kiss."

"Unfortunately, you're right. As much as I wish it was different," he says, without an agenda, without controlling the situation. Just accepting. "I'm glad I didn't kiss you that night because you're right, it would have been the end of us."

He takes my hand and brushes his lips over my

knuckles. "You were always right, Coraline. When you objected to our age gap, because let's face it, you were more experienced in the art of relationships, and I should have let you lead. Even when you objected to our financial differences, I ended up using my money to destroy us after all."

Blame is not going to help us. Because I know he recognizes his errors. Because rehashing it won't help us move forward. "Xander—" I try to stop him.

"But despite all of it, Coraline, you and I are meant to be together. The pain of the past months taught me that. And I'm not going to stop trying."

Chapter 36

Cora

I think I'm dating my ex-husband.

LILY

Are you happy?

SAAR

Sounds like a chick-flick plot twist.

CELESTE

Shut up and pay, van den Linden.

Was there a bet going on?

CELESTE

No

SAAR

Of course

LILY

I didn't participate but I'm glad you're giving yourself a second chance.

SAAR

She's giving him a second chance. One he doesn't deserve.

Yet.

CELESTE

Oh, playing hard to get.

Protecting my heart at all costs.

SAAR

How is that going for you?

Failing miserably.

SAAR

Make him grovel, but for what it's worth I believe you belong together.

I thought you bet against us.

SAAR

Only because I hate his guts for the pain he caused.

I love you all.

The shy winter sun seeps through the window, the curtain billowing. I left the window open last night, and now I don't want to get out from under the soft, warm covers.

I don't have to.

The thought stretches the corners of my mouth into a smile. For years I had been waking up with a frown, a jolt of anxiety, and a rush. Always catching up, always late, always hurrying.

I guess Tuscany is my new paradise. A place where I can shut down the outer world, the responsibilities, and just let my work ripple out to the world with passion.

Fuck, I'm happy.

I grin like an idiot, replaying the past two weeks in my head. The man is dating me. No kissing. No holding hands. No sex.

Only attention, care, laughter, companionship. It's like we're rediscovering pieces of who we were together, but at the same time we dance around it, too afraid to fully dive in.

Okay, I'm the one that's scared, and unlike before, he's just standing beside me, waiting for my cue. For my heart to trust again.

Because let's face it, my body has been onboard, and if the man kisses my hand one more time, I may just combust.

Xander has been respectful.

There is a part of me that is holding back, waiting for the reveal of another manipulation. Everything suggests he learned the lesson, but everything seemed perfect before as well.

Because it fucking was perfect, minus the origin story.

I slide out of my bed and take a long, warm shower. As I go through my morning routine, I spend half the time smiling as I replay our recent encounters, and the other half frowning and deliberating on where we go from here.

I'm so mad at him for what he did to us.

I'm so in love with him at the same time.

I make a cup of coffee and cut a small piece of pistachio Danish and bomboloni from yesterday. Because yes, after that first dinner, Xander started sending both every morning.

I told him to stop sending them, because as much as I love the pastries and the gesture, I don't want to deal with the consequences of this overindulgence.

As every day, right at ten, the delivery truck pulls up to the front, I take my coffee out to greet him.

"*Buongiorno, signorina.*" He shuts the rear door and carries a bunch of sunflowers to me.

"*Grazie.*" I take the flowers from him, balancing them in one hand, waiting for the white box that always comes with them.

The delivery guy salutes me and walks back to his truck.

I stare down at the sunflowers, still cradled in the crook of my elbow, their golden heads brushing my collarbone.

No pastries today.

Just flowers.

He listened.

No pastries.

The small absence carries more weight than all the white boxes before it.

It's not about sugar or calories or restraint. It's about him. About Xander Stone—the man who once steamrolled his way into my life like everything could be bought, solved, or seduced—pausing.

Listening.

Respecting what I asked for without turning it into a debate. Without teasing. Without testing my resolve.

It feels like trust. Or maybe the beginning of it. And it scares me how much that means.

I glance down at the sliver of leftover Danish on my plate and push it aside, my appetite suddenly dulled by something heavier. Something softer.

This version of him—the man who stopped sending pastries, who holds back when he used to push—is quieter. But no less intense. If anything, the restraint makes it worse.

Because now I can't pretend it's all charm and impulse.

He cares. He sees me. He knows me.

And I fucking miss us. Him.

Not the pastries. Not the grand gestures.

Him.

My phone rings, pulling me out of the endless loop of thoughts, pros-and-cons lists, and emotional swings.

"Andrew." I sit down on the porch swing.

"Cora, sorry to interrupt your vacation," my agent starts. "I'm calling with good news. I have two formal offers from publishers."

My heart skips a beat. "That's... that's... oh my God, that's wonderful, Andrew. Two?"

"Yes, I will forward you the details, so we can discuss the pros and cons of each of them. I do have two minor changes to the manuscript. Do you want me to email them?"

More changes? Jesus. "Let me take notes. Just give me a moment."

"Sure."

I fetch my pen and grab the sunflower notebook from my purse. Andrew gives me his ideas as I quickly jot them down.

"Oh, that's nothing major. Let me play with it, and I'll send you the new version later today."

We end the call, and I collapse into the chair, smiling. Two potential publishers? This is really happening.

Mindlessly, I play with the corners of the notebook, letting the joy float through. The notebook flops open at the back.

What are these notes?

Own a private island — Tiny. Useless. Mine.

Oh my God, I forgot I made this bucket list one night after I had a glass or two of Zinfandel more than I should have had.

See the Northern Lights wrapped in a ridiculous fur coat.

Eat my weight in pizza in Tuscany. Maybe live there for a while.

Have my stories published.

Finally give up the bistro.

Be held like someone's first and last choice.

Forgive my mother (maybe).

Fly first class without guilt.

Find a way to matter outside of duty.

I stare at the list, my heart pounding. I own an island. I'm in Tuscany.

Now we eat our weight in pizza. That's what he said when he brought the cats.

My stories are about to get published. I gave up the bistro. I flew first class. I write, and I oversee C.O.R.A., not out of duty but because I want to, because it matters and fulfills me.

And all of it... because of a man whose first and last choice I have been.

Has he read this list? One I forgot about but he made happen, regardless? Because so often, he knew what was better before I found the courage to face it.

With trembling hands, I open the messaging app.

I got a publishing deal.

XANDER

I always knew you'd slay it.

Thank you for the flowers.

XANDER

Are you missing the pastries?
(winking emoji)

Missing you.

I don't get any answer, but somehow I don't worry. I just walk outside and sit on the porch, knowing he's on his way.

Sure enough, his large, expensive truck pulls up in front of the house shortly after. He practically falls out of it, tripping to get to me.

I don't even try to stifle my smile, watching him lose all the swagger and grace he usually carries too confidently.

He stops at the base of the steps and looks at me with such intensity, I'm glad I'm sitting.

"I miss you, too, Coraline, very fucking much."

"Do you want to go for a walk?"

"With you, I would watch paint dry."

I roll my eyes. "Enough with the poetry, young man; I want to enjoy the sunshine." I stand up and bounce down to join him.

We grin at each other for a moment, before I recover and hitch my shoulder toward the vineyards.

We walk in silence. It's kind of comfortable, but also filled with tension. He is giving me space, I know that. I understand the ball is in my court. I just don't quite know how to serve it.

We climb up the hill and turn to admire the rolling hills. The olive trees rustle in the background, and I inhale the fresh air.

I'm content. Almost completely happy.

Just one thing missing. I turn to Xander, and all my thoughts come to a halt when I meet his intense gaze.

While I was admiring the view, he was staring at me. "Are you okay?"

"I'd really like to kiss you," he breathes, his voice low, a little rough.

My breath catches.

He's not assuming. Not leaning in already. He's waiting. That shouldn't undo me the way it does.

The air fills with anticipation, but also something else, like we're worried the kiss may not feel the same.

Like it may bring all the damage to the surface. At least, that's where my hesitation lies.

But we need to leap. I swallow. "Okay."

He steps closer.

His hand brushes my cheek, fingertips trailing along my jaw like he's reading me in Braille.

When his mouth meets mine, it's not urgent. It's reverent. His lips are soft, his kiss patient—like he's testing where it will lead us.

And the moment deepens naturally, our bodies sighing in relief.

My hand finds the lapel of his jacket, gripping it as his mouth opens slightly, deepening the kiss. His other arm circles my waist, pulling me flush against him.

I feel the sharp inhalation of his breath against my skin.

And just like that, the space between want and need disappears.

Too fast.

I press my hand against his chest.

"Xander," I whisper, pulling back just an inch. My lips are tingling, my heart galloping.

He stills immediately, eyes locked on mine, searching.

"I want to take this slowly," I say, voice quieter now. "Not because I don't want you. But because... I do, but I'm still waiting for—" I don't want to say it. I don't believe he'd break me again, but something in me still resists.

My instincts scream at me to have faith, but Ethan and my father broke that inner confidence. And to a certain extent, Xander did too.

His thumb brushes the edge of my jaw. "Then slow is exactly what we'll do."

My chest tightens. With relief. With regret. With the first tender rays of trust.

"Okay," I breathe.

We walk down the hill holding hands. It's strange, and completely normal at the same time.

"Are you hungry?" he asks when we reach the estate.

As if on cue, my stomach growls, and we both laugh. "Do you want to walk to the village and eat our weight in pizza?"

He jerks his head, something akin to fear flushing through his eyes.

"You read my list." I smile, so he knows I don't mind.

He sighs. "You left the notebook at my hotel's spa, and it opened, and I..."

I chuckle. "It has that tendency. It just opened randomly for me."

"I'm sorry."

I grin. "Thank you."

He narrows his eyes. "I fucked up with that island."

"Only because I forgot about that list."

"Shit." He laughs. "So you wanted none of it. I did it for nothing."

"Not nothing." I kiss his cheek. "You did it for me."

Again we grin at each other, until my stomach growls one more time.

After our lunch, Xander drives me back to the main house.

"What are you thinking about?" He breaks the silence when he parks.

"It's so beautiful here. I think I want to stay longer," I say, overwhelmed by the views and the emotions.

Xander plays with the car keys. "That's okay. We can stay for as long as you want."

We?

After a beat of silence, he adds, "I'll stay in the guest house, of course."

Don't.

"You don't need to go back to New York? What about Merged?" I shift in my seat to look at him.

"I sold my share." He shrugs.

I blink. "What? Why?"

"After I left the family business, I believed that building my own firm meant freedom. When you came to confront me in my office, I lost precious minutes in a meeting that seemed utterly unnecessary. I don't want to spend my time doing things that don't matter. Much less if they prevent me from being with you when it matters."

I had resisted this man.

I had married this man.

I fell for this man.

I hated what he did to me.

I divorced him.

A complete circle on the emotional scale. And here I am with butterflies in my stomach.

Smitten by him. Not just the Xander I grew to know and love. But this humbled version of the man he grew into.

Not just for me, but for himself.

He looks at me through his eyelashes. No smirk—just boyish vulnerability he carries like a man. "I thought I could make you happy with gifts, throwing money around. I don't want to change that, but I recognize there is more to a meaningful life than that. And you're a part of that meaning for me.

"I have enough money to last a lifetime. I don't need to make more, because it would never fill the void in a life without you. But I can use my skills to grow C.O.R.A. or similar programs. One cereal box at a time."

And it's like that last piece on the forgiveness puzzle clicks in. Because this might be the first time Xander Stone is not wearing a mask.

The moment grows heavy, and fuck, I need a break from the pent-up, loaded moments. "But then you won't be an entitled rich asshole anymore," I tease.

"I'll still be an asshole." He winks, leaning into our familiar banter.

I bite my lip, my grin splitting my face by now. "My asshole."

He lets out a heavy sigh of relief. "Only yours."

Chapter 37

Xander

I grin like an idiot as I brush my teeth. When I undress. When I slip under the covers.

She wants to take it slowly, so she took me up on that chivalrous offer of staying in the guest house.

I don't mind. I've been seeing her for two weeks now, and today gave me the first glimpse of hope.

I will gladly lie in the bed I made for myself, because at the end of all the fucked-up decisions, I think I'm still getting the girl. Not that I deserve her.

We spent the rest of the afternoon talking. As I was leaving, the weather shifted, and a storm began to stir.

As soon as I arrived, the skies split wide open. Beneath the steady roar of rain, the past two weeks replay in my head on an endless loop.

Her excitement about the book. How she still tucks

her hair behind her ear even though it is held by a headband. Her lips on the rim of the glass, savoring the wine.

How she burped after the last slice of pizza. How she rubbed her belly after the first bite of bomboloni. How sweet that too-short kiss this afternoon tasted. How she smiled at me.

For the rest of my life, I want to be seen by her. It's the most potent drug out there. To have a woman you love looking at you like you matter.

I don't think sleep will come tonight, so I grab my phone and flip through the news. Giving up my shares at Merged didn't hurt as much as I would have expected.

My heart wasn't in it. Not only because it was entirely wrapped up in Cora. Or rather, in her absence.

She showed me there is more to life than making money. The way she took care of people around her, even if some of them didn't deserve it.

Even her cynical skepticism opened my eyes more than any other experience.

Even if she never gave me a chance, service to others would be her legacy in my life. Life I would have wasted if the redhead temptress hadn't crashed into it.

Dropping my phone, I stop the mindless scrolling. I

haven't been paying attention anyway. I sigh, her green eyes flickering in my mind.

A sharp bang against the door jolts me upright. What the hell? In this storm?

I take the stairs two at a time and peer through the front window—nothing but darkness stares back.

"Xander." Another bang is accompanied by Cora's voice.

I almost dislocate my shoulder yanking the door open. A flash of Cora sparkles in front of my eyes before I'm soaked wet, because she jumps at me, wrapping her arms and legs around me and crashing her mouth over mine.

Her lips taste like rain, and the sweetest memory. I stumble back and kick the door closed, pinning her against it.

I'm half sure this is a dream, but when her moan penetrates my mind, I pull away.

"How did you get here?"

"I ran."

"In the storm?"

"It looked like a drizzle when I left. But then the wind snatched my umbrella. And you said it's just behind the pond—"

"A driving distance."

"I know that now." She fuses her mouth with mine

again, and I surrender to her sweetness and her need. Our need.

I fist her hair and angle her head, taking all I missed for the last however many weeks. Our breathing grows labored.

"Why are you here, Coraline?"

Shut up, idiot. She's here.

"Maybe I don't want to take it slow."

This time, I seize her lips, but her teeth chatter. "Fuck, you shouldn't have come on foot."

"I don't have a car."

"You should have called me."

"That didn't feel very romantic." She bites her lip, shivering.

"There is nothing romantic about catching pneumonia."

"Then warm me up quickly, Xander. Get me out of these wet clothes."

I kiss her, hoist her higher, to hold her better under her ass, and carry her to the kitchen.

Sitting her on the island like the precious cargo she is, I peel off her jacket. "Arms up."

She obeys, and I take off her soaked sweater.

No bra.

I groan and latch onto her erect nipple. She moans, arching her back.

Pulling down her wet leggings is neither sexy nor graceful. It's like the water glued them to her skin.

I swear, and she laughs through the entire ordeal, but finally, she is naked in front of me. My cock is painfully hard in my flannel pajama pants, but I pause, admiring her.

She is here; sheis really here.

I grip the neckline of my T-shirt and yank it off. Cora sits up, her nails raking down my pecs.

"I missed you." She wraps her legs around me, pulling me closer.

"I missed you too." I reach between us, dipping my fingers between her thighs. I smirk. She's fucking soaked for me. "Looks like the rain got everywhere."

I flick her clit, and she gasps, dropping her head back.

I need to rail her on this counter. The need is overwhelming and animalistic.

But somewhere on the edges of my mind, a red light flashes to warn me.

"What's wrong?" She cups the back of my neck, but I step away.

"I'm not doing this, Coraline. Not until you tell me you're fucking mine."

I might be pushing her too soon, too hard, but she came. She said she doesn't want to take it slowly.

But recovering from her—like I had to try after the funeral—that's not an option.

"Fuck, Xander, what do you want from me?" She slides down from the counter. "I'm here."

She is here. And she is very naked. And so fucking beautiful.

"I'm not having a pity fuck, or hate fuck, or any other *just* fuck with you... I can't do that, love."

I'm an idiot. I'm having the woman I love practically begging for my cock, and I'm choosing to discuss the definition of our relationship.

But the same woman doesn't trust me yet. She got spooked earlier today, when our lips knew this was inevitable.

"You said you would be around anytime I need," she snaps.

I sigh, bowing my head. "And then I had to live with the oozing wounds after." I walk toward the window, my erection throbbing. "Tell me you're mine," I tell the darkness outside.

"I'm here," she repeats, whispering.

I turn around. "Not fucking enough."

She shakes her head. "We said slow."

"You took that back when you showed up. I know I don't have your trust. I understand I might never win it again. All I'm asking is for you to commit that you will try."

"You're asking for way more."

"And I'm offering everything."

She stares at me for several endless beats, and then she shocks me.

Cora drops to her knees, licks her lips, and leans on her hands. She proceeds to crawl to me.

She fucking crawls to me.

Her hips sway.

My cock is so hard, I might blow just from the sight of her.

Fuck.

She is not playing fair. Just like I didn't so many times.

Our gazes lock, full of hunger. My words, objections, survival instinct—they all travel down with my blood flow.

She straightens up in front of me, staring up at me. "I'm here. I will be here for breakfast. And definitely for the rest of this month before I have to return to New York. Are you going to miss out on that, or fuck me?"

The way she took over the control is fucking intoxicating and arousing. I grip her hair and pull her up with my other hand, whipping us around.

Her back to my chest, I knead her breast, nibbling at her neck. The feel of her is everything.

Who am I kidding? Even if this was my only time

with her... I have no power. She won. She won a long time ago.

And for the first time in my life, losing tastes sweet. Maybe because when Cora wins, it doesn't feel like my loss.

"Hands on the glass," I growl. "Bent over."

I grip her ass and grind against her. She pushes into me, my cock dripping with pre-cum.

"Fuck, I need to be inside you."

"Finally, we're on the same page." She looks over her shoulder, smirking.

I pull my waistband down, and my cock bounces against her ass. I grip it and push inside her.

We both groan, the feeling of her walls around me like nothing I have ever felt.

The feel of her body in my arms, of her skin against me, spurs me to action, pounding her with all the frustration and desperation pent-up inside me.

When she comes apart, pushing off the window and sagging against me in my arms, I pick her up.

Taking her back to the island, I ease her down to the edge and enter her again, circling my hips.

"Eyes on me!" I demand.

This time, I go slowly, building us both up as we gaze at each other. It's like we're re-committing with our bodies before we're ready to move forward.

My orgasm hits me like a freight train, my legs

giving in. Cora pulls me with her, lying on her back on the marble surface. Collapsing on top of her, I try to even out my breath.

"I love you," I pant.

She grabs my face, her eyes sparkling like they used to when we were still us. "I'm yours, Xander. I'm here to stay." She finally says the words I craved. "And I'm scared shitless."

I kiss her deeply.

"We're on the same page, Coraline. Losing you was the worst nightmare. I'm ready to start dreaming with you."

Epilogue

Cora

"You're sure about this?" Tessa fidgets with a spoon, stirring her cappuccino until it's a sad beige mess.

The bistro smells of saffron, baking, and bittersweet nostalgia. A soft drizzle taps the windows, the way it used to on the slow weekday mornings when my dad would hum old songs while restocking the pastry case.

I lean against the familiar counter. Or in the familiar corner, because this counter is new, and the dents and scratches on it are prefab to make it look aged.

The original counter is at our house in Chelsea. Just a memory—one I want to keep.

I run my fingers over the polished surface, standing

where I stood so many times before; only this time I'm not drowning in receipts, or wondering how to make rent.

I eye the folder of papers open between me and Tessa.

"I'm sure." I slide the signed paperwork across. My voice is steadier than I expected. "This place needs someone who still dreams of it."

"You think it's me?" She gives me a skeptical pout.

"It's you. Dad built this place, I babysat it for a moment, but you took it to a completely new level."

Tessa studies me with her half grin. "I still can't believe we survived working together, with no homicide involved."

"Because I locked away the knives," I deadpan.

She snorts. "Or more like you didn't show up much."

"Touché."

I glance around. The new lighting softens the edges of the space. The updated menu on the wall still has the biscotti recipe in Dad's handwriting. The chairs have been reupholstered, the wall behind the counter painted a deep olive green.

It's no longer mine.

It's better.

I take a breath, the kind that makes room in my

chest. "I think I held on so long because I thought walking away meant I had failed him."

"You didn't," Tessa says, quieter this time. "You made him proud."

My throat tightens. I nod, because words would tip me over.

Tessa wraps her hand over mine. It's a strange feeling—being at peace and letting go in the same moment.

"Okay, I'd better go and get ready. I'm so nervous." I collect my bag.

"You'll be great. We're both finally where we should have been, right from the start."

I smile. "I'll see you tonight?"

She shoos me toward the door. "Of course, I'll be there. Off you go. I need to open."

When I leave, I don't look back.

Xander

The school still smells of pencil shavings and overripe bananas. That distinct scent of childhood chaos. I smooth my tie, not that it matters—I'm surrounded by a sea of tiny humans who couldn't care less that I'm a Stone.

The C.O.R.A. initiative banner flutters above the stage.

My Cora stands by the podium, her red curls loose over a pale green dress, notebook in hand. Her fingers tremble. Only I would notice.

Only I know she's scared out of her mind even though she's read this story to me a dozen times at home—out loud, under the covers, half-asleep, fully brave.

Declan's daughter, Zoya, tugs on my suit sleeve. "Is Auntie Cora going to cry?"

"Maybe," I whisper. "She cries when she's proud. It's like a superpower."

"She's pretty," Zoya's brother, Zach, adds with his usual deadpan solemnity.

"She's ours," I say, a bit more gruffly than I intend.

The kids settle. Cora steps up and begins. "Once, there was a fox who..."

Her voice is soft at first, but it grows, line by line, until the room hushes into one single breath.

The story unspools like thread around all of us, binding laughter and wonder into something whole.

The teacher beside me wipes her eyes.

The moment Cora finishes, the children burst into applause. She looks up and finds me in the crowd. Our eyes meet, and I hope she sees the pride in mine.

Before Andrew ushers her away for the signing, I make my way to her and pull her to the side.

Wrapping my arm around her waist, I hold her

closer, kissing her hair. I would do more, but the room is full of children and parents.

"I'm so fucking proud of you, Coraline."

"I feel like I'm dreaming. Like none of this... this life is happening."

"It's happening, and it's a dream. You better get used to it, Mrs. Stone."

She giggles. "We're divorced. I got myself a younger side piece, and his memory is failing. You can't rely on anything these days."

"Call me a side piece again, and you will regret it," I growl into her ear.

Her smile stretches. "Promise?"

"Go sign your books, woman, so I can deliver on my promise."

She turns, and is immediately surrounded by her fans, small and big. I linger back and watch her light up for every kid, every parent.

She belongs here.

And I get to be the man who sees her shine.

Cora

The city hums below us, muffled by the thick windows and the weight of domestic comfort. An uneaten cupcake from the book launch sits on the nightstand.

My socks are mismatched. One of Xander's shirts

hangs off me. I haven't taken my makeup off. And yet I've never felt more like myself.

Xander returns to the bedroom, two mugs in his hands. "I had to research how to froth oat milk. You're welcome."

I giggle, and ogle. He didn't bother with a robe, his body on full display. "Is that the look of a man who used to pay someone to pour cereal?"

"That was one time, and I should have never told you that." He hands me the decaf latte.

God, the man should stay naked forever.

"What are you smirking about?" He sits beside me, taking a sip.

"I might have a new job for you."

"You do?" He looks at me, unimpressed.

"You'll be my personal sex slave. I will keep you here all the time, naked, so I can play with you anytime I fancy."

He puts his mug down and takes mine from me. Before I can react, he yanks me to slide me onto my back and covers me with his naked body. "How is that a new job?"

I laugh, running my nails up and down his smooth, sinewy back. "Currently, you do get dressed sometimes."

"I don't want my balls to freeze, woman. You need them."

"Do I?"

"No sex slave without balls, I'm afraid. But I'm an exemplary employee. And you?"

"What about me?"

"I'm naked and hard, and I want you naked and wet, love." He kisses my neck, and then bites and licks his way into my cleavage. When his mouth closes around my nipple, I moan and arch into him.

"I like wearing your shirt."

He hums, and looks at me with that boyish grin that I foolishly thought, at one time, I could resist. "It's not a bad look, but I prefer you naked."

His fingers trail up my thigh.

"You still need a job."

I'm not sure why I'm bringing it up now. I don't want him to regret that he gave up things. I know it wasn't for me, but I still feel responsible. He will get bored soon.

"Stop thinking about what happens when I get bored." He bites my nipple, so attuned to my body, and apparently my thoughts. "Stop thinking about what I might need." He pinches my clit. I gasp. "I have a job. There is a long list of causes that might benefit from my attention." He shoves two or three fingers inside me.

"Xander!" I almost bounce off the bed, lust cruising through me like electricity.

"Besides, my soon-to-be wife is a successful writer. She will take care of me."

"Soon-to-be wife?" I moan, as he pumps into me relentlessly, his eyes watching me closely, studying every reaction.

It's like his arousal grows every time my body responds to him. Well, the feeling is mutual.

"Of course."

I writhe, trying to get away and closer at the same time, while he just casually observes what he's causing, his head propped in his palm.

"Is that your proposal, Xander Stone?" I pant, closing my eyes. "I don't think you're doing much better than the first time."

His fingers stop moving, and I snap my gaze to him.

"Do you want us to get married again?" There is tension in his voice, but I don't think it's because of what we're doing... or were doing.

"I was so close." I whimper.

"Coraline, we're divorced, and I wasn't planning on proposing, because... well, the first time didn't really..." He shakes his head, like he needs to rid himself of that memory. "I need your lead on this one. Do you want us to get married again?"

His voice trembles with need and yearning.

Demand and desire.

Urgency and hope.

I pull him to me, and our lips meet. It's not fireworks or wild passion—it's quiet, assured, the kind of kiss that says this is forever.

Outside, the rain taps the glass in time with my heartbeat.

This is the story I never knew I was writing. The one where the girl doesn't need saving, but someone shows up anyway—and stays.

"Ring or no ring. Wedding or no wedding. I'm yours forever, Xander."

He smiles at me. "Forever."

Thank you for reading A Tainted Proposal. I can't let you enjoy four Merged partners without adding Roxy to the mix. She deserves her own book.

And while you're waiting, dive into another of my billionaire romances:

***Reckless Deal** is a workplace, billionaire, enemies-to-lovers romance readers call "incredibly captivating," "satisfying to the last page," and "an absolute page-turner."*

Do you want more Xander and Cora? Have a peek into their life ten years after their HEA in the bonus scene here:

www.maxinehenri.com/xander or scan:

Author's Note

How often do we live stories we didn't even choose. Stories handed to us by society, family, those close to us… or, most often, stories we quietly wrote ourselves?

Cora believed her duty was to the family business. She believed Xander was too young, too rich, too spoiled. She buried her feelings to live a version of her life that felt "right", forgetting to question the narrative, or change her perspective.

I believed *Merged* would be a four-book series.

I'm glad I listened to the insistent voice in my head that said: *not yet*. This isn't a goodbye note. And while the next story waits just around the corner, let me spend a few more moments with this one.

Oh, Xander. I hope you loved him. I hope you suffered with him. I hope he made you swoon.

I'm happily married to Mr. Henri, the man who

completes me. Maybe that's why I find it hard to write grovel... or maybe it's because I don't forgive easily, so imagining it doesn't come naturally. I truly hope I pulled it off with this story. I certainly tried. Never have I rewritten the last twenty percent of a book so many times.

Of course, I didn't do it in isolation.

To my incredible author friends—Kat Bammer, Mila Kane, and Sienna Judd—thank you for letting me talk your ears off while I tried to untangle the story.

To Becca Mysoor, my thoughtful developmental editor, thank you for asking infuriatingly good questions about Xander and helping me shape him.

To Kathy at Indie Editing Chick, thank you for your sharp eye (and for reminding me that Cora needed to rest longer after getting sick—ha!).

To Dan, for proofreading the final manuscript. To Jaycee DeLorenzo, for the beautiful covers.

To Nat (@the_endlessTBR), thank you for bringing this book to life online, and to you and Heather (@sponkles_reads) for taking such wonderful care of my amazing content team Maxine's Billionaire Babes.

Babes and all the influencers who posted, shared, cheered, and omg-ed this book. Your voice matters, and I see you.

And most of all, darling reader, thank you for

spending time with Cora and Xander. I know there are countless brilliant books and talented authors out there, and I'm honored that you gave a few hours of your life to this one.

I hope you stay around.

With love,

Maxine

Also by Maxine Henri

Reckless Billionaires Series

Reckless Fate (Massi and Gina's Second Chance Romance)

Reckless Deal (Gio and Mila's Grumpy/Sunshine Bosshole Romance)

Reckless Hunger (Andrea and Ivy's Age Gap Romance)

Reckless Bond (Paris and Finn's Accidental Pregnancy Romance)

Reckless Vow (Brook and Baldo's Marriage of Convenience Romance)

Reckless Desire (Sydney and Hunter's Single Dad Romance)

Reckless Dare (Lo and Dom's Fake Relationship Romance)

Untamed Billionaires Series

Fall in love with the morally grey heroes obsessed with their women

Chosen by The Billionaire (Art and Violet's Enemies

to Lovers Romance)

Chased by the Billionaire (Ness and Rocco's Age gap/Innocent Heroine Romance)

Stolen by the Billionaire (Phillip and Lena's Forbidden Love Romance)

Tempted by Charlie (A Fake Relationship Novella)

Merged Series (Billionaire Marriage of Convenience Novels)

A Temporary Forever (Cal and Celeste's story)

A Forgotten Promise (Saar and Corm's story)

A Convenient Secret (Declan and Lily's story)

A Tainted Proposal (Xander and Cora's story)

Book 5 (to be announced)

If you loved this book, please spread the word and leave a review. One sentence is enough to help other readers and make me very happy.

About the Author

Maxine Henri is a contemporary romance author who infuses her stories with steamy passion and complex characters. When she's not crafting stories that will have you swooning, she can usually be found sipping on a cup of black tea while reading a good book. Or traveling to new destinations.

Maxine believes that stories matter. They facilitate emotional journeys, inspire and entertain. And when it comes to books and fiction, stories are a great escape and probably the most beneficial addiction on this planet.

Her billionaire romances are the perfect escape, offering a taste of luxury and adventure. Maxine introduces heroes who may have a dark past, but are always balanced by a lighter side. And her leading ladies? They're strong, independent women who may be a little broken, but always find their way in life.

You can connect with her on any of these platforms:

facebook.com/maxinehenriromance
instagram.com/maxinehenriromance
bookbub.com/profile/maxine-henri
amazon.com/author/maxinehenri

Made in the USA
Coppell, TX
20 January 2026